LISA L. HANNETT has had over 70 short stories appear in publications including *Clarkesworld*, *Fantasy*, *Weird Tales*, *Apex*, and *The Dark*. Her work has been reprinted in several *Year's Best* anthologies in Australia, Canada and the USA. She has won four Aurealis Awards, including Best Collection for her first book, *Bluegrass Symphony*, which was also nominated for a World Fantasy Award. Her first novel, *Lament for the Afterlife*, won the Australian National Science Fiction 'Ditmar' Award for Best Novel.

You can find her online at http://lisahannett.com and on Instagram @LisaLHannett.

Also by LISA L. HANNETT

Bluegrass Symphony
Lament for the Afterlife
The Female Factory (with Angela Slatter)
Midnight and Moonshine (with Angela Slatter)

SONGS
FOR
DARK
SEASONS

SONGS FOR DARK SEASONS

LISA L. HANNETT

T≋
p≋ Ticonderoga
publications

For Chad

Songs for Dark Seasons by Lisa L. Hannett

Published by Ticonderoga Publications

Copyright © Lisa L. Hannett 2020
Introduction copyright © Helen Marshall 2020

Cover by Vince Haig
Designed and edited by Russell B. Farr
Typeset in Sabon and Kabel

A Cataloging-in-Publications entry for this title is available from The National Library of Australia.

ISBN   978-1-925212-00-6 (limited hardcover)
         978-1-925212-01-3 (trade hardcover)
         978-1-925212-02-0 (trade paperback)
         978-1-925212-07-5 (ebook)

Ticonderoga Publications
PO Box 29 Greenwood
Western Australia 6924

www.ticonderogapublications.com

10 9 8 7 6 5 4 3 2 1

#62

Many thanks to the editors who first published several stories from this collection: John Klima selected 'The Coronation Bout' for *Electric Velocipede* (2013); Michael Kelly chose 'Snowglobes' for *Chilling Tales II* (2013); Mark Morris picked 'Sugared Heat' for the *Spectral Book of Horror Stories 2* (2015); Mark Beech included 'Something Close to Grace' in *Murder Ballads* (2017); Nick Gevers chose 'Surfacing' for *Postscripts 36/37* (2016); Sean Wallace and Siliva Moreno-Garcia kindly took 'The Canary' for *The Dark* (2015) and also 'Little Digs' (2017).

Thanks also to Flinders University for granting me a short but crucial period of study leave, which allowed me to complete the new material included here.

My deepest thanks to Helen Marshall for her incredible introduction to *Songs for Dark Seasons*; I count myself so lucky to have such a brilliant, inspirational, and wonderful friend, and the perfect travel companion. I'm hugely grateful to Angela Slatter, Kirstyn McDermott, Kim Wilkins, and Ellen Datlow for their insights and feedback on early drafts of these stories. As always, none of my work would ever have been written without Chad Habel's love, patience, and delicious cooking.

CONTENTS

INTRODUCTION

HELEN MARSHALL

Often the lonely one longs for honors,
The grace of God, though, grieved in his soul,
Over the waste of the waters far and wide he shall
Row with his hands through the rime-cold sea,
Travel the exile tracks: full determined is fate!
"The Wanderer," translated from the Exeter
Book dated to the late 10th century

ISA L. HANNETT IS SOMETHING OF A WANDERER.
I first met her in 2012 in Toronto where she was celebrating a World Fantasy Award nomination for her debut collection of short stories, *Bluegrass Symphony*. Already I knew it was a find, one of those collections I'd return to, just so I could turn the words over again, harrow them like a plough sifting soil. Rare are those stories that cut keenly and deeply. Rarer still is the storyteller who hones that sharpness.

She and I were kindred of a sort: both obligingly Canadian, both tenderfoot medievalists. Back then I was in love with the refuse of the fourteenth century—doggerel saint's lives and romances, scrappy bits of penitential verse—but you could see right away she was made for fiercer stuff. She had an otherworldly presence, half scholar, half-Valkyrie: with sea-green eyes, hair like wound copper and a smile that invited you to listen. I was more than a little in awe.

The next place we met was foreign turf: the Norwegian fjords. By then I had finished my thesis and was living in Oxford on a fellowship, wading my way through the salt marsh of my first novel. She was teaching creative writing at Flinders University in Adelaide, publishing blood-red stories that glittered like garnet. She had snagged some funding for a research trip. Aimless and in want of inspiration I agreed to come along.

The landscape was magnificent, carved up by the slow retreat of glaciers. Lisa—of course—was in her element. She knew that country from the words of its poets. As we travelled, she told me tales of feuds and feasting; of shield-maidens who became queens; of the great wolf Fenris, born of the giantess Angrboda, whose children were destined to devour the sun and moon; of the *draugar* who guard burial mounds, dying a second death when some vagabond hacks their body to bits. Despite the dark cast of those stories, in all that tale-telling I could sense something vibrant, something desperately urgent and alive.

Canadian by birth, Australian by choice, Lisa has since become one of the vanguards of the Antipodean weird, a radical border-crosser, zigzagging across genre boundaries. Yet for all that, she might better be praised as a *wyrd* writer for what binds her work together is an interest in the winding and unwinding of fate, of the natural—sometimes terrible—consequences of one's own actions.

Coming to this gorgeous, unsettling new collection, I cannot help think of Norway's remote hinterland and the hard-scrabble lives of the farmers who once dwelled there. How they must have struggled against deep snow and scouring rain for barely an inch of good soil. What links those hungry, unflinching northfolk with the denizens of her secret South is the sense of a culture balanced on a knife's edge. A culture soaked in blood, where vengeance is needful, not borne from depravity. Where either you hold the line or else watch all you love swept away by the storm.

There is an Anglo-Saxon word—*ofermod*—which these stories call to mind. Overconfidence, it means, arrogance, hubris, high courage, even greatness of spirit. Satan had it. So too did the tenth-century warrior Byrhtnoth. Facing a thunderous force of Viking raiders, he promised them spear tips and sword blades rather than the tribute they demanded. He gave up his advantage to fight them fairly but in the end his shield-wall broke. Headless, the raiders left him when the fighting was finally over. Was he a good man? Did he act wisely?

So too is it with the inhabitants of Chippewa country. Morality for them is a moving target, salvation little more than a song snatched away by the wind.

No one here rests easily. Not Tub the blues eater, taking into himself all the town's unpleasantness. Not the Reaper's star quarterback, willing to trade his trophies, his home game glory and all his dauntless brawn for a pert pair of breasts and a fish-girl tail.

Miss Tina-Marie Dalton, haunted by her memories of past lives lived as the brawler Halvdan Daggson, as Hoelun, mother to Genghis Kahn, as Catherine the Great with all her riches, the splendour of her winter palace. Now her trailer park children and two-bit rodeo wrangler of a husband seem dizzyingly small. Vicious fucks, you might call them but they are no more vicious than life itself; and at least they have their pride.

See, if language were a blade, Lisa L. Hannett would be the queen of short swords and butterfly knives both; sincere as iron, coarse as rust. She has a poet's ear for the perfect turn of phrase and a scrapper's sense of timing. These are dirge songs of longing, heartthrob and violence. They slip inside you with a quiet, artful twist.

To northerner and southerner alike, fate can be grievous. It can bleed you dry, scatter your kin, leave your homestead wrecked and ruined. But these stories, oh, these stories. They are true myth-stuff: like the gleam of silver in a hidden pocket, like a trashcan fire when the frost lays waste.

Yes, these are tales to get you through the dark seasons, songs to help you find your way home.

∞

SOFT SISTER SIXTY-SIX

E THOUGHT THE RAIN WAS A BLESSING.

For three seasons longer'n our Zeb had started as quarterback, our wheat had withered on the stalks. Our cornrows had grown further and further apart, their pointed leaves dry-curling, ears sprouting smaller than the field mice what chawed their hard little kernels. All the alfalfa grass we'd baled in our fields wouldn't feed half a herd for the winter. Hides sagged on our beef cattle, while the dairy bessies' udders hung like empty leather gloves. We got by, *just*, on coupons and canned-food drives—but our boy never wanted for nothing. Not pork 'n' beans nor streaky bacon, not coin for the school canteen, not new shin pads nor cleats nor, God forbid, a decent cup and jockstrap to keep his family jewels intact. We'd ourselves go without for a year before it ever came to *that*.

A blessing, we thought. This rain.

Before the clouds rolled in, there'd been town hall meetings about the drought. Weekly prayer groups in St. Martin's basement. New moon gatherings in the Lady's grove. As a community, we drew up irrigation schedules. Padlocked our water towers. Debated over reservoirs and dams. Someone floated the idea of making a lake out of the Lower Horn catchment—but there weren't a soul in Athabaska keen to turn on that particular faucet, so to speak, and soak so many dusty acres once and for all.

Meantime, we lit candles. Recited catechisms. Poured ale on parched riverbanks. Painted birch and yew with yearling blood. Tossed silver dollars over our shoulders, whistling spirit-summons as the coins flew. Everyone had their theories, of course, about which of these measures finally greyed the blue torment above, finally drew down the water, finally healed the cracks in our soil. Reverend said it were the Lord Almighty's mercy what saved us—no great surprise there—while Mayor Keesey claimed it were time and patience what wore the skies down 'til they broke. Most folk reckoned it were them other gods what heard our pleas. Them fickle, hidden, oft-cursed tricksters that laughed at and worsened our woes.

Only they *could of sent this deluge,* we whispered behind our hands. *Not to mention the son-stealing lasses what came swimming in with it.*

~

Our homestead suffered them trickster floods worse than most. The nearest crick became a brook, a stream, a whitewater river. It boiled over the rough banks, churned across miles, devouring our pathetic alfalfa, our wheat, our corn. Currents gnawed at the church house's foundations, swirled furious through the ancient mound-yards—churning up headstones, restless ghosts, old bones. At the far edge of our acreage, our dirt road plain disappeared under them brutal currents. Our yard became a swamp, then a full-blown lake. The stables creaked and moaned against buffeting waves. Bessies lowed, full-disgruntled. Chooks *bocked* in frightful screeches.

Perched on a small hill, our house had a good vantage of the destruction.

Ours was the clearest view, we reckoned, of them algae-skinned gals what swum in with the wash.

Closer to town, folk must've been too busy shoring up corner stores and sandbagging streets to notice all them slinky-strange silhouettes rippling under the surface. Down here in the basin, we seen things better'n most—but even so, these were no more'n glimpses. An eel-like flick of a tail. A slender arm knifing through the dark water. Firm rumps and broad shoulders emerging, slick and shiny, torsos twisting as the creatures frolicked, flashing pert breasts, before rolling, diving, silently slipping away. All while their eerie songs echoed long and low like muted trumpets, each note felt more than heard.

Even now we can't rightly say what clinched it—which ballads snared our boys, what promises lured the whole varsity team away from us—but God knows them mermaids must of been conniving.

After all, come football season our Reapers was daily showered in rally-girl love. They was accustomed to being adored. Even the rookies. Even the ugly ones.

Now, never let it be said our Zeb weren't something to behold, on-field and off. If it were pure looks them sea-gals was hunting, well, small wonder our boy was one of the first they took. But damned if he weren't born for better things than chasing tail and rutting. With that height of his, them powerful guns, he were built for throwing pigskin. By sophomore year he were varsity QB1, fiercely huge but still faster than most running backs. Quicker on his feet than in his noggin, true enough, but we'd always thought him sensible.

Until them sea-lasses came. Stark naked, wriggling like they was already between the sheets, they was too blatant to be sexy. Too desperate to be seductive.

Too easy, we said when Zeb set off across the paddocks with our prize ox that day, humming some lah-di-dah tune. *Our boy ain't one for plucking low-hanging fruit*, we told ourselves. *Wouldn't of made QB1 if that were the case, wouldn't wear that 'C' on his six-six jersey. Nope*, we decided then and there, *our boy ain't weak. Our boy don't take the easy grab. Our boy ain't into no skinny-dipping whores. Our boy's got hisself some pride.*

Oh, the lies we cling to when suddenly life is gone wrong.

ᴧᴧ

We waited three days before rowing into town to report Zeb missing. It weren't exactly fear, nor embarrassment, what kept us from talking that long—more a mulish certainty he'd of found his way back to us by then. Our Zeb had his wild side; he weren't allergic to mischief. Most likely, we told ourselves, he'd whoop it up with them slutty lasses a whiles, dip his wick a few times, then spend the next week sleeping off the fun. We'd waited him out before, and so we would again. Even God gave His own Son sufficient time to come home after a long weekend, despite all the fuss His absence had caused. How could we presume to do any better?

In the meantime, we prayed. We were patient. We left butter and beer on the stoop for whatever hidden folk might exchange it for news of our boy. We played hand after hand of gin rummy. We argued about football. We climbed the grain silo, took stock of our stores, tightened our ever-loosening belts. We spent far too long tending the cattle, swishing through the barn-tide, saying *The place needed a good wash anyway* while building risers in the stalls, coaxing bessies up onto mucky planks, out of the wet.

Don't give up, we told ourselves, filling the hours with busywork and hope.

But when another grey dawn washed in without carrying our boy in its wake, we reckoned a recon mission was in order. *Might be he's at the stadium with the other lads*, we thought, packing corn beef sandwiches for the trip, filling a couple thermoses with black coffee. *Might be he's playing pranks on the young bloods joining the team this season. Might be he's camped out on the football field, basking in the memory of last year's glory.* We could still see it: the Reapers all lined up for a 4th and 26 play—only 72 seconds left on the clock—and our Zeb was hauled off the bench, our Zeb launched a 28-yard bullet over the middle to Kane Malicksen—Lord, that boy had a pair of hands on him!—our Zeb kept the team's drive alive. Reapers went on to win 20-17 in overtime, defying all odds. Athabaska County Champions, now and always.

Might be they're playing for the home crowd as we speak, distracting folk from their worries with a good old-fashioned game of pick-up. Wouldn't put it past 'em, we said, *to think of others ahead of theirselves.*

Good lads, they was. Good men.

For a spell, the thought cheered us.

⌁

When we got there the stadium was teeming, busier even than on homecoming weekend. Rain had swallowed the prime sideline seats, the waterline now risen to the bleachers' third tier. Canoes was tethered to the goal posts alongside a handful of bright rubber dinghies, and a raft strung together from plastic kegs and grocery store pallets. Folk in yellow life jackets and gaiters carried clipboards up and down the stands, stopping every few steps to take down the names and numbers of all the boys what'd gone lost.

Near the scoreboard, Reverend and Mayor Keesey stood under golf umbrellas, supervising as Coach and half the girls' swim team slipped on flippers and goggles, plunging pale faces underwater to test their snorkels for holes. *What's going on,* we asked, demonstrating why our Zeb was hisself so slow on the uptake. We gave our boy everything, no doubt about it. Clearly, the search had begun without us. Clearly we was late to the party. *Any sign of the lads?*

There's tea and coffee at the fifty yard line, Jo-Beth from the school canteen said, pointing a chubby arm halfway up the east stands. A trestle had been set up on the concourse there, supporting a couple of them big metal urns, Styrofoam cups stacked in the drizzle beside 'em. *Help yerselves.*

But the boys?

Jo-Beth sniffed, wiped the steam from her oversize glasses. *Talk to Adeline yonder—yeah, Cooper's mama. The blonde with the poncho there. She's keeping track on who's gone, updating the list, taking details on folks' movements. Chatting with Sheriff and them scuba folk, letting 'em know where and when the guys was last seen.* Liaising *she calls it. Triangulating a position.*

Reckon Miss Adeline's watched one too many cop shows, we said, but went to give her Zeb's details nonetheless.

As we sloshed through the rain, we weathered a downpour of cold glances. *Nice of y'all to show up,* the townsfolk said with side-eyes and sneers. *Y'all hiding something? Where's your Zeb been? Our boys'd follow yers anywhere, wouldn't they just. Where's he led them now?* We kept our heads down, stepped careful onto the concrete stairs. Didn't dignify their accusations with answers.

Nothing like an emergency to bring out folks' meanest knee-jerks.

As captain, our Zeb ain't never led them Reapers nowhere but to the championship. He sure as hell led them boys true on the field, didn't he just, but *off* it? Well, he weren't no ringleader. At the worst of times, we knew, our lad became a sheep.

So when Miss Adeline asked after Zeb, we told her only what she needed to know and not a whit more. *Three days gone, that's right. He took old Angus—our best ox—over to clear the corn-mile without so much as a feedbag on his back. Seen hide nor hair of either of 'em since. Nope, weren't none of the Reapers with 'em.* She jotted a few notes, ticked a few boxes on sheets she'd printed up herself. Squinted at our faces overlong, then waved us over to the last semi-dry benches.

There, hunkered under a good-for-nothing awning, we ate our sandwiches. Sipped cold coffee from our thermos lids. Passed on the orange wedges someone rustled up from the locker rooms. Blocked our ears against the hooting and hollering of young girlfriends; the histrionics of young mammas, wailing about *trauma* and *victims* and *suing for damages*. The attention-grabbing farce of it all.

As if their boys was the only ones missing.

As if this disaster were all about *them*.

Forcing our food down, we fixed our gazes on the snorkelers. Kept ourselves to ourselves. We wouldn't entertain no talk of *victims*, we decided there and then. Not 'til Coach brung up some bodies.

⌁

Only corpse the swim team found was two tons heavier than any of our lads, and a sight worse for its time in the water. Bloated and crow-pecked, old Angus looked like he'd been bobbing in the flood-stream for a month, though we knew it couldn't of been more'n four days.

What're we supposed to do with him, we asked when Coach floated the poor ox to our pickup, parked close as we could get it to the school grounds. *Why not leave him for the birds?*

Well, didn't Reverend go and cross himself at that, muttering nonsense about tending *all God's creatures*, as if this sack of rot and gas was anything He'd want stinking up His kingdom. Adeline rolled her black-lined eyes. Ushering folk toward their cars, she steered 'em this way and that, anywhere but in our vicinity. As if suddenly we'd soaked up some of old Angus' stench. As if, no more'n a few weeks ago, Miss Adeline herself hadn't been pining for our attention. As if the whole grinning lot of 'em hadn't been sidling up to our Zeb at the butcher's or Betty's Diner or the gas station, shaking his game-winning hands, hoping some of his good luck on the field would somehow rub off on their own kids. As if they didn't wish their sons was even half so golden as *our* boy.

In dire times, folk always seek out effigies to burn. Scapegoats to draw the devil's own wrath. Tributes to appease fickle gods.

We got it.

Meanwhile, Coach peeled off his diving suit and mask. *Leave no man behind*, he said, the red suction ring on his face accentuating the glare he shot our way. Parade-ground stiff, he scowled then shook his head. As if *we* was the queer ones for not seeing humanity in this here dead cow. As if we'd killed it ourselves.

Thanks for your trouble, sir, we said. Them back-to-back tours Coach'd done in the desert had left him raw in unexpected places, so we didn't say nothing snide. *If anyone could of brung our boys home, we know it would of been you.*

Only, that weren't entirely true.

There were still as good a chance as any the Reapers'd come rolling home tomorrow, we thought, with mud behind their ears and grins smudged on their goofball faces. Still a chance they'd left of their own volition, still a chance that's how they'd return.

It was premature to talk funerals, we reckoned, no matter what Adeline's clipboard had scheduled. Our boys were fighting-fit, they were athletes—goddammit, they were *champions*—but that didn't mean they weren't young. Sometimes irresponsible. Often stupid. Weren't a single one of 'em who hadn't gone AWOL when the pressure was on, wasting exam days at the honkytonk, glugging lunchtime pints when they needed to blow off steam.

Whether it were sooner or later, whenever the lads finally showed up we knew our anger—and sweet Jesus, we was *angry*—would tatter like last year's grandstand banners, and simply drift away.

We hoped it'd be sooner.

We feared for later.

It's too much, we said, a full week after our Zeb disappeared. What with the yearlings to break, veal to slaughter, drainage holes to bore in the home-fields—not to mention the roof wanting new shingles, the shed's hinges wanting repairs, the chain on the grain elevator wanting an upgrade—what with the damp already settling into our lad's room, the dank smell of blue-mould overpowering all traces of his aftershave, that clamminess replacing his warmth. *It's all too much*, we said, spitting into the foul waters what stole him.

We spilled extra salt onto our supper that evening. Stooped over our taters and beans, we indulged and just let despair flow. Once the plates had been cleared, the oats set to soak overnight, we went out to the porch swing. Uncorked a bottle of Jo-Beth's smoothest brandy. Sipped and wept and gazed out on our drowned patch of dirt 'til the world hazed before us. Heads and hearts wilting, we slept where we sat, blanketed in booze and woe.

~

Our Zeb shook us awake.

Come in from the rain, he said, the edges of his body blue-blurred in the wan sunrise. Grip gentle, his fingers snagged our arms like loose strands of riverweed. His hair was grubby, dangling in soaked rattails. Longer'n it were before, the tips grazed his shoulders, once-beautiful brown locks now replaced by manky green. A cheap dye-job, we thought, what with the colour bleeding down his forehead like that, sliming his temples and jaw. Algae pooled in the dips of his collarbones.

Where's yer jersey, boy?

Hardly a day passed when Zeb weren't wearing some version of his winning six-six, showing off that 'C' sewn above his heart. A cotton T- or a sweatshirt for ploughing. Tank top for gym sessions. Long-sleeve mesh for pep rallies and the real deal when he were out on field. Crimson for away games. White for home.

But now his jeans were no better'n rags, frayed and short as Daisy Dukes, and on the rest of him not a single stitch was left hanging. Mottled blue-white, his skin was cold as a trout when we hugged him close. Gone rubbery in the rain, it absorbed the *thwack* of our palms as we patted his back. As we knocked him upside the head.

Where you been, boy? Where the hell you been?

Our Zeb weren't never one for shrugging. Silent, he blinked at us.

Did y'all have fun while we was here worrying ourselves sick?

You could say that, he said. What little focus he'd had now slipped from his gaze, and a flush rose in his cheeks. He half-turned away, watched gouts of water spilling over the eaves. A smile played on his lips, both wistful and proud—an expression we'd seen time and time and time again, after he'd tumbled some local gal, popped some cheerleader's cherry.

Is that what this is? Y'all were out getting laid?

Took a while, this time, for him to answer. Not that he were ashamed—we could see, by the uplift in his chin, the hands-on-hips pose he struck, it weren't that. More like he were lingering awhiles in the memory. Keeping it to hisself just that much longer before sharing it. Pondering the right words to explain what he'd done. Or what had been done to him.

The moment stretched, unbearable. In the yard, a pair of mallards paddled above the flowerbed, the drake's glossy head vibrant against the grey sky, the hen speckled and drab as the weather. Clouds darkened the heavens from here to the horizon, but still we looked for brighter edges overhead. We looked for cracks of light. Any sign the storm would soon break.

Did you get one of them sea-lasses in trouble, son?

Good Lord, what would we do with a muddied guppy like that? Put it in a tank and feed it bloodworms? Put it to work in the drowned fields? Would it have fins or feet? Lungs and legs or goggle-eyes and gills? Should we keep it, raise it as kin? Throw it back in the water like any other fish too small and frail for the plate?

Our Zeb weren't cut out to be a daddy, that's for certain.

Our QB1 had hisself a *future*.

Sorta, he said eventually. Was that a full grin now? There and gone in a flash, it made foreign the face we'd adored all these years. It slitted and smoked his baby blues. Curved and coyed his dimpled cheeks. Plumped and paled that strangely whiskerless mouth. Made the whole picture more girlish somehow. Coquettish, even.

I suppose, he admitted. *But it ain't what you think.*

♦♦

Half the team came home that same night. The rest returned in dribs and drabs, drenched surprises popping up across Athabaska over the course of a week. One and all, our beloved Reapers came back for pre-season training, ready to the very last man.

Only, they wasn't really ready.

Nor really the same Reapers.

Nor men.

Not really.

Clad in his mesh jersey, once proud sixty-six, our Zeb now stood on the sidelines all through practice. Caring not a whit about the freshmen churning up the field, rookies fumbling every goddamn pass, dumb colts set to ruin the team's pristine win-loss record. Ignoring Coach's whistle and jeers from the players what hadn't gone a-swimming that summer. Refusing to put on his cleats. Paddling his bare feet in the deepest puddles instead. Peeling down to his jocks so's to better feel the rain. Letting it wrinkle all the touch from his expert hands.

Either yer in, Coach threatened our Zeb after three days of this nonsense, *or yer out*.

Weren't much of a choice, really. Not with all the tough washing clean out of him. Not with the hard-pumped triangle of his torso and waist melting into an hourglass shape. The broader hips now offsetting a sudden new roundness in his chest. The sheer power of them pile-driver thighs draining into delicate, pointed toes. Not with the flip-flap of his now-dainty wrists. The round little suckers pocking the length of his slender fingers.

Might as well bench him for good, we reckoned. Our QB1 wouldn't throw another spiral to save his life.

〰

For a while, we expected Zeb's piece of fishtail to come a-knocking on our door, knocked up. Sooner or later, we reckoned there'd be a splash on the lawn. A trail of telltale bubbles tracing the sea-gal's passage from sluiceway to storm-gutter to stoop. Between canoe trips out to our swamped pastures, between repairs on the house, between failed attempts to get our lad to eat something, *anything for Christ's sake*, we kept an eye on the stream what used to be the main drag into town. We watched shadows darting like minnows around our well, watched 'em slurp round the cedar hedges and the boundary fence. We waited to catch a glimpse of flippers and fins, tangleroot hair, scaled limbs slicing the floodwater's surface. Sooner or later, we thought, Zeb's sea-lass would slink up to our place, newborn guppy in tow. Sooner or later, we'd finally see her.

Face to face.

Reckon our lad believed the same, though lately he'd fallen quiet and empty as the water-shadows hisself. Hardly uttered a word since he got back, truth be told, except to request we set up a bathtub for him right there in the living room. *Don't look at me like that*, he'd mumbled afterwards, long pretty lashes sweeping over sad eyes.

Never let it be said we ain't always had our child's best interests at heart. Never let it be said we couldn't tell the difference between one of his stupid pranks, his goofball whims, and something *other*, something *important*. Never let it be said we didn't know when our kid was pining for something more'n we ourselves could give.

Never let it be said any of this were *his* fault.

On the weekend we bought the last claw-foot in town, towed it home on a raft borrowed from Coach. After some grunting and a pulled hamstring, we managed to plunk and fill it right there on Nan's hand-me-down carpet, angled so's Zeb could look out the bay window over the lake of our yard. *She'll show,* we said, dinner plates balanced on our laps, taking our supper on the couch so's to be closer to our tub-ridden boy. *After all, what kind of lass would take a man 'tween her legs, then just* leave *once he'd spilled his life into her? What kind of lass could even do such a thing—*

Enough, Zeb said in a voice what echoed long and low, like muted trumpets, the sound of it felt more than heard. His skin now the colour of porridge left out all week on the counter. Ribs jutting under—we hated to admit it, but there they were anyhow—a pair of pert breasts. Belly caved something awful, and no sign of a tum-button. For our sake, he wore boxers when he weren't submerged, but even these got shucked once his scales came. By now the bath he soaked in must of gone cold, but he weren't shivering none, not even when he hoisted hisself half out the water. Palms and rump squeaking against the porcelain, he turned to give us a full-frontal view of his nakedness. The smooth greening of his body, the haired layers sloughing off, scumming the surface. The new sensuous hunch in his posture. The bulge of his nethers deflating, dripping like wax between his thighs, sealing them fast together.

She's done her part, Zeb fluted at us, mournful-like. Hollow. *She's already spawned. Can't y'all see that? There won't be no other orphan left on yer doorstep, understand? There's only me.*

Outside, the rain eased.

We didn't mean anything by it, son. We just want to help.

Weak sunlight trickled in through the window, playing on the ripples in our lad's bath, brightening her delicate features.

Then stop talking, Zeb said, briefly turning her floodwater face away, letting her gaze drift back to the sunken yard. *And help.*

Between us, we wrangled our mer-lad out the tub, slid her onto the hammock of our outstretched arms, and carried her outside together. It took a few paces to get our steps timed right; Zeb weighed no more now than he did as a toddler, but the tail she was near-finished growing were big and unwieldy. The suckers spreading from her fingertips to armpits kept attaching theirselves to our necks and shoulders—a slimy, ticklish suction what didn't hurt so much as throw us off-kilter. Even so, before either of us was quite ready, we was out on the porch. Down the warped steps. Belly-deep in the wash, twigs and plastic bottles and other garbage swirling round our legs underwater. Feet sunk in mud up past the ankle.

Now the rain was more haze than shower, the air so muggy it were right hard to breathe. Our eyes misted. Wetness mussed our wrinkled cheeks.

Go long, we said, swinging our Zeb as we hadn't done since he were in kindergarten, tossing her out far as our poor arms could manage. No seventy yard bomb, that throw. An awkward freshman lob, a fumble and splash. God only knows where our quarterback had got his talent, his strength.

Go deep, we said.

And looking to the clouds, we begged the sun to hold its blaze in a while. For the floods to rise a while longer.

Please, we prayed to any gods bored enough to listen. *Please*, we whispered as our Zeb exhaled, submerged, and vanished under the slow-moving tide. *Swim our boy swiftly, secretly back. Guide her safely home to her soft sisters.*

∞

THE CORONATION
BOUT

MOTHER WAS THE SEVENTH OF NINE BORN TO MY Nan, but the only one to survive infancy. "This chick's a fighter," the midwife had said, helping the town's next Chanticleer latch onto the current one's breast. And when Nan felt the newborn's gums clamp round her nipple, when she heard strength in the little hen's snuffling, she was compelled to agree. "A real fighter," she'd said, so named the baby Claude—not after the girl's father, Argent Attell, but after Claude "One-Shot" Kilbane, the man who KO'd Argent at the coronation bout, securing him the district's featherweight title—and Nan's respect—once and for all.

Claude Jr lived up to expectations. Her tongue was quicker than Pop-Pop hitting the canvas, her singing voice rich as the champion's purse. She was lithe and feisty—a real pugilist child—and when it came time to take Nan's place, she did it with her namesake's surefooted grace. Claude governed with a loosely clenched fist, as liable to wallop a person as she was to chuck him under the chin. Her timing was down-pat: she knew when to act pretty, when to strong-arm, when to bed men into boxing for her causes. Wily thing also knew which situations called for all three.

Most seemed happy with Mother's version of even-handedness. At least, any who weren't hadn't the stones for an open challenge. But whether they loved Claude or not, everyone played sad after the bloat took her last week. Her gut swelled so big, seemed she was starting a new round of life, not hearing the clang of its final bell. Ballooned as she'd been two decades earlier, when she'd brought me and Nettie into this world. What luck, all had agreed then, having two hens at once. What a feat. She'd pushed us out in the swelters of August—barely breaking a sweat—and was back tending her garden that same afternoon. She was a force, our Claude. Prevailing and permanent as the elements.

∿

Nettie got Mother's looks. Plump in kissable places, lean everywhere else. Right iris the colour of sunshine, the left one dark as Jim Gallant's homebrew—and one pupil horizontal, like a goat's. My sister had no trouble with her sideways-slit eye, but Mother's wept constantly. At dawn each May Day, we'd find a basket of hankies on the stoop, stitched with roosters, rings, nosegays; finery that would spend the next year getting scrunched into the Chanticleer's canthus one after another. In her final hours, steady streams had trickled down both of Claude's cheeks, but even through the blur, Mother still saw more than anyone.

On the first of three funeral days, people remembered this all-seeing orb, hidden now beneath blue-tinged lids. They dissected Claude in tributes, raised gourds of Gallant's best, and tied giblet garlands around her wrists and ankles. Remember how tight she was in that swimsuit, way back when? Small but curvy—fitter than other ring-girls. And the length of those legs! The span of those far-reaching arms . . . Mother basked in the compliments silently, death locking away her voice but not her get-up-and-go. You're full of it, the lot of you, she seemed to say with a girlish flick of her hand. Then she'd grin and pinch cheeks and bottoms, her brittle fingers rasping on denim. Even lying on a cold hard bier, Claude knew how to rub warmth into rough-bearded fellows.

And who's next? someone asked. Crass and disrespectful, given the context. Nettie or Regina?

My sister painted herself bashful by blushing, but I could see her eyeing the gents, currying favour the way Mother taught. Swishing her skirt absentmindedly. Perking her cute arse. Frumpy in coveralls, I put on my best tones and simply said, "Me."

Soon enough, mournful talk and flirty gave way to touching eulogies—touching and fondling and prodding. Mother's scalp was smooth as custard, her skull so compact it could fit inside a gutted half-cantaloupe. Powdered with chalk and cinnamon, it practically begged to be stroked; so I stood back and let them. Many had waited so long to cup that bareness in their palms, to feel its naked power. No harm in giving them a grope, I thought, letting them paw for luck.

Nan's white crown, a faded full moon, rested on the slab near Mother's blue-brown shoulder. It used to fit perfectly, snug as gloves. But in the past couple of months, it had started to loosen. Beneath its rim, shadows had yawned at Claude's temples while she chewed. When she laughed, it'd slid up her forehead. Sometimes, as she leaned forward in her rocker to peer across the boxing green, it clunked against her binoculars. Mother thought doctors were quacks; flat-out refused to see them, even though her bones were contracting. Her skin obviously sagging. Her flawless half-melon withering bit by bit.

Judging by the recent trills in Nettie's singing, she'd noticed it too. Mother's lessening. No other reason my mouse of a twin would pipe up so conspicuously, so regularly. Asking Jet the blacksmith and the boys if she might front their band, inviting them over to practise one evening—then suggesting extra lessons alone with the blacksmith. Just like that, Jet was coming round our cabin more than the milkman, armed with a tuning fork he'd forged himself. Nope, no doubt about it: Nettie was gearing up to succeed Mother. And with her scrawny figure, she'd be stiff competition. I mean, Claude could wizen to a cornhusk and still be bigger than Nettie. Lovely, tiny Nettie.

It was a real worry, this diminishment. This dwindling. Soon, I'd thought, Mother'll be wearing a walnut shell instead of Nan's crown. A fine enough legacy for my twig of a sister, but for a lumbering oak like me? No way. No how.

I needed every inch I could get.

~

I did what I could to stall the shrinking. Plied Mother with tisanes steeped overnight, new-and-improved elixirs and cordials. Brewed teas by the bucket-load, herbals plucked from Claude's own plot, guaranteed to stop her from wasting. Toward the end, I kept her so hydrated it's a wonder she didn't float.

Don't go overboard with the sugar, she'd instruct, sicker and sicker by the day. *You make it so I can't taste anything but sweet. Give me something tart. A bit of lemon, a bit of juniper.*

Handing her a steaming cup, I'd told her to hush. To watch she didn't burn herself. To sit up and avoid spilling. To trust, for once, that I knew what I was doing.

Before the bloat stole it, her voice had been hollow; vowels blown through a reed-flute. I heard echoes of Nan whenever Mother spoke.

Blunt that tongue of yours, my hen, the two said. *Like as not, you'll cut yourself on it.*

I'd pressed the cup to her lips, tilted.

While she drank, I clenched my jaw and did my best impression of Nettie. Gentle smile, gentle tune to lull the woman to sleep. Music and charm always were my sister's forte; mine were bargaining, tactics. By fourteen, I'd negotiated trades with the Taskers upriver: six Jersey calves per season for as many bouts with our bantamweights; a brace of our foxes for every barrel of their trout; a cartload of bones for six months' worth of darning needles. Important deals, the lot of them. The promise of continued prosperity, clinched with a Chanticleer's cunning. That's what a town needed in its leader. The willingness, the ability to inspire change. A firm hand when stability was needed.

Nettie, however, only offered distraction from the day-to-day. She didn't improve our lot in life; she entertained. Saccharine plays, sonnets, sestinas, Sunday carolling—our Nettie was a regular nightingale, and just as useless. What good were songs when the dark season came? Show me a poem that could stave off starvation. By nineteen, parleys had won me three boxers, including Thom, the butcher's son—southpaw, welterweight, ugliest harelip you ever saw—who I'd picked for champion on account of his know-how, his scars. Nettie's talents had earned her nothing but fans.

Words are the Chanticleer's greatest power, Mother always said, so much like Nan, if I closed my eyes I couldn't tell them apart. Words spoken, I'm sure she meant, not warbled. Unlike Nettie, I'd paid attention when our dams shared their wisdom. I'd worked hard. I'd listened. I'd learned.

But as Mother slurped down my tonics, I knew it wouldn't be enough. *My crown will never fit you, Regina,* she'd said, as if reading my thoughts. From birth, my head had been shaven, like hers, and bound in strips of silk—Mother's fondest caress was a razor blade rasping my stubble. I had her wits and, yes, her sharp tongue. But mine was a brawler's build, stocky as the bull that killed Argent last spring. Firstborn I may have been, older than Nettie by a full hour, but I was ungainly for a Chanticleer.

And I couldn't negotiate myself smaller.

～

For three days and two nights Mother's body stayed in the smokehouse.

The roof was sound, slatted with a single vent, and the door had a sturdy lock. Every family in town had a key, of course, but they respected our privacy, entering only when we gave the say-so. Small and dry, the space was infused with scents of peat and salt, cod and winter herring. Whenever I could, I'd pop in to remind Mother she wasn't alone.

She wore the cotton nightie I'd scrubbed for the occasion. Tansy dust still stained the ruffles, though I'd bleached the fabric as best I could. In our house the fatal herb's leaves and petals were everywhere. It kept pests at bay, Mother had said, clustering the weeds to hang from the rafters. As they dried, seeds rained from the bunches and she'd sweep them up for replanting; wild thatches now grew all over town, easy to find even after the snows. On my way across the boxing green, I'd plucked several of their snap-frozen stalks. Fingers clumsy with cold, I'd plaited them into a circlet to slip over Mother's head, an offering and a reminder. But when I ducked inside, she was so tranquil, so composed, I changed my mind. No point in riling her yet.

Palms yellow, I trudged down the lane to the fox pens. Wire mesh enclosed an area five times the length of a horse trailer; nowhere near big enough for the number of skulks Old One-Shot had crammed into cardboard dens. The vixens sniffed me coming a ways off. Nose-first, they hurdled the reynards, brush-tails flailing. Red fur flew as they snapped and snarled. I picked up a pail of feed, scattered a handful of the rancid meat through the fence, saw the gobbets devoured in an instant. Another few chunks through the gaps and the bucket was empty.

"That's it," I said. "Greedy guts."

The foxes licked their chops. Kits yipped, appetites scythe-sharp. Scrubbing my hands in the snow, I kept an eye on them through the links. They could smell the blood on my fingers and wanted a second helping.

"Too slow," I said to the pups. "Got to be faster off the mark, else you'll be left wanting."

They barked as I scoured my flesh deep pink, unable to get the stink out.

~

Twilight at the smokehouse, the third of our vigil. Once more the room was packed, but tonight there were no gourds filled, no canons sung, no tears shed. Avarice made everyone serious as they filed past the bier, saying final farewells, grabbing mementos of the Chanticleer. The young and ambitious had lined up from midday, hoping a wasted afternoon would nab them the most potent keepsakes. At sundown, Nettie and I'd gone to make sure Mother was ready. Once we got the nod, we let the rest of the town in with their scissors and knives.

No one dared touch Nan's crown; it belonged to Mother, and would be cremated with her remains. Next, the Chanticleer's tongue was most prized—but my sister got there first, greedy as a fox, and pried it out with the blacksmith's tongs. After that, any detachables were fair game. Teeth, ears, nipples, fingers, toes. One by one, they were snipped and snapped and stuffed into reliquaries, tucked inside censers and jewel-boxes and lockets. Latecomers settled for leftover moles, birthmarks, a sizeable wart on the back of Claude's neck. Curls were yanked from nostrils, underarms, cleft. Tradition kept the mismatched eyes in their sockets, but brows and lashes were plucked bare. Finally, Jade Pilvery took pinking shears to the nightgown we'd peeled off earlier, clipping it into postage-stamp squares for children too short to reach something better.

Mother didn't resent these pilferings.

"It's a real honour, hens. A real gift," she'd said, when we'd gone to Nan's picking-over. "You should be so lucky."

Now, skin greyed and slack as lard, body stripped thin, Claude waited patiently for the scavenging to cease. She'd never looked more regal.

"Go on, Net," I said to my sister, after the vultures had gone. "I'll meet you down at the Bingo."

For a moment, she feigned deafness. Stringing Mother's tongue on a cord, she averted her eyes and tied it round her neck. Runes appeared and disappeared in the tastebud florets; Nettie froze, reading Claude's last words.

"Regina," she breathed at me, startled-deer. "What—"

"Go on," I repeated. "Get the banquet rolling."

Hell, Nettie was a good actress. Clutching the talisman, she sniffled and pecked Mother once on each cheek. Shaking like a tambourine, her sorrow almost believable.

"You think I can eat? Now?"

"Have a cup of tea then," I said, talking over Nettie's yelp. "It's the least you can do."

"You're a real piece of work," she mumbled, and I laughed to take the edge off her jealousy. My sister could fight me for the crown all she wanted, but she'd have no part in this. As eldest, it was my duty—mine alone—to escort the Chanticleer to her unravelling.

Without a second glance, Nettie lifted her grey hood and hightailed it out of there, boots squeaking across fresh-fallen snow.

"Watch your step," I called, repeating the warning as I eased Mother off the table. Elbows linked, we shared the burden of balance while crossing the icy threshold. I guided her along the dark lane outside, a slow careful shuffle. In no time I was huffing and Claude was purpling to black, her corpse growing heavier by the foot.

"Nearly there," I panted. "Don't give up on me now."

I blinked fat flakes from my lashes and peered at Mother sidelong. Wan moonlight strobed through flurries, glinting off the powder on her skinny shoulders. Oh, what a sight. Gouges and gashes rimed with frozen lace, she hobbled like a troll. A rising snow-cap made her seem taller and taller.

Nearly there, nearly there, nearly there . . .

I didn't realise I was smiling until Mother started to chuckle.

"I've earned this," I said, face falling. "You of all people should know that."

She patted my arm, condescending even without fingers. Save yourself the headaches, her touch said. Give Nettie the crown.

"And what would you have done," I snapped, "if Nan'd said the same to you?"

Mother raised her chin, defiant. A true Chanticleer.

I snorted. "Exactly."

She smirked, but held me tighter.

As we approached the pens I signalled for One-Shot, who'd long ago hot-footed out of the ring and into the gamekeeper's racket. Orange flared at waist height on the yard's far side, guttering until he put flame to wick. The lantern bobbed towards us. Iron jangled on his leather belt.

"Evening, Claude," One-Shot said, rattling a cough, singling out the rustiest key. "Reg."

Mother mimed an uppercut, gently clocking him on the jaw. Then she palmed his jowl, punch turned pat. Gave him a look that said, Guard up.

We opened and closed the gate in one swift movement so the foxes couldn't skip out with Mother's entrance. Undaunted by their excited, ethereal barking, she turned and faced me through the fence.

Arms crooked in position, she smiled. Guard up.

⌁

"Nettie stopped in on her way past."

Lamp held near his chest, One-Shot's face was lit ghoulish. His cauliflower ears and truffle nose cast weird shadows, obscuring his expression.

"Is that so," I said. My thick legs kept pace with his nimble ones as we traipsed down the road to the Bingo. The double-peaked hall was decked out in streamers and paper lanterns; golden light spilled into the parking lot, turning slush to lemonade. Later on, Jet and the boys would sing Mother's soul to the hereafter, but for now, cutlery clinking against crocks was music enough. It seemed One-Shot agreed; his belly growled louder than mine.

"She had some thoughts on the Chant's sudden passing," he continued. "And on the outcome of tomorrow's bout." He picked at his teeth with a sprig of rosemary then chomped the needles. His breath was no less rank for it.

"Nettie's a singer," I said. "She makes all kinds of empty noise, just to keep her vocal chords limber."

One-Shot shrugged, never one to engage in a fight he wasn't sure to win. "Guess we'll see, won't we?"

"Guess so."

Behind us, the foxes' howling reached a crescendo. Wincing, I hunched into my coat and kicked my boots against the Bingo's scuffed steps. Before climbing up, I stomped and thudded until every skerrick of snow was knocked loose. It did little to muffle the caterwauling.

"They'll make quick work of it, Reg," the gamekeeper said. He snuffed the lamp and hooked it on the railing beside the others. "Vicious fuckers. Winter brings out the worst in them."

At the door, I waited. Warm scents and sour wafted from within. Spit-roasted lamb, onions, yams. Gallant's ale, unwashed bodies, lavender perfume. Smoke from a hundred Zig-Zags.

"They're just famished," I said, peals of laughter inside blending with feral yowls. "They've been waiting on this feast a long time."

~

At cock's crow, Nan's cauldron was simmering on the hearth. I skimmed dross from the surface—old shreds of bryony, tansy, belladonna—and tapped it onto the grate. When the water was boiling pure, I replaced the lid and went outside to fetch pail and barrow.

Wheeling deep ruts across the boxing green, I dodged cornerposts that wanted padding and ropes that needed slinging before this evening's event. Yesterday's clouds had fallen overnight; I trod on their fluffy corpses, the pale sky so barren I knew we were in for a cold one.

By now, I thought, repressing a whistle as I approached the pens, the starvelings will have gnawed her to sinew and bone. A couple hours in Nan's kettle and she'll be rendered clean for chopping and burning. Plenty of time for the square-circle to be cleared, stools for the cutmen to be found, the announcer's table to be set up proper. Plenty of time to tighten my skin with witch hazel and cucumber. Plenty of time to practise my lines.

Everyone still talked about Mother's coronation speech. How clever it was. How innovative. Instead of boring the town with platitudes, she'd dolled-up in hot bathers, scribbled her ideas on placards, and paraded them round the ring between bells. With Nan's crown and Argent's swagger, Claude was pure class. A real hard act to follow.

For weeks, I'd planned my own debut. I didn't have the strut for Mother's brand of show-ponying, but my voice . . . Well, she'd said it was honest. Reassuring. Trustworthy. A voice to smooth all manner of ills.

But also unyielding, I remembered, clanking to a halt outside the gate. And nowhere near as sweet as Nettie's.

The foxes were sedate, dark copper patches curled around the carcass. Gluttons. Must've gorged themselves into a coma. To be safe, I slopped some meat from the bucket, made kissing noises to get the beasts' attention. Fat and full, they didn't move a muscle.

The body, however, sat up.

"Mother," I said, heart spasming. "You're still here."

Every last giblet had been nibbled off; the flesh around them was slashed but not bleeding. Chunks were missing from her limbs, a wound yawned in her side. Her mouth was a coagulant mess. Otherwise, she was whole. Undevoured.

She crossed her arms as if to say, Obviously. Glowered like it was my fault she hadn't gone yet. Like I had kept her waiting, shrivelling in the cold. Like I hadn't done all I could to see her off. She held my gaze and, gradually, started to hunch.

"Stop it," I said. She pulled her knees in close, flaunting how compact she could make herself. How small. "Just hold right there."

I ran for One-Shot, who was supposed to help shovel the bones. He was snoring on an armchair by his cabin's woodstove, shirt unbuttoned, pants puddled round his feet. The room reeked of stale goon and the old man was heavy with it, his legs deadweight as I rummaged for the keys. By the time I got back to the pens, Claude had huddled herself so tiny, even Nettie would seem huge beside her. "Mother, please."

While she pretzelled herself, I snagged entrails from the bucket and launched them over the fence. Never trust a fox, I figured. Sure, they looked placid enough with their bellies bloated, but offer them a chance to bite and they'd gobble it. I raced in to wrangle Claude before the animals snapped—but they didn't stir. Not even the vixen who usually had such a mouth on her. They just laid there in packs, thin veils of snow blowing over their russet fur. Not a breath among them. "What happened?"

Mother shrugged, impish. Seems I wasn't to their taste.

"Probably too tough," I said.

"Mamma!" Nettie ran to the front door when we came home, stopped just shy of hugging. She ushered Claude onto a blanket box, well away from the fire. "Here," she said. "Let me get you some tea."

Mother shook her head, pursed what was left of her lips.

"Oh," Nettie said. Last night, she'd pegged her new necklace by the mantle; now she retrieved it. Slow-traced a finger along the runes. Reading, the sunshine in her right eye darkened to match the gloom in her left. "So it's true."

"We've got less than eight hours," I said, snatching the tongue, tossing it into the pot. It sank into the boiling water with a squeal. "We have to get Mother ready."

"You can't—" Tears spilled over Nettie's delicate cheeks as she studied the flames. Her skin drank in the firelight, softly burnishing. She glowed with a veneer of warmth; but when I patted her arm it was more frigid than Mother's.

Selfish Nettie. Taking everything in, giving nothing in return. Can't even bring yourself to exude heat.

After a minute, she cleared her throat and gestured at the cauldron. The jars of bryony, tansy, belladonna. The truths blistering off Mother's tongue. "You can't expect me to keep this a secret."

"Grab her ankles."

"No, Regina," she said. "Enough."

Mother once joked that Nettie must've been an out-fighter in a past life—always standing back, side-stepping, forcing her opponent to take the first jab. Whereas I, apparently, was a brawler. I got in close. I loomed.

And I jabbed, quick and hard.

My sister dropped on the third punch, still moaning. She had the figure all right, but not the gumption to be Chanticleer. On the sidelines, Claude rolled her eyes—You're no One-Shot—but cowered when I reached for the tansy. Two handfuls stuffed into Nettie's little mouth should keep her well-gagged, but to be sure I jammed in a hankie and tied the lot in place with another. Four more served as makeshift fetters, wrists and ankles hogtied with tatting and lace. I pushed Mother off the blanket box and shoved Nettie inside.

"She'll be fine," I said in my honest voice, lowering the lid. "Look: she can practically stretch out in there."

Mother laughed as I dragged her to the fireplace. A few prods, a few twists and the corpse climbed into Nan's huge iron pot, conceding defeat. Instantly, the reek of her was atrocious; offal with an undertone of bitter greens. It didn't trouble Mother in the least.

Until tonight, hen, she winked, splashing me as she submerged.

～

Ringside at dusk. The town gathered to put Mother to rest, and celebrate her with a few black eyes and cut lips.

To my left, the announcer tapped his bullhorn, flinching as the thing screeched. "Lights," he boomed, sending the lampboys shimmying up skinned pines. They squirrelled from bulb to bulb, sky-high, weightless, fearless. Flashes of brilliance at their fingertips conjured an almighty glare. Half-blinded, I watched until tears blinked me back to the brazier on my right, to Jet stoking the embers blue-white. Cast-iron, three feet tall, the firebowl slicked the blacksmith with sweat while the rest of us were left shivering. The evening air was icebox. Folks folded hands beneath armpits, snuggled into scarves, tightened hoods. Fighters were puffed in down jackets, high-tops laced to the shins. Thom's knees were blueing beneath his red satin shorts; he jogged on the spot beside me to keep the blood pumping before his bout. Behind him, everyone— everyone—was staring.

Where's Nettie? they asked.

Mother was unrecognisable, just a pile of yellowed sticks on the announcer's table, empty sockets gaping.

Where's Nettie?

With the blacksmith's tongs, I moved Nan's orange-hot crown then stacked Claude's bones on the coals beside it, making a tepee out of the ribs. Old One-Shot sidled up to pay his final respects.

Where's Nettie?

"Withdrawn," I said at last, throat seizing as I met those stares, saw the brown and gold badges on so many hatbands and lapels. My sister's colours, ale and sunshine, in overwhelming majority. Murmurings and restlessness sifted through the crowd, separating red rosettes from the mottled. The crown is mine to try first, I wanted to shout, but tremors shook the words from my mouth.

Across the boxing green, shadows twitched at the front door of our cabin.

My gaze snapped back to the pyre, so small for such a large spirit. She is gone, I told myself, releasing a ragged breath. She is gone.

Mother's skull had a porcelain tinge, more blue than cream, and was light as a teacup in my hand.

Door hinges creaked.

Thom the butcher-boy passed me a hacksaw, eyebrow raised. He'd spent a lifetime with bones, chopping them to fit into crockpots and stoves. He gauged the size of this one without even touching it. He knew it'd be a squeeze.

Please, I prayed. Let it fit.

I pinned Mother's dried-melon in place. Hand spread over the nasal cavity, fingers plugging earholes. I cringed as the mandible wriggled, certain I was suffocating her. Footsteps thudded on our porch, hinges creaked. The tool slipped from my sweaty palm. "Focus," Thom said, ever the fighter. Exhaling, I nodded and tried again. Now metal teeth chewed an uneven line across Mother's forehead, nibbled through the temples, bone dust went flying. Footsteps thudded, frantic as my sawing. Closer. Closer.

Nearly there, I thought, rotating to get at the back of the cranium. Steady.

With a snap, the lid broke away. A smattering of applause from the reds as the crown skidded across the table and dinged the regulation bell. My belly fluttered as I picked the thing up—not even a cantaloupe, a half-grapefruit—and ran a finger along its jagged edge. The break could've been better, much better. It'd be torture until it wore smooth.

"It's supposed to hurt," Claude had told us, years ago. "Being Chanticleer. Speaking for these folks. Watching out for them. Bearing the brunt of their loves, their hates. It's a right royal pain. And if it isn't . . . Well. If it isn't, you're doing it wrong."

Ring-girls shuddered in their dainties as I lifted the crown to my head. One-Shot fixed me with a rheumy glare, sprigs of rosemary bristling from his lips. Fathers lifted kids to give them a better vantage. Armed with enswells and balms, the cornermen crept up behind me, poised to daub. Thom, butcher-boy, boxing champ, judged the first lacerations impassively. Blood trickled warm on my brow.

Guard up, Mother, I thought. I glanced at our cabin. Shadows danced round the front door.

Gashing, forcing, I wrenched the flimsy cap on. Deep breath, lungs filling with charred air. Pulse throbbed in my head, footsteps thudded on the porch. Don't crack. I twisted my fingers slippery, sight sheeting red. On the stoop, shadows wavered. Please don't crack . . . I scratched and dug long after the crown was secure, my skull near-crushed beneath hers.

I did it.

The door slammed shut. Shadows and footsteps stilled.

It fits.

Mother parried two beats later—and I didn't have a puncher's chance.

The world doubled, trebled. One-Shot half caught me as I buckled, my mind clobbered by Mother's memories—bargains wheeled, trades brokered, lovers toyed, walks wiggled, ballads crooned—pummelled by thoughts of Nettie—singing, wooing, struggling against embroidered bonds—and KO'd by visions of me.

Mother's little brawler, getting in close. Towering. Looming over the bed. Plying her with tea. Goat-gaze seeing everything in hindsight, Claude lowered her horns and bucked.

Hail, Regina, she said.

Head pounding, I staggered upright and shook off the gamekeeper's grip. Had he heard her? One-Shot squinted, face unreadable. Footsteps thudded on the porch. Boxers shuffled near the ring, sloughing their coats, eager to get on with it. Leaning against the ropes, bookies butted their smokes, subtly giving me and Thom the once-over. Fingers twitched, heads bopped. Odds were accepted and rejected. The butcher's kid will take the purse, given the shot.

"Hail, Regina," said Thom. Mother chortled at this echo, laughing me nauseous as the boy genuflected. Down and up without wobbling, a circle of snow clinging to his bare knee. "The floor is yours, Chant." Ugly Thom strutted, impatient, flexing every visible muscle. My speech came first, then the champion's bout. Symbolic gestures, promises before the fight, but necessary to seal the deal. "Grace us with a few words. Any bets on who'll win?"

All my plain, heartfelt sentiments fled as the crowd livened, out-shouting each other's wagers. The cabin door creaked, slammed.

Go on, hen, Mother said, triumphant. Poisoned fingers clawed down my throat, pried at my teeth. Death had stolen Claude's voice; my coronation offered her a new one. Open up. I'm feeling downright chatty.

Beside me, Jet stirred the bones, fishing Nan's red-smoking crown from the brazier. Breathing down my neck, Claude Kilbane rolled his shoulders. The old man hocked up milky phlegm. Cracked his bashed knuckles. One shot and I'd be down, just like Pop-Pop. One shot and my crown would be Nettie's. Footsteps thudded on the porch, crunched across snow. Closer and closer.

"Speech!" cried the reds.

"Speech," said the brown-and-golds.

Choking on bile—tansy-flavoured and rue—I stared at them all, and kept my sorry mouth shut.

A GRAND OLD LIFE

FAR AS SHE REMEMBERS, TINA'S PAST LIVES CAN BE named in this order:

Aelia Pulcheria
Halvdan Dagsson
Hoelun
Şehzade Mehmed

Next, and last before this one, before she were born as our own Tina-Marie Dalton, is her favourite, most brilliant time-being:

Sophie Friederike Auguste von Anhalt-Zerbst-Dornburg, she who became Ekaterina Velikaya; that is, Catherine the Great.

Of course, betwixt such vibrant moments in eternity, I tells her, there were bound to be blackness, gaps. All those shapeless centuries she spent floating in utero, failing to stick for nine months, much less get squeezed out into the light. Decades when she were recycled as stillbirths. Countless miserable months when she weren't barely more than an infant—over the years, I tells her, she were *so many* different babies—falling to fever, pox, plague. So many other, unnamed, forgettable cot-deaths. All them long stretches between real lives won't amount to much in the way of memories, I says—good, bad, or otherwise. They're nawt but a series of present absences. Long sleeps without any dreams.

For ages, I reckon, she can't have known much but calm darkness.

But time and again, Tina tells me she don't need no Leather Jenny to tell *her* what she can and can't recall. Says she don't need some old soothsayer reading *her* lives—the way I always done for everyone else on Chippewa land. No sir, *she* sees powerful enough visions her own self, Tina says. *She* sees all them bright thens before she was born, and born, and born again. All them glorious bygones twinkling throughout her forevers.

Pulcheria. Halvdan. Hoelun. Mehmed. Ekaterina. Tina-Marie.

Mind and gut, she remembers every one of them.

She wears their memories in muscle and spirit.

If there's one thing she don't suffer from, Tina says, it's past-blindness.

And yet here she is any-old-how, knocking on Leather Jenny's front door. Wayward and suffering. Seeking my own brand of help.

⚡

"Brought you a pie," Tina says, shuffling from foot to foot on the stoop, holding out a tinfoil-covered plate. Morning's bright but damp with the onset of autumn. The gal's shivering, I reckon, from more than the chill. "Bumbleberry and apple. Still warm, if you fancy a piece now. Got any ice cream? It'll melt right nice into the pastry." She stops, flustered. "Not that I'm suggesting it so you'll serve me up some, too. I just thought . . . "

Wavering on the threshold, she works a pretty flush into that blunt face of hers. *Miss Piggy,* I always think upon seeing her. Uncharitable, maybe. But with them thick-mascara blues, them long curls so over-bleached they're pale and dry as straw, that rose-coloured powder caked on her cheeks, that upturned nose of hers, it ain't far wrong neither. Top-heavy and tall, she's ever-plump from bearing Ger Stout's latest piglet—reckon she's popped out four or five little bastards since she turned sixteen. Of course, when it comes to this gal's looks, it don't matter much what old Leather Jenny thinks. Tina-Marie's opinion on herself is even higher than the collar on that old-fashioned dress of hers. She ain't here for flattery, that's for certain.

Stepping back to let her in, I nod at the two-man table beneath the cabin's main window. A round tin of gingersnaps sits there already, lid sealed tight. A few cans of collard greens, black-eyed peas, white hominy. Fine red cabbages wilting in a bowl. Plastic containers filled with rice krispie treats. Pecan tarts. Coconut jellies I always wind up tossing outside for the squirrels.

Offerings, of a sort, intended to keep this ancient body of mine ticking along. And if I'm honest, folk round here are more generous than they rightly knows. *Gratitude*, so the saying goes, *turns what we have into enough.* Lucky for them I'm more grateful than greedy.

I only ever takes what I really *needs*, and not an inch more.

"Thank you kindly," Tina says, clicking across the boards. The pie plate clunks on checkered cloth, then crackles on old crumbs as she fiddles with it. Pushing it an smidge this way. Dragging it back. Failing to centre it between the chairs. "Smells lovely in here, Miss Jenny. What's that you've got burning? Frankincense? Myrrh?"

Breathing deep, she lifts her chin. Rests peach-lacquered fingertips on the table's edge. Gazes up at wooden shelves laden with jars and bones and other trinkets, at rafters clad in antler and herb-garlands. Keeps her back turned. "Reminds me of the smoke and steam-pots Father's priests once placed around my chamber, when I was young and bed-ridden. Sweet-sharp citrus, bitter pine, a hot haze of soot—perfumes to waft a soul pleasantly into death."

Shuffling across the low-ceilinged room, I keep my trap shut while Tina reminisces. While she's gabbing, her demeanor subtly changes. Pudgy shoulders lift demurely, toes turn inward; she fidgets like the five-year-old she was back in ancient Rome. Poor little Pulcheria, daughter of Theodosius I, expiring in her little bed like that, quietly and without reknown. Not like that *other* Pulcheria—she were the Emperor's famous niece, Tina says, who inherited the dead girl's name but not her bad luck—*that* one grew up. *That* one became Augusta Imperatrix. Saint. Virgin.

I snort. No way *that* Pulcheria could ever have been Tina-Marie. Been a dog's age since Ger's gal came anywhere close to virginal, but I know she ain't here today for a dose of pennyroyal tea. If it were just another womb-emptying she was after, she wouldn't be acting half so skittish. So humble. *No scarier than getting your ears pierced*, she said to me that first time, after I'd given her the strongest ridding infusion I knows how to steep. *Some pinching, some pain, some throbbing, some blood. Worth it, though*, she said, tone rising like it were a question. *In the end.*

Ain't my place to judge, I told her then and tells her every time since. You do what you gotta do to get by.

There's a bit of black coffee left from breakfast, so I crouch by the fireplace, stir up the coals. Lingering near the table, Tina-

Marie's picking at hangnails and foil. Still rambling about her short stint as that Emperor's kid, that Roman stiff who sounds as boring as he were powerful. On the warm hearth, the enamel pot starts to pip, inviting with scent and song. While the brew reheats, I pry off the lid and splash in a good snifter of apple brandy. Pungent vapor soon sneaks out the spout.

"It's hot as a harem in here," Tina says over her shoulder. "Mind if I crack a window?"

"Go right ahead," I says. She nods and stretches over the small table. Soon as the sash is lifted and propped on a stack of tarot cards on the sill, the gal continues her chattering.

I listen, and stir, and enjoy the small breeze drifting in.

Folk eventually talk theirselves round to the crux of matters, I've learned, if given enough air.

∿

Don't take too long for Tina-Marie to drink herself maudlin enough to turn honest. It's the brandied coffee what draws out truth—not like gin, what makes folk too weepy to talk, nor red wine what stains 'em sleepy, nor moonshine what riles 'em into stupid fights—and the caffeine keeps her alert. Pacing in front of the hearth, she drains her mug then holds it out for a refill. Though I don't fancy meself nobody's servant, I oblige. She stares into the cup's pottery mouth with a booze-blurred sneer.

"In the Winter Palace I had more champagne than I could quaff in ten lifetimes," she mutters. "Poured into delicate, cut-crystal glasses, served alongside sugared fruits and meringues stacked on pretty cake-tiers . . . The plates on my banqueting tables were gilt porcelain, the cutlery polished silver, the salvers and serving trays fashioned from mirrors. Everything *gleamed*. There was so goddamned much gold, Miss Jenny. Rib after rib of it was leafed on vaulted ceilings. Engraved on double doors. Carved into reliefs in pale blue and white corridors. Flecked through ballroom tiles and majestic staircases. Framing masterpieces hung in my very own galleries—galleries jam-packed with giant paintings, paintings *I* bought, some even bigger than this whole wall. Gold was ribboned around epaulettes and across satin bodices. And still, whenever I wanted, it was poured bubbling into my glass . . . " Tina sighs, gazes wistful into the past. "We *needed* so much splendor, you see, to combat the grey world outside."

"Y'all might think I look a tad like him," I says, backhanding a cinder off my apron. "But I ain't no Rumpelstiltskin, gal. I spin hide, not gold."

That raises a brow, a chortle.

Frankly, out of us two, I'm much closer to Great Catherine's short stature. Beneath its stitched skull-cap, my shorn head barely reaches the mantel while Tina-Marie's, even swaying with drink, is held high, refusing to accept it ain't topped with an imperial crown. Meanwhile, she's a match for the Empress when it comes to fat. Her broad torso is less regal than it is Viking-built; in that respect, she's still Halvdan through and through. Them muscled arms of hers is made for wielding war-axes. Launching spears. Pulling oars.

Rickets has left my limbs awful bowed, putting a lifelong hitch in my gid-up, but Tina's stride is long and sure. Hers is a horselord's gait. Designed for travelling across grass-blown steppes, riding or running or both. That there's Hoelun's influence, I reckon.

All told, the tips of my toes lift like an imp's, my smile's holier than Mary, and my skin's cracked and brown. Top to toe, I'm tough as the buckskin strings looped round and round my forearms, the oiled strands braided round my chook-neck, the overworked cowhide what lent me its name. Leather Jenny, that's me. Even a blind man wouldn't call neither of us beautiful, but that opinion don't bother *me* none.

Go ahead: call Leather Jenny a gnome, a dwarf, or any other magic runt imaginable. She won't argue. She won't complain. She ain't got unreasonable expectations, no far-fetched aspirations.

Better than most folks, I knows my rightful place in this world—always have—not to mention how to stay in it.

～

"There you go," Tina says, white-knuckling her mug, turning to waggle a finger at me. She huffs over to my ratty couch by the fireplace, green corduroy rubbed pale on the arms and cushions, then stomps back to the table. "That's exactly my point, Miss Jenny. What more can anyone expect from Chippewa—or any other place now, in this godforsaken time, this godforsaken country? What can I hope for here? *Nothing*, that's what. *No straw, no gold*."

"Y'all forever want a magic fix," I says with a shrug. "Straw into gold? Please. Show me a man with more than ten deer-free acres of corn, and I'll show you the only true alchemist these parts ever will know. Now park yerself a whiles, jitterbug." Joints creaking, I lead by example and lower meself onto the sofa in a whump of dust. "All that to-ing and fro-ing's driving me batty."

"It's not just the gold," she says, stopping. "Not just the palace, the fancy champagne. It's—" Her mouth guppies as she grasps for words.

There's this foreign notion I heard spoke on the wireless once, what describes that gut-ache folk get when they's homesick for times they can't never go back to, or missing places they ain't never really seen. Never could wrap my tongue round the word—it's a bunch of aitches and breathy nostalgia—but I reckon Tina-Marie's tone just now captures it perfect. *Yearning*, felt deep, in all its pain and hopeless confusion. It lifts her voice up to the cobwebs, keeps her focus from fixing on these unvarnished walls of mine. Turning slowly, her sights skim across star-charts painted on timbers, over chalked timelines and moon cycles, past maps and genealogies for every possible where and when I've yet fathomed. Leylines criss-crossing here on Chippewa land don't seem to register with her. Histories lock horns with futures all around her, but she don't see none of it right about now.

She pays no mind to the iron cauldron I gots hooked under the flue. The chains of rue and mugwort and chillies pegged on the fire-shelf. The wax drippings on that mantel, the rune marks, the scattered bones. The miner's bench tucked between chimney and sideboard, my sleeping-quilt draped messy across its hard length. The teetering stacks of faceless photographs. The hair-wreaths.

She's looking beyond my withy brooms and the gabled porch they've swept. Beyond the well dug outside in my pine-needle yard. Beyond the barrier of maples, birches, and sticky blue spruce that separates my wild half-acre from a county flattened into concrete lots and paved streets. Beyond stone circles on graveled hilltops, sacred groves of ash and cedar, sigil-marked teepees and the feather-clad folk what dwell in them. Beyond the coal-riddled mountains hemming us, one and all, into this forgotten valley.

Far as Tina's concerned, there ain't really nothing here and now to compare with all that's beyond, and beyond, and beyond.

෴

"I was in the Varangian guard," she says after a moment, expression wonder-filled. Perplexed. "I served in Mikhaēl III's personal retinue—*me*, a Norwegian nobody's son. I was favoured in Miklagarðr long before Harald Hardråde sailed south from our strong Northern lands. I owned armour, understand? What I wore into battle was *mine alone* to wear out, mine alone to die in. Good quality stuff, shared with no one. I had earned my very own helmet. My very own. Today, traces of my name—*Halvdan*—remain in that famous city. Over a thousand years ago, I etched it myself, deep and permanent, into a parapet on the top floor of the Hagia Sofia. Those rough letters have outlasted the hand that carved them. They've survived the blessed man who taught that hand to write."

Tina shakes her head. "I don't get it, Miss Jenny. Once I was also the greatest khan's mother, and his trusted advisor. Later, I was first son to Sultan Suleiman the Lawgiver, most beloved of his children. After I died that time, my good father's grief spilled into beautiful poetry:
The people think of wealth and power as the greatest fate,
But in this world a spell of health is the best state.

"Important verses, don't you think?" Tina-Marie turns, a picture of drunken befuddlement. She's squinting, blinking too much. Tears have melted runnels into her face-paint. "Don't you think they mean something?"

"No doubt," I says. "I gets it."

Now she looks at me proper, half-lit. Frowns. "How the hell did I end up here?"

I knows she don't mean *here*, wasting a morning in Leather Jenny's cabin, so much as *here* in a broader sense. Trapped in Chippewa territory, at the country's arse-end, powerless and poor, with a head full of impossible riches. By *here* Tina's really saying *now*.

This shiftless era. This hopeless state. This century of empty abundance.

This long dark gap between short periods of brilliance.

"Let me help," I says, patting the couch cushion beside me, getting to the crux of it all. "I'll untangle them timelines, straighten 'em out. Settle that uneasy mind of yers, get you back on track."

"Thing is," she says, "I don't want to know. Everything my selves have done, everything we've achieved? Everything we've lost." Then, quiet and true: "I don't want to know how I got here. I don't want to know any of it anymore."

"Well," I says, thumbing the charm-knotted cords wrapped round my arms, the many pasts that string me together. "Y'all know I can help with that, too."

〜

Folk never ask about Leather Jenny's own early days.

Would've disappeared ages ago if it weren't for y'all, I'd tell any who asked. If only they'd ask.

Bound in their problems, their own little lives, they don't bother. They don't care. Not now, not then. Generations of ignorant, lucky fools. All they see's an old bald woman, shrivelled and crooked but still limber enough to look after herself—to look after them, when she comes a-calling. *Always been here, the soothsayer has*, Chippewa parents says to their frightened young'uns, smacking the nail on its skull without even knowing it. Without knowing how very long that *always* has been for me in this county, so long I can't rightly recall the full of it myself. Not rightly. Not anymore.

Maybe, once, there was a Jenny-gal who cured deer hides on the banks of unspoiled rivers, a Jenny whose black braids were silken nightmares to brush, a Jenny who was smooth and smart and learned real fast, a Jenny who soon read cloud-currents and bark-peelings and sap-secrets, a Jenny who witnessed the first tall ships bringing all these cursed folks' folks ashore.

Maybe, later, there was a clever-Jenny who attracted shadows, a Jenny who was welcomed into grove and glade and coven, a Jenny who traded kin and company for hexcraft, a Jenny whose nimble mind and nimbler fingers sifted through lives once-lived and lives sometimes-remembered, a Jenny who ruthlessly stole strands of those years to lengthen her own.

Maybe, there was a solitary Jenny who watched whole fleets arrive by water and leave by wing, a Jenny whose time-tressing weaved her through celebrations and civil wars, a Jenny who snipped folks' time just a bit and stashed the freight of their years inside her own skull, a Jenny who soothed by seeing everyone they'd ever been, then wrenched her own plaits out by the root, desperate to forget what she saw.

Maybe, there's a Leather Jenny whose life is bits and pieces pilfered together, magpied snatches of other folks' memories, other folks' strings, a Jenny who is tough and tired-out as this here couch, worn almost beyond use, yet stubbornly holding on.

Maybe, there's the forever Jenny who wants always and only to be herself, somehow, somewhen, no matter who or what she takes to be so.

∿

Tina's head lolls heavy in my lap, weighed down with brandy and bother. Shoes off, she's stretched full out on the sofa. Hands clasped over the rumpled round of her belly. Heels fretting against fabric.

"Reckon I'm soused," she giggles, slipping into the crass accent she's tried so hard all these years to suppress. "Worse than Mikhaēl III ever was—never mind that folk in Miklagarðr took to calling him *The Drunk*." She snickers. "Them Byzantine richlings wouldn't know a real drunkard if he walloped 'em on their hook noses. The Emperor was a booze-hound, but highly functional; constantly but only ever mildly pissed. Nothing close to what Ger's like after a night at the rodeo, I can promise you that."

Any other day, she'd die of shame before admitting what other folk already know: that Ger's a lout if ever there was one. An ale-sponge first, a seed-spreader second, and coming third—by a long mile—a two-bit rodeo wrangler. Ger still gots enough flick in that wrist of his to rope a longhorn come Saturnsday nights, but somehow he can't manage to loop nothing whatsoever round Tina-Marie's wedding finger. Now his once-firm rump's been flattened on too many of The Short Go's barstools; all them bottomless cups he's swallowed has turned his once-fine figure to suet. Unlike the man she won't never call husband, Tina don't often pursue such liquid escapes. Nor numbing powders. Nor needle-veined oblivion.

Them habits don't offer more than temporary black-outs, which simply ain't long enough for her.

"Slip this on," I says, fishing a lavender-filled sleeping mask from my apron pocket, followed by a fine-toothed ivory comb. As any teenage girl or secret lover knows, everyone's more honest in the dark. "Close yer eyes. Rest a spell."

After she fumbles the faux-satin elastic around her head, I work her tresses loose with my fingers, riffling the frazzled strands across my thighs. Memory knots cluster close to her scalp, filthy bunches of 'em, obvious as black roots in platinum blonde hair. Small wonder she's been so agitated, I think. What with all them shadow-nits roaming, burrowing, laying pesky eggs so near to her dream-maker. Practically begging me to yank 'em free.

"This pressure all right?" I ask, but with the very first scrape of my comb through them overburdened snarls, I knows it ain't.

All right.

The pressure.

First off, the tines snag on pieces of Halvdan's life—these ones are closest to the surface, I reckon, since Tina-Marie was only just thinking on her Viking days—and I tug firm, drawing a thread out to arm's length. What a tangle! What a mess. Combing, pulling, I haul them stringed recollections and twist 'em all out of order. *The Hagia Sofia! Battle-steel and blood! Miklagarðr in its heyday! The Forum of Theodosius with its basilica, its triumphal arch! Constantine's magnificent god-topped column, porphyry cylinders stacked one atop the other, defying gravity! Stone pretending to be a great shaft of light.*

Exposed like this, stretched and combed across my lap, Tina's long lives begin to harden. Unfurled, her memory knots turn into my own life-giving leather. Watching for frayed filaments, for potential breakages, I pluck whole strands root and all. Won't do neither of us no good if I leave wisps behind to burrow into her head once more, to wriggle in deep and start to fester. Careful, careful, I snare and tug and take. Immediately she breathes a bit easier. So do I.

While I work, the morning broadens into afternoon. Day spills thunder-grey through the open window, diluting the fireglow inside. A lulling light, it washes round us, soft as the hush of my comb through Tina-Marie's oldest and dearest recollections, dull as the much more recent memories I leave stuck firm on her pate.

Rasping the comb through Tina's coarse hair, I gather enough life-yarns to weave an immortal tapestry. Pinching and pulling, I unfurl a stiff cord of buff leather long as my arm. The follicle is misshapen and hard: a tenacious, tear-drop pearl. Tina stirs when it finally pops free. Her sigh is a farewell to St Petersburg.

Another strand, slightly shorter, is yellow as a sprig of wheat and twice as flexible—it twangs loose from her scalp, flails, then recoils snug round my forearm. Immediately I'm weather-bitten, scoured by katabatic winds. Hooded falcons shriek, tethered on my wrist. Frustrated hunters, their talons dig in, sharp and tense, as I absorb the ache Tina has for that nomadic age. The steppe-words stop whirring in the deepest pockets of her chest, horsewhipped out between teeth and lips. *Chitt, troot, añoolt, miitsuuk* ... Phrases summoned like herds with a *whoosh*, a *shoo*, meanings galloping away before she wakes. I gulp 'em all down like fermented mare's milk, soaking up all them moments, them honour-driven years.

I coil these detached strands round my biceps and forearms and wrists, skin against skin. While I'm wrapping and knotting these extra days onto my lifeline, I touch-read each remembered event in the leather, stark as a headline. *Hoelun abducted by Yesügei! Proclaimed chief wife! Birthed five strong babies!* For a moment Tina-Marie stirs; she starts babble-whimpering beside me. Rattling off the names of all her many bubs, then and now—*Alexei-Paul, Hümaşah, Gudrun, Honey Blossom, Joelene*—blacking the cords they're attached to with her guilt. It ain't that Tina don't love her current kids. Only, maybe, she should oughta love 'em more. Resent 'em less. The way Hoelun did her son *Temüjin, my brave blacksmith!* The way Flaccilla Augusta—more so than Theodosius—had loved her daughter *Aelia Pulcheria, my short-lived Gallaecian gal.* The way Emperor Sulieman had loved Tina-Marie when she wore the shape of his eldest son, Mehmed.

The people think of wealth and power as the greatest fate ...

So unfair, Tina reckons—I can feel the frustration in her stubborn knots—so goddamn unfair that she died in Constantinople before Mehmed had seen the end of his twenty-second year. Before he could follow his father again into battle. Before *he* could become Caliph of Islam, Amir al-Mu'minin, Custodian of the Two Holy Mosques, Sultan of the Ottoman Empire, Padişah, Shadow of God on Earth.

... in this world a spell of health is the best state.

So unfair to be stuck here in Chippewa county.

Doing nothing worth the effort of doing it, nothing worth remembering.

Enduring the longest, healthiest, poorest now she's ever known.

~

In this today, Tina don't teach her sons tactics, nor negotiate clan rivalries, nor dole out advice about conquering rival tribes. The only wars she mediates are her fool kids' petty squabbles. Whose turn it is for the TV controller. Whose turn to hose down the trailer. Whose turn to go to bed hungry.

In this today, Tina's daughters ain't draped in lace nor ribbons. They don't stand proud in quilted wool robes, fur-lined and hemmed to the shin. Tina's gals ain't got sharp eyes, narrowed to keep out demons. To a one, theirs is wide bunny-peepers, ever startled, ever stupid. She don't expect them to become bank managers or sportscasters or even book-keepers, but wishes they'd at least finish school.

In this today, ain't no dynastic marriage going to drag Tina out of the trailer park. She ain't no-one's consort, no-one's lover. She ain't got endless streams of men come a-courting—no Sergei, no Grigory, no Alexander, no Stanisław—no cashed-up movers and shakers advising her, lifting her up a class or two, keeping her there. Sometimes, she gots Ger Stout. Most other times, she dallies with ghosts.

In this today, what Tina-Marie Dalton gots most of all is a history of greatness and a future what can't and won't never compare. Even so, she can't stop comparing 'em. Comparing is all she gots. Comparing is what she does.

~

Combing and tearing, plucking and scoring, I sort Tina-Marie out better than any city shrink can. Leather Jenny only untethers what holds folk down and not a strap more. Too much greatness is a diamond-crusted suit, I reckon, too big and heavy for any old body to bear, much less this scrawny rack of mine. So I remove only the fetters. The sense of entitlement Tina's carried from cradle to grave and back again. The soul-deep belief that she's been ripped off. The *injustice* of being born a have-not.

The longing for real happiness.

One last pale wisp whistles through my grasp—*No scarier*

than getting your ears pierced, she says—but I let that one fall right where it is, alongside a thick ponytail of protected thoughts. Recollections of her upbringing here in Chippewa, her kin-ties to folk in neighbouring counties, her job at the chip wagon, her choir songs, her young'uns, even her lout of a man. These all stay where the gods put 'em first. These stay right where they belong. Ain't my place to uproot the gal completely, after all. Only to nip out the blighted parts so's she can grow.

᭡

Tina rouses just as I'm putting a crock of beef stew on for dinner. The pot ain't mine—a loan from someone or another who'll make themselves known once I've gobbled the gift inside it—and it's heavier than I expect. Sprightly as my new strappings have got me feeling, it's hard to lift the thing onto the woodstove without a wakesome clang. Behind me, Tina's sock feet thump sleepily to the floor.

"Must of dozed off," she says, squashing a yawn with her fist. "Seems I ain't gots much of a head for brandy."

"Hope I didn't disturb you," I says quietly. In the stove's iron belly, coals clunk against the grate. On the rooftop, a nightingale trills. Slow-stirring garlic into the slop, I sneak a glimpse over my shoulder. The window's a rectangle of blue twilight, the hearth burnished copper, the couch almost pretty in the warm glow. Tina's frumped on the middle cushion, lacing up her shoes. Mascara smudged and hair haystacked, dress so creased it's practically smocked, the girl ain't never looked so composed. So calm.

"Sweet dreams?"

"Not a one," Tina says, smiling wide. "Slept like a log. With five kids, that's dream enough. Gots to give thanks for the little things, I reckon."

"Amen," I says, clanging the spoon against the pot's rim. "Hungry? There's more food here than I can chew through in a lifetime. Shame to see it spoil."

"Gots to scoot," Tina says, shaking her tousled head. "Promised the bubs mac 'n' cheese tonight. Y'all going to be alright out here on yer lonesome?"

"Hunky dory," I says. "Just grand."

"*Grand*," Tina says, snorting. "When'd you start talking so fancy? Putting on airs with me now 'cos I flaked on supper?"

Feels so good to laugh, I keep at it a while without even wheezing. Getting hold of myself at last, I nod her toward the door. "Take care of yourself, princess."

Tina-Marie flushes. "You too, Miss Jenny."

Leaning over the stove I take a deep, rich breath. Steam hides my grin. "Always do," I says, waving as she leaves.

For what it's worth, I ain't touched none of Tina-Marie's savvy, nor her gift for learning—won't hurt if she's a history buff, now will it? Won't hurt if she retains enough facts to win big on *Jeopardy*— but I *did* take her firsthand know-how of all those beautiful pasts, the taste and smell and feel of all her wondrous back-thens. So there won't be no more highfalutin talk out of Miss Tina-Marie Dalton. No more diplomatic concerns. No more being pen-pals with French philosophers. No more scratching her name on balustrades in famous temples. No more sailing nor sword-fighting nor conquering. No more champagne. No more gold.

Let someone else play Catherine the Great for a spell, I reckon.

Let someone else raise Genghis Khan.

Let someone else hope for the better.

∞

FOUR FACTS ABOUT
THE URSINES

THEY ARE ALWAYS HUNGRY.

No matter what y'all are told, now or later, *this* is the fact to remember. Got it?

Of course they don't eat day in, day out. Ursines can go weeks, months—decades, even—between feeds. How quick they digest depends on how much they gorged, which in turn determines how long they'll doze. In other words, the biggest gluttons is the heaviest sleepers. A couple of babies might knock out a grown buck 'til morning. A busload of you kids might set a few Ursines to dreaming for a month, maybe two if they're still cubs. Teams of young men caught pick-axing in the mountains might keep a full clan snoring in its den for a year, give or take, so long as the Ursines in question are small to mid-size.

Our vitals make for powerful soporifics, I reckon, more potent by the swallow than a full copper vat of moonshine.

But once the beasts start a-tossing under twig-and-moss blankets, once they start a-turning over the marrowless bones littering their cave floors, y'all can expect their drowsy arses to roll right out of bed. Roll right back down the slopes to our valley, our camp. Right ready for their next meal.

Now, y'all are probably thinking (as most fools round here will, and do) that surely Ursine bellies is only *so* big. Surely they must get full up *sometimes*. Or food-poisoned. Or simply bored of the same-old, same-old snacks. Gold-miners, rodeo-riders, leather-workers, log-drivers: ain't the gluttons sick of gobbling these four courses and nothing else, year after year after year? Surely the lot of us must taste like scraps of rawhide, thrown horseshoes, hot-rusted steel? Surely *one* of us is bound to twist their guts, sooner or later. Surely they can't chew through every last tender body without some wizened chunk finally sticking in their craws? Some rotten specimen choking them off?

Enough with the giggling, little skeptics.

I know what the lot of y'all are thinking; it's writ clear in them dimples you're grinning, and the roll of them sweet, oh-so-innocent eyes. *Ain't no Ursines in Big Kalhoun, silly Nanny. Yer making this up.* Hmmm? Next you'll swear the world ends at the tree line, that it stops dead where the mountains' blue peaks blend in with the summer sky. Don't scowl so, little darlins. I don't mean to tease. We're all of us born with that same Columbus complex—nothing and no-one exists beyond our realm of knowings, not 'til we discover them for ourselves. Believe you me: we've all of us been the very first explorers of our age. We've all of us unearthed brand new mysteries other folks already dug up countless times before. Sooner or later, everyone in these here ranges finds it's second nature to dig. Can't blame no-one for doing what comes natural. Doing whatever they can to survive. To thrive.

As I was saying.

The Ursines is a god-awful, ravenous lot.

After all this time—more than four dozen years by my reckoning—they're stirring in their hollows again. Shucking coverlets, rubbing yellow crust from snouts and lashes, turning bleary gazes to the Big Kalhoun-shaped pantry we've been so busy replenishing for 'em. Took 'em that long to sleep off their last feast, and exhale all the treasure their kind produces in slumber. No doubt their lairs is hell-shiny with it; the rough stone walls closing in, grown thick with the gold of Ursine's petrified breaths. By now, I bet they're feeling awful cramped in there. I bet they're aching for a good stretch.

Yes, smart-mouth: *even more cramped* than in this here burrow of mine.

No, sirree. Y'all can't go a-roaming yourselves today.

Believe you me, soon the Ursines will break loose of their rich covers and come roaring down to our valley once more. Breaths cold and empty as their stomachs. Toting sickles, scythes, hessian sacks. Hankering for breakfast.

Think this is nawt but a tale I'm spinning? Some trick to coop the wretched lot of y'all inside, forcing you to keep old Nanny company?

Hmmph.

Your folks ain't done you no favours, keeping y'all ignorant. They're doing you no favours at all. Trust me.

So tell me, little experts. Indulge me. You think I'm *that* lonely? You think my noggin's gone soft as warm suet? Maybe it's crammed with fogged memories, nonsense stories, and old lady fears? Well, I may not recall my own Mama, but I sure as hell didn't pop from her nethers hunched and shrivelled like this, I can tell you that much. My hairs weren't always like milkweed fluff, my skin weren't always thin as birch bark. I didn't always have this limp, this crutch.

Once upon a time, I was pink and fresh and just as delicious as you.

The Ursines couldn't *wait* to sink their teeth into kids like me.

Like y'all.

And folks is ever keen to let them.

⌁

Hard to say who came first to these mountains: us or them. Could well be *they* were already tucked in their dens, hibernating, oozing ore, long before giant Nathaniel Kalhoun ever piled picks, prospecting kits, pegs and pans into that famous mule-drawn cart of his, long before he drove it overland from the prairies. Could well be there was all this prime territory here for that digger's kin to claim because any and all other would-be settlers was even then lining Ursine bellies. Then again, it could just as well be the steady influx of pioneers strapped into covered wagons—old-fashioned meals on wheels, they were—that drew the beasts out from whatever dark womb spawned 'em, and lured 'em straight to these ranges.

Either way, the fact is, Ursines ain't known to share.

They reckon this land is *theirs*. Far as they're concerned, there ain't no negotiations, no bargains, no stake on this turf sharper than their soul-crunching teeth. And that's one damned compelling argument, if you ask me.

But that's the trouble, ain't it? No-one really has. *Asked*, that is. Even though I once escaped the foulest of Ursine dens—the very *kitchen*, where the worst eating happens—not merely one of them abandoned nests your folks sneak into nowadays. Armed with chisels and axes, your parents hack chunks of hardened breath-gold into barrows, then slink away with wheels squealing under the weight of that theft. Not that they see it as such, of course. Stealing.

Season after season, they just keep tramping upslope, taking what the Ursines won't willingly give. Again and again, no questions asked. Never getting caught. Never punished. Never learning what it means to lose more than ever they gained.

They don't *really* know what it means to survive, your folks. They ain't never wriggled out from under Ursine paws. Never felt that rank, oh-so-precious, honey and pork-scented breath on their cheeks. Never heard claws gouging swift trails to our camp, never seen them deep dirt-grooves scummed up with human gravy. They don't know what it means to really fear.

Listen.

Quit your fidgeting—there's room enough on this bunk for everyone. C'mon, snuggle in close, little poppets. No, we can't light a fire. Last night I clambered up the grassy face of this here lonely burrow, and clogged the smoke-hole with rubble and scree. Took some doing, that did, what with this gnawed leg of mine twisting every which way it shouldn't, this crutch better at tamping down chimney-junk than holding an old woman upright. Then I nailed shut the only window, welded its hinges flush into the schist. Rigged the passage door so's it only unlocks from the inside. And all that *after* I'd already trekked round to the beast-riddled side of the mountain, *after* setting and sparking a couple well-placed fuses, *after* hobbling back home with pebble and mortar blast still rattling my skull.

(I could of been a decent engineer, you know. I'm none too shabby at planning ahead, predicting outcomes, figuring and calculating. Shrewd, folk called me, after I eluded the Ursines that time. Cunning, they said.)

Plus, we've run out of logs and I sure as stone ain't going out to chop more. No, children, neither are you. Few things ring louder than axe-echoes in this valley, and it's best we don't hook the beasts' ears right about now. Grab another quilt from the blanket box if you're cold. Jam your hands under your rumps. Make do.

Of course, ain't nowhere warmer than inside Ursine guts. If y'all don't behave, I could roll you in syrup, leash you outside as a tantalizer . . . That's what your folks' folks use to do, you know, when the growlers kept a-coming. Thick and fast and *hungry*.

At first, it was the tunnel-dogs what went missing, snatched straight off the chains pegged outside prospecting tents. Then horses. Then the burliest miners we had, my own gruff Pops included. The Ursines tore through our outlying camps, randomly munched their way inward. Raiding harsh and unpredictable. By the time they reached Big Kalhoun proper, there weren't much in the way of large meals left. Orphans well and truly outnumbered their elders, clever widows outnumbered the men who'd dragged 'em here. You'd of thought, wouldn't you, that those Mamas would of fought back—flint and flame women they were, like your old Nan. You'd of thought they'd wield stakes and steel—whatever they had near to hand—to lay waste to immediate threats, to lay claim on a safer future. You'd of thought they'd sacrifice *anything* to survive.

And in a way, I suppose, they did.

When I was a young'un—yep, just like y'all, except my folks was already both scorching in the afterlife—I sure ain't had a cozy room like this one, nor a soft bunk to cower in. Stray children like me were lucky to snag a bit of mattress in some widow's hallway; more often than not, *bed* was nawt but a thin towel spread out on her cold storage floor. Where I was boarded—near the crick, at Mrs Masterson's place—there was just two other orphans, twins too young yet even for talking. For a short while, the three of us shared a threadbare sleeping bag laid on a scrap of foam.

Next door, Widow Ross were stuck minding a bunch of Big Kalhoun's tykes. Nine, I reckon, which weren't *so* many, since she started off with none of her own. Even so: *Ursines can't snatch ye if yer harnessed to the porch*, I once heard her say to the girls she'd taken in, little Junebug and her sister Thelma-Rose. *They ain't got the thumbs to undo buckles and knots.*

Of course, Widow Ross had it nowhere near as hard as Widow Jameson further on down the road. Already *she'd* birthed seven bubs herself, but got saddled with four more on account of her cabin having a good-sized living room. *A burden*, she often mumbled into her brandy. That's what us kids was to them. Heavy reminders of what they'd lost.

Not a one of them ladies had it in her to care for young'uns what weren't her own. Not *really*. Not like your old Nan.

Hush, you. Make believe y'all are those baby boys I shared a bed-roll with—quietest things I ever did meet, those two. Didn't grizzle one bit when Mrs Masterson wrapped 'em in her floral apron, plunked 'em out on the stoop, and strapped 'em to the railing with a set of reins she didn't need no more.

Ursines don't care for the taste of leather, she'd said, when she caught me spying through the fly screen. She whistled for her loyal guards—sleek, muscular mutts with vicious snarls—and clipped their collars to chains nearby. *There*, she'd conveyed with a smirk and a lazy wave. *Don't say I ain't never helped.*

Bullpucky, I'd shouted (ever the bold creature), right before she hauled me out by the ear, tethered me next to the droolers. Just beyond reach of the hounds.

We'll see, she said, then went inside, pretending she couldn't see nothing at all.

That night, the twins made punctured kick-ball sounds in the pitch darkness: two sharp squeaks, a whispering whine, and that was it. They were gone. Gulped down. Leather and all.

To be honest, my own clobbering wasn't that much noisier. I would of shrieked my throat raw, if only I'd sensed the bastards coming. My hearing's as good now as it was then, but still nowhere near sharp as *theirs*. If only I'd seen 'em creeping out the forest, across the grass yard, lurking up to the house . . . But when they grabbed me, the moon was worthless as a silver dollar in a wishing well. Black clouds rippled in a soot sky, heavy and low, as good a blindfold as you're ever like to get. Mountains merged with the woods round Mrs Masterson's cabin, each one dark as the other. On the porch where I was hog-tied, sometimes numb, sometimes aching, there came them two squeaks, double whines, then a sudden dim absence where the twins should of been. Silence where there should of been dogs.

Now, I ain't going to lie to y'all the way Mrs M did me. Ursines ain't got no problems with harnesses. They love the taste of leather and denim just as much as cotton bibs and aprons and flannelette. Porch rails ain't no goddamn barrier. Neither is darkness.

Ursines don't eat with their peepers, after all.

Whimpering or wailing—whatever the volume—calls them quick as any dinner bell. Yeah, they must of listened out our location, the twins' and mine, traced the frantic flutter of our breaths. And in the split-second before that foul skin and bone—hand? paw? long-fingered *something*—clamped over my face, before it smothered me from jaw to brow? I *must of* hollered.

Lord, I still hope it set their ears to bleeding.

I hope it *hurt*.

Y'all have *got* to understand: ain't nothing more fearful than being snatched. To be suddenly vanished from your old life without warning. Without a word. Without a *why*. And there ain't no reasoning with the Ursines—we can't talk our way out from their jaws, not now, not then—especially not if you're little and helpless like I was, like all of y'all are. Ain't no escape whatsoever but to close your damned eyes. Hide in plain sight. Play dead while they feast on the living.

But y'all don't have to worry about that now. Every last one of you is safe, aren't you just. Tucked warm inside, truly safer than houses. Ain't no other way y'all could stomach stories of these beasts, ain't no other reason y'all would be begging to hear 'em. Tell me I'm wrong.

To you, the Ursines are only ideas. Fodder for harmless nightmares. You ain't never been carried up to their warrens. Ain't never had their greasy digits rubbing, prodding, insinuating. Ain't never felt the rasp of their honey-snot tongues on your neck. Ain't never been tossed on a wet, cold pile of chopped twigs and logs—make that boulders and bricks and shards of stone—*no*, make that ribcages. Gnawed torsos. Thighs, elbows, chins, knees. (Over there was Junebug, always and still in gingham, Thelma-Rose in her dungarees.) Y'all ain't never crawled under the decaying shells of your hollow-skulled playmates. (White leather booties for the twins, who'd never learned to walk.) Y'all ain't never worn dead bodies for cover.

None of you's ever been struck by the notion—even as arrowhead teeth pierce the stupid leg you left sticking out from that edible heap, even as *the pain the pain the pain* burns up your shin, even as you bite your tongue and play corpse, even as chomping leads to spurting to gulping to slurping and, thank holy Christ, to burping and hiccupping and finally to drunken-loud snoring—y'all ain't never *known* that the Ursines ain't really to blame for your being there, crippled and near-senseless, bleeding out on a dirty cave floor. It ain't really *their* fault at all.

So, no. To answer your question: I ain't never seen 'em clear-like. Maybe they're part bear, part pig, part giant. Maybe they have talons or tusks or boar-bristle spines. Maybe they wear children's skins, maybe they have pelts of gore and shadow and stink. But I do know one thing for certain: they ain't fiends. They ain't *inhuman*.

They ain't never devoured one another.

~

Fact is, Ursines ain't got any real family.

They ain't loyal. They hunt solo or in packs, whatever's convenient. Between breakfast and bedtime, they rut out of instinct. Boars on boars, sows on sows, sires on siblings; ain't no boundaries between them, no morals, no lifelong mates. They don't love, so don't never get lonely. They don't *need*. They hunger, that's all. So they feed.

They birth plenty of offspring, but their young don't stay that way for long.

All right, out with it: what's squinting them peepers of yours?

Hmmph. That some imagination you got there, punkin. Ain't no parents *never* come a-calling when our foes is set to rampage. Trust me. When them beasts get a good hunger going, it's every kid for herself.

After I got snatched, the Ursines ransacked Big Kalhoun. Wiped out more than half the town before sun-up, snapped up all but a couple of orphans. Of course, I ain't seen the devastation myself for nigh on a week. While the gold-spitters slunk from their lairs, I stayed behind in the den, a prime brisket stored in their fridge for later. I was in no condition to walk, much less run, but damned if I wouldn't escape. I could still writhe on my belly. I could slither.

Slowly, slowly, hugging the dank stone walls, I gained the cave's mouth, then slid like a tongue over its split lip. Dribbled down the gravel and dirt path, into the woods, to the shelter of crackling undergrowth. Already there was smoke on the air, but what that meant didn't register. Not then. Feet and paws and hoofs juddered past, so close I should of been trampled, scooped up, hauled back into Ursine maws or dragged down to our rallying camp. Should of been, but wasn't.

I always was good at hiding.

In a prickly hollow, I lay still and senseless while torches were lit far below. While jerry cans were filled with cheap whiskey and gasoline. While rags were stuffed into the tanks' red plastic spouts. While rifles popped, closer and closer. While shrieks combatted snarls—near, then on, then up the mountainside. While claws and teeth fought bullets. While predators contended with prey.

The Ursines will forever outnumber us. We can shoot at 'em, we can burn out their dens, but ain't no chance we'll defeat the whole army in one go. With sharpened shovels and hatchets, the widows made a good dent in their ranks that night, walloping what shadows had dodged fire and shotgun spray, what gold-growlers had lumbered into camp past the rifle-slung gents. None of the Ursines cared a whit about their fallen kin. They galumphed right overtop of 'em to get at our screamers and snivellers. They trampled any and all bodies into puddles, into muck.

And yet.

Even so.

It ain't lack of kin what makes you a monster, believe me.

∿

Weapons only do so much in these circumstances, if y'all want my opinion. The smartest fight is the one waged in secret. Wait the brutes out, I reckon. Act by not acting out—not for a good whiles anyway. Least of all when they expect it. Withhold the youngest, tenderest, best part of the feast while Ursines race round stealing, hoarding, glutting themselves dumb on larger, slower treasures. Mind you, there's bound to be casualties with this approach—ain't no such thing as a bloodless war—but, with proper planning, with foresight, you can manage it so's only them what deserves it get snuffed. Might well be we can put right the imbalance what's been tipping Big Kalhoun off-kilter all this time. Ever since.

This ain't just a theory, but a work in progress. Here's hoping we can pull this off, the whole lot of you and me. Together.

At one point—when the Ursines was sleeping, a blood-hot huddle all round me, and there I was, cold on my back, staring up at the yellow ore on their cave's ceiling, centuries of stalactites shaped from their putrid breath—my eyes were so blurred with exhaustion,

I swore all the gold up there wasn't stone. Wasn't honey, neither. No, I thought. Up there was a county's worth of haloes, one small shining circle for each life folks had ransomed so's they could stay here in Big Kalhoun. Yep, that includes your folks. And their folks. And mine.

Why stay, I wondered, knowing the dangers? Surely there were other dig-holes to plunder. Surely there were other, Ursine-free ranges. Why weren't our folks striking camp there and then, packing up soon as dawn pinked the sky? Why didn't they put the torch to their dead, say prayers and farewells, and make the swiftest possible tracks elsewhere?

Why were they still here days later, when I finally stumbled, half-mad with fever and infection, onto Mrs Masterson's ruined porch?

Why are they still here *now*?

Don't bother answering. Sixty-odd years it's taken me to figure it out; we ain't got that much time left for y'all to reach my conclusions. Soon as the ruckus dies outside we'll be hitting the road, so I'd better lead y'all straight as I can to the end.

Just for a minute, imagine yourself out front of the log cabin your great-granddaddy built with his own two hands. Picture them peaks across the valley he settled as more than just great humps of pine-covered rock. See 'em instead as your own personal lock-box, filled to the brim with treasure. Know down to your very marrow that there, *right there*, is a legacy fit for any of them high-rolling city folk. Believe yourself an adventurer, a pioneer, a trailblazer. Convince yourself security always comes with risks. Look at them mountain troves and decide you can slip in gentle enough—you're stealthy, you're resourceful—and you can slip back out again, rich and unstung. Full *proud* of what you've done.

With pride comes overconfidence. *The Ursines ain't attacked in years . . . We'll mine only the oldest, least-used caves . . . Shame about the kids we lost but, heck, we still gots the makings to git us some more . . . Plus, now we gots the coin to support 'em . . .*

You think I'm exaggerating. How would you know? You weren't around then. All you've got is my word on how greedy we got. How greedy we are still.

Just to clarify, so's we're seeing eye-to-eye on this, by *we* I mean *them*.

All them folks in Big Kalhoun. Razing forests where once upon a time the Ursines slept in peace. Knocking together pretty wooden boxes for all the orphan-breeders to live in. Building a whole town full of people-coops. (Folk laughed when I tunnelled into this here hillside. Nigh impossible to break into, this little hidey-hole of mine, I said back, and still they laughed. We'll see who's crazy once the beasts arrive. We'll see who's laughing then.) What's worse, though? *Breeders.* Folks having more kids, *here.* In *this* world, this country, this day and age. Pure selfishness, that is. All they're doing is cluttering up the landscape with precious dumplings. Tidbits born to distract the Ursines from bigger, more filling mouthfuls.

Clean the crud out your ears, children. Ain't no-one else truly cares for your whereabouts. Only me.

〜

This is a real-life telling, not some folk tale; it takes more than three neat parts to unfold. Today y'all are getting four and a bit. Tomorrow? Who knows. We can tell it again on the road, if you want. Embellish and refine it together.

Don't worry, now. We'll make it through fine 'til morning. Mongrels they might be, but only one Ursine part is hound—and it sure ain't the snout. They won't never sniff us out in here. Fact is, their noses are blunt as concrete.

Their *ears*, though. Well, we already know how sensitive they are, don't we just? Top-notch canine. Owl-keen. Good thing these walls of mine are three yards thick, not to mention muffled in turf. Even better: that door there is fit for a fortress. Not much will penetrate it. Not claws, not battering rams. Not some lonesome Nanny's voice responding to a bunch of children's wee ramblings. Air will sneak in through the shuttered window, sure enough, but little else will undermine them bolts. We're well away from the action, darlins. From here, we'd be unlucky to hear the slaughter.

Dry them tears, sweetness. Stop that sniffling. Clench the quiver out of that chin.

We'll be safe 'til it's over. Safer than houses. Those gunpowder blasts (one hell-cunning diversion, that was, if I do say so myself) did double duty: not only waking the Ursines from their overlong sleep-in, but also throwing them off our sound-trail. Even now, a ruckus of loose boulders and pebbles is avalanching down the mountain's

— 77 —

westernmost face. Directing those terrifying ears away from this humble hideaway. Pointing them, once more, at Big Kalhoun.

We'll be safe so long as your folks keep on hollering.

Keep your voices down 'til theirs give out.

It's all right, my darlins.

Hush, now. Hush.

I've got you.

I've got you.

Listen as night falls quiet. Listen to me.

The Ursines are coming.

They are nearly here.

And they are hungry.

∞

SOMETHING CLOSE TO GRACE

FTER THE MULE DIED, MOSE SCROUNGED AN OLD pickup off Ruddy Jickson's lot no more'n a mile down the interstate. Once it might of been a sweet oyster blue, but now the junker's well-chewed by time. Its rounded panels and fenders is doilied with rust, the paintwork's red-brown from lid to belly, much like them jugs of sour mash Mose is been known to swig on a homeward drive. Hopeless as sin, that truck of theirs, but Perch were glad enough to see it.

Ain't half so good as swimming, she'd thought back then, watching Mose pull up on the gravel out front. *Still . . . Reckon it'll go further than the donkey ever done.* That poor waste of flesh weren't hardly able to shoulder groceries from Bisbee's market, much less a woman grown, nor the four kids Mose'd got on her. But a truck! A *truck*. Well, now. *That there's a four-wheeled promise of freedom.*

Except, like so many joys Perch is known in her twenty-odd years, this one's short-lived. With holes wore clear through the floor, handles what don't open on wet or cold days, and axles hee-hawing to the high heavens, the thing ain't barely fit for the road. No more'n twice a week, it whines up to the lookout off Chillins Bluff, metal guts rumbling while Perch idles there, watching gallon after hypnotic gallon swan-dive to the Saccattaw river below.

Once upon a time, she swum them deep wide waters all the way from Tapekwa County to the falls right here in Plantain. That trip would of took most folk half a day by boat, but Perch weren't most folk. She *weren't*. Before she met Mose, she could see clear through silt-choked shallows and frothing rapids alike. She could make it from one muddy bank to the other without once needing to surface. She could hear the currents whisper, and understood what they was saying. *Go this way. Go that way. Git away away away . . .*

Underwater, she breathed better than ever she did on land. Only when she were fully doused could she enjoy the hint of gills on her neck, the sheer strength of a double-finned kick, the fish blood of her Mama's kin. Submerged, she were cold powerful. Sleek and firm. Shimmering speed.

Before Mose, Perch's very own flippers drove her upstream and down whenever the mood struck. She ain't never *quite* achieved Mama's endurance, nor her perfect tail, nor the school of tiny fish that were always flittin round it—but she were getting close. So close. She *were*. A few months more and she'd of been ready—oh yes she would of—just a few more months and she could of taken the plunge, could of full-dunked herself into a pool of Tapekwa's magicked waters, could of turned mer-lady for good if she'd wanted. Before Mose, Perch reckoned maybe she *did* want it. That legless life. Sun-up to set, she'd splashed around in the drink without ever feeling tired. Or lonely. Or lost.

Since Mose, though, she ain't been herself. Now she's weak as warm piss. Her riverskin's dried out, hidden in the trailer somewheres. Without it, she can't go no further than where this sad old pickup takes her. To Bisbee's when the oats run out. To the gas station on Sunday afternoons so's she can use the phone box there. To the liquor store when the money tin's full, or to Ruddy's private still when it's rattling—whichever will keep them in easy spirits.

Eight or nine times in ten, the truck brings them back home safe.

But when them wolf-nosed Marshals sniffs the fuel on Mose's breath—as they did again, night before last—well, that pickup of theirs just ain't gots the grit to outrun them. Some Marshals gots extra speed in them furry hindquarters of theirs, extra stamina in the shapeshifted tickers pounding inside them. Put them wolves behind a patrol car's wheel and, sure as shit, they ain't gonna be slow. The way Perch heard tell of it, the chase that evening were over before them troopers' cherries even started a-blinkin. A few *whoops* of the siren and the junker were locked up in the local impound, and Mose hisself in Plantain county clink.

Once upon a time, Perch would of raced on down to the jailhouse to free him. Faster even than them hound-dog Marshals. Come hell or high water, ain't nothing would of stopped her. Once upon a time.

⌁

Keep yer skin to yerself, girl, Mama always told her. *Don't give it up to just any old someone. Once it's gone, it's gone. Ain't no easy way of getting it back.*

But for a while there, Perch couldn't wait for Mose to shuck her right out of it. For a while there, he cleaned hisself up right nice when he came a-calling. Black hair parted almost straight, hat in scrubbed hands, yellow silk shirt carrying only a whiff of mothballs. For a while there, she were drunk on the salt-smell of him, on his sweet liquored looks, on being so fiercely chased. For a while there, Mose sure were fierce.

It weren't the presents what won Perch over. The posies. The rhinestone brooch shaped like a magician's rabbit, cute little ears poking out of a gentleman's hat. The fox-fur muffler Mose'd prepared and sewn hisself. It weren't the promises of silver—*trappers catch decent coin*—nor even, eventually, the solid band of gold. It were how hard he loved her, how wild.

It were the thrill of being known so deep, so close. So often.

Keep yer skin to yerself, Mama said, but soon Mose had touched every inch of it, from the thin scar at Perch's hairline to the webs between her fingers and toes. Whenever they was alone—and sometimes even when they wasn't—he'd palm her bare shoulders, cup her bumps, squeeze her round cheeks, lick the pinkness above and below. The usual, sparrow-twitch of his gaze calmed right down when he looked only at her. With jagged nails, he'd gently trace the dolphins inked on her forearms, the twin fish circling her belly-button, the pretty waves cresting at the base of her spine. He'd take swig after swig then pass along the brown-papered bottle, purpling her neck with love bites as she swallowed and swallowed and swallowed. At last, when both their heads was swimming, he'd burrow into her. He kept at it 'til her belly was full, bullfrogged. So goddamn often.

Keep yer skin, Mama warned, but by then Mose had already gone and stole it.

— 81 —

~~

Come daybreak, Perch is cracking boiled eggs at the sink when Ruddy swerves round the mailbox at the end of the long drive, Mose's pickup hitched to his tow-rig. One headlight fights the grey dawn. Its single beam yellows the gravel, the hen-scratched yard, the bonfire pits, the trailer's corrugated side, the small kitchen window. Perch squints into the glare, looking through her own thin blue silhouette on the glass. Paying little mind to what her hands is doing. After borning this many young'uns, she sure knows how to peel an egg. Could do it with her eyes closed.

Outside, clouds of exhaust mix with tire-spun dust as Rud eases up on the throttle. This ain't the first time he's brung the pickup home for Perch—far from it—though she reckons it might be the last. Less than a yard from the front door, he kills the engine. Lumbers out into the haze. Beard a steel wool pelt that scraggles down his chest, splitting around the bulge of his gut. Coveralls spotted with grease, ball-cap brimmed with sweat. A Saint Nick shine on his nose and cheeks. Between draws on a cigarette, he mouths the words to the same tune Perch's got wailing on the wireless above her stove. If the baby weren't chirping so, if the kids weren't yawping, she might even of heard him singing out there.

"Shhh," she whispers. The bass in that twang o' Rud's always were a comfort, each note twice as deep as Mose's were high. After the right amount of whiskey, them two struck up some decent harmonies, the older voice ever carrying the younger. Perch tosses a naked egg into a plastic bowl. Imagines herself outside for a spell, soaking in the morning music. "Hush now. *Please.*"

Behind her, the kids is flapping round a small melamine table, rowdier'n a bag of squirrels. Three boys under six. The baby in a hand-me-down highchair. Another's growing under Perch's floral apron, or so says the pinch in her waistband. The sinking in her belly. The whole lot of them wears Mose's features—waxy green eyes a smidge too far apart, sharp noses even more'n a smidge too big for such narrow skulls, hair flat as cornsilk and blue-black as the sky between midnight and moon-dark. None gots her own bright hazel irises, none her loose blonde curls. In summer, they all toast up like marshmallows while she keeps herself out the sun.

Her mother-of-pearl flesh too pale, too translucent for its harsh glare.

If she hadn't squeezed them bubs out herself, she'd easily believe they belonged to a stranger.

Perch taps another egg against the metal basin, slides her nails under the shell. Hard bits cling to her fingers. She gives them a good flick while the boys complain, spitty beaks wide, squawking for breakfast. *Bird-brains*, she thinks, catching reflections of their sleep-feathered heads in the window. *Y'all is just a flock of rusty blackbirds.*

Weren't none of her water-magic passed on to any of them— Mose seen to that hisself, didn't he just. Stealing her swim like he done. Trapping her much the same way he did game. Skinning her. Filling her with stone after stone after cold stone.

Ain't a one of them kids could float worth a damn.

As Rud goes round to unhook the pickup, he spies Perch through a gap in the frilled curtains. Standing there, sleeves rolled to the elbow, smashing a whole brood of brown eggs. She returns his nod. Not his smile.

⌁

It's a twenty minute drive to the county jail. Straight down the interstate, no sharp turns, only a steady curve 'til they hit the parking lot out front of the cement building. Perch knows the route that good, half the time she don't even see the road no more. The view's a regular blur. A long stretch of asphalt pointing nowheres. Stands of pine and blue spruce whipping past on both sides. Fields swaying thick with corn. The same weatherboard farmhouse, over and over. The same faded red barn.

Beyond the crossroads, she vagues out. Fiddles with the radio. Starts counting the number of songs it takes to reach town.

Jinx, her oldest, is cross-legged on the front seat, thumbing a dog-eared deck of cards. Nostrils chapped, sniffling. The two middle'uns, Toph and Gibbs, is hunched over a comic book in the back. Snickering at the gaudy pictures, grunting and slapping if one or the other tries turning a page too soon. Slung across her chest, the baby's wriggling for another feed. "Hang on a sec," she says, then shakes her head at the expression. As if the bub ain't done

— 83 —

nothing but hang on these past few months—as if any of them ain't latched onto her like a clutch of zebra mussels. Suckling her all out of shape, sagging and stretch-marking what's left of her original skin, so's it don't look nothing like her own no more.

About a third of the way to Main Street, the Saccattaw rushes up alongside them. Only the road's gravel shoulder, a steel rail, and a bush-covered slope is between them and the water. It's a two or three mile splash to the far shore. A scattering of fall leaves spins with the waves, quick as the honkytonk man's guitar-picking fingers on the radio. With that cloud-high warble of his, Mose sung this tune all the time: *Red Clay Halo*, one of his favourites what Perch don't despise. It's got that fast bluegrass tempo, them uplifting lyrics. All that talk of mucking through life's waters, passing through them Pearly Gates even if a soul's good and muddy—well, it gave a gal hope, didn't it just. Not much wrong she could do in this world, she reckons, that won't be forgiven in the next.

Easing up on the gas, Perch jostles the bub so's it'll hush. *Hang on.*

"Make her stop," Jinx complains, drawling the 'o' long. Face screwed up worse than the baby's. "Can't hear meself think through all that naggin."

Perch flicks the blinker and swerves off the road. *Boy don't know what he's saying.* She brakes more sudden than she intended. *Just playing at mockingbird, echoing his daddy's song.* Cards fly as Jinx topples into the dash. Small bodies thud into the back of her seat. Surprised shouts become giggles. Accusations. *You was scared! No you was!* The pickup's front fender kisses the roadside railing.

"Don't move a muscle," she says, scrabbling for the handle, slamming the door behind her. Outside, she turns and glares in at her green-eyed boys. "I mean it. Y'all stay put."

She walks along the highway 'til she can't hear them no more. Their fussing, their whining, their laughter. Keeps on 'til the baby's lulled into shallow sleep. After a good while, she stops at a break in the barrier. A black-tipped stake is driven into the dirt there, a wreath of fake flowers bleached thin at its feet. Swaying to settle her stomach, Perch stands in the gap between posts. Watches the brown river flow steadily away, so far, so fast, so deep.

"Have to start charging y'all rent soon," says the uniformed C.O. behind a reinforced window, inside the jailhouse's reception and waiting room. Hairy jowls wobble as the half-man chuckles, ugly snout curling to reveal coffee-stained teeth. Eyebrows extra shaggy, overcompensating for the way his noggin's started balding up to them wolfish ears. Donut-gut giving them khaki shirt buttons a run for their money—only part on him what's been running in ages, Perch reckons. He grabs a pen and clipboard, slides a piece of carbon paper under the topmost form. Mottled tongue jutting out the corner of his mouth, he leans over the page. Presses too hard while scratching Mose's name on the release form.

"Surprised you ain't taken that show on the road yet, Hink," Perch says, deadpan. "Highlarious, that is."

"You know the drill," Hink says, flicking the sheets to make sure the copy's coming through all right. "Show us what you got."

Perch draws a dented coffee tin from her purse, upends it on the counter between them. A handful of coins rattle out first, then a feathering of faded green bills. While the clerk scowls, she thumps a hessian-wrapped bundle atop the miserable pile of cash. Unknotting the cord, she flips back a corner of the fabric. Reveals a stack of stiff hides—jackrabbit, groundhog, black-ringed raccoon—with them furs brushed sleek, shining pretty under the long fluorescent bulb overhead. She strums a finger down the ragged sides. "Take yer pick," she says.

"You think some mangy old skin's enough to get a soul outta this place?"

Perch shrugs, plucks a nice winter hare from the pack. "Reckon one oughta do it," she says. "What do you say?"

⚬

A free man once more, Mose gets in a high mood that lasts all morning. Before hopping in the truck, he grabs a couple cans from a cooler roped in the back, cracks one, and drains it with full-throated gulps. He takes another, just to be on the wet side. Play-punching Jinx on the shoulder, he tells the boy to scoot over. Slides in next to him on the front seat. The whole way home Mose slurps and belches, crow-calling out the window—a shrill taunt to them wolfish Marshals what caught but couldn't keep him—and trilling tune after tune with the kids.

"Truck stop's coming up," Perch interrupts after a few miles. "We could pull on in and give Ma a shout. Won't take her but an hour or so to swim over, what with the autumn current . . . " Already she's picturing it. The lacework of sunlight skimming Mama's back as she darts underwater. Glimmers on flesh and fins. Taffy-ribbon hair streaming long behind her, weightless and strung with minnows. Those effortless strokes of hers, drawing her ever closer. Then, on shore, that easy transformation from mer-queen to plain old Ma. "Maybe she'll whip up some of her brandied apricots when she gets here? Make this a proper welcome home. A real occasion."

But Mose says there's party enough with just them two and the young'uns. He don't meet her eye the rest of the drive, only turns in his seat and pulls faces 'til the kids is crying with laughter.

What a Pa he is, Perch thinks, feeling that same flush in her cheeks, that same warmth in her belly, that same clench in the nethers what got her flayed in the first place. Soon as they's home, the trailer unlocked and the boys plunked in front of the tube, Mose steers her to their bunk. Pulls the bulb chain. Peels her again.

When he's done, she's tingling from lip to lips.

Naked as a jaybird, Mose gets up and cracks the bedroom door. Pokes his head out. Down the narrow hall, the kids is fighting over what channel to watch; he sneaks across with them none the wiser. Pulse slowing, Perch lies back on the thin mattress. *Baby's gonna want a feed*, she thinks, pulling the skirt back down over her hips, adjusting her bra. She rolls on her side. Doesn't go no further.

A hum through the wall says Mose is hopped in the shower. His warbling keeps time with the exhaust fan's whirring. Some flaw in the design sucks steam from the bathroom, blows it out through the vent above their bed. Musty air turns humid, unbearable for more'n a minute or two. Finally sitting up, Perch itches everywhere Mose is been, new skin tender where he's rubbed off the old.

Noon fights through orange curtains, suffusing the room with dim light. Perch blinks, sure the gloom's fucking with her eyes. There's a burning around her navel what her fingernails can't seem to scratch out. White welts appear where she's been digging, even paler than the flesh around them. The unmarked, un-inked flesh. Stumbling into the hall, she pulls at her belly to get a better look. There's still that awful bulge above the waistband—sure, Perch ain't lucky enough to get *that* suddenly disappeared—but where has her pretty fishes gone? Might be there's the faintest trace of their scales, just above the belly-button . . . Might be a hint of mirrored dorsal fins . . . But what's left ain't the vibrant Pisces she's wore there since she were fourteen, tattooed in river colours Ma picked out just for her.

"Mose," she shouts, barging into the tiny bathroom. For all its churning, its wrong-way blowing, the fan ain't managed to clear too much steam. "You ain't never gonna believe this—"

"What's that, darlin," he asks, shower curtain rattling across the steel rod. Half-turned, he looks out at her. Water streams over his bareness, glistens on the dark pelt curling from chest to pelvis. Haze billows around them both, then escapes out behind her. As the view clears Perch closes her mouth, scrutinising. Not the tight curve of her husband's arse nor the muscular 'v' leading down to his manliness. But that, *there*, nestled under the swirls on his belly— were that a smudge of green down there? A swoop of blue? Were them black lines drawn from ink, or hair?

"Well?" Lathering them maybe-shades out of sight, Mose turns to face her full on. "What?"

Outside in the yard, a horn *honk-honks*. A car door slams. Boots clomp up the stoop's metal stairs.

"Wonders never cease," Perch whispers as Mose starts rinsing off. *Definitely* some yellow streaks there. Some scalloped orange. Taking a step back, she lifts her gaze to meet his. Forces a laugh.

"Ain't nothing," she says weakly. "Only, Rud's early."

⋀⋀

After a hefty soak in Ruddy's cask of rye that afternoon, he and Mose slapped on wool hats, zipped bright orange vests over tartan flannel, and set off. Smoothbore .45s slung over their shoulders. Plenty of powder and shot on hand for them both. A pair of tin flasks to ward off the four o'clock chill.

"Ain't nothing better after being locked up," Rud said, stuffing a loading rod into an oversize canvas pack, "than hoofin it into the wild."

Sure, Perch thinks. *Ain't nothing better.*

Now alone at the kitchen table, she twists ice cubes free of their tray, refills her glass. Downs the shot in one go, the fumes off Rud's mash making her eyes water. Knuckling puffed lids, she tells herself it's only the fumes what's made such a mess of her mascara. She snivels into her sleeve, quiet as a gopher, so's not to wake the kids. Between shudders, she refills. Swallows. Refills.

Keep yer skin to yerself, Ma use to say, again and again. *Keep yer skin, girl, coz once it's gone . . .*

When did she stop saying it?

Before Jinx come along? Before that? When Mose slipped that gold band on her flipper? Before even that? When she and him come running here to Plantain? With Perch straddling that wretched mule like some latter-day Mary, Mose jogging alongside? Together they went and run here, all the way from Tapekwa County.

Run. Perch shakes her heavy head. *Not swum.*

Even then it had started. *Even then.* Mose's sneaky-slow theft.

The cask blurps as she turns its copper tap, refills.

Swallows.

Refills.

Nope, she ain't sure when Mama stopped warning her, only that she had.

Now Mama don't hardly bother with her gal no more. She don't flap them strong fins upriver—short trip for one such as her—she don't come round to visit. *And why would she?* Swallows, refills. Perch went and gave it up, didn't she just. Willingly, happily. And now . . .

Ain't no easy way of getting that skin back.

Frowning at the tabletop, she watches silver flecks whirl in the melamine. It were the only explanation: Mose must of took her swimming-skin. Sometime before Jinx were borned. Before Perch were gold-ringed. Before she run away from home, from the crick, from Mama. He'd gone and trapped her the way so many other mer-ladies been trapped. That magic smile of his cutting her deep, them magic hands stripping her bare. Then he'd gone and hid her finned self somewheres else, hadn't he just. Her firm, strong self. Why else wouldn't she of took off when he got hisself locked up—if not that first time, then the fifth? The fifteenth? Why else wouldn't she of swum away when he were sauced and raging? When he were laying into her, while promising it weren't never going to happen again? Why else wouldn't she of up and left his lying self yet?

Why else.

Refill.

Swallow.

The glass clunks down hard as Perch sways to her feet. Sun's only just lipping the treetops; the kids is been abed for no more'n an hour. Time enough for her own bit of hunting, she reckons, before Mose gets back from his.

She starts in their bedroom. First she lifts the double mattress, strips the quilt, guts every pillow. One after another the tall-boy's drawers gets pulled open, dumped. She empties the small built-in closet. Tosses the laundry hamper. Pries back the wood veneer where it gapes round the window. Stretching out an arm, she sweeps the mirrored shelf. Trinkets, perfume bottles, photo frames, and Mose's one angling trophy crash to the floor. Perch don't expect to find her true skin sitting there, in plain sight all these years, wedged between her makeup bag and stack of CDs. She ain't that blind. She ain't *stupid*.

Still, right about now there's a spirit caught hold of her, as it does every so often, a fury what leads to shit getting broke.

She smashes kitchen cupboards. Digs into the fridge. Yanks out that useless tray under the oven. Next she tears off the couch cushions, rummages through storage blocks underneath 'til she's good and sure her skin ain't packed up with the extra smokes, boxed away with the puzzles. Chest heaving, she shoulders open the kids' door. Crouches to feel under the plastic piss-sheet on Jinx's metal-framed cot, cranes to peep under the canvas' low sag. A check of the bunk beds turns up nothing—Toph and Gibbs is heavy as logs, torn funny-papers crunching round their skinny legs—and though the crib's a lump of sodden blankets, it ain't been padded with no supple fishskin.

Panic clogs Perch's windpipe. Her mind reels so's she can't catch her breath. *Something ain't right. Something's missing . . .* Dull light slices through gaps in the blinds, throwing shadows on the sleepers. *And whose fault is that,* a little voice whispers to no one in particular. No one at all.

~

"Just making space in the icebox for y'all," Perch yells across the yard, slamming the garage's side door too hard behind her. Fumbling the padlock. Let him believe she were simply clearing a path through the junk inside. Washing dust off the freezer's white lid. Shifting cartons of ice cream, bulk bags of mixed veg, stiff northern geese sheathed in tan stockings. Rearranging all the small carcasses Mose trapped over the summer, making a nice flat surface for the bigger sides of meat to lie on. That's all she were doing these past forty minutes or so. Ain't no other reason for her to be in there, right?

None Mose needs knowing about.

No, she weren't dumping out boxes of wires, sparkplugs, and other metal doodads—finding no sign of her shining scales. She weren't taking every rubber tub off the pine shelves, unlidding them, tossing them aside—smelling no whiff of the Saccattaw among the Christmas ornaments, the macaroni angels and crumbling gingerbread houses. She weren't climbing up to the rafters, flashlight beaming across paddles and skis and a haunted house's worth of cobwebs—spying no tarps, no rainsheets, no folded up mer-lady skins. She weren't crawling beneath the rickety mule-cart to see what might be hid in the undercarriage. Coming up empty-handed once more, she ain't kicked the hell out of the thing, maybe busting a toe and one of its wheels in the process. No, sir.

"How'd the shootin go, love?" Pitching her voice high, Perch aims for cheerful. Disappointment pulls her shy of the mark. *If Mose ain't stashed it in the garage, then where is it?* Walking casual, she makes for the fire-pit nearby. The logs and kindling's already set, bolstered by slabs of foam and strips of stained carpet fossicked from Ruddy's car yard. Crouching, she strikes a match. Gets the bonfire blazing.

Mucked and bloodied, Mose and Rud come grunting down the drive in single file, a good-size deer swinging between them. Must of dressed the thing out in the field, Perch reckons, then bagged the innards. Slung across the towman's body, a canvas pack is full bulging, hanging low and heavy with offal. Mose never were one to risk spoiling a keeper.

"Arright, I s'pose," he says with a modest shrug, fooling no-one. At the doe's heart is a perfect red hole, the shot clean, dead-on. Ain't nobody could of done better.

"Bagged hisself a wild turkey too," Rud chuckles, pulling the flask from his vest, swigging the joke.

"Don't mind if I do," Perch says when he waggles the bourbon her way. Tipping it back, she drinks 'til there ain't a drop left. "I'll get us a top-up," she says, dashing inside for the cask and glasses, leaving the men to string up the carcass from the garage's eaves. When she gets back out, the deer's hanging from its hind legs, black velvet muzzle brushing the gingham blanket laid below to sop blood.

Mose whistles and sings while he separates the doe from her hide. Working from heels to neck, he whisks the sharp blade downward fast and skillful, shuffle-footing round the creature. The pelt peels away in one whole piece, not a nick in sight. As he hunkers to make the final cuts, the skin flops onto him from above. Snorting, he stands with arms outstretched, does a little spin. Proud as any king in a fancy new cloak.

"Fucking idiot," Ruddy says, flinging a gob of entrails at him from the waste. Turning to Perch, he says: "Get that grill hot as Hades, darlin. Won't be long now."

While Mose takes a hose to the naked deer, Rud bags the liver, packs it into an ice-filled cooler in the pickup's tray. Then he winches the garage door open, helps lug the venison inside for ageing. With Perch looking on, the two of them pours bucketloads of salt onto the hide. Folds it all up. Lobs it onto the gritty pile already in the truck, ready for carting off to Butcher's Holler.

"Earth to Perch," Mose says, snapping his fingers. "Stop yer gawking, girl. I'm starving."

"I reckon," Perch says quiet-like, squinting at the pickup. *Ain't checked in there yet*, she thinks, crossing over to the fire. After popping a barbecue grill on the coals, she pours them all a fresh glassful while it heats up. Another drink sees them through 'til Rud's charred the doe's heart in the fire. He turns it for a minute or three on the grate, then serves it up while the meat's still tender, each hunk soft as the riverbed.

Perch gulps her share without hardly chewing. Refills her glass between bites. Rye-rinses the liquid iron and warm ash from her mouth.

◆◆

"Mose," Perch whispers, prodding his shoulder. "You awake?"

The moon's dunked its bloated belly below the clouds, silvering the trailer, the pickup, the mud and grass yard. The two men snore like hell in their lawn chairs, legs outstretched, boots resting on the fire-pit's cooling stone edges. Squatting on a polished stump beside him, Perch watches the man what's kept her all these years. His gob open, throat vibrating a fine ruckus that ain't neither words nor song. Irises flicking to and fro behind his closed lids, looking everywheres for some dream worth catching.

"Mose," she says, jabbing again.

He scowls. Twitches like he's been skitter-bit.

Giggling, Perch pokes a few times more, just to see him writhe.

"You awake," she asks, louder now. Thinking, if he's this dead to the world, she oughta take advantage. Only one place left to check for her skin, and it's parked right over there . . .

"Hmmph," Mose snorts. Shifts position. Gives his gut a good itching. As his fingers scritch, the hem of his shirt inches up to rib height. The hair showing there's thick and dark as always, but in this light the skin underneath looks paler than ever, a ghostly blue-white glowing through the curls. *Except*— Perch leans closer. Narrows her eyes at the smudges of colour, the distinct lines. Riffles her nails across his navel as though she were picking lice. *Except there?*

Can't see shit through all that fur. She lurches to her feet. Looks around 'til she finds the knife Mose used on the deer earlier. Fetches it. Gives it a rinse with the hose. *Gotta thin the forest to see what's lurkin in the undergrowth.*

Careful as a surgeon, Perch places the cold steel above Mose's bellybutton and starts scraping. Three swipes and she's certain. Twin fishes is swimming round that dark whirlpool. Oh yes, there they is: sweet little Pisces. Mama's gift to her favourite mer-girl. Her very own special gift.

Hers.

Not Mose's.

The blade rasps. *Stealing my skin ain't enough? Now you gots to have my ink, too?* Perch keeps shearing 'til there ain't no doubt. Not one speck. There it were, plain as soot, scrawled across Mose's belly. Proof of his wrongdoing.

Her vision blurs. *You sure, girl? That's it?* Propping her knife-hand against his body, she uses the other to push up his sleeves. For a moment, her gaze swivels down to her own forearms. Only that morning, them pretty dolphins of hers was smiling there—she *knows* they was—but now they's gone and vanished, too.

Frowning, she blinks.

Blinks.

Blinks.

Blinks.

Looks up at her husband's exposed wrist, and seethes.

That there's a bottlenose poking out that cuff, I know *it—*

"What you doing, darlin?" Mose sits up so fast, ain't no chance Perch can get away. She's good and caught, right there on his lap, groping his clothes, pawing round his nethers. Surprise whooshes out of him. He gapes down at her. Addled, she reckons, with booze. A *whuff-whuff-whuff*ing sound comes out his open mouth. Ain't laughter. Ain't his usual trilling. No, it ain't that. More like anger. She's trapped, red-handed. That's what it is. Her hands is all red.

"Oh God," she says, but He ain't listening. Not now, not ever. Surely not with Rud snoring to the high heavens, so much louder than Perch's blubbing. "Oh my God."

"Darl—" Mose gasps, the knife stuck in his guts, right up to the hilt, the blade so goddamn sharp Perch ain't even felt it go "—in."

"Oh God," Perch says, broken record. "Oh God." Lightheaded, though Mose's the one losing blood. *Get the gingham sheet,* she thinks, picturing him swaddled in it, the blue and white checks catching all that mess. That mess he were making, that mess what he's made—of everything, again, as always. What a goddamn mess. He yanks out that carvin-stick and it's like he's pulled a keg plug. All the juice is glugging from him now, spreading down past his thighs. Perch presses both palms against the wound, pushing down while Mose struggles to stand. Determined to die just as fast and hard as he guzzled, as he sung, as he loved.

"Jinx," Mose grunts. "Baby—"

"Hush now," Perch says, ducking under his dolphined arm, offering her shoulder as a crutch. Always thinking of them little birds of his, was Mose. First and foremost—after trapping and skinning and drinking—them kids was in his mind. "Rud's right there if they need him."

With their backs to the moon, Mose's life drips black as Perch shuffles him to the pickup. Scooping the blanket on the way, she tucks it tight round him. Buckles him in, then climbs into the driver's seat. Keys is already in the ignition, thank Christ, and there's fuel enough to speed them to Doc's farm.

"Hang on." Hands slick on the wheel, she reverses, tires spewing gravel. Doc ain't but one county over. Close as hell to Plantain. "We'll make it. We'll make it."

They won't.

Mose is whiter'n Perch long before they reach the turn-off. Breaths rattle into him, foul air wheezes out. In between, that broad chest of his conjures up some frightful unnatural humming. Soon the hold he's got on her loosens. Soon she can't hardly hear him through all them sobs. For an instant—one traitorous, hopeful second—she glances at her skinny thighs. Thinks, *Soon they're gonna sparkle.*

—Play us a tune, Mose says after a long quiet while. *By the Mark.* Better yet, *I'll Fly Away.*

She clouts the radio 'til it spits noise. Static, mostly, but Mose don't seem to mind. His head lolls from side to side, a metronome keeping red dirt time. They turn right at the crossroads, away from the Doc's. Away from town. Won't be nothing but trouble waiting there now. Instead, Perch follows the Saccattaw's roughest offshoot. Rolls down the windows to blow out the stink Mose is making, and to hear the distant roar of the falls.

—Where we headed?

"Not far," she says after a minute, insides churning. "Off Chillins Bluff."

—Reckon yer up for a swim, do ya?

"Could well be," she says even as her head shakes and shakes. "And you?"

Mose never were one to decline a challenge.

〜

Hours later, the numb still ain't wore off.

Cold beyond shivering, Perch sits behind the wheel in the silent, empty pickup. Rat-tails of hair drip on her back, wriggle before her downcast eyes. A puddle seeps from her jeans and thin t-shirt, damping the seat inch by inch. The wet she pulled in from the river don't quite meet the stain Mose made last night, his deep red soaking clean through the blanket she wrapped him in. For a while, some of that colour were rubbed off on her. Up on Chillins Bluff, she got her scrawny arms good and smeared with it when she wrangled Mose out the passenger side. Since her man weren't in no mood for cooperating—he just flopped hisself spineless, *whump* on the ground, the same way Jinx did when throwing a fit—Perch had to grab him under the pits, prop him against her chest and thighs, pull him upright like a farmer set to snip the balls off her sheep. She got right messy while she dragged Mose to where the truck's beams was pointing, the yellow 'V's widening and softening the closer they got to the cliff's edge. The light there were blurred with mist, the pebbles slick with waterfall spray.

—Reckon yer up for a swim? he said again, lack of blood making him stupid, repetitive. With her throat lumped shut, Perch couldn't respond just then. Looking away, she scrounged some fist-big stones from the lookout. Tucked some in Mose's pockets, some up his pant legs, another in his mouth. That one didn't stop him humming the same ditties, over and over, while she wound the sheet round his boots and legs and fast-cooling body. She snugged it under his belt. Covered his sweet-singing face. Knotted it under his chin to keep it from wagging.

"You first," she said before kissing the rough fabric where his lips was, kissing it hard. "I'll catch you up."

Mose were a sizeable man, a broad-chested bellower, a relentless hunter. There weren't nothing elegant about him. But as he soared over Chillins Bluff, Perch seen him taper into something truly dainty, smaller than small. She seen something dazzling in that pale checker shroud, the fish-backed angle of his dive, the white roar of his final plunge. Something close to grace.

Now, in the grey light of morning, she can't quite get her head around what she done wrong.

What else could I've done?

While Mose were still sinking, Perch had motored down the bluff to the highway. Quick as the devil, she'd pulled up alongside the low metal railing. Parked so close, she had to scramble out the passenger door. Around back, she bailed out the bundled pelts in the tray and launched them all onto the riverbank.

One by one, she slipped on them skins. Weasel, woodchuck, natural wolf. Fox and deer. Even a Chippewa bear. Some what might of been dogs. Others whose origins she couldn't peg—these last she wore especially, in case hers was stuffed in there too. Stiff or supple, feral or fine, she swum with them all. Holding her breath near long as Mama—she who were second-best and second-prettiest in the whole of Tapekwa County, and had the gill-marks to prove it—Perch watered them peels for hours. She kept diving 'til they was pruned as rotten apples, 'til each bit of flesh were clean magickless as the rest.

She wore every last one of them skins, but weren't none of them hers for keeps. Come dawn, her legs was still split right up to her gash. Still she ain't grown no tail, though Mama swore she would. Could? No, *would*, goddammit. Still the current hauled her ever shoreward, no matter how hard she kicked the other way. Still she couldn't swim for shit.

Now he's gone, she wonders, *how long's it gonna take for that old skin o' mine to turn up?*

~

Now parked in the drive outside their trailer, Perch is struggling to get the facts straight. All them skins at her disposal but here she is, still, forever stuck in Plantain. All that water, and she couldn't breathe none of it. All that splashing and glugging, and still Mose is singing. Loud and lofty as he ever done.

Small wonder the noise ain't woke Ruddy yet.

But the towman's slouched in his chair, head back and snoring, fog puffing from his open maw. Frost's creeping across the grass, whiting everything but the two long tire tracks she made up the drive. Not yet dawn, it's fair chilly out, but Perch reckons Rud's got enough meat on his bones and mash in his belly to warm him senseless 'til the sun punches in for the day. Even so, she wishes Mose would pipe the hell down. His jolly, smug warble—more hum and whistle than words—carries across the yard in bursts and snatches. She ain't got to hear real lyrics to know what he's chirping. To know she don't want no-one else singing along.

—Water's fine, darl.

The tune wrenches her guts, a secret sung in the key of truth.

—Reckon yer up for a swim?

Quickly lifting her shirt, Perch inspects her bare navel. She claws at her dolphinless wrists. Twisting in the seat, she searches for any sign of ink left between her freckles and beauty marks. Finds not a drop. Not a single line.

Mose is got her all her waves. All her fishes. All her swim.

Goddammit, Mama.

Gripping the steering wheel, she rests her forehead on her knuckles. Tears plink from her lashes, happy pennies dropping. Quiet as can be—she don't want to rouse Rud—Perch leans back and laughs herself sick.

Keep yer skin to yerself, Mama said, but Mose got it anyway.

Mose got it.

He's *got* it. On him.

Handed it over my own self. Perch chuckles, swipes the wet off her face. *The very day we was wed, I gave it up.* Ain't no better explanation, she reckons. No greater cause for relief. They *was* man and wife—in God's eyes and man's—and so they was united. One body. One flesh.

One *skin*.

No doubt Mose is had a fine time dallying under Chillins Bluff overnight, laughing at his fool wife, racing the rapids in her best, swiftest fins. Skimming the riverbed. Wave-dancing with them frisky falls. Making wagers with hisself as he plunged and surfaced, guessing how long it'll take her to add two plus two.

Stifling a snort, Perch revs the truck to life. Only thing for it, she reckons, is to go'on down there and get Mose back. Fish him out. Face his music. Let him shout hisself hoarse at this wrong she done him. Let him froth and rant and curse her straight to hell. And when his hate's up, when he's truly set to tear into her—well, that's when she'll do it.

It's over, she'll say, firm on the Saccattaw's muddy banks, louder even than the falls. *We ain't one no more. That skin of mine is mine alone.*

Gives her a thrill, just thinking on it. The power in her mer-fins peeling away from him quick-smart, all that freedom returning to her . . . But Lord Almighty, how Mose is going to holler!

Perch pulls the handbrake. Putting it in neutral, she gets out the truck. Runs up to the trailer. Ducks inside for four last things before heading off.

Mose can't get *that* angry with the kids near . . . S'pose they come along, a flock of green-eyed buffers? Won't do nothing but good, she reckons, having them little blackbirds tweeting nearby when she breaks up with him. Sure, they ain't never flown before, but Perch knows they must have it in them somewheres, just like their Pa. Won't need more'n a nudge—she'll floor the gas pedal, give them a real fast run-up to the edge—and they'll be flapping them wings of theirs in no time.

Hang on, she'll say as they drive to the lookout. Then she'll take her foot well off the brake, press the clutch. Shift into first, no need to reach second. She'll rev the engine good, then —'Let go," she'll say, and they will. All of them.

Ain't that far to travel off Chillins Bluff, straight down to where Mose is swimming, wearing her own skin. A four second plummet, *max*. No longer'n the first bar of a favourite old song—short and easy as that. Perch could do it with her eyes closed.

THE CANARY

LL CRIED AS HER PATHETIC WHISPER GAVE OUT. *No, no, no.* Jac's brother Raif clacked his strong beak against her flushed cheek. Pushed. Cawed. *Shhhh, gal, shhhh.*

Yellow-orange light flickered through the trailer's one window, parking lot bonfires gilding the crow boy's near-sharpest edge. His face-blade pressed close, closer. Black feathers glinted on head and shoulders, *so close.* Springs screeched. Well over six foot, Raif *hulked* over her. A giant perched by her frozen knees. Leaning in and down and *on.* Bare from chest to hips, skin smooth as brown toffee, sooted wings folded against his broad back. Muscles hard in his jeans, legs *hard*, tapering to honed claws. Callused fingers pinning one slender wrist.

Ell sank into Jac's unmade sofa-bed. Her fine hair snarled to knots. *No no no.*

Whoops and clanking bottles in the lot outside. The other coal miners croaked, *hip-hip-hoorayed*, drank to the season's best haul. Slurred through their beaks for Raif.

Ell scrunched water and snot from her pretty face. *Nonono.* Hoped to repulse him soft.

Raif held firm, breath hot, reeking of gut. He stared. He *pecked.*

Ell mouthed *okay* without meaning it. Surely he could see that. Surely he could tell she wanted to wait. Surely he could feel her quaking, crying like a kid.

No

The crow boy climbed on.

᷍

But that were Raif's job, weren't it. Ploughing on when others might stop. Chasing shaft girls like Ell down the mines, rarely waiting for the go-ahead. Spearing after them, danger-fast, nipping their little arses if the pace slowed too soon, too close to the surface, where the veins had long been bled dry. Urging them deep, deeper. Pointing out fissures only slim gals could fit into—cracks too narrow for regular men, much less them with wings spanning twelve foot. Circling as lasses sank into the stink damp, their bright heads gleaming in the near-black. Diving at the first blow of their whistles—*Clear! Clear!*—then snatching them gals, flailing in their coveralls, and hauling them topside before the dyn-o-mite they laid blew its load.

No hesitation.

Nine shifts out of ten, Raif were first to hear the girls' cues: the *snick* of their zippo lighters, the *fizz* of fuses catching, the shrill *tweeeeeeet* of come-get-me calls. He only ever worked with gals what was fit enough to dislodge the priciest nuggets, the stuff buried in the skinniest chasms. And he were first to scoop them chicks in his talons, first to fly them wriggling up out the holes, first to dive back down—*solo*, mind—to glean what them girls had exploded.

Raif were first to cram the ace hauls between his pinions and fluff.

First to carry the heavy loot topside.

First to cash in.

First to choose which gals earned what part of his payload.

᷍

Ell closed her eyes, retreated behind her lids, the only place she could escape now her favourite cargo pants was tugged, kicked, roped 'round her pasty ankles. The waistband on her embarrassing unders tore. Raif shifted his weight. Unzipped. Snapped rubber.

Gotta plan ahead, girl. Now that were Ma's voice rattling inside Ell's mind, chastising. She imagined her in the kitchen, as ever. Apron girding her suet waist. Bleach masking the greys in her once-golden topknot. Scarred arms hugging a huge bowl, mixing batter.

Tone rougher than the spoon scraping round and round on old plastic. Such a small woman for such big opinions.

*Take two sharp borers whensoever you head below: one for drilling, one to keep from being drilled. You hear? Stick to the middle of them shafts, away from mine-shadows. Walk heel-toe, heel-toe along them chutes; softens the tread, keeps you from stirring what don't need to be stirred. And no shorts at work, my gal. No tees or tanks. I know it's stifling down there—*Lord do I know—*but a fair child like you, well, don't you just glow in the dark! Trust me, Ellie-girl, you gotta snuff that shit else you'll blind 'em senseless . . .*

On and on Ma went, blending chunks of advice into each batch of cookies. Ell loved to sit, cross-legged on the linoleum, and watch them blobs swelling into sweet golden discs in the oven. She never could wait for them treats to cool, but pigged them right off the tray. Never did mind the hard bits, the black chunks and grit no amount of chocolate could disguise, the smoky shards what sometimes loosed her baby teeth, sometimes saw her spitting them onto the floor. The sugar made up for the burn, she thought then. The butter for the blood.

Think afore you act, girl. Ma cracked the spoon across Ell's scorched fingertips, then passed a tea towel to wipe the pink from her mouth. *We need you in one piece, got it? Stop and think.*

Ell's innards churned, then and now.

Ma weren't never wrong.

And Ell hadn't planned, had she. She hadn't thought.

No no no

Now Raif shoved himself in 'til it burned.

∿

Outside, Jac sung a tune he wrote just for Ell, though it ain't mentioned her once by name. A ballad about lovers—all his songs was—devised after a half dozen pints, best heard when none else but them two was around. Tonight Jac were far enough into the sauce not to mind what folk made his audience, nor how many, nor to notice its true heart were missing. Fires popped and bottles dropped from drunken hands. Gals giggled and squealed. Men and crows alike hollered for another round. Over it all, her boyfriend's thready voice warbled, high and true. Without shame despite being off-key.

Maybe it were Jac's pluck what drew Ell in the first place. Sure as hell weren't his looks—the little daw's hood and mantle was faded grey, his wings stumped, his yellow eyes bugged like one always surprised. He weren't strong like his brother; Jac's man-parts was shrunken as a boy's, the bird-bits only just past fledgling. Jac and Raif had different daddies, weren't no doubt about it. Folk reckoned the younger crow were part jay, but the elder were quick to snap the tongue off anyone with the balls to say so.

Still, Jac weren't given nowhere near as many mine-shifts as Raif—he hadn't the stamina for it—but he *were* far luckier than featherless men. *His* coffers weren't never empty. He weren't forced into the fields to rustle grub. His clothes-rack weren't hung with scraps and hand-me-downs, but real clothes he bought in town, tailored to fit round *his* particular figure. Already, at seventeen, Jac'd flown enough good coal topside to buy a new trailer all his own.

Not that it were the boy's wallet what kept Ell around. Raif had black gold aplenty, and a house in the foothills that weren't even on wheels. Maybe it were simply Jac's kindness, that he made her feel special for a time.

Jac weren't nothing like his brother.

∿

Last week, Jac'd took Ell to the roadhouse to meet his Maven. *You're my gal, ain't you*, he'd said, the down at his throat proud-ruffling. *Go on, now. Go on in first.*

In a back room with shag carpets and veil-dimmed lamps, a great rook sweated in a floral muumuu, too lard-bloated to get up from her bunk. Incense clogged the small space, failing to mask the reek of old sheets and unwashed creases. More woman than bird, Jac's Ma spent her life flapping fat lips, entertaining what lonely folk dared pay for such a visit. A scraggle of blue-black feathers was plaited on her huge head, dripping grease, adding shine to her plum-glossy skin. Cherub wings jutted above her round shoulders—them tiny things ain't stood a chance of lifting Mave's bulk, though the wizened chook-legs under her slop of a belly sure as hell wished they'd give flight a try. Ell coughed at the foot of the bed, tried not to stare. Stared.

Lashless eyes fixed on Ell and her boy, taking stock. Blue smoke swirled as Jac's ma finally stretched out a dimpled brown arm, grabbed a paper fan off the quilt, waved them closer.

Youse gotta love each other, Mave had said, slow and heavy. Sighing, she slumped against a mound of pillows. Lit a cigarette. Puffed. *Youse gotta be true to each other, no one else. Just youse two.*

But Ell knew she didn't really love Jac, not *really*. Not then, not now. He were sweet and soft but temporary, like them stale candy canes Paster doled out in church on Christmas Day. Jac were scatterbrained, barely a man. He were a *dalliance*, Ma said. Nothing more. *Nothing more.* And Ell were only fifteen, for God's sake. Too young for any real sort of devotion.

Hell, she were still cutting teeth on Ma's treats.

Raif grunted and grunted.

Chafed in and out.

No more'n twenty feet away, through plywood and veneer, someone wolf-whistled as Jac's song hitched back to the chorus.

Ell clenched all over, became thin and flat and stiff as a board. Holding her breath, she pictured a plate piled high with warm biscuits. Not that she ate many, not lately. To help feed the family— she were one girl of three—it were her job *not* to feed, but to keep skinnier than her sisters, to wriggle deeper into the mines, to go farther down them tunnels, to blast out the good big nuggets, them ones what fetched the best prices when hill crows bartered with valley folk. If Ell stayed scrawny enough she might learn to slip between shadows. She might earn a bigger piece of them boys' prizes. She might buy her way out of this place.

She might even sneak up on a way to make Ma proud.

〰

Plan ahead, girl. What with that blonde head of yers, that slink in yer step, yer a real target. Them gimlet-gazed crows gots both power *and* intention, *you hear? Keep them nails of yers sharp, yer wits sharper. You listening to me, Ellie-girl?*

Maybe I should find somewheres else to scrape a wage, Ell had once said, half-floating the notion of following Pa to the fruitlands, hopping whatever trains might lead south, migrating wherever the ripenings took 'em. She could earn a dollar plucking melons with bearded men by day, then plucking six strings for them same blokes by night. But Ma burst that hopeless bubble quick-smart.

She weren't one to waste time on no ridiculous honkytonk dreams.

She wouldn't never drive Ell to open mic nights. Said they started too late. Said she couldn't see the road for darkness. Said she couldn't abide the untried talent with their ukes and banjos and mouth-harps. *A pack of cat-stranglers*, Ma called them, on account of their cheap twangs, refusing to admit her own girl could truly croon.

Sometimes, most times, Ell thought Ma were lying.

She were just fine behind the wheel, *just fine*, never mind what goddamn time of day it were. And there was spangles and sequins tucked far back in Ma's closet. A well-used harmonica. A pair of red glitter shoes—heels so fine only a star wriggler could've earned 'em. A gal what once went deepest and farthest down the tunnels. A woman who ain't got no fear of the dark.

But music weren't nothing but distraction, Ma had decided. No point in Ell rousing cattle-wranglers in the town hall. No real cash to be grabbed there—nothing but dust and spirits was stirred when them bare-backed men clomped sore feet on the floorboards. Bluegrass wouldn't fill a girl's belly the way the mines could. There weren't no future for Ell, not really, but the one carried topside on broad wings.

Hate me now, thank me later, Ma always said, stirring, baking. Ell did neither.

ᑊᐜᑊ

The only songs Ell could stomach right about now was Jac's, them feeble things drifting through the screen, and even them she rathered not hear.

She weren't too keen on spoiling melodies what othertimes brought her comfort, ones she hummed to herself while planting fire-sticks down the mines. She didn't want *them* beats forever keeping time with *this* one's, this particular rhythm of what Raif were now doing.

Ell didn't want to feel this hollow song ever again.

She didn't want it to echo through her soul the way that famous fox-haired lady's tune did—Ell knew all her lyrics by heart—singing how she'd had her own grunt and fumble with her own Raif in her own town, not so many years ago.

Saltwater dripped down Ell's temples, plinked into her ears.

There weren't no lying to herself: she knew her situation were different from that beautiful singer's. Weren't it. Raif weren't no stranger, Raif ain't clocked Ell or pushed her into the back seat of a rusty old car, he ain't held her head down while struggling with his buckle, he ain't pressed no gun to the back of her skull. He ain't *forced* her, Ell thought, not really. Had he. He only wouldn't listen close to what she were saying, only held the scraped-up machete of his beak right sharp against her neck, he only clutched *one* of her wrists overhead—the other were still balled by her side, not punching, not beating him away—he only nipped her a bit with the point of that beak, nipped with each thrust, nothing worse than what she got in the shafts.

And she ain't cried out even when it hurt, even when Raif drew blood in two places at once, above and below.

And she'd followed him to Jac's trailer willingly, hadn't she. Hadn't she.

Hadn't she.

No, Ell reckoned. She'd ruin no music remembering this night. This stupid, stupid mistake.

✿

"Come with me," Raif'd said, and she had. Easy as that. He weren't sloshed like the rest of them boys, neither were she, though she'd had a jar or two, maybe four, *just* enough to feel warm and free and light. Only just.

"I gots to talk to you," he'd said. "Know what I mean?"

And Ell didn't know, not really, though later she'd think she must have, she weren't *retarded*, she *must* have known, but maybe didn't quite at the time, not *fully*, so she'd followed.

Ain't no one forced her, had they.

She were flattered—was that wrong?—that Raif might pay her particular attention. That he might woo her, tell her secret things he couldn't say in front of his friends. He were so popular, so *sure*, he were all confidence, all strut with a hint of danger. Raif never showed no fear. Was it wrong that she were flattered? That she'd left the parking lot, left the party, gone to Jac's trailer because it were much closer than Raif's own house in the woods? That they'd skirted the other crows' tents, dodged booze-driven brawls, avoided moans and slurps in the bushes, and gone to Jac's little place, where once upon a time she'd lain on this very couch and listened to records, where she'd sang unembarrassed, where she'd been safe, and she'd not really loved, but definitely *liked*?

Was she wrong not to have fought back?

Raif groaned, thrust hard, once, twice more, and pulled out. A smear against her thigh. A shift in the cushions, pressure released. A cold breeze across her bareness as he stood, preening.

Ell's pulse thumped where he'd been, nowhere else.

Removed from her neck, the beak now buried itself in Raif's plumes, began rummaging. A shower of coal gravel sprinkled Ell's naked skin, collected in her dips and cracks, before the crow boy dug out real treasure—one, two great chunks of coal, each the size of a fist—and tossed them into her lap.

"Bet you feel weird now." A smile in his tone as he brushed filth from his palms. Zipped and straightened his baggy pants. Raked the proud feathers on head, face, collar. Hooked the screen door open with his taloned heel spur. "Eh?"

"No," Ell replied, pulling up her cargos, retying her shoes, not meeting his gaze.

"No," she said, firm too late.

⌇

After, at home, Ell will hide the expensive charcoal in her wrecked unders—babyish wildflowers on a white field—and cram the whole bunch to the back of her bottom drawer. She'll tell no one about them, or this, not even after the vivid red stains on the cotton have faded to brown.

I wanted to be your first, Jac will say in the morning, when he phones to see why Ell left the party early. Soon he won't write any more songs for her. Won't bring her to visit his Maven. Won't call.

All day she'll lie quiet on her bed, atop Gran's old quilt, new heat throbbing up from her nethers, heat in her mind, and she'll

— 106 —

stay there for hours, so still Ma will have to come down the hall to double-check she's awake when it's high time for supper. She'll stay quiet throughout the meal, then and for weeks after, and if anyone asks what's wrong she'll say nothing.

"Nothing."

"Nothing."

And if they ever *was* to find out—Ma, or Gran, or her chubby sisters—if they ever was to ask about it straight on, she'll fib. She can't do otherwise, no she can't. Can't bear their disappointment. Can't handle the guilt on Ma's face if they was all to sit 'round the table and ask point-blank *What happened to you, Ellie-girl?* Can't take the pain of finally telling them true.

But they don't never ask, so she don't really lie.

Ell will run away when she sees Raif after work on Monday, girlfriends giggling by her side, the chase a laugh to them, nothing but a hoot. Raif will fly fast to catch her up, faster than he did that night, but for once she won't be caught. He won't get why she's running. No one will think to tell him, and he won't never think to ask.

From then on, she'll get the foreman to assign her to other shafts. She'll wriggle the mines more careful. She'll keep from the shadows. She'll plan. She'll be a board, stiff and hard, impenetrable. And when she loosens a bit, months and years later, when she softens *just* enough to meet and marry a guitar-playing wrangler, when they live in a much smaller house than she could now afford, when she accidentally has her own girls, well, she'll bake chunky cookies for them, exactly the way Ma did for her.

Day after day, Ell will feed them, hoping to plump them right up so's they'll be too fat for the tunnels. Secretly she'll lace biscuit after biscuit with chocolate and coal chips, cracking and jagging the girls' teeth so's they's too ugly to catch crow. And when they complain their mouths is sore, when they spit pink and crumble the cookies in their stout little hands, when they try to feed gritty scraps to the dog, Ell will whack a spoon across their knuckles then pass them tea towels to wipe their faces.

"Stop and think," she'll say, taking another hot tray from the oven. Inhaling sugared steam off the toffee-brown treats. Refusing to eat even one single bite.

∞

LITTLE DIGS

THREE GENERATIONS ARE BURIED ON WHEELER LAND, starting with Great-Grandaddy Winston, the only one to live up to the surname. A far-traveller, he was. Crossed seven county lines to reach Napanee, carting a new wife, her faith in the old gods, and a wagonload of beehives along with him. Winston named his first and only child Queenie, back when he still held high hopes for honey riches, but slipped into the habit of calling her Teenie when she grew no bigger than his bank account.

After planting her Pops in the first mound out back, Teenie took root on the homestead, settling it and the household accounts. Had such a knack for numbers, in fact, she saved up for a pesticide rig that kept the larder well-stocked, the fields bug-free and her son in a job for life. In her seventy-odd years, she never took no man's name, nor his hand in wedlock. But, on one occasion at least, she invited him into her bed—and kicked him back out again long, *long* before she birthed that plane-loving heir of hers.

Nowadays, Queenie surveys her property upwards from the wormside of mound number two, while her boy most often sees it from the clouds. When Buddy Wheeler brings that Piper Cub of his in for a landing, stinking of diesel and creosote, his own daughter Bets teases him something merciless. Poking and prodding, she checks him for extra limbs, sudden chemical-spawned tentacles, or indiglo skin. If he minds, he sure doesn't show it: Bets' daddy knows how to take a joke. He's open-minded. He gets the bigger picture. Always has.

Winging hither and yon in that bi-plane of his, Buddy's seen far beyond the confines of this hand-me-down property, this cornbread county. Way farther than Bets or her Mamma ever did.

Once upon a time, before Queenie had wheeled groundwards, Buddy used to haw on the harmonica between harvests. Even gathered a decent following—or so he says—at honkytonks here, there, and everywhere, thanks to the unique style of bluegrass he played. Tunes whined extra soulful against that ugly set of metal teeth he wore, temporary inserts he kept in permanent on account of the sharp glint they gave off, the steel shine they lent his smile.

"These chompers of mine's worth their weight in twenties," Bets' daddy used to say, especially when whiskey-soaked, too numb to fly anywheres much less lift a blues-harp to his lips. Thick-tongued, he'd toy with the bridge, running the blunt tip along silver valleys and peaks. "They's the brightest map outta here, understand? The trustiest, most valuable map . . . "

Mesmerised, baby-girl Bets had watched the thing wiggle in and out of his mouth. She'd read about touch-maps them Artick injuns used, little sculptures that looked every bit like her daddy's teeth, except they were whittled hunks of wood. Those carvings' dips and whorls, Bets later learned, were landscapes shrunk small, coastlines and mountain ranges tucked in pockets or carried inside seal-fur mitts. Portable 3D worlds, in other words, and more reliable than paper or memory. At high noon or moon-dark, travellers could run fingers over them cracks and bumps to get their bearings, certain they'd never be led astray.

Now standing on the back porch her Nanna Teenie built, Bets hefts a shovel and looks out on the hummocked land Great-Grandaddy Winston claimed. Releasing a pent breath, she pats her back pocket for the hundredth time that morning, feels the folded paper's reassuring crinkle. Guts all a-flutter, she sends a silent prayer to the gods. Thanking any and all of them for blurring Daddy's sights with clouds and moonshine, filling his mouth with them precious silver directions. Asking—not begging, she's too reasonable for that—any and all of them to look kindly on her venture, to reward her for putting herself out there, putting on a brave show. *Gods favour the bold*, she tells herself, hoping their invisible eyes have already turned her way. Hoping they'll approve. Hoping they won't leave her stranded.

~

More than halfway through spring, the ground's still almost hard as it was in mid-January. The last shaded knolls of snow finally sank about a week ago, leaving patches of grit on winter-squashed grass in the backyard. Filth gathers like crumbled shadows under the boundary's split timber fences. Weathered barriers divide dirt for the living from that for the dead, keeping ever-fallow acres separate from budding maples and crabapple trees, and from planting-fields in the back forty beyond.

In the distance, a range of low mountains gently curves across the horizon. Each greystone peak is bare and blunt as a molar. Six or seven of the things are pressed close together, so's the ridge as a whole looks to Bets like a broken set of dentures. Closer to home, between the rusted swing-set she used to ride for hours—failing to muster enough courage to leap off the seat at its highest point, to wind up and let go, to *fly*—and the ploughed rows waiting for the new season's crop, three soft hillocks push their swollen bellies out of the earth.

Until last autumn there'd only been the two big ones on the left, bulging side by side, reminding Bets of that joke about Dolly Parton lying in the bathtub. *Islands in the Stream.* Now that the third's been added, a much smaller mound they barely got covered in burlap before the blizzards set in, she thinks the trio looks more like a giant snowman got drunk and toppled over, his soft noggin slumped to the right. It was a hasty job, building that grave, but Mamma only became *more* pig-headed when upset, *less* inclined to listen to—much less heed—anyone else's advice. She'd wanted that soil piled high while the body was still warm, understand? It wasn't *skimping* if it meant getting her own way. Hell no it wasn't. Just get the burial over and done.

Don't cut no spirit ditch round the site, she'd said to the teamsters Daddy had booked for the job ages ago. *Waste of time. Any soul what can scrape its way free from all this ain't going to trip up on a little ol' channel in the ground. Don't be too precious with the backhoe; the hole ain't got to be perfect, just deep. Y'all know the drill. Speaking of which: don't fetch no auger for this dig, no concrete, none of them posts neither, nor them two-by-fours, nor them planks. Why fuss with tombs or chambers when already we're sinking a case of good steel down there? How many coffins does one corpse need, anyways? This ain't ancient Egypt and sure as hell ain't no pharaohs round here. Waste of good money, that's all this burial business is, a waste of good goddamn cash. Go'on and bulldoze the dirt back where it were scooped from; we'll tamp it ourselves later on. Nope, nope. Don't bother stacking no cairn over the whole shebang. Our goats can't graze on no goddamn heap of stones.*

When it came time, Mamma wanted the mess of death scrubbed clean out her house, swept from the yard, put in its place. Out of sight, out of mind.

Red Lucifer'll trade his pitchfork for a halo, Bets knows, before the old lady ever admits she might or should have done otherwise.

〜

There's a whiff of clay in the breeze this morning, damp leaves and workable mud. Bets tucks the legs of her baggy overalls into knee-high rubber boots. Zips her acid-wash jacket up to the chin. Sucks in cool air, breathes it out warm. It's too early yet for the sun to offer much in the way of heat, but already it's squint-making, bright as the bell-song luring folk down the lane to church.

"Ain't going to make much progress with *that*," Daddy had said a few minutes ago—words slurring across his bare gums—before answering that bronze-tongued call hisself. Normally, the cinder shovel Bets swipes from the fireplace set goes unnoticed; it's so small, she's carried it outside three times this week alone, used and returned it, without once getting caught. Today, though, she'd misjudged. Thinking he'd already jammed a cap over his balding head, pocketed a few coins for the collection plate, and hustled off to Mass, Bets had snuck into the sitting room and lifted the tool. She'd made it down the hall, through the kitchen, and had *just* slipped her boots on when Daddy had come clomping up the back steps.

"Forgot my Hail Marys," he'd mumbled. Reaching inside the door, he snagged a strand of beads off the key rack. Stopping long enough to deride Bets' choice of shovel. Not to ask why she was digging. Or where. Or what she hoped to find. Not to make a better suggestion.

Only to offer another two cents out of an endless wealth of criticism.

"Reckon Mamma had the right of it," Bets had muttered after him. "Without teeth, you sound just as stupid as you look."

Now she waits for the bells to hush before setting out across the yard. Blue jays razz her from cedar bushes nearby. Further afield, nuthatches and robins chirrup between the stark cornrows, beckoning her with sweet promises of summer. Smiling, she wonders what tunes birds warble in the city, if their notes are smoggy, thick with tar and rust. She tosses the shovel over the low fence, clambers after it, then trudges round to the newest mound's far side. In the field beyond, cheeping their hayseed chorus, a crew of brown-hooded sparrows scolds her for being late. Bold little buggers, they flit and hop and *pip-pip-pip* as Bets unearths a feast of worms.

Despite the harsh ground and harsher opinions, she *has* made decent headway. Kneeling in the groove she made yesterday, Bets digs into a hole already deep and wide as an apple barrel. The shovel's cast iron pan shunts into cold soil, clanging against pebbles. Scoop after scoop of dirt avalanches down the mound beside her, slow but steady. A regular rhythm of progress.

Few more hours should do it, Bets reckons. Not quite so long as it'll take Daddy to cycle through his Thorsday rituals. Reverend's sermon always runs just shy of noon. Wine and bread comes next. Confession and penance after that. Once all tears have been sopped and hankies wrung dry, the congregation drags itself a half-mile north for a palate cleanser of donuts, cherry pie, and sweet tea. As afternoon shadows start reaching for night, folk dust the icing sugar from their laps, brush the crumbs from their whiskers, drain their cups. A short march through the diner's parking lot and they've left the vinyl and Muzak, but not the sugar buzz behind them. After fetching cats and boars and billy-goats from pickup trucks on the way, they assemble in the Lady's glade beyond the streetlights. Knives come out in the gloaming. Bowls.

By the time these gifts have been offered and accepted, the ale-horn passed round, blood and verses spattered upon ancient oaks, Bets is bound to be done digging. She'll have made it through. And down. And *out*.

All by herself.

All with folks none the wiser.

Bets learned *real* young to keep any hopes to herself. Any efforts. To dream the same way she now shovels. Carefully. Quietly. Secretly. It's the only way to stave off collapse.

Bets must've been ten or eleven when she first recognised that sudden burn in her belly, that hot flutter above her liver, for what it was. Not instinct so much as a flash of true understanding, a gut-deep feeling of rightness, of *knowing* what she has to do, what's to come. Call it a psychic moment. Call it divine intervention. Call it grit. When faced with important decisions—say, whether or not to sing at the Sunday school talent show—Bets felt a blazing hand gripping her innards. Twisting her resolve. Yanking her across the line between *missing out* and *daring to try*.

Silently telling her which path to choose, which future to follow.

Truth be told, the talent show was no big deal. A bunch of local folk and their kids gathered in the church's back room, Reverend on steel guitar and Miss Shayanne on piano. There were no prizes, no ribbons, no certificates. All the same, it was a challenge for a shy gal like Bets. A chance to be seen. To be heard.

To be noticed.

So she'd picked 'Song for the Asking', a number she loved, one that ran well short of two minutes. A minute and a half, really. Next to nothing. In the lead-up she'd practically wore new grooves into Daddy's 45 LP, replaying that tune on the spinner in her bedroom, memorizing the words. Singing quietly, ignoring the strain on her throat. Bets had never mastered any instruments—she could get through 'Heart and Soul' on her plug-in keyboard, and the first few bars of *Stand by Me*—so she'd decided to sing *a capella*. She'd wondered what the phrase meant, so went to the bookmobile and looked it up. *A capella. In the manner of the chapel.* Arranged that way, the familiar letters felt foreign on her tongue. Strange and lonely. Fitting, she reckoned. After all, it's just going to be her voice, open and vulnerable. Just her and whatever ears might listen.

Nerves jittered her down the gravel road to the church, then kept her standing in the small square room while most grown-ups sat on cheap plastic chairs, kids cross-legged on the floor. As other acts drew applause—for *what*, Bets can't recall—she leaned against one of many pin-boards, sweater snagging on hymns and construction paper art. Gaze fixed on her boots, she strained to remember the first line of her song. Grasped for the verses dribbling out of her mind. Blanked at the whole melody.

When Reverend finally called her name, so many faces had turned her way, some clearly bored, some smiling. Jesus and all them other wooden gods frowned down at her from painted bricks on high. Breath coming fast and shallow, Bets had pushed herself away from the wall. Heels scuffing between rows of seats, she'd made it to the front of the room. Swayed there a minute. Searching the darkness inside her skull, desperate for the right words.

Thinking it over I've—
What?
So sweetly I'll make you—
What?

Ignoring the burn, the twist, the knowing yank in her guts, she'd lifted her chin. Smiled at her audience. Chickened out.

~

"I still *sang*," she'd told Mamma later. Her folks hadn't known about the contest; it hadn't been in her plan to tell them at all. Her plan, such as it was, had been to amaze the crowd with her talent. To blow them so far away, it'd take weeks to bring 'em back down to earth. *We heard your gal the other day*, they'd gush to Mamma and Daddy at the Holloway feed store or the Napanee auction house or the gas station at Miller's Point. They'd brag on Bets' behalf. *What a set of pipes she gots! Swear to God, that child's part canary.*

The plan, such as it was, had been to surprise them into being proud.

Once it was over, though, Bets knew she'd missed the mark. *Knew* it but wanted to be told she hadn't done half bad. That she'd come close, which wasn't nothing. That she'd thunk on her feet, even, changing songs at the last minute, choosing a tongue-twisting choir tune folks could tap their feet to, instead of a two minute lullaby. That she'd done *something*, hadn't she just, never mind that she was only a kid.

"I hit all the notes, got all the words," Bets had said. Standing stiff in her bedroom doorway, she'd admitted failure to her mother's back. High up on a barstool, Mamma was hanging wallpaper she'd got on clearance: Christmas green spattered with cream-coloured hearts. Bets had wanted navy, plain and dark and classy. Mamma had said it was too boring. Too mature. Too expensive. It was hearts or Holly Hobbie. Her choice.

"Everyone was right kind. Clapping and whistling like that." Bets had paused, grasping. "Still, I wish I'd done the other song."

"Guess you should've practised more," Mamma had said, without so much as a glance over her shoulder. Cocking her head, she ran her palms over the strip she'd just hung, checking for bubbles. Glue smacked underneath each blister she'd found. The paper bulged, resisting each poke, each prod.

"Hand me a pin," Mamma had said.

〰

The hole's waist-deep when Bets breaks for water and a piece of cold chicken. She swigs out of a dented plastic bottle. Gnaws fried flesh straight from the bone. Sweat's collecting above her lip, trickling down her temples and back, so she unzips her jacket and lets the breeze whisk the salt from her skin. Better that, she thinks, than going underhill like a living salt-lick. Practically begging ghosts to rasp their dry tongues across her damp places when, really, she'd rather they didn't.

Nanna Teenie has only done it the once, drawling a long cow-slurp across the cheek, after Bets had crawled into her grave that long-ago Sunday, determined to sing that goddamn tune from start to finish. Never said nothing, did Nan, but neither did she discourage. As a rule, she nodded way more than ever she shook that veiled head of hers. Like Mamma, she wasn't all that keen on hugging, but showed affection in other ways. She paid attention when Bets read aloud from her library books: atlases, mostly; outdated encyclopedias; dictionaries, so she'll know what's what. While Bets twanged through the entries, Nanna Tee placed a cold hand atop her warm one, squeezing support. And just that once, licking.

"Thanks, Nan," Bets had said, always meaning it, even while inching away. Far as she's concerned, it was a lucky bolt of storm-light that had cracked the middle mound's shell. A garden trowel Bets had wielded *just so* built on that god's work, widening a gap between the metal struts and scaffolding that held the burial chamber up, keeping the space below clear if not always dry. Most times Bets visited Nanna Tee—dropping through dirt, then dank air, then a hole torn in the soft-top of a '57 Buick—she wound up shivering on the car's oversized front seat, wet as clay.

Stuck behind the wheel of her finned casket, the old revenant really listens. Teenie doesn't agree with Bets just for the sake of it, but doesn't patronize. She's there for Bets, body and spirit. She's *present*.

She understands.

⌁

Mamma pretended not to know about the tunnel Bets had followed into her grandmother's chamber, nor the tarp she'd taken from the garage to cover it. She and Daddy never did care much what Bets did with her time, so long as she kept to herself, and kept that sameself *here*. After seventeen years under their roof, she's still cheaper than hiring seasonal labour and, in the long run, easier to manage. Though Winston and Queenie once thought it grand indeed, their farm's really too small to support many hands; the annual yield's not worth the price of extra mouths nor fancy machinery to replace 'em. A full pantry come winter relies on Bets helping with the spring planting, the harvest come fall. If she chooses to burrow into the dead lands in between, so be it. No reason the girl shouldn't always be covered in dirt.

Whenever Daddy was away dusting crops, doors were best kept closed at their place. Eyes lowered. Sketchpads held close to the chest. Notebooks scribbled in at night, under cover. Songs breathed, not even hummed. Unseen, unheard, Bets listened while Mamma grumbled on the phone about the sorry state of her house. Her marriage. Her life.

Sure as sunrise, the Aunties would come over next morning, armed with bottles and casks, to float Mamma out of her funk. They'd have Dolly on the turntable, a glass in each hand, smokes burning between chapped lips. The lot of 'em hooting and hollering, having such fun, it never failed to entice Bets into the living room. Soon as she peeped round the jamb, they'd call her in, put her on the spot, ask after her drawings or beg for a ditty, using words like clever and perceptive and dark-horse when she'd finally relent and pass her rough pictures round. Clutching her calico skirt, she'd creep in closer, passing the couch and coffee table, the uncomfortable rocker, and step up on the cold stone hearth to watch the hens peck and cackle. Searching for falsehoods in their flattery. Condescension in their comments. Finding none.

When they put the sketches aside, Bets saw their honesty, generous and plain. They wanted nothing from her but delight, maybe a song. Puffed as a robin, she'd sing 'til her face was pinker than theirs.

"Enough showing off," Mamma always snapped too soon, shooing Bets out.

"Let her stay, Gayle," said the Aunties, but by then Bets was already gone. Back down the hall, back to her books and paints. Back on her lonesome.

⌁

The cinder shovel's small but sturdy, the worn handle a good fit for Bets' grip. The blade's got some new notches and the shaft is bending, but it's holding up, keeping pace. *Shunt, spill, shunt, spill, shunt, spill.* Bets grunts as she digs, conserves energy by tipping the dirt gently beside her instead of tossing it like a stupid cartoon character. Folk who don't turn soil for a living have some highfalutin notions about work like this—suburbanites and city slickers pay top dollar to visit hobby farms, to crouch in their chinos and pull weeds for a spell, to shove their manicured hands in manure for a weekend and call it a Zen experience. Being in the moment. Focusing on the *now.*

Horseshit, Bets thinks, shunting, spilling. There's nothing relaxing about the pain in her lower back, the crick in her neck, the afternoon sunlight glaring off the dregs of water left in her bottle. With every spadeful, she's time-travelling. Imagining herself elsewhere. The past. The future. Anywhere but the present.

Anywhere but here.

There had to be someplace to start, she'd thought. Some first step she could take. Some way to catch a break.

"Maybe I could get a gig at the Sugar Spoon," Bets had suggested after dinner one night, when Mamma was mellowing on the couch with a cigarette and a bit of cross-stitch. There'd been an ad in the paper the day before, a local ragtime band looking for backup vocalists. Black and white, no pictures, the opportunity had been crammed in a few lines of text, printed between a psalm and a call for pageant judges.

She'd run the idea past Nanna Teenie that morning; the old ghost had nodded, squeezed, flapped her mouth enthusiastically. *No harm in trying*, Bets believed Nan'd said. So she'd dusted off the grave-dirt, gussied herself up, gone down to the saloon and auditioned before she could overthink herself out of doing it.

This time Bets performed the song she'd intended. Start to finish. And she'd done all right, maybe more than all right, her voice trembling only when she wanted. They said they'd call her tonight or tomorrow.

They'd smiled and said she was good.

Every time the phone rang, her belly squirmed.

"I hear they might be looking for singers," Bets had said, aiming for aloof, managing something more like half-contained fidget. Now that she'd already gone and done it, it was safer to broach the topic. Mamma couldn't ruin it after the fact. "Maybe I could try out," she said.

Mamma had tied off a thread, then reached for her smoke, balanced it between her needle-fingers. She took such a long drag, her chest rattled.

"Be reasonable," she'd said, squinting, exhaling clouds. "This ain't but another whim. Ain't it. When's the last time you picked up a pencil? Or played that keyboard of yours? This ain't no different. You ain't no *singer*, Bets. It's just a phase."

"But," Bets had begun. Stopping as the phone rang.

"Get that," Mamma had said, getting up. Heading off to the john. "I've had so much tea tonight my back teeth are floating."

"Got it," Bets had replied. Reaching over to the side table, she'd laid her hand on the receiver. Didn't pick up.

~

She isn't asking much. Not some round-the-world cruise on a ship bigger than Napanee County. Not a million dollar lotto win. Not to be fawned over in fancy-girl dress shops like those snobby ladies did Julia Roberts in *Pretty Woman*—a film Bets had adored, immediately and profoundly, and was foolish enough to say so. While the credits rolled on their TV, she'd sighed happily, hand fluttering up to her heart. "That was *so* good."

"Bets is found herself a new calling," Daddy had said from the recliner, loud so's Mamma could hear it from the kitchen. "Fancies she's gonna be a *hoor.*"

She can still feel the heat of that flush. The lump jagging in her throat. The teary anger at being so misunderstood.

"It's just a movie," Daddy had said, laughing, clicking those damn silver teeth of his. "And you ain't got the figure to make that kind of money."

All Bets wants is to live a while in the city. *Downtown.* In an apartment. A sleek one with granite countertops and stainless steel fittings, picture windows without curtains, and halogen bulbs inset in white ceilings, beaming down like alien spotlights. She wants a place with no yard.

She thinks about the type of someone she'd have to become to match those upmarket joints. A catalogue model. A regular guest at the Grand Ole Opry. A rich man's wife.

Nope, Bets thinks, digging, digging. Scratch that last one.

If she can't find her own shine, she might as well stay home.

Shunt, spill. One little dig after another, accumulating, really gets her pulse going. She braces herself against the mound as the ground shifts beneath her feet. The crest is rising up fast in front of her; if anyone looked out the kitchen window right about now, they'd glimpse her blonde bangs over the ridge, her hair teased up in a wave that's beginning to droop. They'd see the cool arcs of brows she's spent hours upon hours plucking. Pale green eyes that blink too much, fluttering to shut out a world that doesn't yet match the one hidden behind her lids.

Although this third grave's much smaller than the one Nanna Tee's in, it's still big enough to swallow a heavy duty Silverado whole. From chassis to skylight, quadruple headlights to a tray that can haul over 3000 lbs, the pickup's well and truly covered. *No sense burying nothing useful, nothing valuable*, Mamma insisted. *Sink rustbuckets instead of good timber.*

Always was so practical, her Mamma. Never did nothing without a solid reason. Never acted on a whim.

Bets straightens up, cuffs the sweat from her brow. Pauses to take in the familiar view one last time. The flag jutting out from the house's back gable, parachute fabric snapping in the breeze. All those red and white lines pointing nowheres, those jagged stars fading to nothing. At the end of the driveway, the rickety toolshed. She won't miss its oil stink, its spiders, its stubborn door. By the stoop, there's the swan-shaped planters Mamma bought at a flea market, cracked from too many cold snaps. The bleeding-heart bushes have grown wild around them, weird flowers bobbing in grass that was overgrown long before winter, and has now sickened into a yard of pukey yellow-green. *Phlegmatic.* That's another word Bets once looked up: means apathetic, unflappable. Literally, she thinks, looking at that useless lawn. So heavy and dull, even the wind can't budge it.

Nothing shiny round here, Bets knows, but what's underground. Singing low, she keeps digging until she hits some.

∿

Soon as Bets strikes metal, she tosses the shovel and starts using her hands instead. She's not worried about damaging the truck—the thing was a piece of shit long before it was buried—only, she wants to reach the cab without having the whole damn thing cave in. Between each scoop, she packs the dirt walls around and above her, suddenly grateful for the ground-freeze keeping the mound's earthen lid stiffly in place. The sloping tunnel is now twice her width and half again as tall. Cursing Mamma's stubbornness—it'd be so much easier if the pickup had been parked inside a cavern, the way Winston's jalopy and Nanna Tee's Buick were—Bets crouch-claws down to the bottom. Does her best terrier impression. Sprays soil up and out the hole behind her.

Luckily, her aim isn't too far off target. A window's topmost edge is poking up from the ground in front of her: not the windshield she'd expected, but the driver's side door. Scraping her fingers raw, she cleans the glass bit by bit, wiping away grime and the fog of her breath, until the pane is mostly clear. A ragged circle of light filters in over Bets' shoulder, reflecting grey on the panel's upper right corner. In blue shadows inside the truck's cab, a slight figure is buckled behind the wheel, dressed in her Thorsday best. Lace-gloved hands folded in her lap. Permed head bowed as though praying. Refusing to look up.

"Open up, Mamma," Bets says, knuckles rapping on the glass. "Don't make me break in."

Mamma's gaze flicks to the door, then back to her knees. Slowly, she bunches the lengths of her black skirt up onto her thighs, twisting the fabric around a glint of silver. Patting it in place, she straightens her shoulders. Rearranges her tarnished necklace, nestling the cross between ruffles on her blouse. Tilts the rearview mirror and fusses a minute with her hair. Acts like she's alone. As ever.

"Come on," Bets snipes, knocking harder. "*Mamma.*"

The ghost rolls her eyes, unrolls the window. Soon as it's cracked an inch, a dank gust of air whooshes out, reeking of smoke and tar and hospital-grade antiseptic. All the stinks of life that led her into death, clinging for eternity. It wasn't dramatic, Mamma's end. It was efficient. Expected. Not trusting anyone else to get the details right, she'd made all the arrangements herself. Hedging bets, she'd asked Reverend to send her off, *ashes to ashes* and all that jazz, then invited the Lady's diner sect to drive her into the ground.

That's my girl, Daddy had said proudly, before Mamma went and stole his smile for good. Keeping it for herself.

"Got my license," Bets says, talking fast so Mamma won't interrupt. "And a spot on the bookmobile's roster. From next week, I'll be driving the Napanee—Athabaska route. It's not much, but . . . "

Bets stops, swallows. Keeping her gaze down—if the gods are watching, they're watching, whether she's under wide skies or close earth—she wriggles onto one elbow, reaches back with her free hand. Paper crackles as she drags the map from her pocket, then smooths it between filthy palms. Scrawled on a scrap torn from an old sketchbook, the road-lines are messes of crayon, the landmarks smudges of multicoloured chalk, the street names and compass arrows scribbled in illegible marker. No matter which way it's held, the thing's damn near impossible to read. A kindergarten kid could've done better, no doubt about that.

Good thing you're set on broadening your horizons, girl, Daddy'd said when Bets showed it to him yesterday. *Most Wheelers know these roads inside out, but this . . .* He'd shaken his head, turning the map this way and that. *If you ain't inherited my sense of direction, well, you'd better ask yer Mamma for the next best thing. Reckon she'll give it to you easier'n she will me.*

But Bets knows Mamma never gave anything so easily as she did criticism, followed by her own—*the only*—opinion. Death won't have changed her mother *that* much.

She's counting on it.

Steeling her resolve, Bets holds out the drawing, keeping her hand flat and low, close enough for Mamma to lick. It really *is* the worst piece of art she's ever crafted, as appalling in the gloom as it is in full bright, but Bets yammers like she has so many times before when showing off what she's made. Too quick, too eager for approval.

"The bookmobile stops in the city twice a month to restock," she says, pointing. "*Here* and *here* and *there*. Don't know exactly where else I'm headed, but probably we'll follow the river," she wags her finger at a splotch and a purple squiggle, "then motor alongside the canyon a whiles." Brown penciled nonsense cuts across the page, so ugly Bets can hardly bear looking at it. "Reckon this map's going to lead me on some grand adventures, don't you?"

Chin lifted, Mamma rolls her eyes at the thing.

Don't hold back now, Bets thinks, suppressing a grin when Mamma uncrosses her arms, snatches and crumples the page.

How will you ever get by, the ghost's blue sneer seems to say. Magnanimous, Mamma fumbles at her skirt, freeing Daddy's silver-toothed map from the wool's dark folds. With a huff, she tosses it up into the dirt tunnel. *Don't let me stop you.*

"Oh," Bets says, smiling at last, running a thumb over the mouth-piece's worn ridges. A new song tickling her lips. A coal of certainty burning hot in her belly. "I won't."

SURFACING

DOT REMEMBERS THAT POND BETTER THAN TED DOES. The July water, warm and waist-deep. Clear as summer wine if they'd stood still long enough, toes touching, feet sinking in the clay; churned to cloudy cider if minnows had nibbled, if sunk branches had scratched, if milfoil had brushed her shins. Any excuse and she'd squealed, jumped into Teddy's arms, kicked up silt. Any excuse and he'd lifted her, held her right close, goosebumps roughing his skin despite the afternoon heat. Dottie with no varicose veins, no cellulite. The red floral maillot Mama had bought her cupping and accentuating, not digging in. Teddy trim from a season's planting up north, muscles lean from all that hoeing. The two of them, sun-glazed but shivering. Curved hardnesses pressed against soft.

Dinner bells had rung while they swam, crickets droning around them in the long grass. Poplars had rained yellow-green. Old man willow had averted his gaze, bowed his head to the shallows and wept. Teddy had teased and tickled and pinched. He'd hauled Dottie underwater to keep the horseflies from gouging chunks out their scalps. Only then, her squeal had been genuine; all that time spent curling, pinning up her hair, all that wasted effort. They'd emerged gasping, sputtering, speckled with leaves. Teddy had brushed maple keys from her shoulder blades, called her *angel* as the little green wings spun free. She couldn't help but smile.

A fine screen of reeds had spiked the banks, long stems broken where retrievers had ploughed through chasing ducks. In Dot's mind, those shoots are still tall and swaying and backlit, black dusted with gold. She'd been fifteen when they'd splashed into that darkness together, that first time, on Teddy's birthday. Fifteen when she'd torn the leg elastic on her new swimsuit, pulling the fabric too quickly aside. The ripping high-pitched, a whip-crack that had stopped Teddy's clumsy prodding. He'd stopped and looked at her. Waited for her say-so.

He'd waited.

It'd been all the comfort Dottie needed.

Don't worry, she'd said, teeth chattering between kisses. *Keep going.*

She'd bled for him in that pond. Without worrying too much about love or marriage or what Mama would say when she saw what Dottie'd done to her new suit. She didn't care about all the possible *thens*; she was focused on *now*. On Teddy. On not getting caught.

The reeds were magic camouflage, hiding their bare nethers from all but Jesus' sight. They'd kissed in the shade, lips bluing. His thighs beneath hers strong but so cold. She'd flinched as his chill pushed its way up and in. Freezing her from the inside out.

It'll get better, Dottie had told herself, tasting salt and iron. *Hang in there.*

The water had roiled painfully between them for a couple of minutes, and then it was still. After, Teddy explored Dot's smoothnesses and nubs, places where she was now slick or tender or numb. He'd blushed and fumbled to re-lace his trunks. "Here," she'd said, taking the strings, double-knotting them. Tugging to make sure the bow would hold.

Laughing, the bold Teddy she'd always known had returned, replacing the shy. With a wink, he'd clasped her shoulders, puckered for another kiss. Dot had leaned in—and Teddy heaved, dunking her head-first. Water simmered past her nose and ears, fizzing like popping candy. The world was muted, a shimmer of light above the murk. Holding her breath, Dottie had stayed under. Listening to the hollow thump of Teddy's feet running away. Squinting against the grit. Exhaling bubble by bubble. Sinking deeper, into silence.

Her lungs burned by the time she'd heard muted sloshing, Teddy's trophy-winning stroke pulling him smoothly back. A few seconds later, his shadow sailed over her. He'd kicked carefully, arms scooping, reaching down. Grinning, she'd dodged his hands. Made him squirm a bit before surfacing.

✿

They'd taken their honeymoon in a tent by the pond's shores. Drifted their summers away on orange air mattresses. Swam through the sadness after one Baby Boy and two Baby Girl Brantferds were born quiet and blue. They'd gone there so much over the years, Ted used to joke, their skin hasn't grown *old*—it's just permanently water-wrinkled.

But this new puddle on their front lawn, this mattress-sized pool trenched between the begonias and the curb, *this* is not their pond. Theirs was filled with concrete thirty-odd years ago. Capped with a drive-in, then a parking lot, then a discount outlet mall. Theirs is cement supporting cement, smoothed without a ripple.

This one is all wrong, all Ted's.

A lace of white cloud scudders overhead, as if God's drawn Chantilly across His window this morning. Sunlight filters through the gaps, bright but not all that warm. In frost on the porch railing, Dot's handprints melt into her husband's as she huffs down the steps. Slowly, slowly, she follows his trail to the water. It's deep green, impenetrable, black where muck meets grass. She shudders, seeing the night sky trapped in its surface; thousands of stars glinting between ghosted branches of elms, larches, pine. There are no crickets chirping here, no sunny birdsong, just a low-level electric hum. The shore is fringed with ferns, not reeds. Around it, the air smells like rain.

Ted's been gawking at the thing, on and off, for days. Gaze unfixed. Arms crossed or hanging listless. Sometimes rocking gently, squelching from heel to toe, sometimes barely moving. That's how Dot finds him now, standing right where her marigolds and peonies should be, a lone sentinel planted in the embankment. Barefoot and still wearing the same overbleached boxers he slept in. The knobs of his spine showing through a thin undershirt, hardly any meat left on him. She used to love running her hands up under Teddy's work shirts, feeling the heat of his skin, the ridged muscles, the fur on his solid belly—but Ted's mostly wisp now. If Dot scratched his back the way she used to, he'd probably catch under her fingernails, crumble, and blow away.

"Where's your housecoat, love? Where's your shoes?"

Her guts clench when he doesn't answer.

"You'll catch your death," she says, louder this time, just in case. No response. For all his flaws, Ted isn't deaf. Mama used to call him a master of selective hearing—he'd tune out whenever fishing shows came on, or when the in-laws popped by, or when the dishes needing doing—but most of the time Dot couldn't complain. *Teddy's got a head full of figures*, she'd kid, wriggling her arse, *which is why he sticks with me.*

But at breakfast this morning, Ted flat ignored her. Almond milk and rolled oats turned to concrete in the bowl while he stared out the window, not eating no matter how much honey Dot added. Few weeks ago, he'd started drifting when she was only half through explaining what happened on *Days*, and wouldn't clue in again until *Final Jeopardy*. A couple days later, he'd traipsed round their front garden for hours, not mowing the nice little lawn, not picking her any daisies, just moseying here and there. Trampling the impatiens. Snagging his pants on the bleedin' heart bush. Paying no attention to where his feet strayed. And last Tuesday, when she got home from visiting Mama at the boneyard, when she'd hollered herself red at the shocking state of their yard—the grass submerged under God-knows how much water, her blue-ribbon roses lagooned, the little pottery boy and girl disappeared with their little pottery umbrella, and tropical ferns bursting round the shoreline instead of reeds— Ted hadn't said a single thing.

"What you doing out here?" she asks now, quiet as her slippers, when, really, she still wants to yell, *What the hell'd you get this for?*

She can't make head nor tails of it. Ted pale as a fish belly, stringy-legged by this unexpected pool, ready to dive. Ready to go—who knows where. Who knows why. Ted's never been much of a traveller. Come harvest, he'd go where the work took him and no further. He got in good with local farmers, charmed them with his broad shoulders, his stamina. Before long, he got first dibs on the nearest fields; so if he wasn't in by dinner each night, guaranteed he'd be back for bed. And when the crops started growing too thick and fast for his old body to reap, he drove right down to the local carpet factory, took a job assembling samples for other men to schlepp door-to-door. Must've bored him shitless, Dottie thought, being inside all day, doing that fiddly, repetitive work. But Teddy swore he didn't mind. He'd just grin and say he got more than enough excitement each night, right here at home. As usual, Dot would snort or flick him with a tea towel and say, *be serious—*

but she knew, deep down, he was honest. He wasn't a wanderer, her Teddy. He liked things the way they'd always been.

Until this goddamn pool appeared out of nowhere. Smothering her plants. Looking nothing like *their* pond, what with Ted getting the details so wrong. The foreign waters washing him so far away.

"A cup of coffee would go down nice," Dot says, changing tack. She takes him by the elbow, musters a weak smile. "Come on inside. If you're good, I'll even give you a bit of sugar."

Without the punch line, the old gag falls flat. *On the double-double*, Teddy used to say, making a lewd gesture that Dot never quite got—but now Ted misses his cue, distracted by reflections.

"Please." He balks at her touch and for one stupid second Dot thinks, *My hands are too cold.* But they aren't, they aren't. They're spotted and creased, with bulbed knuckles that trap precious rings on her fingers, and so hot they're bloated smooth. He balks, Dot thinks, because she's a stranger. Shrivelled where she used to be plump, more than plump where she used to be taut. Over the years, she's become Mrs Sprat. And poor Ted is more and more Jack.

"Wait," Dot says, but he doesn't. He doesn't. He's up to the hips in water. "Wait." He keels over without a splash. Arms and legs starfishing. He doesn't wait. Doesn't float. Doesn't sink. He dissolves in the shimmering black.

"Wait," she says, knowing she should plunge after him, clothes and all. She should dredge the deeps, tow him out of there with teeth and nails, claw his thin undershirt to ribbons if she has to. She should squeal and jump into his arms—any excuse—but Teddy's not there to catch her, and this pond is his, not theirs.

"Come back," she whispers, reaching out to nothing. Her mind leaps as her body edges. Fighting thoughts of hospital bills and nosy neighbours and what will happen to his pension and how to fill a casket if they don't have a body. She stops well back from the waterline. Afraid to touch that darkness. Afraid of getting lost in it, too. Just plain afraid.

Closing her eyes, she prays so hard her temples ache. *Sweet Jesus*, she thinks, over and over, until a scratchy old voice interrupts.

"Keep your goddamned oats," Ted says, horking a gob of phlegm on her feet.

"You scared me," Dot says, scrubbing the mess off with a tissue. Wishing she could stuff him full of fried-egg sandwiches. Fish and chips. Grease and starch and dripping red meat. Wishing she could dig her fingers into his back, pull him close, press her ear to his chest. Wishing she could hear the dry thump of his heart. Wishing she could be sure he's here and whole and solid. Wishing it was really him.

~

Next morning when Dot rolls over, the bed is empty beside her. The blankets are thrown back, cooling. She gropes at the bedside table, gets her eyes on. Eases her legs over the mattress edge, joints stiff and aching. She swears she can hear them swelling, if she listens hard, liquid slopping around knuckles and knees. Her wrists splash as she takes her pills, two pinks and a blue. Outside, there's a squeal of laughter. Childish and overly loud. More splashing—yes, Dot can definitely hear it—the swirl of limbs through water. She groans to her feet, hips and ankles sloshing her over to the window.

The pond is still there.

A flash of scarlet in the ferns. Floral and ribbons. A glimpse of slender legs bowed. Fronds tremble, leaves scissoring in the breeze. Dot blinks and the colour is confetti. It's red petals lilting. It's vanishing in black water. Another blink and there's only Ted, not splashing. Disintegrating in starlight.

She picks up the phone, dials Mama's number. It rings twice before she remembers.

Cradling the receiver, she concentrates on breathing. *Don't panic*, she tells herself, but her heart is chugging and the rest of her's trying to outpace it. She races past the bathroom on her way to the front door. "Ted?" she calls down the hall—'Ted?"—poking her head into the spare room, the nursery, the kitchen. "Ted?"

It's pointless, Dot knows—God, she saw what she saw—but each time he goes a part of her refuses to believe it. A part is always surprised.

Another part wonders what it'll be like. If, when.

On the way out, she grabs a fleece jacket and throws it on over her flannel. She jams her feet into sheepskin boots, hands into wool mittens. After twenty minutes outside, her beige leathers are soaked dark brown, the frilled hem of her nightie drenched with dew. Circling the pond, she wears a path in the mud where dahlias once bloomed, where the crab-apple tree dropped its fruit, where poor little Whiskers fertilised the roses. All of it, all of it, is covered in water and sludge. All of it drowned with Ted.

Come back, she thinks, then aloud, so he'll know he's missed. "Please come back."

For a second, the pool contracts. Dot calls again, again. Echoes distort her voice, filling her hearing aid with robotic feedback. Words screech and deepen; now girlish, now rasping. Now an exhausted old man's.

"Sorry, angel."

Hunkering over, Dot wrings the damp from her nightgown with furious twists. *Don't look*, she thinks, knotting the pain up in her skirts. Her hands are shaking. His are whittling air. *It isn't him yet. Not 'til he gets his bearings.*

"Where'd you go," she says at last, risking a glance up. Ted is dripping, blue-lipped. His eyes are full of the pond.

"Nowhere," he says. "Right here."

◆◆

They need groceries but Dot just doesn't have the energy. The trolleys are too big nowadays, the carry-baskets too heavy. She can't manoeuvre either while swatting Ted's hands away from the cherries, the shrink-wrapped cold cuts, the colouring books, the cotton undies, the fizzy drinks, the gross milk chocolate eggs hiding cheap toys inside. If she turns her back for a second, just one second, he's gone. Then everyone looks at her funny—*how could you lose your husband so goddamn quick*, they all say, without saying a thing, talking with smirks and side-eyes—and she blushes until sweating, searching for some nice aproned boy to mop up the fern leaves and puddles Ted's left behind him.

Sometimes Dot wonders if a harness would be best, clip a leash to his back the way mamas do when they're too tired to run after their toddlers.

Sometimes she avoids the supermarket altogether, takes Ted to Jim's Surf 'n' Turf instead.

We got enough to survive until tomorrow, she thinks, a brass bell clanging as they push open the restaurant's glass door. Inside, Jim Bluinn's hanging glasses behind the bar. Chatting with the lunch crew. The beer-swillers in fluorescent vests. The interstate drivers.

The girls talking books, their rosy-cheeked bundles asleep in prams. Jim's polite to them all, even when they gawp at his bulging eyes and the badly-stitched cleft above his lip. Mama always said Jimmy was drop-dead gorgeous on the inside, though it took years for Dot to agree. *Doesn't matter now*, she thinks. Mama's gone and Jim's a hell-bent bachelor. He's too old to be serving up drinks, slipping maraschino cherries into Shirley Temples, knifing the heads off overfull pints. Too well-off to be waiting.

"Dorothy," Jim says and Dot mumbles a greeting. He lifts his chin at Ted. Ted grunts, follows a pretty hostess to the furthest available booth.

"Thank you," Dot says as the girl doles out menus. Across the table, Ted's washed out, thin and grey as the early winter light. Beside them, the picture window's blinds are rolled right up to the valance. *What a view*, she thinks, scowling at the parking lot. Jim's shiny new pickup. Three-way traffic lights, pulsing red. Cars taking turns at the intersection. The highway stretching away, away, away, through a light flurry of snow. Dot looks for the little ball-bearing cord to lower the shade, finds it triple-looped around a hook near her hip. She works at it for a minute, but the metal's too flimsy to grip. When the waitress comes over to help, Dot says *It's fine, dear, really—just a whim*, and orders a club sandwich and fries for Ted, with extra mayo on the side.

"And you?"

"Oh, I'm fine." Dot pats her belly, acid burning from bowels to craw. It was a dumb idea, coming here. Another stupid splurge. "Got to watch my waistline."

Staring outside, Ted eats mechanically. Bacon grease and ketchup drip down his skinny wrists as he nibbles instead of biting, packing his cheeks like a chipmunk. Off-white mush foams down his chin as he takes in too much, forgetting to swallow.

"Here," Dot says, wiping, wiping. "Better in than out—right, love?"

A glob of half-chewed bread splats on the table.

Once the plates are cleared, Dot lies and tells the waitress it's Ted's birthday, just for the free cake. A team of fake smiles brings it over, singing and sparkling. They take one look at Ted and refrain from making him stand while they clap and sing. Jim sends over a beer that Ted won't drink, so Dot sips at it until her heart palpitates.

Mashing the chocolate wedge on her plate, she makes a paste that won't need much chewing and spoons it into Ted's mouth. Pale worms of light twist across his face, twitching on his bony beak and slack jaw. Constellations twinkle in his wide pupils, reflected off the pond bogging up the parking lot outside.

"We'll get caught, Dottie," Ted says, brown guck drying in the corners of his mouth. "We're dead meat if we're caught."

"Look here," Dot says, stopping his ramble with another mouthful. She rubs his throat with unsteady fingers, coaxes the dessert down. "Look at me." Palm greens unfurl in her peripheral vision. *It should be reeds*, she thinks, again and again. *Where the hell are the reeds?* A dark sedan skims over the water outside, honking at a blurred streak of red. Ted's gaze swims from the window to Dot and back. A slow, blank lap.

"Come on." Dot licks, thumbs his lips. Tosses a handful of bills on the table and a few coins for the waitress, for Jim. Putting on her coat, she glares at the pool. Prays Ted doesn't fall in on the way to the car. "Let's go for a drive."

~

They'd ridden double home from their pond that day, Teddy steering, Dottie on the handlebars, leaning back with legs outstretched, throbbing between. On her own, she could've raced back to Mama's in fifteen minutes, tops. But Teddy was being extra careful. And Dottie had made him go the long way, just to prolong the moment.

In the car, it takes more than half an hour to reach the old gully; fifty years of commercial development, blocked shortcuts and traffic have done a real number on travel time. On the way, Dot points out where things used to be. The Dairy Queen. The Pop Shoppe. The JP's office where she and Teddy jumped the broom. The Women's & Children's hospital. The drop-in clinic Mama brought Teddy to after Jimmy Bluinn broke his nose that time.

Once in a while, Ted butts in and corrects her. Sometimes he's even right.

"Here we are," Dot says as they pull into the outlet mall's lot. She angles the car between faded white lines, switches off the windshield wipers and ignition. Between hatchbacks and sedans and SUVs, poplars stand naked in curbed cement beds. Willows huddle on raised medians, branches trailing in slush. Maple leaves blanket the knees of pale stick figures painted flat in simple wheelchairs. "We're here, Ted. We're here. Can't you see?"

Static sparks as she squeezes his knee. Twigs rub against twigs. Snow falls but doesn't last; the flakes melt into puddles, small and lined with salt.

"Are you with me, love?" Clutching hard, Dot jerks her head at the window, at the concrete pillars and lampposts and trolley bays. Their pond is long dried, long buried. "Are you with me?"

Ted sighs and unbuckles his seatbelt. Vines curl out of vents in the dashboard. Cattails sprout from the hood. Ferns get tangled in the door as he opens it, letting in a gust of warm cedar air. Long grasses shield the car from passers-by; people checking their phones, pushing carts, crossing the lot with hardly a splash. Well-used to avoiding winter boot-soakings, they skirt the wrong pond's shore without looking up even once. Without noticing it's even there.

Among parkas and dark jeans: frills and red flowers. Ribbons. Sun-browned legs.

"Don't go," Dot says to Ted, leaning over to kiss him. His wrinkled cheek has no firm left to it, the muscle sagged to jowl. Pink lipstick smears on papyrus skin. Flesh presses against bone. Through rough whiskers, she feels the hard edge of Ted's molars.

"Are you sure?"

"Of course," she replies. "Yes, of course."

"We'll get caught," Teddy says, whispering but excited. As he shimmies to get out, Dot yanks on his sleeve, clings. He writhes, bull-snorting, hankering for escape. She scrabbles at his narrow chest, pins it with an elbow. Makes a cage of her hand and traps the seat buckle. Panting, she clips him back in place.

"Shut the door," Dot says and, eventually, he does. She slumps against the wheel. Closes her eyes. All her shock absorbers are shot. Her forehead bounces on her knuckles as the car rocks back and forth—"Don't move a muscle," she warns—then finally settles. Springs in the seat wail, then fall silent. The car fills with a stale scent. Wet cotton dried on the body. The musk of creases, of yeast.

Dot breathes in deep, holds it. Listens to the hollow thump of her heart. Exhales bubble by bubble. Lungs burning, she looks in the rear-view. Wincing, she says, "Let's go home."

Ted smiles and relaxes against the headrest. "Happy birthday to me," he says, a hint of the old charm flitting across his features. Laughing, he reaches over and takes Dot's hand. Threads his fingers through hers.

~

For half a second, Dot considers gunning the accelerator when they pull into the driveway. Forget stopping, she thinks, with the thirsty pond here again, lapping at the asphalt, waiting to drink Teddy in. Forget stopping, letting him step into those waters, letting him go. Forget stopping. Rev through the living room wall instead. Crash through the chesterfield and the TV. Smash the china cabinet with Ted's old trophies inside and the porcelain ladies he bought on their anniversaries, forty-eight pastel dancers with arms and legs stretched to forever. Hurtle through them and keep going. Leave tire tracks across the kitchen floor. Grind through the hessian sacks of oats and lentils, the organic wheat germ, the antioxidant red wine, the jarred broccoli and beets that have done him no good, no good at all. Horse-power through everything, she thinks. Make the house collapse in their wake, trapping them in the bedroom together. Just them—no Teddy, no Dottie, no tiny blue-lipped mistakes—just Ted and Dot. Let them be each other's airbag, each other's emergency blanket. Let them be here, now, alone.

The car rolls to a halt, its bumper kissing the garage door. The parking brake ratchets up between the front seats. Keys click. The engine pings and pops as it cools. Ted opens his door. Braces himself against the frame. Creaks his way out.

Dot sighs and watches him go.

"You too," she says to the mirror.

Dot's joints are rock pools at high tide. Her feet are overfilled water balloons, wobbling as they hit ground. "Is this your fault?" she mutters, getting out of the car, reaching the waterside just in time to see Ted go under. She hates the quaver in her voice, hates knowing she doesn't have it in her to pull him back out.

Ferns stretch into reeds along the shoreline as she trudges back to the car. Poplars replace sugar dates as she fumbles at the visor, finally pressing the garage door opener. Gunpowder breezes waft across the road. Golden retrievers bark in the distance. She heads inside, aims for a shelf Ted half-built, half-propped on boxes of samples. She digs through tents and tarps and sleeping bags. Rustles up dust. Cobwebs. Finally finds one of their old air mattresses, orange plastic patched with duct tape.

It takes hours for Dot to blow the thing up, one shallow puff after another, but she's got time. The snow has stopped, the clouds wandering. By her feet, the pool is black and still, its silver stars shining. When the mattress is finally firm, Dot is light-headed. Her arms shake as she slides it into the water. Then she has to sit, right there in the muck, and take a breather before climbing on. The plastic seams are sharp with age; they bite into her hands as she clings, pushing off without getting wet. Floating on outer space.

Afraid to paddle, Dot lets the breeze take her where it wants. Ear pressed to the scalloped pillow, she listens to sounds amplified by water and air. Ripples thrumming beneath her. Wavelets flapping. Bullfrogs croaking. Electricity crackling from shore to shore. At dusk, she looks up as Jim Bluinn's pickup roars past. She watches the headlights shrink from bonfires to sparks, then lowers her head back down. The temperature has dropped with the sun, but Dot's been cold so long it makes no difference. Arms tucked in close, she shuts her eyes and listens hard.

There, she imagines, recognising the smooth rhythm. *There*, the in and out of Ted's medal-winning stroke.

It will get better, Dot tells herself, shivering, holding her breath. Waiting for him to come find her.

∞

SNOWGLOBES

JIMMY DIDN'T WANT CHILDREN, NEVER HAD. JANIE knew that when she married him. She also knew he wasn't the type to change his mind. Not when it mattered. He's loyal, Janie's best friend, Annabelle, had said, when they were both sophomores and Jimmy was in senior year. He's a goddamn Saint Bernard.

All through high school, Jimmy played hockey; defence, eighteenth man on the team. Ready to fill in whenever coach needed, but in four years he racked up maybe half a day's ice time. Janie didn't care. She went to his games anyway, just to see him riding the bench. He pretended he didn't notice her and Annabelle sitting in the bleachers; gossiping, giggling, whispers hanging in the fog of their breath. Wearing zippered miniskirts, sleeveless blouses, beaded necklaces and elbow-length fishnet gloves. All in white, the both of them, with oversized bows in their frosted hair. Like Madonna. *Like a Virgin*. Even with his eyes on the rink, Jimmy noticed.

～

When Annabelle died—black ice on the overpass, low visibility; the counsellor assured them it was nobody's fault—Jimmy came to the funeral. Throughout the service he'd held Janie's hand, squeezed her fingers until they were bloodless and cold. Janie had squeezed back. She hadn't cried while the priest mumbled prayers, then spoke too quickly, clipping his words during the requiem as if speeding through Mass would make his Latin sound more natural. Every other girl in the class sobbed shamelessly, though, double-thick layers of mascara gobbing down their flushed faces. Janie's cheeks had remained cool, her makeup frozen in place. She looked hideous when she cried. Her eyes puffed like blowfish, her nose swelled and reddened, her lips doubled in size. For hours afterwards she'd taste salt. No, it wouldn't do to cry. Not with Jimmy by her side. She'd weep herself ugly later, behind closed doors. Annabelle wouldn't mind.

"Coffins should be white and smooth," she'd said, as her best friend's heavy oak box lowered into the ground. "Like time capsules, perfect and hard. You know, to keep out the worms."

Jimmy rubbed her palm with his broad thumb and said nothing. So much grief had thickened his tongue. Though mesmerised by death, he could see still see Janie. He watched her blushing from the corner of his eye.

～

A week later, Jimmy pinned an orchid on Janie's floor-length black dress and took her to prom. In the stretch limo, she'd imagined Annabelle sitting across from the mini bar, wearing skin-tight leggings and matching bolero jacket, a babydoll tunic in peaches 'n' cream lace. "You look awesome," Janie said, after Jimmy had stepped out of the car. Annabelle had winked, and shooed her away.

Janie smiled all evening. She'd danced until she was sweaty, then wished that she hadn't: Jimmy's hands had slid on her bare shoulder blades when he'd pulled her in for a kiss. Their heads had collided. Her bony nose connected with Jimmy's left eye. He'd squinted for the rest of the night, tears leaking from beneath his lashes. I guess that's it then, she'd thought, watching the disco lights colour his teardrops gold, blue, orange. She didn't even have a tissue to offer.

They hadn't been crowned King and Queen, far from it. Jimmy looked like a Saint Bernard, Annabelle said so herself. And Janie wasn't even so pretty as that.

～

Janie had studied English literature at university. Shakespeare, Milton, Donne. Four years later, an Honours degree under her belt, she got a job as a receptionist. She worked at an office filled with cubicles, grey boxes carpeted from floor to ceiling, like cells for the criminally insane. The company distributed white goods. To commemorate her tenth year of service, the owners gave Janie a new fridge and a standalone freezer. She would've preferred a raise.

Jimmy took accounting, graduated early, then fast-tracked to become a CA. He wore suits at work, track pants at home. On weekends he played pickup hockey with a bunch of guys from the firm. He took Janie to the movies, to corporate functions, to conferences out of town. Sometimes she'd wait for him at his hotel, surprise him with slinky lingerie and sex in the middle of the day. She'd stopped taking the pill, but Jimmy would always pull out. He loved her, he'd said. He loved her body. He'd pretend to impale his eye on her nose, just to make her laugh. It would be the two of them together, or nothing, he'd said. There would be no children.

~

She'd bought her first snowglobe when they eloped to Acapulco, a cheap plastic dome with a photo of her and Jimmy inside. She'd been so slender then, fit and taut and tanned from a week in the sun. She nearly disappeared between the overinflated muscles of Jimmy's arms. As a wedding gown, she'd borrowed a spaghetti-strap sundress, and her husband was dressed in cream. They'd both worn mischievous expressions when the shutter snapped; Janie more than anyone loved a good secret.

For weeks she carried the globe around in her purse, and snuck glimpses whenever she could. It didn't bother her that there was no snow in Mexico. The flakes were confetti, as far as she was concerned, celebrating their marriage. A perfect moment of happiness, caught in a bubble of water.

~

Janie got fatter and fatter after that, but it didn't lead to maternity leave.

"It's love," joked her boss, patting his own flat abs. He was confidently gay, and so thin you could practically see through him. Every day he'd flit from cubicle to cubicle, flirting with staff of both sexes, telling them about his wild trips to Greece. Freckled and tiny as he was, no-one ever took him seriously. No-one ever felt truly harassed. He smoked too much and puffed when he walked. He'd bulked up to a size o since meeting his boyfriend.

"It's love," he repeated, pinching the taut flesh at his hips, seeing love handles where there were none. "It shows that you're happy."

Janie soon grew so happy she could no longer fit into regular-sized clothes.

~

They upgraded from an apartment on the outskirts of town to a two-storey house in the city. Maple trees lined the streets and in each driveway were parked shiny new cars, four-wheel drives, convertibles that could only be driven in summer. Their place was modest, four bedrooms, two W/Cs—one with a claw-foot tub. Janie loved few things more than wallowing in the bath, books stacked on the tiles, bottles of vodka within easy reach. She'd be in there for ages. Hours and hours, until the water went cold and she'd have to drain some of it, refill it in a scalding rush. Drain and refill, drain and refill, she'd keep everything submerged until the chill left her bones.

Jimmy would chuckle to hear her splashing around in there for so long. He expected the room to be waterlogged after one of Janie's marathon baths, but she always left the place spic-and-span. Once he found a thin smear of blood on the rim of the tub. Only once.

"Cheap razors," Janie said, her arms wrapped around a bundle of clean towels. "Never buying them again."

She smelled like baby powder when Jimmy kissed her cheek. Her skin was a violent shade of red, and shrivelled as a newborn's.

~

Slimming foundation garments filled Janie's wardrobe. Underwear that stretched up to her breasts and extended down to her knees. Janie contemplated corsets but couldn't afford them.

Instead she wore loose dresses with empire waistlines. Low-necked shirts that would accentuate her cleavage. At work, her friends said she looked beautiful. Her boss continued to flirt. But weeks would pass, great deserts of time, in which Jimmy was too tired, he said, to touch her. When he spooned her at night, as he still often did, she'd move his arm so it wouldn't drape across the drooping roll of her belly. And when they had sex, he'd take her from behind, most vigorously after several tumblers of scotch.

~~

Jimmy brought his wife presents, little surprise gifts, just because. Bouquets from the grocery store. Figs dipped in dark chocolate. Curry his personal assistant, Annie, had made. Texan barbecue crackers. Bottles of sparkling red wine. Simple pleasures, and sweet. Treats they shared together after a busy day at work. Jimmy filled up, Janie filled out.

~~

They shopped at Price Club, and later, Costco. Janie always bought in bulk. Saran wrap on rolls so large you could wrap a Rottweiler, if he'd stay still long enough, until the black of his fur looked pale grey—and still there'd be plastic left to cover baked goods for the freezer. Cotton balls in great rectangular bags that could smother a small child if they were mistaken for pillows. Garbage bags sturdy enough to wrap a whole tree in full bloom, to trap the leaves on its branches come autumn. Egyptian cotton towels, all white, twenty bucks for a baker's dozen. Bleach in industrial-sized bottles. Linens will last for years with enough bleach, Janie knew. All stains easily erased, towels and sheets returned to the cupboard pristine. Without a spot of colour on them.

~~

She named their son Ariel after the sprite in Shakespeare's *Tempest*. Immediately, she shortened it to Ari because baby boys should not be confused with little mermaids. Babies cannot breathe underwater, nor can they sing with lobsters.

When Ari was grown, he'd wear running shorts with white piping around the waistband and legs. They'd have built-in mesh jocks, so he could race around the house without flapping about. The shorts would be blue, his t-shirt sparkling white, like the blizzards inside her snowglobes. She'd bought one a year since Ari was born, seven in all, at gift shops all over the world. Paris, London, Québec City, Niagara Falls, New York, Vancouver, L.A. Jimmy consulted and Janie went with him. They travelled business class. Jimmy could afford it, and the seats could better accommodate Janie's girth. Hong Kong was next on their list.

Some days Ari's irises were clear blue, like his father's, others they were soil brown like Janie's. Hazel, she thought, was the way to describe their colour—their shifting, inconstant hue. Occasionally they were almost purple. She was sure they'd darkened over time. She stopped looking closely at his face, after a while. Unsettled by the shadows she saw there.

She named her daughter Hazel, since the girl suffered the same ocular affliction. For Hazel, she bought glass paperweights.

For a while Janie contemplated changing her name to Jade. It was a much more exciting name. Sexy. Daring. More like the Cheries and Krystals and Desirées in the magazines she'd found in Jimmy's sock drawer. It might turn him on, she thought, if he closed his eyes and called her Jade. He might not even need the scotch to get going. And she still wasn't taking the pill, so who knew what might happen . . . But it was the end of financial year, and Jimmy was in no mood for games. What he wanted was Janie. He wanted the woman he'd married.

Hazel wasn't looking well. Ari was much more robust, but even he was beginning to sag. Janie, on the other hand, was healthier than ever. She earned a promotion (PA to the CEO) because of her dedication, her unblemished record of service. But when her babies started falling apart, she did what any mother would do: she called in sick. She stayed home and looked after the pair of them. They weren't rowdy. They suffered in silence. Perhaps they're dehydrating, she thought. Perhaps they need sugar. So she'd bake until the freezer was topped-up with brownies, butter tarts, scones. All the while she'd listen to old Leonard Cohen singles and scratched Simon and Garfunkel LPs. Hazel would like those ones best, Janie thought. The little girl actually vibrated at the singers' deep voices, their carefully chosen phrases. She rattled. She practically hummed. Meanwhile Janie imagined herself as Suzanne, or as the girl who read Emily Dickinson while Paul Simon read Robert Frost. She wanted to be Cecilia for an afternoon. She wanted another baby.

Nobody's perfect, she thought, phoning in to book the rest of the week off.

※

On their fifteenth anniversary, Jimmy and Janie holidayed in the Dominican Republic. Seven days and six nights, a package deal at half price because it wasn't yet full winter. Janie wore sarongs to cover her stretchmarks, billowing gypsy blouses to cover her bloated torso. A broad-brimmed straw hat kept the pregnancy mask from darkening on her forehead. Plastered in zinc and sunscreen, Janie looked as pale as ever. She could've painted herself up like a clown, red nose and all, and Jimmy wouldn't have noticed.

Jimmy's arms had deflated over the years, but his butt still looked good in a swimsuit. She peeled it off him, straight out of the pool, and reminded him why he was lucky to have her. Eight months along, she wasn't up for sex; but her tongue always made Jimmy squirm, and when she swallowed instead of spat the sheer joy on his face guaranteed Janie another few months as a married woman.

He bought her a crystal globe in Santo Domingo. Palm trees and a surfer dude bobbed in waves of sparkles instead of snow. Shards of colour swirled, clutched in Janie's palm—too much colour. It didn't match her set, all ice blues and frost whites. It looked wrong.

"Cheer up," Jimmy said, mistaking the source of her frown, seeing reluctance to go home writ large on her face. "We've still got two more days in paradise."

She forced a laugh and said he was right. But tucked comfortably beneath the soft sheets of a king-sized bed, in a luxury bungalow looking over the Caribbean Sea, she couldn't sleep. Her mind raced. Had she turned off the gas before they left? Had she locked the back door? What if there was a blackout? A full freezer defrosted, and everything spoiled. They hadn't hired a house-sitter—no need, Janie thought, it's only a week—and they didn't own any pets. Her stomach churned. The baby stirred in her gut, all elbows and knees. She stayed awake until dawn, hoping Ari and Hazel were all right. Hoping no-one would find them alone.

～

Outside it was snowing. The city muffled under a blanket of white, sparks of ice catching in the beams of streetlights, the world unsteady beneath Janie's plump feet. We've been shaken, she thought, laughing, then gasped as another contraction wracked her body.

"Be good, be quiet," she told her children in the kitchen. She shifted a few boxes of brownies in the freezer, dug a hard square from one container, stuffed it into her mouth. Warmed, the cake went soft on her tongue. She drizzled melted icing onto her fingertip, smeared it across plastic wrap, revealing the babies' compressed lips. "Hush now," she said, wiping the frost from their nostrils.

"Christmas party starts at eight," Jimmy called from the living room. "You nearly ready? We need to go to the liquor store, and pick Annie up on the way. She's clueless when it comes to directions."

"We've got tons of time," she replied. Janie's water had broken after lunch, and everyone knew third births were the quickest. "Give me an hour or two and I'll be a knockout."

"Ha ha," said Jimmy, flicking on the TV.

"Ha ha," said Janie.

The baby kicked at her ribs, pressed its head hard against her cervix, let her know it was time. Let her know it was now or never.

"Mamma needs to take a bath, my darlings." Janie chucked Ari on the chin, tweaked Hazel's nose. She ate the last of the brownies, clearing a space in the freezer. "I know you're excited—I am too! But I'll be back soon, all pretty in my dress. And then you can meet your new little brother or sister."

"Hush, hush," she whispered, closing the heavy white lid. "Enough chatter. We don't want to disturb daddy."

BLUES EATER

TUB NEVER MAKES HOUSE CALLS. FOLK KNOW WHERE to find him: beached, as always, on the brown striped sofa-bed in his one-man trailer, parked at the farthest end of Mama's long drive. Armed with cans of corn relish, plates of butter tarts, rhubarb pies, heat-sealed jars of gooseberry jam, his callers stop in at Mama and Gene's place first. Without knocking or ringing the bell, they wait on the stoop until she joins them. Trod on so often, the timber planks are worn and tired, whining at the lightest step; Mama hears folk skulking out there long before she opens the front door. When she does, they skip the small talk. Voices quiet— softer than the whoosh of Gene's CPAP machine in the living room, hosing life into his tar-clogged lungs—these visitors ask after Tub.

Is he free?

Has he already eaten?

Does he have room for one more?

No-one goes into detail with Mama. All she wants to know is how many cookies are in those plastic containers of theirs, and do they have nuts? Tub can't abide nuts. What kind of jelly is inside those donuts? Blueberry's his favourite. Is that pie Key lime? Homemade or store bought? Topped with whipped cream or meringue?

Tub isn't all that picky, really. He'll take what's brought. Always has.

Mama just wants to make him happy.

Hand hovering near, but not touching, elbows or the small of backs, she steers Tub's guests past the rusting swing-set he used to love as a kid, past the junked cars Gene never got round to repairing, past Wendy's banana-seat bike and the cardboard lemonade stand she set up outside his trailer years ago, past the half-blind pitbull chained near the windowless door. Lifting his old head, the dog whuffs until Mama shooshes him. She knocks with the great ugly ring Gene gave her, then walks in without waiting for Tub's say-so. She knows he's home. Of course he is. Where else could he be?

"Thought you might be hungry," she says, every single time, barely pausing to gauge his reaction. Doesn't matter much if he shrugs or shakes his noggin; she's quick to turn back to the entryway. Quick to beckon folks in.

Today it's a guy, late-twenties or early thirties, the skin on his cheeks a red mess of acne scars. He's short as Mama; so short he's got to roll up the legs of his blue coveralls. Still wearing a tool-belt, he whips off his hard-hat and clutches it to his chest. Bows his head, almost respectful, like this was a church or courtroom or something, instead of a dust-quiet, low-ceilinged, wood-veneered caravan. Gaze lowered, he holds out the hoagie he brought for Tub. Family sized, melted cheese and mustard seeping through the paper wrapping. When Tub doesn't get up, the guy looks to Mama for a cue.

"Go on," she says. She waits until he scuffs his work boots on the welcome mat just inside the door, then leaves them to it. On the gravel outside, her sneakers crunch a hurried retreat.

"Don't mind her," Tub says. "She's always discreet."

The guy winces. Partly out of embarrassment, Tub knows, partly at the feathery pitch of his voice. Such a girlish noise produced by such a monstrous blob of a man; it's hideous. Repulsive. Even Tub shudders to hear words whispering through his thick lips, lisping around invisible scars, cursed runes burnt into the tender flesh of his mouth. Ridged reminders he'd rather forget. He doesn't talk if he can avoid it.

Instead, Tub smiles his thanks for the sandwich. Invites the man to dig into it himself. *Go ahead*, he says with a nod, pointing at the lone stool tucked beneath a card table. *It's lunchtime.* Whatever's left over, Tub will gobble up when he's alone. For now, he watches nervous nibbles become open bites, the muscles in his guest's temples throbbing in and out as he chews. Grease loosens the tongue better than liquor, Tub knows. Soon enough, secrets will spill like crumbs down the repairman's front. All it takes is time.

When the sub is half gone, the guy's posture stiffens. He rewraps the offering, puts it aside. Brushes scraps of bread off his face. Stands and walks over to the ever-unfolded sofa bed. Tub pats its wide armrest—there's no room on the mattress beside him—and waits for the man to climb on.

Once he's straddling the support, boot heels thunking into the upholstery, he begins, as they all do, by mumbling some variation of *I don't know how long this has been going on . . . Don't rightly know how it started . . .* In the scheme of things, this guy's sins are far from the worst Tub's seen. A telecom worker, he jacks into the cables he's supposed to be repairing, jacks into porn hotlines, racy 1-900 numbers, then spends too many of his billable hours in public johns, jacking off. Missing appointments and call-outs. Coming home late without ever earning overtime. Spurting his sex drive into scrunched toilet paper, saving none of it for his wife.

"I feel awful," he says at last. It doesn't matter if Tub believes him or not. What matters is he's here now. A supplicant only Tub can help. A burdened soul begging to be lightened.

Squinting, Tub searches for the deepest hues of the man's guilt, the heaviest blooms. Around his palms, on his lap, in his crotch, the air is contused, blue and black and purple, wavering like steam off a fresh-baked loaf. Each person's regret carries its own shade, its own awful whiff. Without really meaning to, Tub catalogues them by colour and stench. This guy's is a vinegar bruise. It wells most densely at the sides of his head.

Tub opens his mouth.

"Hush," he says, gripping the line-worker's skull, pulling him close. "Hold still," he says, slurping all traces of the stain from around the man's ears. Gulping it down like oysters, swallowing the slime whole. When he's done, only a milky-blue scum remains, just another smear on the guy's uniform.

Immediately, the added weight bulges in Tub's gut, an extra roll flabbing dimples around his middle. Ten pounds of shame, he'd guess. Give or take.

"Don't mention it," Tub says as his guest smiles wide, springs off the sofa-bed. They always feel better—buoyant, carefree—after bloating him with their worries. Glutting him with their problems. Keeping him fat, obscenely well-fed.

"Really," he says. "Don't."

He'd still been skinny—delicate, even—that night Mama came into his bedroom and found him bawling in the dark. Wrung out, incoherent, somehow made scrawnier with tears. Wearing nothing but his little boy swim trunks even though he was almost thirteen then, almost a man. His piss-soaked undies bunched at the back of his closet, buried under the shoes he'd outgrown but couldn't bear to chuck out. The sleeping bag wet beneath him.

Just a nightmare, she'd said, pulling her fake satin robe snug. Drawing its ties in hard around her tiny waist.

Just a nightmare, she'd said, after he'd choked back his sobs, mustered his nerve, and told her.

Finally.

Mama's tone was tighter than the springs on his single bed that night, straining as she perched beside him. *Hush now.* Tighter than the arm she'd wrapped around him. *Hush.* Firm as the kisses she'd pressed into his temple and forehead. Rigid reassurances. Dry and cold.

A nightmare, she'd said. *That's all.*

He'd thought, then, she must be right.

It had just been the once, hadn't it?

Hush, hush.

Maybe he'd misremembered? A week had already passed, seven sleepless nights since— Seven nights shivered away in the dark, hour after hour afraid to close his eyes, to hear the door hinges wheezing open behind him, the linoleum floor shuddering, to feel that stumbling, *stop start stop*, that fumbling at his quilt, *stop start*, to smell that whiskey fog grunting closer, *closer*. Afraid of that rasp, of stubble, of zippers. Afraid of that sickening *tug*. That tobacco grip on his lean face. That unreal taste.

Unreal.

Maybe Mama was right.

Just a nightmare.

It couldn't be real.

Maybe he's always been wrong.

But.

All those wakeful nights later, a residue of chlorine and salt-coated fingers still squirmed on his tongue, dribbled down his chin. Right then, he didn't get what it was, what it meant. Why the blue cloud of it dragged him down, why it made him feel so open. So exposed.

Oh Toby, Mama had said, sitting, pulling him to her chest.

From the hallway, a thin bar of yellow light angled into his room, slicing across the bed. The streak cut across Tub's face, severing Mama's head and shoulders from her torso. In that moment, he noticed cobalt lines pooling along the sharp bones of her sternum. A maroon blob pulsating between her breasts.

Cheek pressed against Mama's skin, Tub had wept himself hollow, puffy and hot, while she stroked the sweaty hair off his brow. Her hands were dried out from bleaching Gene's work shirts, her fingertips starched, rasping. He recoiled at their touch, then covered it by forcing himself to hug her. Snuffling, he breathed in a strange mix of spices Mama had never worn before. Black pepper and aniseed. Sour cherry. Tonguing tears and snot from his upper lip, he tasted something else, something that stung like jalapeño. Something that set his eyes watering once more.

Carefully, he licked again.

Hovering above her heart, Mama's disbelief was a smoked chicory coal that burnt all the way to his gut when he swallowed it. Her excuses were gobs of overboiled Swiss chard. Over these clung a wispy mesh of self-reproach, sticky as cotton candy. Without thinking, he'd sucked it all in. Filled his face, his heaving belly. Forced it down.

Better, she'd sighed after a minute or so, once the air was clear. Tub knew it wasn't a question. As his middle pudged out, some of the stiffness had left Mama's spine. Lard swelled around the elastic waistband on his swimsuit while her embrace had gone limp. Lips curving with relief, she'd nodded. *Just a nightmare.*

Making breakfast the next morning, Mama had sung her favourite hymns. She'd opened the window above the sink, hooked the gingham curtains up to let sunlight stream in, flung the screen door wide. Puddles on the back porch reflected a clearing sky. Gusting into the kitchen, the breeze was fresh but damp, carrying the dregs of rain.

"Every new day is a brand new start," she'd said, piling the square table with flapjacks, bacon, bowls of maple syrup and whipped cream. For Tub, she'd baked a dozen chocolate cupcakes. Mama must've been up for hours, he'd thought, as she served him up one of the paper-wrapped treats, letting him dip the buttercream icing into a plateful of colourful sprinkles. Meanwhile, Gene had guzzled black coffee, chain-smoked strong cigarettes. Asked for a poached egg, runny. Mama'd smiled, unfazed, as the pancakes went cold. After she'd clunked the dish down on Gene's placemat, he'd shaken a small blizzard of salt onto the soft white mass. Punctured the yolk with a nicotine-stained finger, stirred.

Once Gene had left for the service station, Mama told Tub to stay put, eat his fill. *Eat, EAT.* She'd holler him outside when she was ready.

She had a surprise for him.

Four rashers of bacon, a buttered short stack, and three cupcakes later, Tub heard barking in the backyard.

"Toby," Mama called. "Come on out!"

Too full to run, he'd thudded outdoors, down the crooked steps, thumping to a stop at the sight of Mama playing tug-of-war with a lively, grey and white pup. "Remember Mrs Ennis telling us about that scrappy little fighter of hers? The one she'd housebound a few months back? Well, this here's one of six reasons why." She'd huffed a bit as the young pitbull strained against the leash. "This is Wally."

Stocky even then, the dog had more muscle in his blunt jaw than Tub had in total. His brown eyes were pointed slits, but Tub liked to think they were smiling. Hard to tell, though, since Wally's snub snout was wrapped tight in ugly leather straps.

"So, listen. Mrs Ennis and me were talking just now . . . " Mama had paused, checking and rechecking the contraption's buckles. "She's mighty keen to pay you a visit. Just to see how Wally's settling in. Just to *chat.*"

Looking up, Tub had seen the lady from two lots over ambling down the long drive from the highway, green rainboots mud-spattered, the hood on her red slicker pulled up to cover her curlers, half-concealing her face. A foil-covered pie plate was balanced on her mittened hands. Unable to bark, Wally whimpered excitedly. Mama patted his wide head, riffled his short ears, then turned to Tub. "Leave this muzzle on the whole time Mrs E's here, okay? But, otherwise? Feel free to go'on and take it right off when you're alone. You got me, Toby?"

⁂

Tub's more than twice as old as he was then, not to mention seven or eight times as heavy. 600 lbs, give or take, at his last weigh-in a year ago. Doc Rennalds said he'd soon grow too big for the scales in his office, if something didn't change—and quick. *You can't keep eating like this, lad,* Doc had told him, frank and clinical. After scribbling contact details for a nutritionist, he'd looked Tub up and down, then added a referral for the local shrink. *The strain on your heart alone . . .*

No point hauling himself back into town, Tub had thought at the time, just to be gawked at. Scorned. Told what he already knew.

Not that he can make it there now, even if he wanted to. The cab of Mama's pickup isn't built for folks like him, and hiring a taxi-van is out of the question. Too expensive, Gene says, by which he really means *too goddamn embarrassing.* Doesn't really matter: even the short trip from Tub's trailer to the car is more than he can manage nowadays. The motor in his mobility scooter gave out not long after his knees did—and since there's no way in hell he'll ever ask Gene to fix the thing, that's pretty much that.

Using canes, he can lever himself from one side of the sofa-bed to the other when Wendy comes in once a week to change the sheets. But by the time she's finished, he's sweating so bad onto the fresh cotton, she may as well not have bothered. Ditto when Mama helps wrangle him into clean track pants, clean T-shirts, clean boxers. Ditto when she gets him up to the john. Ditto when she makes him strip every second day so's she can hose him off on the bathroom tiles.

He's too big now to fit in the shower.

Only Wendy still calls him Toby. By now, everyone else in Kaintuck County knows him as Tub.

Even Mama.

Even *him*.

◆◆

Mrs Ennis was the third grown-up to bring her blues into Tub's bedroom.

"It's nothing, really." She'd forced a laugh, discomfort blotching the soft folds under her chin. Sitting next to him on the little bed, just as Mama had the night before, Mrs E stared down at her hands. At the threadbare toes of her sweatsocks. At Wally, whose warm side was pressing against Tub's bony shins, tail whacking as he wriggled and waggled, trying to get at the apple crumble the lady'd put on the bedside table. The spicy-sweet scent of cinnamon and brown sugar *almost* overwhelmed the pall of antiseptic and sour grapes clinging to her scratchy wool sweater. She cleared her throat. Plucked a bit of fluff off her jeans. Looked anywhere but at Tub.

Realistically, Mrs Ennis explained, *realistically* she knew he couldn't magically make her start winning. That wasn't why she was here, though of course she wouldn't say no to an upswing in her luck. Having said that, she was *sure* to make back what she'd lost. Just one more trip across the river to Chippewa Springs Buffet and Casino and she'd recoup all the mad money they'd socked away, her and Mr Ennis. And she had more than enough time to play with— Mr E wouldn't notice the coin tin was empty before Friday night, when he went to grab a few bucks for his after-shift bourbons— it wasn't *time* that was the problem. Not even a problem, she'd corrected, so much as a *hitch*. Sure, she'd spent every last token she'd had, but it wouldn't take many to get back on top. One of Mr Ennis' retirement bonds would do the trick, and he'd never even know it was gone, he never checked those accounts, and he'd be more than grateful when she tripled its worth. Really.

"Yer Ma mentioned . . . " Mrs E said, fingers twisting on her lap. "She said you could . . . "

Tub understood. Most folks are slow to change secret habits. It's always so much easier to beg forgiveness than to ask permission. But it's even better not to feel the urge for forgiveness at all.

"Slip this arm out your sweater," he'd said, pointing to the one closest to him. As she unbuttoned the cardigan and lifted up her shirtsleeve, Tub saw the pert muscles, the sinewy forearm, taut from pulling slot machine handles over and over and over. Holding her hand, he leaned in and gently gnawed the purple knotwork guilting her limb, slurped its loosened strands like spaghetti. When he was full, her bicep was soft as an empty leather wallet. She was the happiest loser this side of the Manatawk river.

Nowadays, Mrs Ennis drops round once a month. Sometimes bringing meat trays she acquired at a silent auction, baskets of sugarplums she snagged at Bingo, brandied fruitcakes she won in some raffle. Other times bringing heavier mouthfuls, sharp and desperate, tainted with unkept promises. Gutful after gutful of edible complicities.

Sweet or sour, Tub accepted them all.

On a scale of, say, white lies to genocide, gluttony is definitely less sinful than murder. Willing blindness is on par with oversight. Enabling is better than crushing a spirit. Anything beats feeling starved.

Between guests, Tub thinks about such things.

Scooping chocolate ripple into a salad bowl, he ranks remembering as worse than forgetting. Feigning ignorance as worse than fessing up. Shifting blame as worse than taking responsibility for wrongs done—but that's a tricky one. That one's hard to decide.

There's a see-saw in his mind, ever-creaking as he tries to strike a balance between bad and deplorable. Between heinous but bearable, and irredeemable soul-blistering crimes. Between what happens, what has happened, and what should never be.

Between nightmares and reality.

He abandons the bowl. Spoons ice cream straight from carton to gob.

"Opportunity makes the thief," Marty from the Buy 'n' Save quips while Tub nibbles at the store manager's fingers, gaining forty pounds of his kleptomania. The sin's grimiest at the ink-stained tips, clumped on cuticles and hangnails. Tub munches the coconut rush of not getting caught, the pineapple thrill of pocketing things he don't and won't never need. When he's done, Marty leaves a twelve-pack of Twinkies on the bedside table. Visibly struggles not to sneer.

Next afternoon, Kaintuck Public's sophomore quarterback comes over with half a box of the same. Clement's skin is dark, but not so dark it conceals the blush that accompanies his last-minute, part-eaten, unoriginal goodies.

"Why are you even here," Tub asks, not snooty. Not insulting. Genuinely curious. The JV star shrugs, 250 lbs of steroid-swelled muscles and nonchalance. "Momma's outside," he begins. "She made me come."

Acutely aware of the jiggle in his every movement, Tub cautiously waves the boy over. "What's she think you done?"

At home, the QB finally admits, there's a hole clear through the wall between the bathroom and his bunk, no bigger than a pencil's eraser-end. *He* didn't drill the thing—it was already there when they moved in, ages ago—but Momma found it the other day. Now she's accusing him of being a Peeping Tom. Of being a *pervert*.

"I don't do motivations," Tub says. "Only consequences. If she's wrong, you might as well go."

Clement shifts his weight from foot to foot. "Ain't no arguing with Momma, Tub. She'll know if I ain't been cleaned."

"If you say so." No Mama watches her son *that* close, he thinks. No way could she distinguish between shiners Clement got on the field, and ones he guilted onto himself. "Might as well get it over with, then."

Ideally, the boy would lie flat beside him on the hideaway, stare up at the stucco, and try not to blink as Tub licked the tarnish off his eyes. *Ideally.* But it's been years since he could bend over. Best he can do is grip Clement's broad face with pudgy hands, thumb his lids open, tell him to hold still.

"Sorry," Tub says before taking a deep breath, holding it. Knowing it feels so much worse, this unwanted closeness, when fetid air comes wafting out of an unbrushed mouth. Cautiously, his tongue flicks across lashes and eyeballs, lapping up the sight of Clement's cousin's full breasts. His mother squeezing into a lacy bra and underpants. His older sister in the bath shaving long, marathon-runner's legs. Over and over, he sees the dark curves, the circles, the clefts of every woman sharing Clement's house.

The young perv is trimmer than ever when he leaves.

Tub's going to need another 'X' in the size of his shirt.

The screen door doesn't quite shut before it swings open again.

"Mind if I have a word?" Clement's old lady asks, coming right in. Hot pink from the silk threads wound through her cornrows, to the fitted tracksuit, to the three-inch daggers she calls nails. She looks much younger than the quarterback gives her credit for, Tub thinks. Much lovelier with all her clothes on.

She doesn't offer anything but her worries, but Tub lets it slide. He simply asks her to zip her velour jacket all the way up, then to lean in as if for a kiss. "Whenever you're ready," he says, closing his eyes as she talks. Her voice is sweeter than any cake, her forehead radiating cocoa butter and humiliation—not at being spied on. At having to be *here*, with *him*. Having to ask . . .

Precise as a cat, Tub laps the furrows in her brow, easing them smooth.

What was her boy's reaction, Clement's momma silently asks, when he seen her starkers like that? Was there a minute—a second, even—when he didn't think she was completely gross?

∿

Tub prefers folk's disgust. The scowls, the fake retching, the barely concealed judgment. *How could he let himself get so bad? Ain't he got no shame?* He's earned this unhealthy insulation. This blubbery armour. He *deserves* it.

Better them than the ones who think he's blessed, a big fat Buddha puffed with luck from toes to earlobes. Without asking permission, a few of Tub's regulars rub his belly while he feeds on their woes, though it makes his skin crawl, his nuts shrivel. It's all over faster if he says nothing, if he just lets them do what they got to do. He never tells them to stop.

He wishes they would.

He isn't after flattery. Admiration. Intimacy.

He'd much rather repulse them. If he's huge as a boulder, Tub thinks, he'll be insurmountable. Way too big for anyone to climb.

∿

Mama doesn't really visit him, not anymore, and never *that* way. Ever since that first time, when he was a boy, skinny in soaked swim trunks, her conscience, Tub thinks, has been clear. Now she pops in to take out his trash, drop off the day's groceries, plug in a new air-freshener. Chit-chatting away the whole time. *Wendy got promoted at the Buy 'n' Save. No doubt she'll make Head Cashier soon.* She gets Tub's canes and Zimmer frame positioned at the end of the foldaway. *Did ya catch that cliffhanger on* Survivor *last night? Wasn't that a doozy.* She kicks the bed's metal legs out so the mattress buckles, tipping into a sort of slide to help Tub teeter forward. Fighting inertia, she uses whatever she can to get him to his feet. *We had an appointment at Doc's this morning.* Always saying *we* when talking about Gene. She's done it so long now, Tub

— 157 —

doesn't think it's on purpose anymore.

Sometimes, he can't help himself. He waits for her to elaborate, and when she doesn't he grunts himself upright, stands there sweating and heaving, hands propped on bowed sticks, and asks: *And?*

More and more, Mama just shakes her head. Shrugs. *What can you do.*

Tub sighs. Says nothing as she hoses him off.

Lately, Mama mostly leads folks to his door, often clutching a lemon-scented dust rag, giving the impression his callers have caught her mid-clean. As if to say, *Ain't nothing a good bit of elbow grease won't scrub away.* As if to say, *Ain't no mess in my house.*

"Cup of coffee?" she always offers, knowing how drained folk feel after offloading. Tub has a bunch of plastic-wrapped humbugs in an ashtray by the door; it's one of those antique glass jobs on a brass stand, ugly but functional. *A housewarming gift*, Mama had called it, but Tub knew she'd pinched it from Gene. One of many failed attempts to get him to quit smoking. After their sessions are done, his visitors pluck a candy or two from the bowl, a bit of sugar to sweeten the experience, then head up to Mama's for the caffeine that'll buzz them on down the homeward road. To let them feel normal before they get there.

"That'd be right nice," says a frosted blonde lady Tub's never met before. She's in high-waisted slacks, a frilly sleeveless blouse. Beige hairband, beige ballet flats, beige expression. "Thank you, Ma'am."

"See you in a few, then."

The latch clicks shut behind her.

Boredom is better than excitement, Tub thinks. *Better plain than eye-catching.*

Lies are the hardest guilts for Tub to choke down. Many folk carry them like tumours in their throats, hot clusters of pain at the base of their necks that make it hard to talk straight, hard to swallow. The way this oatmeal lady paws at her necklace, fiddling with the tiny cross in the dip between her collarbones, Tub knows that's her deceit zone, too. *Is it a lie if no-one finds out?* As she unbuttons her shirt, peeling it halfway open, so many falsehoods spill out—ruffle after ruffle of palpitating untruths, smears black as the universe's furthest corners—Tub shudders at the stink of them. Backseats in strangers' cars, *lots* of them, behind the gas station, vinyl slick with sweat and cum, scorching in summer. Dumpsters in town alleys, fumblings on rusted metal, rubber undertones, fryer-oil. Antiseptic, hand-sanitizer. Geranium shampoo. Gardenia body lotion overpowered by the husband's cheap cologne. SpaghettiOs microwaving for the kids' dinner.

Tub can't throw up. Not during, not afterwards. If he does, she'll only come back, angry instead of abashed, frustrated at having all this rancid lard returned. She'll come back, not demanding a refund but a redo. She won't stop coming until he gags. Until he does it right.

"Take a candy on your way out," Tub says when it's over. Too tired, almost, to speak.

∿

Every so often, Tub dreams of Wendy when she was young. When she thought riding a banana-seat bike was fun instead of *retro*. When she sold lemonade to stuffed toys instead of manning a cash register for five bucks an hour. When she was still his little sister instead of his nursemaid.

Every so often, he dreams there's still room enough for her to snuggle beside him on the couch. That they can *sit* instead of recline. She brings ten-cent comics from the corner store, pulp novels from the book-mobile, Sci-Fi movies already more than twenty years old. She brings bottles of milk, sometimes chocolate. She brings silly stories and songs she has to practise for choir. She brings her own happiness; she brims with it, she has loads to share. A daily peck on the lips is more than enough to see him through until morning, but Tub scrubs his mouth hard the second she leaves, sends the goodness back. He won't never deprive her of it, not ever.

Every so often, Tub remembers compliments whispered across his pillow. Sneaking into his room in the moondark, the words are laced with strong rye, aimed at his ears alone. How lean he is. How svelte. How firm.

How perfectly beautiful.

Always, Tub wants to roll over, away, to snatch back his lost goodness, but can't.

Sometimes he thinks he never could.

〜

Exhausted, he doesn't hear the dog bark outside. Doesn't hear the door squeal. Doesn't hear the *step-shuffle-step* of moccasined feet on linoleum. Doesn't hear the floorboards creaking underneath. What wakes him, instead, is a tangible shift in the air. A sense— elusive but undeniable—of being stared at. A musk and smoke presence hovering close. Too close.

The hydraulic hiss of artificial breath whooshing in through ridged plastic tubes. Shushing out. A glottal stop in between, the airflow obstructed, thick with phlegm and the promise of death.

Whoosh. Stop.

Shush. Stop.

Whoosh.

Stop.

Gummed with sleep, Tub's eyelids snap open. Immediately, the noise registers, a constant reminder of his childhood. Hollow inhalations, ever-present. The man's dark force still powerful after all these years.

With his back to the door, lying as much on his side as he ever gets, Tub stiffens. Too late to pretend he's still asleep. His breathing, like Gene's, gives him away.

"I can't take this no more," the old man whispers. Tar rattles in his lungs, louder than the CPAP's motor. The machine quietly thunks, placed on the floor. Gene's joints pop as he straightens, wheezing.

In Tub's mind, the see-saw teeters. *The past is worse than the present*. Totters. *The present is worse than the future*.

"Look at me, Toby." More plea than demand. "I feel—"

They never want forgiveness, Tub thinks, rolling over. Only to forget.

"I feel rotten."

It doesn't matter if Tub believes him or not. What matters is he's here now. A heavy soul begging to be lightened.

Lifting his gaze no higher than the pleats in Gene's slacks, Tub opens his mouth. He shoves his hand in, steadily, right up to the knuckles. Jamming fat fingers deep, he pushes until his throat spasms—then stops, swallows noisily. *Old habits*, he thinks, slurping pale dribble as Gene shuffles closer. *Die hard*.

"I feel so damn rotten."
Jaw wide, Tub pushes until he pukes.

SUGARED HEAT

THEY'S BUILDING THE BONFIRE IN A FIELD ON THE forest's southern fringe, a two minute trudge from camp. They's piling fuel high—if there's one thing they got in abundance 'round these parts, it's wood—close enough to the tree-line to make a point, far enough not to set the whole woodland ablaze.

Huffing and cursing, cousins Bren and Gerta, skirts hitched high, roll fat logs with crooked feet, their arms too stunted for lifting. Cousin Willem's reach is longer'n both twins combined, but his legs is useless stumps that flop below the hip; he's parked on a wheeled crate next to the kindling, baling fagots. Soon as Wil's knotted the twine, a herd of young 'uns runs the parcels over to a large stone-ringed pit, tosses 'em in, darts back for more. On a trail off to the right, Clint and six or seven other cousins is approaching, each hauling bigger, thrashing bundles across the dry grass. Dark boys, the lot of 'em, fit-bodied from working the slaughterhouse—but, far as Mert can tell, somewhat lacking inside the noggin.

"Vicious fucks," he whispers, watching the butcher-boys sneer and drag broken dryads behind 'em. When the ladies trip or fall, tangled in the ropes binding their branches, the cousins turn 'round and stomp on 'em with glee. Soon the trail is littered with busted twigs and leaves. Streams of glistening sap.

Pastor says these tough fellas ain't never used the good sense God gave 'em, Mert thinks, but who's he to judge? No doubt Kaintuck's holyman is off in the icebox, drowning his disgust with cold gin, leaving Mert's own ma to take charge of the burning.

Not that she's unsuited for the task, mind. Dirra's wider than she is tall, but every round inch of her is plumped with know-how. To be seen, she has to climb atop one of the benches planted 'round the fire pit—but even hidden in green shadows a hundred yards away, Mert can hear her short, sharp commands.

"We oughter go," he whispers, cuddled up to a trembling sugar maple. Gently he tugs at her straight waist. "C'mon, Sammie."

Around 'em the forest shivers. Birch, alder, oak, slender beech—all manner of gorgeous dryads copsed together, all crowned autumn red, all reaching for the sky. All open-mawed, gaping. All shaking like his own sweet gal.

Mert rubs a scaly palm against the maple's rough bark, then scratches the back of his blistered hand. It takes all his willpower not to chafe the sores on his forearms against her coarse trunk. There's no time to peel off overalls and flannel, nor grind cracked, weeping skin against the incredible balm of the dryad's syrup. Later, Mert promises hisself, when Sammie's safe.

When no-one else can harm her.

"C'mon, darlin. Let's git."

Sammie's gnarled locks twist in the wind, leaves flailing. Grackles and nuthatches chatter in her auburn canopy; the birds hop and flap, snipping 'copter-keys with their beaks. Mert presses close, wriggles. Looking *way* up, gazing on the dryad's mottled features, he catches a falling seed in the eye. Vision blurred, he thinks for one crazy second that his gal is dead. That her slack face—so hollow now, so skinny—her blank stare, her immovable trunk, means she's fixed to this spot. That she's up and lost her soul, traded it for permanent roots.

⌒

It was the boars and goats what led Mert's kin to the dryads.

With those tusks and that pungent meat, them hairy pigs was a good supplement to Kaintuck trade. Them beady-eyed buggers made a person work for their hides, mind. Faster than the nannies folk raised for milk and wool, and they was daredevils in the scrub to boot. Snouts down, hoofs trotting, they led gun-toting hunters on a wild chase through the trees. Even with rifles primed, Bren and Gerta was lanky enough to slink through the hogs' narrow tunnels; legless Wil was low and right quick, powering through the undergrowth on his wheel-board, spear rigged and ready. Wielding pistol and lasso, Mert hisself had a go—though he was much happier crawling directionless through the scritch-scratchy bush than he was killing. Still, him and the cousins bagged a fair amount of bacon before Dirra ever joined the party, and showed folk what *true* bounty was in them woods.

All summer, hogs nosed truffles and mushrooms 'round the base of poplars, hornbeams and hazels—but Mert's ma raised everyone's sights, lifted it from the scrub 'round fleet dryad ankles, focused instead on the rich moss of their clefts. While folk craned their necks, awestruck at the timber-gals' beauty—their firm curves and placid whorls, their impenetrable calm —Dirra squinted, taking stock. Acres and acres spread green 'round 'em. Near and far, saplings sprang up fierce, regardless of season. Never mind how quick some folk were with an axe.

"These chicks is damn fertile, ain't they?" she said.

The others grunted and nodded, reaching to pat dryad thighs and papery rumps. But with sacks full of warm hog, their attention again drooped to the path, and turned campwards.

Next day, in no mood for shearing, a randy buck bolted from Dirra's goat pen. It skittered between tents, dodging cook-fires and guywires, clip-clopping across the wide field, long gone fallow, and into the woods.

Mert's ma belted him into fetching the dirt bikes; soon the two of 'em was revving through the gloom after their best cashmere, worried he'd be gored by oinkers. As they churned grooves through the brush, pigs squealed away from their tyres. Crows screeched blue murder overhead while boughs creaked and thwapped up a storm of leaves. Dryads never was fond of the hunt: the flying knives and zinging bullets, the engines fuming, the dogs pissing on territory what ain't theirs to claim.

Turns out, though, the gals *was* fond of dairy.

Sure enough, upon riding into a clearing Mert and Dirra found their rascal goat rutting hisself empty on a sweet little pine yearling. The dryad was splayed on the grass, calm as a pail of water while the buck had its way on her. From the looks of things, she were lulled senseless by the stench of nanny-milk on its coat, the gentle tickle of its pointed beard.

Before winter had full-melted into spring, the young pine creaked and moaned her way out of the drowsy woods. Gait thrown off-kilter, due to the lopsided bulge at her middle, she shuffled a path through the snow, into the circle of trailers and tents. Stinking of panic, the dryad lumbered up to Dirra—who were busy fixing porridge over the communal hearth—and squatted.

As she pleated her limbs, needles showered from the gal's lofty head. Squirrels clung to her quaking shoulders, but she paid 'em no mind. The owl-hole of her mouth sucked in air, expelled gusts of feathered breath. Grunting like a spooked hog, she bore down once, hard, conjuring up an almighty *crack*.

"Give her some room," Dirra said needlessly. Folk were none too keen on approaching the pine madly swishing her nethers, scraping the distended gash, flicking sap. All stood, unblinking, or sat well back.

A minute later, a steaming wet bundle plopped on cold earth.

It had took Mert's ma nigh on three days to push her own bub out, nearly losing him with half her life's blood, but this gal made birthin look easy. There were no cord to sever, no placenta, just a coating of amber goo to wipe clean. The kid was small, sure, but well formed. Goat from nipples to cloven toes, everything upper were made of the most darlin brown-skinned girl Dirra ever seen. She had a set of lungs on her, no doubt about it, and a kick with plenty of spring. One strike of her tiny hoof took a chunk of pine from her ma's shin, which slowed the dryad not one iota as she rose to her full height, raised her arms to the clouds, and returned to her grove. Pulp still sludging from her split. Sap slicking her inner thighs.

"What kind of mamma would do such a thing," Dirra cooed. "Leaving a teeny babe afore it's even dry."

Bending, she scooped the grizzling child. Lightly bopped its upturned nose. Kissed its matted hair. Holding it at arm's length, Dirra took a solid gander at the little doe's condition, and nodded. "With teats like yers, kid, bet you'll make the sweetest cream for miles."

⌁

The dryads spook as flints strike steel.

"Git a move on," one slaughterhouse cousin snarls, veins in his thick neck bulging. A lithe oaken gal struggles against the leash knotted 'round his right hand. From afar, Mert can't tell if the guy's talking to the writhing tree or to Gerta and Bren, who's both kneeling by the pit a few feet away, shooting sparks into dry tinder. The twins is usually skilled fire-starters—they both cook a mean hot-stone bannock—but with the butcher-boys stomping close, the girls fumble. The lighting-kits slip from their stubby fingers, forcing 'em to belly on the dirt like salamanders to gather 'em up again.

Meantime, the timber-ladies is giving their wranglers a hard workout. The beech and aspen thrash like they's caught in a cyclone, near tearing the arms off the tattooed men holding their restraints. The poplar trots to and fro like a penned billy goat. Nostrils flared, she tips her crown and attempts a head-butt; her mate dodges, weasel-slick, hooks an ankle 'round a loose root, and throws her down.

"Hang onto this bitch," says Clint, hair black as sump oil, passing the hazel's lead to his brother, before running back to camp. Already burdened with the beech—a fine pale lady like Mert's never saw— the younger cousin sets his feet wide, digs in his heels. Holding the two ropes like reins, he whips the dryads 'til both he and they's frothing, only stopping when Clint returns. Over his shoulder, a canvas tarp is slung like a hobo's sack.

"Take a couple." He opens the satchel, holds it out like it's filled with autumn candies. Moving from butcher to butcher, he doles out iron tent stakes, their points still mucked with dark soil. "Use one to hammer in the other—got it?"

At the forest's edge, Mert dances from foot to foot like he gots to piss. "Sammie," he mewls, clutching the bole above her hip. "Sammie, please . . . "

His gal blinks with each *clank* of iron against iron. She leans forward as the cousins crouch to drive the long pegs into the ground, as they try to tether the dryads' ropes to 'em, as they fail. The leash-twine is too thick for such slender rods; the loops keep sliding up over the nails' heads, threatening to loose the frenzied dames.

"Fer fucks sakes," says Clint, snatching a picket from his pal. Quick as, he kneecaps the closest dryad—the youngest, gentlest birch—and when she buckles, he clomps on her shin, whacks her leg 'til she timbers. Soon as she's down, he drives the stake through her mashed limb. Hammers it home.

"Got it?" he asks again, chest heaving.

The clamour of nails being pounded through wood echoes across the field.

"Babe," Mert says, pulling and pulling on his sweet maple. "Jesus Christ."

At last, Sammie rouses, takes an unsteady step forward.

~

"You still climbing atop that Lellie-girl every other day?"

Dirra tipped a barrow next to the stock pen, spilling a great pile of brambles and blackberry greens she'd trimmed from the forest that morning. On a three-legged stool nearby, Mert flushed, half-dropping the kid feeding on his lap. The tree-goat was a healthy little eater; she slurped, sucking back the bottle jammed 'tween her gums.

"Not so much," he managed, hot to the very tips of his bristles. Felt like months since he'd last had blind Lellie Horner flat on her back, bruised legs spread, calico dress unbuttoned to the waist. Last time he'd gone calling at her Winnebago, the goat-sprout had only just dropped. Proper riled from the kid's birth—the opportunity it promised, the *possibilities* —Mert had gone to Lellie's to unwind. Once he got there, it'd been hard to relax. What with the girl singing stupid songs and gabbling rot while he was in her, biding the minutes 'til he spurted. What with the image of that pine's sap-dripping nethers clear as new ice in his mind.

The bub had plumped from infant to toddler since Mert and Lellie'd quit their wriggling sessions.

"Good," Dirra said, a grin in her tone. "Save yer juices. Reckon you'll need 'em, my boy."

Whatever plan she'd cooked couldn't of been worse than the jellied red blob he and Lellie'd once made together, so Mert listened to her thinkings, listened close.

Took no longer'n burping the kid to convince him.

"Worth a go," he said.

Mert followed his ma a-knocking from trailer door to tent flap to hammock. He watched her honey ears with talk of *propagatin the future*—that's what Dirra called it, fancying up her lingo to impress—and *proliferatin our root stock*. He seen the clever hook of her idea pierce she-folks' hearts, and tug at he-cousins' loins.

Mass-milkings started that same afternoon.

Shallow bowls and tins was filled to sloshing with the goats' whitest and brightest, then gently laid, one by one, on the grass. By the dinner bell's clang, a dotted line of saucers connected camp and woods. By dusk, the first dryads had took the bait.

Aspen and beech, birch and hornbeam. A robust, budding maple.

"That gal there's for my Mert," said Dirra, watching the ladies wake, and walk. Foliage rustling, sun-licked orange and red, they emerged from thickets of dozing relatives. Slowly, like as though they was caught in a dream. Heads tilted, they come on over the field with a crunching, creaking tread. Nostrils twitching, sniffing cream on the air. "Reckon he'll take a fancy to them samaras her boughs is wearing—shaped like perky arses, ain't they just."

"More like cock 'n' balls," muttered Bren.

"More like Bren's jugs," said an acne-scarred cousin, cupping invisible tits to snorts of laughter.

"Dumb as deer, every last one of 'em," Willem said when the ruckus died. Whistling through his teeth, he squinted as dryads knelt to drain each dish. "But twice as pretty."

After a moment, he wheeled hisself over to a timid sprig of an oak. Dipping a callused hand into the milk, Wil paddled his fingers to catch her focus, then *flicked*. Pale droplets splashed the gal's face, dribbled down grooves in her cheeks. She giggled, drunk on musk and butterfat. "She's a real looker, this one is."

Dirra smiled. "Take her, then. She's all yers."

~

At last Bren and Gerta's got the sparks flaring. All the logs is coned like a grand teepee, fattest boles angled 'round stacks of kindling, slenderest sticks poking at heaven. It's last year's timber, mostly dry, laced with hunks of fresh spruce. Perfect flame-swiller. Plenty of heat and crackle and pop.

While Dirra circles the fire—checking for what, Mert can't rightly tell, but she's intent as a spaniel sniffing out a shot duck —Pastor staggers on up the road. Smirched with mud or shit, the old man's cassock is unbuttoned and slung on crooked, his whale-gut bulging over wide-waisted jeans. Heedless of thorns, gravel or embers, he goes barefoot. He heads straight for the clearing, a puckered-arse look on his face.

Sammie lurches, pulling Mert forward.

"C'mon, darlin'," he says, yanking one of her many elbows. "This way. Follow me."

The dryad shakes him off.

Pit-side, the twins is doing their utmost to haul Pastor off a quivering birch. The rector's holding firm, though, hugging the tree's mashed thighs, blubbering into her crotch. His prayers is muffled and whiskey-slurred; the only word Mert can make out is *Sin! Sin! Sin!*

"Enough is enough," Mert says, more growl than anything. *Ain't no great Almighty looking down on Kaintuck folk*, he thinks, digging into Sammie's ridges. Tugging and jerking, he grinds the raw rash on his palms into the maple's trunk. The scratch of her rough bark is so fucking good, he can't help but stiffen. *Ain't no one fit to judge or save no one else*, he thinks, rubbing and rubbing, while Pastor grovels on the far away ground like a hog. *No sense getting worked up about it now.*

Soon the bonfire is roaring, smoke seething upwards, oily grey streaks untroubled by wind.

"Let's go, Sammie-girl." For one stupid second, Mert thinks of cartoon injuns. Shirtless red men in buckskins, hunkering beside the fire. Flapping wool blankets over the flames. Sending signals ain't no one can read.

"Let's *go*."

⚡

"Reckon she's excited to meet you proper," Dirra said, ushering Mert into the goat run behind their shack. The enclosure were chicken wire roofed in places with corrugated tin, the walls so tall even the springiest billy couldn't over-leap 'em. Not quite high enough, though, for Sammie. Pacing the narrow pen, the maple bent like there were a fierce wind a-blowing, head bowed so's Mert could scarce see her face. Her canopy were squashed, new buds and unfurled foliage alike jutting in all directions, snapped branches scraping metal with a god-awful screech. Dirra clicked her tongue, shooed miniature angoras away from the dryad's wandering feet. "She near tore my arm out the socket, what with her eagerness to get going."

With a thick-knuckled hand, Mert's ma massaged shoulder, bicep, forearm, then paid special mind to her rope-burnt wrist. Frowning, she tried slackening the twine tying her to the maple; but with the gal's fussing, the cord was soon stretched taut and chafing once more.

"Maybe this ain't the best time," Mert said, turning to go. Dirra hushed him with a smirk. From all 'round camp came a chorus of belly-laughing and grunting and hurried, first-time friction. Half-strangled moans, storm-lashed leaves. Proud *whoops*. Applause.

"No one likes a tease, boy. Samara here's been waiting all morning for ye to come—haven't ye, girl? Go on now, Almert. Fetch that pail, and give the lady a drink."

Mert reckoned the goats'd churned the dirt to rat shit; *that's* why he wobbled so, crossing the pen. In the far corner, he crouched to collect the full bucket, gulping air to slow his jackalope heart. No use. Chest heaving, he stood too quick, slopped milk on his best flannel, felt it soak through to his inflamed skin. Spots jigged in his vision as he about-faced. When he spoke, his voice sounded distant, like it were someone else altogether scuffling there in the muck, working up the grit to graft with a goddess.

"Ye thirsty, Sammie?"

He didn't look to see the dryad's expression. Head down, he held out the offering, and heard the keys rattling in her crown. Whether she were shaking her noggin, whether she were saying *Yes, sir*, or whether it were the breeze stroking her noisy, Mert couldn't say.

Focused on Sammie's trunk, the scabrous bark of it, the soft patches of moss, he inched close, closer, 'til there were nothing between 'em but the springtime music of her trembling, the sugared heat of her breath.

"She's ready, kid," Dirra said, stepping as far back as the space allowed. "Feed her good."

Mert blinked. Now the pail were empty, now it were rolling on the ground. The milk must've hit the dryad's veins instantly; one second she fidgeted and twitched like she were flea-bitten, the next she laid stiff as driftwood, tense and silent as Mert climbed on.

At first, he felt modest—shy, even. What with his ma right there, clucking happily. The herd bleating, snuffling his boots, chewing his cuffs. Mert unbuckled his overalls and shoved 'em down only far enough to free his cock. Ashamed of the vivid red blotches on his backside, the weeping sores on his hips. He groped the dryad's main cleft, fingered blindly for the right slot. Found a likely hollow and pushed hisself hard into it.

No sooner than the humping started, Mert's awkwardness fled. Between thrusts, he stript shirt and pants, jocks and even socks. Gusts of late-spring air played across his rash, soothing cool, but it were the gal's *touch* that got him going, the harsh of her timber, the bucking *scratch* of bark against bad skin.

Screwing Lellie Horton never felt like *this*.

A minute, tops, and Mert were moaning and groaning louder than any other tree-climber in camp. The burn in his blisters, in his flaking cracks, in his chapped creases, felt good, *oh so good*, hot spreading along his every part, *oh mamma*, he never wanted to stop, but *oh* the hot, the hot, the hot *spurting*, hot fit to set the maple alight . . .

Dripping, Mert exhaled and slunk up Sammie's length. Belly to belly, he scraped and sighed 'til his head were aligned with hers. Sparrows tittered in her branches. Striped chipmunks clung to her twigs, staring. Nanny goats cackled below while billies rammed their horns into Sammie's side. Hinges squealed, then the gate slammed behind a whistling Dirra.

Finally alone with his girl, Mert wanted to say something, something powerful and pure as that moment, but he never was no poet. Instead he stretched to his fullest. Kissed the white smudge blurring the dryad's closed lips.

∿

"Ma ain't stupid, Sammie. See how she's grilling Pastor? Snapping Bren's head off? Needling Gerta 'til she bawls? Won't be long 'til she adds up one and one, figures us two ain't coming. And the cousins ain't got no reason to protect us, now do they? No sirree. They seen us leaving, sure enough. Greasy-Clint were overly keen on our doings—he always did have a hard-on for you, darlin. The second Ma turns on 'em, them fuckers is gonna give us up. No doubt."

Despite the day's warmth, Mert's palms is sweaty. Muscles spasm, making claws of his fingers; he doubles the chain 'round his hand, grips tight as he can. The fetters is cold and slippery, the iron rough-hewn. With hanks of wool, he's padded the links circling Sammie's neck, hoping they won't shave her smooth. Her wood splinters regardless. Fragments chip away as she presses forward, the leash buffing even as it gouges. The maple *pulls* Mert toward the field, the staked ladies, the ravenous fire. She breaks cover, poised to run.

"Wrong way," Mert hisses. "You trying to get us caught?"

Sammie shoots him a brief, indecipherable glance. Keeps pulling.

⋀⋀

Same as always, pigging season hitched into Kaintuck on summer's tailgate. The forest were crawling with the beasts, promising sausage-filled winter larders; but with ready flesh snared in their lassos, the boys ain't had much mind for extra hunting. What hoglets wandered into camp would suffice, they reckoned, the troupe of 'em smug as emperors, spearing boars and babes in their very own backyards.

For a spell, weren't no one happier than Mert and his ma. Sure, Dirra and them she-cousins had one hell of a time keeping the dryads in milk. The gals was damn thirsty creatures—what's worse, seemed the goats was addicted to the trees' wild stink. Gone right feral, prized cashmeres hardly stood still; they played mule when the milking stool come out, refusing the pail. Even so, Dirra sheared the beasts' matted hair and spun it into decent skeins while Mert was off courting his Sammie-girl. Needles clicking to the rhythm of the boy's exertions, she knitted tiny blankets and bonnets and booties for the half-and-half child that would, she believed, join the family any day.

Once she'd knitted the goats bare, Dirra whacked a cradle together, using straw and sheets of old gyprock. Truth be told, it was a lopsided thing, but seeing how Mert goggled at his gal, she thought better of building a bed for his sprout from bits and pieces of Sammie's dead relatives.

From forest to highway, other folk hammered and glued basinets, crocheted and stitched dainties, tilled special gardens for the timber-mammas' rest. Dairy was scarce, and bacon rashers were flimsy, but any day now, any day, they believed—they *knew*—they'd all be richer than ever.

Any day now.

Any day.

Any week.

～

"Reckon these sticks ain't got the guts to bear us no bubs, my boy," Dirra said over a dinner of jerky and biscuits. She pushed away from the card table they shared for meals, climbed a footstool to peer out the shack window. Outside, autumn had nearly bled summer's corpse dry. Lost in thought, she stood there awhile, arms crossed, fingers drumming, while Mert finished his grub. After licking the plate clean, he carried it to the washtub. Itching fit to burst, he were eager to see Sammie, but something in his ma's stance gave him pause. The tilt of her black brow, maybe. The dark angle of her squint.

He sidled up next to her, followed her gaze. Evening's curtain were falling on the smallhold; in the gloaming, weren't nothing out of the ordinary. Oil lamps glowed on tent-poles, flashlights bobbed back and forth from the shitter. A cigarette cherry flared, floating at knee height, as Wil rolled from yard to yard, checking locks and rattling cages. Embers winked in the central hearth, the cook-fire banked until morning. Beyond, the forest were a jagged silhouette, blacking out the rest of the world.

Dirra reached over and scratched Mert's shoulders, drawing circles down his lean back. This, too, weren't nothing new. For seventeen years his ma'd eased the itch with hook and claw—but that night, he went rigid at her touch.

Immediately, she snatched back her hand. The glaze in her eyes sharpened, turned scowl.

Mert cleared his throat. "Best I pay our gal a visit, I suppose."

"She's playing us for fools," Dirra said, glaring. As if it were *his* idea to lure the dryads out their groves. As if it were *him* what wanted a whole new brand of young'uns. "And not just Sammie, God help us. That first one flat tricked us with her pine-kid, the sneaky bitch. And the rest followed suit, pretending to y'all they was something they ain't. Fuck 'em. Better yet, *don't*. Let the whole frigid lot of 'em burn in Hell."

"Never pegged you for a quitter, Ma," Mert said, though he knew snarking were useless. From the stubborn clench of her jaw, Dirra's mind were already set. "Think what you like, but I won't abide no talk of *burning*, ye hear? Keep that sick shit to yerself."

Out in the goat run, Mert peeled off layer upon layer of tension, and stood naked before his gal. Sammie needed a good hosing; curled in her own filth, the shine were all but gone from her leaves, the dirt littered with molted maple keys. At his approach, she scooched herself into a corner.

"It's okay, darlin," he said, lying down, pressing his backside into her coarse front. "I'm here."

Flexing and relaxing, Mert shuddered against Sammie's body. He jerked up and down, almost the same as when they was humping, but without it being over so damn fast. Spooning like this, he could be with her for hours, the pleasure of her skin raking his a thousand times better than blowing his load. Quietly, so's Dirra wouldn't come out with torch blazing, he scrubbed hisself to groaning-point, thinking, *Baby, oh baby.*

〜

The fire's roaring white, hotter and more devastating than love.

Upping-stakes, Bren and Gerta and all them cousins haul the gals one by one to the blaze. The boys is walking funny; there's a hitch in their giddy-up from so much humping, from the day's struggles, from fey gashes torn into their gams.

"You can't stop nothing," Mert says, grasping tangled twigs, failing to get a solid hold. The chain is cutting off his circulation; blue fingers throbbing, he *yanks.* Sammie tows him beyond the wood's thinnest edge, their passage so far gone unnoticed only on account of the commotion pit-side.

Mert's stomach turns as the flames catch. The aspen goes up first, *whoosh!*, just like that, then the lovely hazel, the spitting young pine. What a racket the dryads make, with hair and sap sizzling, when once upon a time they scarcely uttered a sound!

Mert falters, wanting—but afraid—to close his eyes. He can't bear the thought of *his* Sammie on that there pyre. Amber and ruby licking all the places he's claimed for hisself. Greed scorching her black.

In his gut, buried deep, he knows that's the end *she* wants. The fire. The agony. The nothingness.

Sammie wants to be a fucking martyr.

Oh, what an almighty ruckus.

Half-shadowed, Mert looks at his gal's profile, the beloved bumps and crags outlined with flickering gold.

"You can't stop nothing," he says, sobbing. "Not unless there's a egg in that nest of yers what's ready to hatch. A bub to call our own."

No answer.

She's playing us for fools, Dirra had said, and might be she's right. Ain't no mixed kids come from none of Kaintuck's dryads. Last Vinesday, Clint's pet laid one shrivelled nut, tough as a peach pit, human hair whiskering its only bone.

Only one.

That's it, sum and total.

It weren't enough.

"Git 'em," Dirra had hollered—*No*, Mert realises, *she's hollering*. His ma's perched atop her step-stool, one eye on the burning, the other fixed on *him*.

"She seen us, darlin."

Huffing, she clambers down the rungs. Sprawled on the ground, Pastor's bawling nonsense, catching flurries of ash. Taking up a flaming brand, Dirra yells and kicks the holyman out the way so's he don't catch fire when she runs past.

"Won't be but a few minutes 'til she's here," Mert whines. "Hoof it, love. *Now*."

No chance. All sudden-like, Sammie's got herself a bronco-rider's expression, his cocksure posture, and more than his fare share of balls. Bracing herself against Dirra's attack, the dryad plants her feet wide, raises her boughs. Smiles.

For a second, Mert admires his lady's tenacity. Despite the slightness of her frame, the tonnes of weight she's lost since they first met, Sammie still reckons she's a heavyweight. That she's bigger than she truly is. That she's midsummer fireworks, set to go off.

What a mamma she'll make.

In Mert's grip, the chain is gone slack, the tug-o-war with his gal nearly over. With no other option, he fossicks through the ferns and thistles until he finds a stone with just the right heft, just the right jag, then clobbers his gal good and hard. A swift, sure blow to the burled skull.

Crackling farewells follow as Mert drags his withered gal into the deep, safe dark of the woods. Huffing, cursing. Minding he don't trample Sammie's twigs.

Shouting louder than the dryad's sisters, brandishing death, Dirra trails after the retreating pair—but she's too late to catch us, Mert tells hisself. Too slow.

Fallen, Sammie's limp body whispers through the scrub, roots sighing along the ground behind 'em, nibbled by pigs.

THE WAIL IN THEM WOODS

PROPER FLITTING TAKES PRACTICE, THE ROADHOUSE madams used to tell Sperritt, back when she was a starling-voiced up-and-comer. There's a particular rhythm to working a crowd before a performance, they'd explain. A knack not everyone masters. (*But you will*, they'd promised. *Yer timing is hell-good.*) Treat it like square-dancing without a caller, a hoedown without fiddles. Keep a light tempo. On the balls of yer feet, get out there and *promenade* from one cluster of folks to the next, *dosado* around couples, *chain down the line* without ever scuffing yer soles. Whisk yer skirts round those slender thighs God gave you. Show off the pretty cut of yer calves, the prettier cut of yer smile. Make yer presence known, but not lamented. Chit-chat only, y'hear? Talk small. Don't over-linger in any one place, no matter how tempting: remember yer a warbler, girl, not a conversationalist. Save the knock-em-dead lyrics for later, when it's just you in the spotlight, belting out songs you adore. And even then, only give *so much* and not a speck more. An impression's always strongest if it's short, a wow instead of a wail.

Flit, girl.

After yer name's called on stage, go on up and sing yerself breathless—but then make yerself scarce before the final note dies. An echo's ever more haunting than the voice what first shaped it. The more you hold back, the old madams insisted, the more folk'll want from you. Remember that, if nothing else.

Nowadays, the lure of a different deep-country wailing yanks at Sperritt; it snags her, right down to the core. She can't resist the slightest whine of it, much less its full-throated holler. Whenever and wherever she hears that particular kind of cry, loud and lonely and screeched, it seems, just for her, Sperritt can't help but chase it.

Nowadays, she's got *that* flit down cold.

∿

Paper birch, Wil decided weeks ago, is far too short-lived a lumber for the piece of carpentry he's got in mind. Sure, he'll admit, it's workable stuff. The boughs are pliable enough for rungs and curves, the pale planks patterned with delicate grain—and birch sure is *available*. These groves tangling the Kaintuck county line is fair wild with it. Wouldn't take much grunt to hack a whole barrowful, he reckons, swinging a hatchet in one callused hand. Even less effort to wheel that load home before the dew lifts.

A few short steps away from the highway's gravel shoulder, he's plunged in shifting shadow, surrounded by ghostly trunks. Rank after skinny rank of birch trees traipse off into the forest's own twilight, their tattered white skins fluttering like grave-lace, whispering secrets in the cold wind. Stopping to listen, Wil hears mostly taunts in that breeze. Words half-spoken, melodies half-formed. Verses and choruses shaped by leaves he can't and won't never understand.

Maple and spruce are the wood-songs Wil knows best, willow tunes coming a close third. Sturdy, reliable fiddles get born from them timbers; gorgeous things with bodies strong as they are hollow. No doubt about it: what instruments Wil crafts from *them* will long survive their maker. Hundreds of years from now, he reckons, some other man's son will tune pegs he hisself carved, guide horsehairs over f-holes he hisself jigsawed, play reels for grandkids Wil hisself can't and won't never know. Imagine the wails all them everlasting bodies will produce! All them beaut Southern cries drawling across ages! Angelic notes fit to make a soul weep.

Hitching his axe through a denim belt loop, Wil ploughs through the undergrowth, aiming for a distant stand of trees. Today he ain't after young, teasing birch. No, he can't—*won't*—rely on nothing so flimsy, so washed-out, so fickle, not for this last keepsake. Only his

— 180 —

trusty-faithfuls will do this time. Maple. Spruce. Pine. Familiar voices humming ballads just for him, singing lullabies he knows by heart.

~~

Night after night, Sperritt barefoots it in and out of the bedroom without waking Wil. She flits without so much as creaking the floorboards. Silently, her blue terry-cloth robe slips off the bathroom hook and onto her flimsy shoulders, snugs in tight round her frill-edged nightie. Faded cotton floats above the carpet as she flutters across the living room; her shape now moon-silvered, now shadow-blurred. On her way through, Sperritt pauses here and there as if to straighten the couch cushions, fuss with the curtains, adjust photos in their dusty frames like she used to. Her gaze slides over dozens of small, stoic faces. In the flesh, Wil's kin are scattered from one side of Kaintuck to the other, but right here there's dozens of 'em hung on the walls, propped on the pianola, cluttering up the liquor cabinet and side tables. Seven older siblings and three younger all captured in Kodachrome, plus the ever-growing brood of cousins, nieces, nephews, step-sisters, second uncles once-removed. Generations of solid, small, shiny-paper kin. Every last one of 'em sprung from Wil's family tree.

In her own lifetime, Sperritt never really had no-one worth saving like that, pressing 'em flat between glass like precious wildflowers, no-one's memory to preserve. All she really wanted in life was what she'd had, for a while. Just her and Wil. Just them two.

Flit, girl.

At the end of the hall, she hesitates outside Wil's workshop. The door's ajar, but she doesn't go in. Brushing fingertips across the varnished frame, she closes her eyes. Imagines him in there, whittling and hammering with the radio on. Tapping his boot to Emmylou Harris. Linda Ronstadt. Tammy Wynette. Cranking *Stand by Your Man* over and over. Filing and lathing and steaming planks into shape, conjuring up a heady fog of pine-dust and furniture glue. Heading into the forest, axe in hand, whenever the wood was too knotty, the grain too dark or too light, the timber not perfectly *perfect*. Determined to finish every goddamned job he started, no matter how long it took. No matter how useless. No matter how overdue.

Wil ever did build fiddles better'n he played 'em, she thinks. He had a fine eye for detail. A pitch-perfect ear. Only his timing was forever off.

Outside, Sperritt skims over the parched grass round their little house—and it *is* a house, mind. It's never had nor been towed on wheels. It stays put. Grey brick and weatherboard, it's more than twice her and Wil's ages combined, at least sixty years if not seventy, and draughtier than a barn door to boot, but it was *theirs*.

Further on down the road, the few nasal notes what had drawn her outside keep whining out of a double-wide parked near the dried crick bed. The pain in that sound is one she knows well, one she can't help but follow. Canting her head to better catch it, Sperritt dashes from yard to yard in the near-darkness, whisking over gravel driveways and cement paving, steering clear of porch lights and motion sensors and dogs. Hidden crickets *scree-scree-screeeek* for their mates, high-pitched and incessant, hounding her all the way to the trailer's corrugated side. In polite company, *shrill* is how the old roadhouse ladies would've described them creekers. *A god-awful racket* they'd have whispered for Sperritt's ears alone.

After so many years in the honkytonk—hobnobbing and two-stepping to old-time bluegrass; shouting over banjos, hee-haws, steel guitars; voice straining for Patsy Cline octaves (*Heavenly*, agreed them sequined know-it-alls, *but well outta yer range, girlie*)—Sperritt has lately changed her tune. Lately, she's stopped her singing and become a powerful listener. She ain't adding to the din no more—at least, not when nobody else is around. Now she's quiet as a black hole. Now she listens. Now she listens and hears more than ever she did before. Poor, unhappy little wailers, crying their hearts out all across town. Ain't no-one but her need to hear such misery, Sperritt reckons. Now she's compelled to do everything she can to soothe. To bring folk a bit of peace and quiet. A few precious hours of hush.

~

Wil never could stand the quiet.

Far back as he can remember, the passing of time was marked with hammers, chisels, band saws. His daddy's baritone forever underscored the *rat-tat-tat* of tools, his catalog of Chippewa field-hollers expanding along with the family cabin, always trying, ever failing, to keep up with the latest swell in Mama's waistline. When he weren't breeding or building or baling hay for the winter, Waylon was teaching hisself the six-string. Then penny-whistle and mouth-harp. Ukulele and mandolin. Got so good over the years, them big-shot honkytonk folk roped him into playing at regular gigs there. Hoedowns and square dances, Vinesday hootenannies— Waylon even sat in, once, when the Grizzly Mountain Boys brung their famous bluegrass set to town.

In his workshop, Wil turns up the radio. Don't matter what's on, he reckons, so long as it's loud. Returning to the cluttered bench, he picks up a pencil. Sketches gentle curves on the maple boards he's glued into a stiff sheet, eyeballing the angles instead of using a stencil. Formed round a pattern, the shapes looked too neat, too perfect, like they came from someone else, which Wil simply cannot abide. After all, life ain't but a collection of mistakes, some small, some big, all eventually clumping into the greatest fault what finishes it off. Everything Wil touches comes out off-kilter, reeling to its own rhythms, stopping dead when he least expects it. This new piece he's making shouldn't be no different.

A table-saw blunts the wood's sharp corners, then Wil turns to hand planes and old-fashioned elbow grease for more precise work. Sitting on a low stool, he clamps the plank between his knees. Slowly shaves off the rough edges, smooths away the excess inch by inch. Getting into the tempo, Wil grunts up a sweat. Around him, sweet maple curls onto the linoleum. Each pass of the tool stirs up primal tunes, a haze of timber-dust and memories.

The halls in Wil's mind echo with the slide of steel guitars, the screech-laugh of gals swanning round the roadhouse, deep beer-soaked voices shouting for their sweet attention. Soon as they could stay awake past eight, Waylon dragged his young'uns to the honkytonk, introduced 'em to board-stomping, drum-thumping, head-swimming ale-songs—and the barroom gals what poured 'em.

The file stops rasping as heat rises from Wil's belly, knots in his throat, clouds his vision. He turns to the wireless and cranks the volume. Drowns out the deadwood's awful keening in his hands. Squashes unwanted thoughts under quick-tapping toes.

What Wil wouldn't give to go back to them smoky roadhouse days. Pops strumming for hours on the stoop, cigarillo champed in the corner of his mouth, a twang in his nose and fingers. Mamma barking at Megs, Lucy, and the little ones, the girls too busy squealing and hopscotching and wrestling to listen. The newest bub baying for another feed. Marv pulling up the drive on soft summer evenings, honk-honking the horn on Reverend's borrowed hearse. A tinny *Glory Hallelujah* piping from the car stereo.

Wil snorts at his oldest brother's nerve. None of Waylon's other sons ever did match the first one's gall. Such *borrowings*, Wil knows, is what led Marv down a lonely road to the state pen—but in those days they were a lifeline. Marv's gift for hot-wiring bought them all, Pops included, a few blessed hours of freedom. Away from fallow fields, away from scrawny cattle, away from their cabin's ramshackle walls and the opossums scritching within 'em. Before the horn's blast faded, the lads all piled into that corpse-mobile, Nate and Arch and the others sounding off about who'd get first dibs on what gal, Wil punching a path to the front seat. Wielding elbows and fists—teeth if needs must—to avoid riding in back with the coffin.

What he wouldn't give to hear them same musics now, full raucous and sweaty and blithe. Songs of togetherness and kin and belonging. Songs of hope.

When the file's rasp changes timbre—less mosquito whine now, more bumblebee drone—Wil runs a thumb over the maple's edge, feeling for splinters. Half an inch along the track, his skin snags.

"Jesus H. Christ," he hisses, sucking the cut to stop it bleeding. Head shaking, shaking, at the stupidity of it all.

He'd wanted to share those good times more than relive 'em.

He'd wanted to make new songs for a new family.

Using socks for sweepers, Wil clears a space by his stool then balances the curved wood upright on the tiles. Gently, he nudges the thing with his toe. It sees and saws—once, twice—then falls over with a muffled *whoomph*.

Wil's sigh catches, stifled before it can become a sob.

What he wouldn't give for a houseful of noise.

～

Drifting up to an open window at the trailer's far end, Sperritt cranes her neck to peer through the mesh. A plastic sun plugged in near the baseboard adds a soft yellow glow to the pale blue filtering through half-raised blinds. In the dim light, a skinny gal in cut-offs and a sloppy T-shirt droops on the single bed. Candy-pink hair clumped with at least a week's grease. Formula puked down her right shoulder. Breast-pump and bottle toppled in her lap, a pair of milk-circles blooming on her chest. Leaning against the wall's pine veneer, the gal's head is sliding south. Jaw slack, her lower lip's glinting dribble. Bare leg twitching every now and again, she snores while a plump baby cries in a Moses-basket at her feet.

A good stretch of silence, Sperritt reckons, is a blessed gift. A goddamned jackpot for young mammas like this one.

At this time of night, ain't no-one else roaming the neighbourhood. No-one to spot Sperritt's pewter-hued hands popping the gal's screen out corner by corner, then guiding the glass pane quietly along its track. No-one to see how easily she floats up and over the sill. No-one to out-cry the baby.

"Shhhhhh," Sperritt coos, tiptoeing to the bedside. Her shoulders ratchet up with the child's unhappy pitch. From neck to nethers, her muscles tense as the bub gets a good howl going. Guts roiling, she hunkers beside the new mamma. *You don't want this*, she thinks. Cringing, she stares into the basket, mesmerised by that gaping maw. Tiny but terrifying, she reckons. That toothless devourer. That dream-destroyer.

Believe you me, honey. No right-minded soul wants this.

The mattress groans as the snoring gal stirs. Charms on her ankle bracelet jingle as she hauls her legs up, relaxes into a slightly more comfortable position. With her neck kinked like that, Sperritt reckons that young mamma will be aching soon. All the same, when a body's that tuckered there ain't no fighting sleep.

Shhhhhh, Sperritt says again. Wrapping her arms round the straw basinet, she drops to her knees, thin face sinking lower and lower. Leaning in, she resists touching the squirming bundle inside, only inhales its talcum powder and damp jumpsuit stink. Its milk and pabulum screeches.

Leave her alone now, y'hear?

Whisker-close, Sperritt sucks in every note of the child's uproar. She takes in its sniffles, its grizzles, its quavering breaths. She cramps her hollow belly with its unwanted noise. Swallowing tears, she draws in another deep lungful. Clamps down. Gulps the babe perfectly quiet.

Do folks a favour, them retired songbirds had told her: *commit. Give it yer all. Rock their worlds hard and fast.*

Fuchsia gloss bleeding round wrinkled lips, the old biddies parked their bony butts on barroom stools, smoked their own voices to ash, and spat advice through tobacco-grimed teeth. *Hit 'em hard*, they said, *then git yerself gone. You want to make yer audience reel with a single song, y'hear? Just one. You want 'em crying into their bourbons once yer done. You want 'em to holler after you. You want 'em to yearn. You want to leave 'em bereft.*

Even now, it still sticks in Sperritt's craw, so many folk telling her what she should have accomplished on this here earth. What God made her for and what He didn't. What she *wants*.

Lately, all Sperritt hears is crying.

Lately, all her time is spent doling out favours.

What she wanted sure as hell ain't *this*.

The broom whisks gentle across the wood-littered floor. Wil leans into the sweep's slow-soft rhythm; each tired push whips up a comforting, hypnotic sound. A rake combing through dry autumn leaves. Wheat fields rustling in a moonlit breeze. A kind mamma shooshing her restless bub.

Behind him, a ballad croons low on the radio, a song Wil ain't heard since his sweet Sperritt first took the stage. She couldn't of been more'n fifteen at the time and a pint-sized creature to boot, but her figure were already full-womanly. Lord, how his brothers had dog-howled at the sight of her! Lord, how he'd wanted to join in. But the gal's sashay had stole all the wind from his whistle. The flick of her gaze had bullwhipped him silent. The smoulder in that too-brief glance of hers had left him full-parched, chugging ale like it were fresh air. Didn't bother him none that she could hardly carry a tune in a bucket. She had gumption, getting up there like that, with God and sun-reddened men like him looking on. Wooing the crowd with that one single number. Robbing hearts, stealing breath with hips and lips and pure grit.

Good Lord, his gal had such spirit.

Wil crouches to fill the dustpan, fills it again and again, then fills the trashcan with sap-spiced scrapings and shavings. *That's pretty much all I'm good for,* he thinks, joints creaking as he stands. *Whittling things down, filling things up. Making a goddamn mess in between.*

It's late. Near midnight Wil reckons, now the radio's upbeat pop-country selection has gone and slipped into golden oldies. Carter and Cash. Hank Williams. Sammi Smith's *Help Me Through the Night.* Sad songs written for after-dark hours, a perfect fit for his black bourbon mood. Overhead, a fluorescent bulb shines harsh white on the room, its sheer brightness almost too much to bear. The light buzzes, bleaches the almost clean floor, chases shadows under workbench, toolbox, and stool. Merciless, it reveals how useless the place is now. How empty. How bare and lonely.

Of course, even with the curtains drawn and the lamps switched off, it ain't much better down the hall. Everything in the living room's arranged *just so* on account of it not really being lived in no more. The kitchen's a storehouse for formula and sterilized bottles and tiny jars of food what won't never get ate. And then there's their room. His room. The chill in there just gets worse with each passing night. The silence just gets heavier.

Wil sweeps 'til his palms blister.

If only she'd come in and say, *Tools down,* as she used to, ages before he were ready for bed. Even if she did it to spite him. Even if she wanted to cut his work short, the same way—she accused, when she were in a snit—he'd done with hers. *Time to focus on family,* she'd say, shoving whatever fiddle he'd half-crafted aside. Distracting with an honest twang, a straightforward tongue. *There'll still be music tomorrow.*

Wait, he'd say. Just as she'd said when first he'd broached the topic. Babies, and lots of 'em. A family tradition he were keen to continue.

Just wait, she'd said, again and again. *Can't it just wait awhiles?*

Only, they'd made such a good start together, Wil reckoned. They'd practised so much and neither one of 'em wanted to stop. His instruments swelled her performance. Her act swelled his business. For a time, pleasure and love swelled 'em both.

Then she'd swelled even bigger soon after they'd wed—and beside her, Wil's pride were huge.

Man, he'd been so goddamned proud.

Of them.

Of himself.

Mostly of her.

Lord, she'd had such grit. Such strength. Every day, she gave up her song. In the end, she gave him her everything.

Lord Almighty, how he wishes he could give it all back.

◆◆

Sperritt flits.

From the pink-haired lass's trailer to a second floor apartment across town. Twins await her in a rickety crib there—one boy, one girl—but at least the parents had the sense to put 'em in their own room. The air reeks of chamomile, diaper-cream, desperation. Both bubs are colicky, both crimson-cheeked, but only the little guy bellows for Sperritt's attention. His screams are ragged, erratic; the pauses between cries are just long enough to keep his folks abed, hoping against hope that this one, *this one* will be his last shout.

There, there, Sperritt murmurs, lifting the boy from the cot. Shooshing him good.

Next she's called to a ranch up Butchers Holler way. By car it's a twenty minute drive, but even on foot Sperritt gets there in jig time. At the sight of it, she whistles long and low. Prettiest double-gable farmhouse she ever did see. No less than a dream home plucked from her wildest fancies, built right there by the highway for some other, luckier family to live in. Bright white siding with green trim, lantern-shaped porch lights attracting moths and June-bugs, windows shuttered and doors barred against the night. Passing a red-flagged mailbox at the end of the drive, she tilts her head and follows a woeful sound-trail around back.

There, hulking beside a field of summer corn, a weathered barn harbours fifteen prize heifers, two handsome ponies, and a quartet of vagabonds up in the hayloft. Gentle as a lullaby Sperritt climbs the barn's ladder, palms and soles barely touching worn rungs as she rises. There's a rustling of straw overhead, rat-like scritching, air squeaking from snot-noses and rank arses. The loft is no more'n twenty feet deep. Plenty of space for two guitars, a fiddle, a squeezebox, not to mention the folks curled beside these instruments, their coats and cases striped with what moonlight's slipped in through the boards. Lying in a snug row, a travellin' man and his three girls steal a few winks of shut-eye. All but the tiny one is dead to the world.

The baby's wide-open eyes roll this way and that, searching for relief, glinting with tears. Nestled tight between her sisters, the child ain't got much wriggle-room. Winding up, she arches and flops, thumps her swaddled legs, but can't quite muster a good thrash. Frustrated and hungry, the chick's miserable squawk turns shrill.

Now, now, Sperritt says (*Keep a light tempo!*) balancing on the balls of her feet. Reaching out, she strokes the child's fevered brow. Cups the small sweaty skull. Steadying herself, she draws a deep-bellied breath and starts spooling the bub's awful ruckus onto her tongue. Though she chokes wad after wad of it down, the young'un keeps reeling more and more of it out. Sperritt gags, swallows.

Calm yerself—

"Who's there?" comes a frightened voice to her left. High and sweet, despite being sleep-gummed (*Oh, what a singer she'd make!*) it calls out, "Mamma?"

No, Sperritt thinks, gone painful rigid.

Propped on one elbow, the girl knuckles her lids. Shadows under her wispy bangs bend to a scowl as she peers into the gloom. "That you, Mamma?"

No no no.

"Roll over, Bee," another lass mumbles, face buried in a makeshift pillow. "Yer dreaming."

Shaking from toe to tip Sperritt clenches, everywhere. Gaze locked on the mute bundle in her hands. *Willing* its sister to shut up, goddammit, and go back to sleep. She feels the girl concentrating beside her, *reckoning*; hears each click of the child's lashes as she blinks, thinks, blinks. *Shhhhhh*, Sperritt wants to urge, but she can't. All the unhappiness she's already stomached is wreaking havoc on her innards; if she cracks so much as a lip, she'll spew it out, all that chaos she sucked in; she'll shit all that blubbering muck stuck within her.

This is all yer fault, she thinks, staring, *staring*, seeing—

"Mamma?"

No no no—

Sperritt wants to run now, now she wants to run, but she's stiff-squatting, she's aching, now it's too late to go back, now heat's tinkling between her thighs, again, now her nightgown's sodden, again, now she's grunting, now the still baby drops, it slops, it *flops*, it's too late now, it's out of her grip, out of her reach.

It's gone before she ever got the chance to take care of it.

It lies there still and quiet.

Not again, she thinks. Not again.

"Will you still be here in the morning?" Bee asks, a yawn burring the words.

No no no.

Jamming both fists against her trembling blue lips, Sperritt recoils from the mess she's made. She retreats down the ladder. *Flits.*

᠅

Alone in the woods, she opens her mouth and wails.

As always, Sperritt were near-bursting before she'd quite made the county line. Her lungs burnt with pent notes, belly desperate to wring itself into a bellow. Veering off the main drag, she'd dived into the forest. Star-spangled leaves had clapped overhead, lariat branches thrashed along the trail's edge, none grazing her as she'd ran. Flying, ever-quick, ever-certain, she aimed for the same copse night after night, the same sheltered grove. The one with the very best wood.

Wil had took her there hisself, more'n once—when? Sperritt can't rightly say; it was a lifetime ago, now. Time and again, they'd gone to this grove to picnic and plan and, in between, make love. Time and again, they'd picked a few chords, sang *Old Dogs, Children and Watermelon Wine.* Wil had turned to her, time and again, he'd turned to her and said *Darlin, stick with me,* he'd said, *This ain't but the beginning*, and he'd hacked through maple and spruce and pine, and he'd promised that these here trees would supply her the best backup music a man could fashion. The most haunting resonance.

He'd split trunk after trunk, rubbed callused fingers over that beautiful blond pith, and grinned. *See? Smooth as the horizon*, he'd said. *Nary a knot. Nary a hitch.*

Now the grove's studded with stumps, a flat chorus of all the fiddles Wil's harvested here. All the woods Sperritt's soaked in the sweetest, saddest songs.

Maple drinks in a dirge better'n any other lumber. Pine grows powerful sharp with keening. Right down to its core, rosewood absorbs a good howl. Cedar leaches every last quaver from her voice, while spruce clings closest to moaning despair. Wil ain't fond of birch—too *flighty* he calls it—but time and again she woe-betides whole stands of the skinny saplings anyway. Just in case.

Wait 'til you hear the wail in them woods, she thinks, wishing he'd accompany her here one last time, wishing he'd listen. Wishing he'd hear.

The final notes of her night-song rise full mournful, then slowly dip into the softness of dawn. Around her the copse warms from silver to rose-gold. Owls quit their *hoo-hoot*ing, bats their *click-chitter*ing. Moths whirr after the retreating darkness. While buntings and cowbirds burble daybreak melodies, Sperritt's loud sorrow bleeds into dull disappointment. Bleeds into the trees. Bleeds out.

~

Come morning Sperritt's awful ragged, flimsy from the night's efforts. Retracing her steps, she scraggles past that rich homestead, spies the farmer cutting tracks through the dew as he tramps over to the barn. From inside the house, a woman's sifted-flour voice wafts out behind him—them green shutters now thrown wide, welcoming the sun—her wordless tune soft as churned butter. *Flit, girl*, Sperritt tells herself, but she's too goddamn weary. Time has caught her like a loose thread and it's pulling, *pulling*. Bedraggled, she skirts round the twins' apartment building, shrinks into the hedge across the road as a familiar red-cross van signals and turns into the drive. No sirens, no lights flashing.

No point now, Sperritt knows, for urgency.

It's too late once the spirit has flown.

Onward, she scuds along gravel and asphalt, her steps unraveling over the miles. Bits of lace and terrycloth tumbleweed in her wake as she climbs the crick's dried banks. The bathrobe she uses to hide the muss of her nightie is hardly worth wearing no more, yet she still can't take it off. She *can't*. It clings, Sperritt reckons. Even as it falls apart.

At the edge of the trailer park, she pauses. Closes her eyes. Listens.

Now *there's* a chart-topping heartache, she reckons, drifting over to that same double-wide in the overgrown lot at the end of the street.

"But he were just fine last night, I swear," cries a tear-snotted voice. "Just fine! I don't get it, Ma. I just don't get it . . . "

Oh, the anguish in that whine! The gal's lament is pure agony, Sperritt thinks. Pure soul-stirring gold. Imagine a fiddle wrought from *that* grief-struck timber! The young mamma's holler has ten times the vigor that bub of hers did, a hundred times more inspiration. Despite the morning's weak hour, Sperritt finds herself tempted even closer. Suddenly she's hovering at the trailer's window. Now she's clawing at the screen—

"The Lord works in mysterious ways, darlin. Thank Him for what time y'all had together, precious short though it were, and take comfort in knowing that yer little lad's in a far better place now than we are. Hush, child. Hush. Wailing ain't never done no-one a lick of good."

Sperritt recoils at the older ma'am's calm, her know-it-all advice. The very *wrongness* of it spurs her on down the road, back home. After all, where would she be without doleful tones? Where would she be without the pluck of loss, the screech of horsehair on gut-strings, the music she and Wil first noised together, and what they now wrought apart? Where else would she be without that sorrow?

Where else *could* she be?

Where?

～

The house is still when she gets back.

In the entrance, a frosted glass lamp dangles dark from the ceiling. Wil's muddy boots slump on sheets of newsprint she'd thrown down months ago, the paper now browned with age more than dirt. Photos hang crooked on their nails—no amount of fixing ever rights 'em—and the narrow hall carpet is bunnied with dust. No steam or shower-songs sneak out under the bathroom door. The wicker-framed mirror on the wall is shrouded—with black lace or cobwebs, she can't tell which—so's she can't see her reflection. There's a swamp whiff to the air, damp and stale with a hint of mothballs. It's a smell of old folks and emptiness. Of quiet but certain surrender.

Nowadays, it's almost like she'd never been there, Sperritt thinks. Almost like she'd never been there at all.

Wil? she calls, but of course there's no answer.

Quickly, she drifts past the workshop. Stops. Turns back. The door is flung open, the lights cold, the blinds hitched all the way up. Though it was always his habit to get working long before she herself rolled out of bed, Wil ain't at the sawhorse. He ain't straddling his favourite stool. He ain't firmly twisting no vise. The floor's been swept and cleared of all clutter. It's so clean, in fact, she could very well bob a curtsey, *thread-the-needle*, and *swing-yer-partner* round and round it without brushing up against a single thing.

Wil? she calls again, worried now. It ain't like him, she thinks, to be so tidy. When she'd left, the place was a pigsty—fiddles mid-warp, scrolls half-traced, scraps of wood strewn all over hell's half-acre—but now the tabletop's free of sheet music, diagrams, designs. There ain't a single purchase order thumbtacked on the board. The radio's been unplugged.

Shoved up against the walls, a dozen or more unfinished fiddle shells collect dust in open cardboard boxes. The lot of 'em propped on their lower bouts, one leant against the other, fronts gaping like tiny unlidded coffins.

Oh, Wil, she sighs. Don't give up.

Sperritt hears the mutter and smack of his sleep-talk before she slinks into their room. The quilt is twisted and bunched, the blankets dream-tossed, pillows crammed under the headboard. And knotted somewhere in the middle of that cotton chaos is Wil.

His hair's a rats-nest, grown much longer than she remembers. Worry furrows deep lines into his brow. Each outward breath carries a hot gust of whiskey, each toss of his head turns out a sour sweat breeze. Sperritt goes to smooth the frown from his mouth, to cool the flush from his cheeks, but stops mid-reach.

Sperritt?

Mumbled so quiet, it's hard to tell for sure.

Hush, she says after a minute, hardly making a dent as she perches on the edge of the mattress. Hush, she repeats, trying to think of a song to ease his troubles. A dose of good country spirit to rouse him.

She trills the first bar, then stiffens, thrown off-key when she sees the thing he's built, the awful overdue thing he's set up right there in their room, right there on her side of the bed. An accusation hewn out of maple and pine.

Oh, darlin, she whispers, nudging the cradle with her toe. Wincing as it rocks. What a sorry wail them empty woods wreak! Back and forth, the timber moans and cries and squeals like so many babies, like one in particular, a pink song Sperritt hadn't wanted 'til it was lost.

What a dreadful lullaby, she thinks, kicking the thing again, letting it shriek, listening to that harmony of blame what she herself helped to shape.

I tried, she thinks, rocking, rocking. *Didn't I?*

As the cradle whines, she hears her own voice echoed back twofold, threefold, sounding from every timber at a frightened, breathless pitch. As the cradle creaks, so do the bedsprings. Wil tosses and turns, sighs *My baby*, then buries his face where hers once rested. He reaches into the curtained darkness, he reaches, but don't grab nothing but air.

Sperritt palms the cradle quiet so's to hear him better. She waits for him to go on. In silence, she listens.

∞

BY TOUCH AND BY GLANCE

NEVER WERE A LESS BLOODTHIRSTY SLAUGHTERMAN than Butcher.

Ever since he were first bearded, Butch has used his daddy's saws and axes, his granddaddy's bolt-gun and riverside abattoir—but he ain't inherited none of their zeal for whetting blades, slicing, carving up joints. Long as she's known him, Mag ain't never seen him bash in bovine brains the way Butch Snr used to, ball-peen hammer in fist, splattering cow juice hither and yon. In fact, not once in her sixteen years as Butcher's neighbour has Mag even seen the roller-doors on his killing-shed winched open, not even in mid-summer when the whole damn place reeks to high heaven and sure could use a good airing. Thing is, Butch ain't keen on letting death-moans yawp across the valley, nor the sick rhythm of pumping hydraulics, the dirge of so many popping skulls. Everyone knows Butcher's granddaddy enjoyed all of that, and worse. *Much* worse. But Butch hisself? Well, he don't relish killing dumb beasts the way his forebears so obviously done. He simply does the job, quick and painless, keeping the endings quiet and to himself.

So when Butcher's eyeballing the countless acres of Maberry's pasture, the way is he is just now, when he's sizing up the precious cattle grazing there, his expression is ever a grim one. Beyond the roadside fence, dozens of would-be steaks is dragging their hoofs on soft autumn ground, snorting away flies, twitching their tagged ears, and chomping their way closer to where Mag and Butch is both leaning up against the roadside fence. The herd's at least a hundred head strong, a mixed bag of Black Angus and belted Oreo, one or two Charolais bulls to breed ruggedness into the calves, plus a handful of Hereford bessies forever drawing their rich owner's praise.

My heifers is docile as they come, Maberry has bragged more'n once. *Pretty as they get.*

Propping her elbow atop the nearest fencepost, Mag whittles a splinter of ox skull with her jackknife and looks hard at old Maberry's stock. She gauges the density of the beasts' big shoulder blades, the length and girth of their thighs, the translucence of knee-balls and vertebrae. She tugs the brim of her hat low against the morning glare, so's not to confuse it with that telltale glow she's searching for, the light Gran taught her to see shining inside all them lumbering bodies. Squinting, she judges which of them walking carcasses might be lugging the best and brightest bones.

Reckon that one'll do, Mag thinks, studying the closest black 'n' white cow. Measuring the thing's potential. Its peepers is a bit yellow, a bit small, not sweet and brown and fringed with cute lashes. Kinda rheumy, really, from the looks. Lowing, she turns. Her udders is empty, she's knock-kneed, and winged critters pester the raw sores on her rump. This bessie sure ain't nothing special, Mag thinks with a sly grin. She ain't beautiful, nor shapely, nor tall. She ain't quite awful, not yet. For now, she's still perfectly *bland*.

Mag wonders how many pins this bland bessie's bones will yield. Will they fix the hex-pattern she's been quietly working these past few weeks? Will they finally finish it off?

Maybe, she thinks.

Hopefully.

"What about her?" she asks Butcher, casual-like. "Looks fit for the chopping block, that one does."

Beside her, Butch grunts. Follows where the tip of her blade's pointing. None of this livestock belongs to Butch, not a single steer. Most everything round here's tied to the Maberrys, one way or another: the cattle what gits trucked off to market after Butch is done his bit; the bessie-bone pins Mag bespells to keep lasses like

Penny-Jane, old Maberry's precious daughter, *glammed* throughout pageant season. This here's a field rich in portable wealth—and that's the very best kind of owning, she reckons. A fortune that ain't rooted in one place, but moves on many feet.

Money ain't worth shit if it's tied up in farms or mills or land. All them crops and houses and waterwheels, going nowheres, is easy pickings left out for any folk to thieve. Any banker to foreclose. Any stupid kid to burn down to nothing.

"Well," she says. "Whatcha reckon?"

As always, when it comes to killing Mag waits on Butch's decision. It's only right. After all, it's his trade what keeps food in their bellies. If it weren't for Butcher's inflated cent-per-pound rate for slaughtering and selling the flesh old Maberry bank-rolled— well, Mag don't like to think on where she'd be without him. Ever since Gran passed, hardly a day goes by that she don't answer the call of Butch's lunch bell next door, ringing her over for some grub.

"Well?" Mag says again, lifting her chin at the two-toned Beltie. It's Butcher's choice, she knows, but that don't mean she can't help steer it. "Think she's near ready?"

He takes another gander at the creature, then horks into the dust between his boots. "Give it time," he says. "Bit lean yet."

Mag smirks. She closes the jackknife, slips it into the back pocket of her coveralls. Swats a fly what's been gitting in her ears ever since they crossed the cornfield an hour ago. As ever, Butch were the proverbial tortoise when it come to chopping cows for the plate. Never putting that bolt between their eyes a minute too soon, nor taking a head more'n what folk truly needed.

"Slow and steady," Mag jokes, stopping short of calling him soft.

Watching him jog across the road toward home, she knows Butcher's about as soft as a weathered ox. Strong-shouldered, bull-bellied, brown head streaked with gold and beard silver-curled, he leaps down into the grassy ditch on the highway's far side and clambers easy over the field's wooden fence. Huffing a bit, he lands, light on both feet, and glances back to make sure Mag's set to follow.

Always looking out for her, is Butch.

Looking *out for* not *at* her, ain't no question about that. No matter what them vicious biddies in town whispers. Butch is fond of her, sure enough, just as he were Granny Brawm once upon a time. Fond, but not *fond*. Ever grateful for the favours old Gerta done him, but never confusing that gratitude with loving. He had more'n enough wife waiting at home, more'n enough to keep him from wandering. So his friendliness with the Brawm women weren't ever hot, but it sure as hell weren't ever cold. Far as Mag knows theirs were a happy, practical arrangement.

A *mutually beneficial situation*, old Maberry with his fancy words might call it, before spouting some shit about securities and bonds.

One way or another, all folk agree, it won't do no harm to stay on a conjure-woman's good side.

Leaves scritch and shiver as the big man pushes through the corn, silk tassels waving as he passes by. This late in the year, the field is gold as the harvest-goddess's braids, fair begging to be reaped. Overlooking the crop, a ragged crew of latter-day Saviours is nailed high on sturdy crosses. Part effigy, part offering, part guard, them scarecrows stand vigil until the combine finally chaws up the cornrows, swallowing ripe ears, spitting husks. Their faded Stetsons carry a whiff of cumin and salt—a preserving mix Butcher parboils their cow-skulls in before staking 'em up, hoping to extend their afterlife. Strips of rawhide and beef jerky dangle from scarecrow collars, offal and other tidbits is bagged round their middles to keep attacking black-beaks preoccupied, well-fed. Moving from one hay-man to the next, Butcher gives their posts a good shake. Straw spills from hessian sleeves, but he grunts approval as ropes, stakes, and wires hold fast.

Before the slaughterman gits too far infield, Mag trots across the road after him. Ain't just her magicks what keeps her under the big man's watch. Fact is, she thinks, ducking between splintered fence rails, Butch is hell-bent to keep *all* his gals safe and out of the public eye—not that Mag were *his*, not by blood, not like Daisy—and that were just fine by her. Finer'n fine.

Weren't nothing she wanted more'n to be overlooked awhiles.

You're special, Magnolia, Gran use to lie while twisting and pinning Mag's awful red curls atop her head, fixing 'em like a wreath or a crown. *Ain't no-one else like you. No-one at all.*

Talk about soft.

At least, that's the image Gran conjured. Gerta were just a regular spinster surviving by her craft. Pins. Bones. Small trinkets and tisanes. Just a pudding of an old woman, gone wobbly after the blaze what destroyed her only daughter, her son-in-law, their home. Taking Mag in when she weren't but three—*What a burden for a widow like her,* folk had said, never calling Gerta *witch* nor *hag,* never aloud anyway, though Gran somehow heard it, *What a sacrifice!*—ever fussing over her little darlin, saying how *lucky* Mag were to be here, how *blessed.* Only for Mag did Gran blunt the barbs on her tongue, freeing it of double meanings. Unlike them snarks in town who took special joy in observing how *bright a spark* Mag were, what *fiery* plaits she wore—that, and any other such puns about fire they could bleat—Gran talked direct to her sweet Magnolia, her poor orphan gal.

Lies slipped through the gaps in Gerta's greying teeth, Mag reckons, easy as commonplace spells.

But that were the trick of staying family, weren't it? Smiling around falsehoods. Repeating heartfelt untruths. Spreading 'em thick as lard if needs must, thinner'n rancid butter if not. Either way, expecting 'em to git swallowed whole. And as for them who's doing the swallowing? Well. Amazing what folk can git use to. Much like Mag hardly notices the gusts of Butcher's blood-yard wafting through the trees between their properties. A quick wrinkle of the nose, a short whiff, and *poof*—the stench dissipates and gits absorbed. Blending in with all them other, everyday rots.

— 2 —

Ain't much makeup left, but Daisy's crafty. She knows how to stretch what she gots. Add a drop of canola oil to the foundation bottle, screw the lid back on, *wrist-flick.* Don't use swabs to git at what's swished up—waste of good paint, that is. *Use the smoothest pad of the weakest finger,* Mama use to say, standing at the tarnished mirror, back when she still had breath to fog its glass. *Toby Tall or Ruby Ring. The others is too tough, no matter that they's smaller, on account of 'em being stuck on the outsides. Believe you me, they'll pull yer tendermost skin to ratshit.* Middle finger it is, then. Cotton only soaks up what's better smeared on Daisy's cheeks, and down over the tight pink scars on her neck. When the tube of concealer's run low, she snips the pinched end off, dips her pinkie in—amazing how much more can be got at that way. Buys her another week's worth of coverage, maybe two if the weather's cool, before Daisy gots to git inventive. Talc mixed with a bit of water makes for a half-decent substitute, but the colour ain't quite right. Too white for her ruddy skin. Too clumpy. And sometimes the fake lavender scent makes her eyes water, even if she don't pancake it on the way Mama use to before going on stage.

Sitting at a little TV table in front of the full-length mirror Pa hung for Mama's primping, Daisy digs through a quilted bag full of plastic pots and heavy glass bottles, smiling at the clatter under her rummaging hands, the familiar music of beauty. Picking up a wonky pin—a reject Miss Maggie let her keep, one of many she said weren't sufficient perfect for selling—she scrapes into a round compact, loosing a few precious chunks of finishing powder. Crushing the pale grit onto her jaw, she rubs downwards to dull the shine of old wounds. Tilting her head this way and that, she takes a gander at her handiwork. In the low kerosene light, her skin looks almost peaches 'n' cream. Almost smooth.

Almost half so nice as Magnolia Brawm's.

Needs a bit more colour, Daisy reckons. Brighter patches to draw attention up and away from the scorch-marks mottling her neck. Eye shadow, definitely. Liner and mascara's also a must. But first—

As if reading her thoughts, Mama's ghost plucks the fattest, softest brush from the bag. Ruffles its long ermine bristles with her blue nails. Daisy snatches the thing before it's ruined, just like that pretty blush she'd been hoarding. She still ain't sure what stirred the ghost so, why Mama were driven to grab the rose-tinted case right out from under Daisy's applicator, why she fumbled it, why she let it smash on the pinewood floor.

Jealous, most like. There ain't no amount of *rose silk shimmer* can bring life back to Mama's dead-suet skin.

"Don't y'all want me to do this?" Daisy whispers now. "Ain't this what you want?"

Mama's ghost rolls her eyes. Drifts a few paces back 'til her calves bump against the bed she use to sleep in. Sits on the patchwork quilt she won at her first pageant, the blue and white mariner's compass skewing under her weight. Folding one long leg over the other, Mama smooths creases out of the ruffled nightgown she died in. Lifts two fingers to her lips. Draws on a cigarette only she can see, slits her gaze, and blows invisible smoke at her daughter.

"What," Daisy asks, hesitating before crushing blush-chunks onto the apples of her cheeks. "Why you giving me that look?"

Shrug.

"Either tell me how to fix it, or keep them glares to yerself." Daisy duck-faces, admires the effect on her features. Adds a touch of glimmer to accentuate the slight jut of her cheekbones. "Them head-shakes ain't helping neither. Don't you want me to git better at this?"

No response.

"*Fake it 'til you make it*," Daisy continues, parroting Mama's living voice. "*If God don't want us improving on His design, He wouldn't of invented cosmetics.* Ain't that right?"

Mama's ghost grinds out the cancer-stick what killed her, searches the pockets in her housecoat for another one. All the while avoiding Daisy's eye.

"Ain't no other way I'm gointa win myself the hell out of here, Mama," Daisy says, fishing out her favourite blue palette. She tries closing one eyelid without squinting the other. "And you know it."

Holding up a finger—*wait, girl*—Mama's ghost reaches under the bed, pulls out a shoebox. Inside, there's a satin sash or two she wore in her time. A tiara what's lost its sparkle. Dried carnations and Queen Anne's lace knotted in a tatter of ribbons. These she dumps on the bed, along with a pair of dangly earrings Daisy instantly covets. A gold-plated charm bracelet. Two rings grown too big once the sickness drained all the plump from her small hands.

Scraping her chair closer, Daisy cranes to see what other delights the box holds. What trinkets Mama's ghost might share, what extra dazzle might help clinch a title. *Miss Butchers Holler.* And from there, *Miss Athabaska County.* After that, she'll go All State.

Bet she's gitting me a choker, Daisy thinks. Strings of pearls to cover the flaws—

Mama's ghost smiles and pulls out a speckled brown feather. A falcon's, maybe. A roadside hawk's. Too big for a songbird, too small and drab for an eagle. The quill sharper'n any of Miss Maggie's pins.

"What you saying, Mama? I'm bird-brained?" Daisy turns back to the mirror. "Thanks for the vote of confidence."

If she could, Mama's ghost would be sighing disappointment from them perfect nostrils of hers. Instead, she lets her shoulders rise and slump, sketching frustration. *Nest,* her reflection seems to say, tucking the feather under the blanket, patting it in place. Or was that *rest*? Her mouth moves too quick for Daisy to decipher the words. *Give it a rest? Give it yer best?*

"Slow down," she says.

Purpled lips press shut. A grey hand flutters as if to say, *Git on outta here.* As if to say *fly.*

"I'm trying," Daisy mutters, plunging into the bag for mascara. She unscrews the lid, withdraws the coiled wand. After spitting into the tube, she jams the brush back in, out, in, out, 'til the bristles is wet. "You of all people should git that."

Quickest way out of Butchers Holler is on the pageant circuit. Bird-brained or otherwise, most gals learn that fact early and fast. Most gals is keen to take advantage. Most gals, Daisy thinks, slicking layer upon layer of black onto her white-blonde lashes. But not Miss Maggie.

Behind her, Mama's ghost makes *whoa whoa whoa* motions. Or were it *go go go? More is more, the best charms ain't subtle, you gots to mesmerise as them witches does, spread yer magicks by touch and by glance—*

Puckering, Daisy cherries up her lips. Blots. Adds more red. Repeats 'til her smile's gots a PVC gloss.

Still ain't got nothing on Miss Maggie's shine.

Weren't much she begrudged her pretty neighbour—not Butcher's taking Mag under his wing, not old Gerta's doting on her above anyone else, not even the damage she's done since she showed up here in Butcher's Holler. Absentmindedly, Daisy reaches to her neck. Grazes the scars no-one talks about, like there ain't no-one else but her recollects how they got there. Exhaling, she lets her hand fall. She gits that the sweet old witch must of pinned new memories into folks' hatbands, keeping 'em from accounting for them finger-shaped burns on Daisy's neck, or even wondering whose hands fit them marks. What she *don't* git is how Mag never took more advantage of her granny's kindness. How she ain't hightailed it soon as her crime were covered up. How she never took them gorgeous curls of hers, them fey-tilted eyes, and hit the pageant circuit. How she ain't got no *ambition*. No exit strategy.

Almost, God forbid, like Mag were set on staying put.

Fact is, Daisy can't recall a time when Mag weren't here in the Holler, setting this dim corner of the country alight. It's been how many years, now—twelve? fifteen?—that the pinmaker's been stuck in these boonies? Yep, far as Daisy reckons, Mag's set to stay that many more again. Even with her luck 'n' all. Even with her glowing looks.

It don't make one whit of sense.

~

Since Pa's still out calculating the days Maberry's cows gots left to roam God's green earth, Daisy fixes to do a bit of roaming of her own. First she puts on a knee-length dress, careful not to muss her face paint as she slips the floral thing over her head. The summer cloth's a tad too flimsy, but hangs nice on her lean frame. And if she unbuttons the collar *just right*, then cinches the waist-ties *like so* . . . Well, she reckons it has a *desiring effect*, don't it just. No doubt the talk-show ladies would agree.

Mama's ghost ferrets a cardigan from the trunk at the foot of her bed, holds it out. Hovers closer and closer 'til Daisy can't pretend not to see it.

"Prude," she says, shrugging the oversize thing on. When the busybody gots her back turned, Daisy slinks a gold-sprayed belt round her middle. Poses a minute with hands on hips, imagining she cuts an hourglass shape. Now, she wonders: boots or shoes? Spinning on the balls of her feet, she eyes the polka-dot heels she's practically wore flat, sashaying up 'n' down the long concrete aisle in Pa's chop-shed. Them pumps make her walk better'n any fashion model, Daisy reckons, but she ain't so sure they'll survive the cross-country trek to Jax Kellermin's place.

Let Mother Nature decide, she thinks, popping outside to check the weather. Northerlies gots teeth this morning, full-snapping at the grey sky. Downwind from the abattoir, Daisy wrinkles her nose, snorts out a lungful of steaming innards, iron, earthworms. Underneath that stank, though, is a different scent—the sort what lifts the spirit, makes the air crisp like apple pie and somehow just as golden. Maple and oak leaves turned to spiced mulch. Wet stones doused in the river's spray. Mushroom rings squishing up through moss-covered loam, dank as cheese left out the icebox.

Most folk is happiest lolling through sultry dog days, but Daisy ain't overly fond of sweating. Summer wipes the artful colours clean off her face, leaving a clownish mess. But *Fall*. Fall smells like cinnamon and cloves and hot ale. It's fresh-mown hay and goose down and, sometimes, if winter's too antsy, snow-dusted wool. Soon, nights will darken long before supper and drag on 'til well after breakfast; cold hours best spent snugged under blankets.

Spinning tales by the woodstove. Cuddling up to other bodies, warm and clean as soap.

Daisy breathes deep. If that's Fall brisking the air, then welcome change is a-coming. The promise of an end before the next beginnings.

Goose-fleshed, she goes back inside.

Boots it is.

Don't take much more to finish gussying. She scrubs her teeth with sassafras powder, her pits with lemon, her fingernails with juniper and lye. Widens her smile with a swish of petroleum jelly. A daub of honey goes behind each ear and in the faint shadow of her cleavage, a bit of secret sweetness for Jax to discover, to nuzzle, maybe to taste.

Sure, she's a *tad* younger'n him, but that don't matter. She's pink in the right places. She gots handfuls above and below her braided belt. Small handfuls, but worth grabbing all the same. Nothing wasted.

After helping herself to a couple T-bones from the icebox, Daisy plastic-wraps and double-bags 'em. Now certain the steaks won't juice down her dress, she tucks the parcel under her arm and sets off. Primed to barter with Jax the colourman for some of his winningest dress fabric.

And if Jax ain't hungry for beef this morning? Well, Daisy thinks, she gots herself other meat to offer.

— 3 —

On the far side of his cabin, Jax's drying shed stands on a concrete platform long and wide as a barn. Built it hisself, he did. Tall sturdy pines serve as columns and beams, timber felled from the woods ringing his property. Corrugated iron caps the open-sided structure; under a plastering of leaves, the roof's green ripples and ridges is slowly succumbing to rust. Still does the job, though. In springtime, it sluices off the worst of the rain. All summer, ain't no colour-bleaching sunshine can git through it to ruin his cloth. Come winter, Jax nails up sheets of ply or gyprock to keep snow and sleet from blowing slantwise under the pergola, soaking his wares. But while the weather's fair he don't hang so much as a shower curtain from the eaves. Simply lets the wind blow where it will, doing the hard slog of drying all that fresh-dyed fabric for him.

From afar, ain't nothing fancy about the place—a kid could of drew it with no more'n a stick of charcoal. Beyond its four corner posts, everything's fading. The forest's in its dreariest brown outfit, the river's traded diamond sparkle for mud, the sky's forgotten where its blue cloak is, so's put on a grey hood instead. But *inside*, strung from the rafters, is a labyrinth of colour Daisy loves gitting lost in. Eyes wide, she drifts quiet as a cloud, floating in a rainbow dream. Lengths of cotton, hemp, flannel, linen—even *silk*—billow round her as she wanders. Dye drips and patters gently alongside her as she tiptoes from one end of the shed to the other. Purple splats on the cement floor, yellow plinks into ever-growing puddles, every possible hue *pat-pat-pat*s on her head and shoulders. Wending her way through bright pumpkin and cranberry and tie-dyed passages, she slowly follows the smoky trail of Jax's whistling.

In each cloth corridor, the air is damp and close. There's a tang Daisy can't place, can't shake. Pungent as witch hazel, sharp as copper, with fumes that tickle the back of her throat. Struggling not to cough, she swallows. Once, twice. Holds her breath. She ain't quite ready to let Jax know she's here.

Reaching the maze's far end, she peers through the narrow gap between a candy-striped blanket and five or so metres of satin—a gorgeous bit of material, that, ever changing colour in the breeze. One second it's black, the next it's plum. The next it's a shimmering bruise.

It'll cost a lot more'n two T-bones, Daisy reckons, to git her a dress sewn from *that*. She looks up at Jax—hunkering over his workbench, warbling as he siphons dye into Mason jars—then back again at that first-place-winning satin. Finer'n anything folk sell in Main Street boutiques, and here it won't cost near half as much. Although, at this time of year, when rich fabric merchants is overwhelmed with contestants' custom orders, it ain't like they don't hire Jax hisself to tint their overpriced wares! And when they does, well now, they all expect Jax will trim a few yards off the bolts for hisself, then colour these scraps and sell 'em cheap to the backwater gals. Ain't like them fancy vendors is keen on serving the likes of Daisy anyhow, nor having her plain face dulling their swanky joints. Even better: Jax ain't opposed to trading goods for goods, services for services. And since the work he does is *that* good, the money he makes them shopkeeps *that* considerable, they don't refuse him an angel's share of their cloth.

Hard to refuse him anything, Daisy thinks, gaze fixed on the broad-shouldered colourman. Smiling, she takes in the curls scruffing his tanned neck. The muscular, pot-stirring arms, on full show in a flimsy white tank top. The nip of his waist. The perfect fit of them rolled-up cargo pants.

For a second, she watches a possible future unreel before her like a picture show. The *maybeness* of the next few minutes project from her mind onto a layer of wish-gauze clouding the air between her and Jax. In this vision, a better version of him turns, sensing she's there. Flashes them rugged, uneven teeth. Beckons her over with a wink. Lifts a jar of starshine, the liquid sparkling and twinkling like a bedazzled gown in the spotlight, spitting disco-ball sparks round the room. Says, *Made this one special. Just fer you, Daisy-gal.* And then—

A silvering black sheet flits across her vision, then falls away with the wind. Daisy flutters through as many dream-frames as she can before blinking back to the here 'n' now. She can't hardly breathe, she wants it all so bad. Wants it to be real, and true.

"Jesus Christ," he says. Glass clunks on the stainless steel workbench as a jar slips from his grip. Scarlet water splashes up his front and all over the counter. "Scared the shit out of me, kid."

Heat rises up Daisy's neck as Jax nervous-laughs. Don't let him rile ya, she thinks. You got this. Plastering a smile on her face, she exhales slowly so's the old scorch marks won't go livid under her makeup. With a fair swagger, she sidles up to the table. A series of dye-filled kegs is lined up along it, amongst a mess of steel ladles, dishes of salts and powders, bottles of vinegar, beakers and urns and screw-top containers. Nothing sparkly. No *Miss Universe* glitter.

Casual-like, Daisy leans against the cold metal.

"Brung some fine cuts for ya," she says, looking up at Jax through a flutter of lashes. "Thought we might make a trade."

On the trip over, the steaks had gone a mite warm but Daisy holds the package out anyway. The plastic crinkles between her fingers, the meat flopping soft. Soon as Jax gits a hand on it, she yanks the bag back, aiming to reel him in at the same time. Licking her lips. Tensing for a kiss.

The maneuver don't quite work the way she'd pictured it.

Instead of Jax stumbling into her—immediately feeling the heave and thrust of her bosom like them chisel-jaw guys does every week on TV, giving in to them urges Daisy knows they both gots, taking her in his powerful arms, tearing the buttons off her dress, aching to git her naked and on her back—instead of all *that*, well, Jax just *lets go.*

Staggered, Daisy collides again with the table. Jars rattle, spoons clatter, and shallow dishes slop their jewel-hued liquids. Within seconds, the spillage soaks through her skirt, straight to the butt. Defiant, she refuses to wince.

"Porterhouse?" Jax nods at the bag. "How much is Butch asking?"

"What? No." Forcing herself not to frown, Daisy lifts her chin. Straightens her spine. Puffs out her chest. Thinks *seduction.* Locking her gaze on his, she prays to God her voice comes out steady.

"This here's just between me 'n' you," she says, pressing the package into his hands. Pressing close. "I thought, *y'know.* We might have some fun."

Soon as the offer's spoke, Daisy starts to shiver. Clotheslines creak as a chill rushes through the shed, setting the hangings all aflutter. Some negotiation, she thinks, mentally kicking herself in the arse. Should of mentioned the silk first. At the very least, she should of laid out the terms of their trade. Only fools jump straight to the final offer.

Can't unspill milk, Mama use to say, *but ya* can *replace it with a dram of moonshine instead.*

"Oh, darlin," Jax says after a minute. *Now* he shifts closer. Rough fingers brush hers as he accepts what she brung. Catching his grin, Daisy throws it back twice as wide. Moonshine indeed. No *way* he ain't felt them sparks.

"That's mighty kind," he says, clearing his throat. Bare feet slapping concrete, he turns away and crosses to the blue plastic cooler parked in the shed's corner. Crouching, he knocks the white lid off. Ice clatters as he shifts tinfoil-wrapped bundles, unloads a couple bottles of soda, then nestles the steaks inside. His knees pop when he stands.

"Now ain't ideal," he says, firm but not unkind. Even so, Daisy's traitor lip starts a-trembling. She bites down, hard, as Jax bends and scoops up the drinks. "What with the harvest nigh, the county fair looming, and all them would-be Miss Butchers Hollers to dye for . . . " He passes two bottles to Daisy. Wrenches the cap off a third and takes a swig. "It's hell busy, see? Ain't got no time for dallying—no matter how enticing that may well be. Gots to earn my bit of fun, y'know?"

Daisy nods, clutches the cold sodas with fast-numbing fingers.

"Speaking on which," Jax continues. "I needs Mag—"

"Course you do."

"—to double my last order. Four lots instead of two. Reckon she can handle it? Hardest nails she can make, soonest done. Ain't nothing she ain't managed before . . . "

Again, that trembling lip.

He ain't even looking at me no more.

Before the moment can, she lets a bottle slip through her fingers. It smashes with an oddly hollow bang, and a surprising geyser of fizz.

"Daisy!"

How she loves her name on his tongue.

Jax dashes to the nearest hangings to check for backsplash. He skims the candy-stripe, lingers on the luxurious black. Palms grazing the swelling, sighing, oil-slick satin. Finding no damage, he releases pent breath. Cants his head and takes a step back. Looses a long, low whistle through the gap in his teeth.

"Real beauty, ain't she?"

"Sure," Daisy whispers. "Sure is."

— 4 —

Drought's shrunk the cornfield so's it ain't half so big as it were last year. Mag scoots through it in no time, them slack-jawed scarecrows spying on her all the way to the forest. Up ahead, Butcher's red 'n' black flannel marches in and out of view as he heads for the narrowest curve of the river, the shortest path home. Around them the woods is gitting ragged, scrappy. Great gaps of grey morning sky is opening where once there was blossoms, cobwebs, vine-garlands strung between trunks. Paper-bark birches, sugar maples, sticky-sharp cedar is all shucking their pretty summer green, all turning feral, stripping to bare essentials, arming theirselves to survive. Now they's mostly sporting dagger-tipped twigs. Spear-pointed branches. Hardened needles to stab and stab at winter's cold guts 'til, at long last, it bleeds spring.

Mag dawdles, boots skidding on a damp carpet of leaves, as she wends through the forest. She runs her callused hands over rough bark just to feel the life rumbling beneath. Scrapes lichen patches off boles and boulders, whispering a rhyme as she crushes the orange flakes with her nails. A second later she's plunging her fists into the riverside muck—*quick quick!*—snuffing the tiny, flame-feathered phoenix suddenly roaring off her fingers. Wrist-deep in the mud, she rocks back on her heels. Shuts her eyes. Tries to squash the panic, the flutter of dread, fast as she done that traitor firebird. Breathes in time with the water's slow, swirling rhythm. Sucks in lungfuls of cool, open air. Listens to the rattling wind.

Git ahold of yerself, girl. Rein that shit in.

Her filthy hands is still shaking when she reaches the split-log shack Granny Gerta built. Plywood hutches and a chook shed prop up the place's forest-side wall, where a winter's worth of fat cotton-tails is fenced in with half a dozen bantams and one screwed-up leghorn with no beak on its featherless face. From pens further out back, three fussy angoras bleat unhappiness at gitting their hoofs wet. Round the house's foundations, railway sleepers box in Gran's thriving herb garden. A shadowed patch at the end of the drive regularly turns out pumpkins, carrots and spuds for Butcher's cook-pot.

Ain't nothing fancy, this cabin of hers, this workshop, this home. The planks is dingy and frost-split, the eaves blistered with wasps' nests. The stone chimney tilts too far south for Mag's liking, while the other cobbled-tin smokestack is crazier'n a whistling Dixie. Peak-roofed and moss-shingled, the shack's got a single window under the gable and an off-centre door—and a twelve-year-old Daisy propping up the jamb.

In tights wrinkling round her ankles and grass-stained at the knee, Butcher's daughter strikes a sassy pose. Slim hip jutting like it were sheathed in sequins, not a simple calico dress. Blotches of dye marring the shoulders and sleeves of her cardigan; when she twists to grind her boot into the stoop, Mag sees the colourful mess also spreads down the girl's back. Don't seem to bother Daisy none. She wears her wrecked sweater prouder'n Joseph done that dreamcoat of his.

Not for the first time, Mag peeps the scars poking out from Daisy's collar. Some neat piece of hexwork could easily camouflage them mutilations, she reckons. Maybe a bone-pin bowtie? A fancy filigree necklace? A chain of bone snowflakes might do the trick—it were one of the first spell-patterns Gran ever showed her, one Mag's practised over and over, so she gots the jabbing sequence and varnishes truly down-pat. Would that be enough? Or maybe she should fashion something so common, it don't bear noticing? A bib of some sort? A white ribbon to knot beneath Daisy's throat, flexible despite its being covered with smooth, plain pins? Dip the whole thing in clear, vanishing-resin . . . Would *that* cover it?

Too easy, Mag thinks, lowering her gaze. Butcher's girl were a lesson, weren't she just. One neither of 'em could ever afford to forget.

"Jax brung this round for ya," Daisy says, blushing, lifting a bottle of fizzy orange-water. "Said I should have it meself if you wasn't back before the ice melted."

"Did he now."

Daisy smirks and drains the sweet drink. "Says it'll cost ya some hard nails." She tosses the empty bottle into a hedge, then filches a smoke from a pouch hung just inside the door. Lights it and takes a drag. "Says he wants *two* today and the rest spread out, come as they will. Reckons we can handle it."

"Did he now," Mag says again, emphasis on *did*. Girl's fibbing something fierce, she knows, but ain't no pinpointing the what nor why of it. "Best git to it then."

Inside, she kicks off her boots and jams her feet into a pair of slippers. Goes to the sink to scrub the forest from her hands. "Leave the door open when you're done," she says. On the porch, Daisy half nods, keeps puffing.

Using a broomstick to jimmy open the window, she lets in a charcoal and iron-tinged draught, a stream of much-needed bright. With a potbelly stove in the front corner and a fireplace yawning in the back, it gits damn hot in this hut. Mag's small bunk is tucked between stove and entrance, snug in winter and sweltering in summer. A long narrow worktable runs almost from one end of the room to the other. Around it, the walls is hidden behind bone-filled apple crates, materials ranked and stacked by colour and density and size. Taking pride of place above the mantelpiece— where most folks is got their bull-skulls hung—Mag's nailed up a polished mahogany plaque. Once upon a time it were the lid of a piano bench, but now it's a shiny showcase for Gran's original, one-of-a-kind, and most popular styles of pins.

There's the smooth and straight ones—bestsellers, these—cheap staples for sewing. Quilt pins, corsage pins, pleating pins for delicate fabric. Some with flat heads, others round, a range with coiled ends, others capped with pearls and rhinestones—pageant gals save their pin money for these sparklers specially. For rich bridal trousseaux, Gran mastered the art of silver-dipping—hatpins and hairpins and bobbin-lace pins—though she were never that keen on this cold finish. Below these is a row of short stabbers, delicate as whiskers, whittled from the ribs of catfish Gran hooked from the river every second morning. And bracketing the collection, long as knitting needles, is a handful of engraved beauties Mag ain't never been able to copy.

No question: Gran would hate Mag keeping 'em on display like this. Glued in one place. Useless as fossils.

～

Most of these ain't here for the long haul, Gran had said, deft fingers turning, turning, turning bones into beauty. She'd schooched her tall stool closer to Mag's at the table they use to share. Handing over a straight razor and a few softened bone wedges, the old lady yakked up a storm while they worked. Hands deft as her mind, gesturing at the padded vices and rows of sharpened files already, always, set to rasp them sherds real fine. *They ain't needles, ain't meant to pull threads what might outlive the hand who sewed it. Pins is . . .* She blew away dust, flicked the shaft for strength, kept trimming the point. *A quick fix, that's all. Weren't never supposed to last.* Careful and slow, she dipped the neat stick into a series of uncorked jars, watched it soak up charmed resin. Held Mag's eye, made sure she were watching, memorizing ingredients, recipes that don't never git writ down.

In 'n' out: pins git the job done and disappear. Just like magicks.

With a wink, she pocketed the hexed product then moved on to a humdrum standing order. Acting for all the world like the other didn't exist.

Ain't nothing permanent in this world, my sweet Magnolia, she'd said, fetching another fistful of knucklebones. Load after load of them blue-white shafts spilled from her palm, clattering onto the worn tabletop like soothsayer's runes. *Let them broken ones go. Sweep up the mess. Start again.*

～

Mag don't often git a free minute to herself. If she ain't stompin across fields with Butch, sourcing skeletons for her trade, she's simmering what bones already she's got. Soaking and shaving 'em. Sharpening and inscribing 'em. Measuring and fitting 'em for whatever buyers stop round. Dropping off filled orders and collecting new ones. Keeping Daisy in line—the girl gots a decent eye for detail, but she sure does fidget, can't settle on one task without eyeing a dozen others—and traipsing across hell's half-acre to Jax's property. Buying his bottled colours to dye the posh brooches them pageant gals is such magpies for. Steeping a bit of shade into less visible pinnings.

Hunched over a vice, slow-filing with a fine-grain, Mag thinks about the code hidden in the soda-pop message Jax had Daisy deliver. *Wants me to show up at two, does he? Fixing for a fast tumble with his favourite beck 'n' call gal?*

Mag snorts.

Daisy's gaze flicks up. Her chisel stops. After a few seconds, when it's clear Mag ain't inclined to share the joke, the girl continues *chip-chip-chipping* at a tiny fragment of toe-bone.

It's not that Mag wants Jax to treat her special. *Not at all.* She's a roll in the hay, not a soul mate, not a goddess. She ain't even a romp—that sounds too exciting, and she ain't keen on exciting nobody, not like that. Ain't nothing good ever come of sparks flying.

She 'n' Jax is just means to each other's ends, so to speak. Nothing more. That's what she bargained for. Nothing special.

Still.

Don't mean she gots to come running the second he calls. And definitely not when she gots to take care of some first-things-first.

"Go'on git some grub," she says to Daisy, though it's only just gone midday. "Finish them shorties up when you git back. Which'll be . . . when?"

The girl's features turn fox as she offers, "After the one o'clock soaps is done?"

Mag raises an eyebrow. "Nice try. You gots an hour, tops."

Butcher's daughter scrunches that over-wide forehead of hers, searches for the catch. Ain't often Mag sends her off early, nor gives her so long for lunch . . . But them dull eyes of hers ain't made for inspecting the mouths of gift-horses, and Daisy sure knows it. Off she scuttles, quick if not smart, leaving Mag alone at the workbench.

Humming quietly, she takes out a couple hairpins she's been hexing—an easy piece of sabotage for that gorgeous Chippewa lass who can't *quite* beat runner up in any contest. Rosa? Dora? Don't matter her name; won't no-one ever need to recall it. Dumb chit, Mag thinks, painting the gal's baubles with Gran's second-most potent shimmer. Poor thing don't realise Penny-Jean's purse is bottomless; that no matter how good these here pins is, Maberry's daughter can and will buy even better. Sooner or later, that rich snoot screws everyone over, if it means gitting her way. Against Penny-Jean, that Chippewa gal won't never stand a chance.

But a customer's a customer, Mag reckons, no matter how hopeless the cause. Ain't her place to correct delusions, only to poke these here pins in reality's eye. Git it to see things slantwise for a spell.

Whatever keeps 'em happy, she thinks, keeps *her* in business.

Precise, she daubs and decorates, singes and scores. Like most of her magicks, this one's a small curse, nothing what'll git no-one burnt for working nor wearing it—not one more soul's gointa blaze on Mag's account—but it's effective all the same. The stuff she's brushing on fair reeks for now; but once that wannabe winner tucks these twigs up into her long black braids, ain't no-one will seem sweeter. Mag ain't never tested the glamour on herself—she don't want or need the extra attention—but she's worked it sufficient times to know how it leaches the lovely from every doll-face in the vicinity, makes it seem there ain't enough makeup in five counties to pretty them up again, while all of a sudden the wearer's turned more stunning than ever . . .

But only for a while.

Only 'til the judges raise them numbered paddles, giving her a row of tens. Only 'til the sash is slipped over her shoulder, the tulip and bluebell bouquet thrust into her arms, the crown nestled on her charmed head. Only 'til the limelight's snuffed, and folk blink away the stars in their eyes, wondering how *she* could of won, thinking excitement and homebrew must of blinded 'em all.

Or, truth be told, only 'til Penny-Jean takes advantage—as always—and gits folk a-talking. Gits 'em to cry foul.

With tweezers, Mag lifts the finished pins. Always careful not to handle the pretty things too boldly, too directly. Always keeping an eye on what she's wrought. Doing whatever she can to not ruin everything with a reckless touch. Each charm draws a teensy clinker out of Mag's heart-furnace; every lost spark helps dampen the wildfire inside her. Ain't no *controlling* the flame inside her, not really. Only *managing* it. Channeling it into these here bones.

A beeswax stub burns on a tin plate between her bit of tabletop and Daisy's; one by one, Mag runs pins through the flame, hoping the small heat will be enough to seal in the magicks. No need to stoke the hearth just for this. She ain't got much oil to refill her lanterns, and when it comes to government wire-power, well, she prefers affordable darkness. That said, she's happy to take what candles folk offer, and any other goods that'll keep her in business. One fancy lady's maid brung garnets and moonstones for her gown decorators, another a ceramic nail-file perfect for honing appliqué pegs, and one even made a gift of her slippers, so soft and simple a treasure. Little comforts is Mag's common pay. Nothing overly practical. Nothing to fill her belly or free her of the trade what keeps her on the outskirts of town, near the river and pastures, beside the butcher what keeps her bone-boxes well-stocked.

High county folk'll use her, sure enough. They'll come visit her rundown cabin, they'll give her the slippers off their pampered feet—but that don't mean they want her as neighbour.

Finer'n fine.

Once Mag is sure Daisy ain't gointa pop back in saying she forgot something—gots a rabbit's memory, that girl—she puts the soot-coated distractions aside. Hooks a finger on the ball-chain round her neck, pulls a key out from under her shirt. Shifts her stool away from the timber table and walks down to its furthest end. Hunkering, she unlocks the top drawer without removing her necklace. Tumblers clunk. Wood scrapes against wood as she slides the thing open.

The types of spells Mag crafts is often little conceits, often for moneyed and disgruntled gals. Unlike the ladies, most cowboys round here wear vanity same way they does holsters—tucked near their vitals, not fully on show, but never *quite* hidden. Mag reckons them wranglers is too big with pride to ask for her small fixes. But every now 'n' again she hexes larger wearables for the gals. Petticoats so thick with pins they don't never need stitching. Corsets so stiff ain't no fatness could ever roll through. Girdles and garters and criss-cross suspenders for wearing under loose pinafores. And smocks.

Yeah, she charms the hell outta smocks.

Gran warned her never to pin nothing for herself, nothing for keeps. Testing a glamour were one thing, she often said; that were just quality control. But taking the work home with you, so to speak, letting it linger at the end of the day? That were another thing altogether.

Worst harms is domestic, Gran said when she were feeling spiteful, or when Mag were whining for hex-garb of her own. Rapping a spoon across Mag's smoldering fingers, the old witch clicked her tongue. Swiped pins and tools out of reach. *Worst accidents happen at home*, she'd scold, wetting a towel to keep Mag chill.

As if Mag don't know *that*.

As if she don't know the cost of magicks gone awry.

As if she don't remember what got her here in the first place.

As if she don't see another piece of her shame rolling its eyes at her each 'n' every day.

But *this*, she thinks, gently lifting a heavy smock out from the secret drawer. *This* is worth the risk.

It's taken months, cobbled together whenever she could steal a moment alone, but now the garment's click-clattering, near covered with enchanted pins. Carefully, Mag slips it onto a seamstress's dummy then stands back to admire her handiwork. Two thick straps hold the boxy apron-dress up. The motley fabric—offcuts she'd wriggled out of Jax after a few minutes wriggling on him— were now almost invisible under the sharp, intricate patterning. For each poke she takes from Jax, for each prick she receives, she spends that many hours sticking in bones her own self. Cornrows stripe the smock's skirt, chevrons point up 'n' down from neckline to waist, pinwheels spin between the gaps. Every line stiff as day-old grits and much the same hue. The overall shape styled after Daisy's own clothes, but the cut's even humbler.

If she dresses frumpy like them forgettable gals, Mag reckons she'll be overlooked, too. Unremarkable. Invisible.

She adds a flourish to a paisley detail, hoping it'll quash the burning in her belly, the niggle that something ain't right. Something's missing . . .

A screen door slams in the distance; Butcher's daughter won't be long in coming back. With no time left to try it on, Mag simply adds a tiny arrow on the spine, then lifts the dress off the mannequin. As Daisy comes whistling across the yard, Mag holds it up against her chest, feels the magicks already doing their thing. Ain't no mirror in here to confirm the sensation, but she reckons the embers freckling her cheeks must even now be winking dark. Them blazing curls of hers is washing out straight and drab. The squint-wrinkles round her amber eyes is digging deeper than ever before. Her mouth twitches.

Time and again, she seen this spellcraft work in reverse—pin-patterns making dull gals shinier than they's ever shined—so ain't no reason it shouldn't ugly her right up, if the sticking's done backwards.

For a second, Mag smiles, picturing how *bland* she's gointa look soon. Won't nothing be fiery about her when she puts this plain-maker on. Nope, she'll be see-through as water. Ordinary as milk. About as striking as a goose-feather pillow.

Finer'n fine.

— 5 —

If she hurries, Daisy reckons she can make it to Jax's and back before her lunch hour's up. Soon as she's off Miss Maggie's porch, she hightails it down the long gravel driveway, set on making a quick pit-stop at home before running upstream to the colourman's. Won't take her long at the cabin: food ain't top priority right about now. Besides, she never did eat much. Scrambled egg whites for breakfast, a few carrots for lunch, a fist-sized lump of steak for dinner. High protein, low carbs, just like them glossy mags at the market prescribe. Gots to keep super-trim, don't she, so's she can impress the bikini judges.

So's she can wow Jax.

Most important is fixing her face before he sees her again. It's so muggy inside the workshop, her mascara's bound to be running, her eyeliner smudged to shit. If her belly gits the growls, she can swipe some veggies from old Gerta's garden, chomp 'em on the way, maybe wash 'em down with another of them soft drinks at the drying shed . . . But there ain't no doubt Jax'll send her scampering, faster'n a raccoon, if she shows up looking like one.

Her stomach sinks a bit, thinking on him. It don't feel right, how things was left off between them that morning. What must he think of her now? After she fumbled her come-on. After she acted such a fool, throwing herself at him like that. Sweet Jesus. Everyone knows a gal gots to play hard to git, especially with older guys. If it ain't a challenge, if she don't give chase, well, ain't no-one gointa want her, least of all someone like Jax.

So she'll just drop in, all breezy-like, to show him how little she cares.

Taking the front steps two at a time, Daisy clomps inside. The screen door screeches, bangs shut behind her. Half a dozen strides and she's across the living room, into the kitchen. Early soaps is showing on the tube; Mama's ghost gots the volume down, the TV blaring nothing but technicolour from the liquor cabinet it's set upon. On a low stool beside the hearth, the ghost gots her back turned to the screen. Slowly tearing old newspapers into long strips, she's dropping frayed shreds into the fire. Each crumpled ribbon flares briefly, blue, gold, then shrinks to a puff of orange-rimmed black.

"Watch yerself," Daisy says, edging round the dinner table to reach her parents' room and the makeup she's stashed in there. Her own space ain't fit for such finery. A camp cot beside the pantry is her only bed, an old suitcase jammed under its sagging canvas her only closet. Figuring it shouldn't go to waste, she's borrowed some of Mama's storage. For now, anyways. Once she wins her first comp—hell, once she so much as *places*—she'll buy herself a new tallboy dresser with her earnings and, eventually, a room of her own to put it in.

The ghost don't look up as her daughter darts past.

At the mirror, Daisy whips a brush through her hair. Gouges the black goop from the corners of her eyes. Buffs the smudges from her lower lids. She don't usually indulge in a second round of gloss, but today's special. Nothing says *easy-breezy* like a pair of lips what never lose their shine.

"Mama, be *careful*," Daisy says once she's back in the kitchen, ready to go. Kneeling, she pulls the stack of papers further away from the embers, tucking the nightie's hem between cold ankles while she's down there. With a few firm tugs, Daisy scrapes 'n' gouges the stool—and the ghost slumped on it—out of harm's way.

Back outside, she's halfway across the rear yard when Pa's voice comes a-bellowing out the chop-shed, making it clear to anyone within five miles how this neck of the woods got its name.

"Annabelle," he hollers. "Annabelle come give me a hand!" Forgetting, in the heat of the slaughter, that Mama ain't fit to answer no more, much less come haring soon as Pa calls.

For a second, Daisy considers pretending she ain't heard him. After all, it ain't like Pa knows she's home, much less within earshot. Nope, he thinks she's still at Miss Maggie's earning a crust. If she dekes round the slaughterhouse, aims for the river from the stable-side instead of taking the direct path past the shed's front windows, he won't even catch a glimpse of her shadow flitting by. Squinting up at the sky, she tries to guess where the sun's at behind all them clouds. Couldn't of been in the house for longer'n five minutes, she reckons, which leaves about forty for her to spend at Jax's, assuming she gits there in ten . . .

Guilt gnaws at her guts.

What if Pa's hurt? What if he's hacked off a finger, fallen off the cattle ramp, been trampled by a feisty bull? Chopping up bessies is a two-man operation, but Butcher's only ever had one and a gal . . . And ever since Mama's lungs phlegmed their last breaths, he ain't even really had that.

Fine, Daisy thinks with a sigh, trotting over to the shed. Let Jax miss her a whiles longer. Absence makes the heart grow, right?

The southernmost door is easiest to roll up, so Daisy cranks it to hip height and wriggles under, stepping onto a metal landing. Three open-backed stairs lead down to a catwalk running right up the middle of the rectangular space. Suspended a good metre above the floor, the walkway's iron grating bounces and clangs underfoot, no matter how light a gal treads. But it don't git too slippery and dries quick after regular hosings, so there ain't no real reason to complain. A long open stall—about the width of a healthy bullock—butts up against it, the closest steel side serving as a bannister for Butch as he stomps to 'n' fro, failing to prod or wrangle a hefty black cow inside.

"What's the ruckus, Pa?"

Butcher's rubber boots squeak as he turns. Blinking, he scowls in Daisy's direction 'til she moves out the door's half-light and into the naked glare of the bulb overhead. *That ain't her*, says the droop in his expression, there and gone almost before Daisy sees it. Almost.

"What happened," he asks, pointing with the cattle-prod at her stained clothes. "Rainbow pissed on ya?"

"Yer one to talk," Daisy replies, though there ain't nothing but red on Pa's overalls, spattered on his button-up shirt. "Were you yodeling for help, or weren't ya? Ain't like I don't got better places to be."

"That so." Scritch-scritch-scritching at his beard, Butch looks her up 'n' down. Eyes narrow. Nods a slow, silent *a-ha*. Don't take much for Pa to cotton on when Daisy's trying to hide things, he knows her that well. Knows, equally, that telling her to stay clear of Jax were about as useful as ordering their backwater stream to flow townwards instead of washing shit downriver.

Still, he *had* told her so, hadn't he just. Couldn't help hisself. *Don't go gitting yerself mixed in that one's affairs*, he said, time 'n' again, like any meddling Pa would. *Fix yer sights on the stage, my girl, just like yer Ma. Or on work, the way Mags is done. Y'all gots options*, he said. *Don't fritter 'em away for some good-for-nothing colourman.*

Daisy reads Pa's wishes writ in each 'n' every furrow in his face, but for once he don't give 'em voice. *Now* weren't the time to shame her for ignoring him.

"Git over here, darlin," he says instead. "This bessie's one hell of a stubborn bitch."

Edging closer, Daisy instantly sees what he means. The Angus is gots her head and forelegs fully in the stall, but she's digging them front hoofs hard into the packed dirt. Rounded flanks heaving, hindquarters thrashing, back legs pounding the ramp—the gal's refusing to go a single step further, and she's too stupid to go back. Rocking side to side while Butcher pushes her rump, growing wilder when he yanks the lasso round her neck. She's bound to do herself damage before all's said 'n' done.

"*Move*," Butcher barks, climbing onto the stall's steel ledge. Poised there like a possum ready to spring. Focusing on the panic-lathered bessie, searching for a pattern in her erratic motions. Looking as he must've, once upon a time, a clean-faced rider showing off on rodeo nights, instead of a bloodshot old wrangler what spends his days slitting cow throats for a dime.

"Got it," Daisy says, knowing without being told what Pa needs done. With Butch looming over her, the heifer's started bucking something fierce, smashing her skull every which way. Ain't likely to break nothing—the beast's that well-padded—though the thundering of meat against steel sure is an ominous racket. Sprinting down to the opposite platform, Daisy grabs the suede belt Pa normally gots slung round his waist, the *Cash Knocker* snapped in its holster. Carrying it back, she tries to ignore the pounding echo of her feet, another fat cow in the stampede, and that god-awful moan knotting her innards, the high-pitched *Hail Mary* whining out of a dumb creature what ain't got no hope in hell of ever really being heard.

"Hold tight," she says to Pa, hopping down into the emptier end of the stall. While Butch ropes the cow's head still as he can, Daisy edges close, closer, 'til she's face to face with it. Dodging its sorry gaze. Sucking in its sour-grass breath.

Now, Daisy may be scrawny—hell, she may only be just shy of thirteen—but she's Butcher's own and only *real* daughter. She's swung ball-peens and sledgehammers. She's worked cleavers and cimeters, breaking and boning knives, sabre saws and coping saws and even chainsaws when the bones is real tough. She's roped 'n' bolted more bulls and bessies than most rodeo clowns. When needs must, she gots the know-how to stagger an unruly beast.

The thing ain't gots a prayer, so she whispers one for it.

Gripping tight, she presses the bolt-gun against the flat black swirl of hair between its huge eyes. "Shhhh," she says, and frees the gal from her misery. "Yer alright now. Yer good."

— 6 —

"How come you ain't never put yer name in for Harvest Belle?"

Mag snorts. Gripping Daisy's dainty hips, she turns her this way and that on a rickety footstool, trying to git a better angle on the corset she were decorating. "*Please,*" she says round the pins clenched 'tween her lips. Already it's half past two. Ain't no chance she'll make it to Jax's this side of three. "Get real."

Arms outstretched, Daisy's holding a saucer of sequins, another of short pins. She tilts one dish after the other, faster'n Mag can snick 'em onto the stiff velvet panels. *Make that more like four.*

"Ain't no-one ever told ya how *striking* you is, Miss Maggie?"

Mag pauses. Were that a dig? *Striking*, like, *flint 'n' striker*, like *makings of a fire . . . ?* Daisy offers another thin aluminum disc, not yet noticing the pinning is stopped. Playing bashful, the girl flushes like a robin. "Reckon I wouldn't stand a chance against ya," she says quietly. "Yer smokin hot."

Now that *were* a dig. In certain lights, Mag's freckles glint like crumbs of lakeside mica. In others, they's coals seething against her toasted brown skin. And with that hair of hers—red-tipped, yellow at the roots, middles orange as a devil's paintbrush—she's vibrant, all right. And with them magicks she gots burning inside . . .

Striking.

Smokin hot . . .

"Hush now," she says, focusing on the waist-cincher. Yanking on the laces, rougher than need be. "Yer yapping the lines all outta shape."

Daisy's trap clamps shut. Ain't no way a willow switch like her could skew the corset's stiff dips and curves, not when Mag's fitted the ribs to perfect measure, but the girl ain't got the spirit to argue.

Dull little mouse, Mag almost snaps, but can't talk for jealousy. Even if she *does* say it, or worse, Daisy won't do nothing. All on account of one disappointing fact: *striking* gals gits away with things what no-one else can. Lying, cheating, stealing, blackmail, fraud. Don't matter who knows, who sees, who suffers. If the culprit's sufficient pretty, she could murder her own parents—just for example—and ain't a soul would punish her for it.

No matter how much she deserves it.

"Stop yer gawking," Mag murmurs, pinching another pin and jabbing it through a hundredth sequin. Cheeks hot, she don't bother looking up at Daisy's empty gaze, emptier head, nor the spoilt neck it sits on. The girl ain't got a single trouble in that melon o' hers, nor a second thought. Ain't never had to git away with nothing. Ain't never had to avoid a sideways glance. Ain't no-one cared in a long, long while to waste no gossip on Butcher's daughter.

More lucky, her.

＊

Must be 'cause she ain't yet gots her bloods, Daisy thinks, that she ain't gots no real magicks like Miss Maggie. Not that old Gerta ever explained it so. No, Daisy's figured that fact out her own self.

Weren't so long ago—six years, maybe seven—when Mag were the young one standing up here on the footstool, trying not to git stuck with her Gran's pins. The cabin just as stuffy then as it is now. Shutters and door latched tight to hide the goings-on inside. Birch logs popping in the woodstove, fragrant turf smoking in the hearth. Enough candles to fill a parish church melting onto pottery dishes and enamel tins, balanced on any surface Gerta wanted brightened. The workbench, the kitchen table, the mantel and bedhead. The witch lit all them fires to spite fickle fate-weavers, or so Pa once explained—without explaining *nothing* so far as Daisy knows— and to rub their divine noses in her own earth-bound powers. To taunt 'em with her lack of fear.

Back then, Gerta's rafters was strung thick with bushels of dill and rosemary, twined clusters of shiver-tree branches, dusty bunches of nettles, tansy, mistletoe. Garlic chains dangled from home-crafted nails, spider-bead necklaces hung beneath, a huge wreath of feather and bone capping the lintel. Garlands of fluffy rabbits-paws was looped from the beams waiting for the old lady to fix their luck to strips of leather. It were all so cluttered, so dingy and close. As though Mag's Gran were intent on burying them in monsters and weeds.

But even with the weight of Gerta's collection pressing down from above, even with shadows ever-creeping in from the cabin's corners, even with the tiers of apple crates looming so—even barricaded as she often were behind a wall of mismatched chairs, tethered to the front leg of an immovable hutch, its shelves stuffed with glass vials and books and liquid-filled jars—even *then*, five or six-year-old Daisy reckoned the place were more open, somehow, when the shawled old woman were there. Far more honest than things was now, anyways, without her.

Back then, Daisy ain't never felt this squeeze in her chest—a squeezing that ain't got nothing to do with being corseted, and everything to do with being ignored. Shut out.

Daisy reckons she seen how things was, then and now.

She pays attention.

For one, she knows it weren't no accident, Pa sending her daily to the hexwoman's house. Too small yet to turn a lathe, much less wield a chisel and file, Daisy trucked through the woods and over the little crick to Gerta's soon as her morning eggs was eaten. Not to make pins—she wouldn't spin a bone 'til she were nine, the old woman long gone, and Miss Maggie in desperate need of an apprentice—but to make her scarce while Mama lay dying. Fat lot of good that done. After seeing Butch put so many bessies out their misery, swift and gentle as he could, Daisy coped alright when it finally come time to kiss Mama farewell. All the same, she wouldn't of minded being spared the ending itself. The spirit leaving with the last crackle 'n' hiss of red breath. The botched returning.

Old Gerta ain't never failed to glam pageant gals, to magick 'em onto so many winners' wagons, but when it came to sticking dead spirits back into cold fleshsuits, well, the witch's pins sat *much* better on silk sashes then ever they did winding sheets. They worked wonders on tiaras, not so much on shrouds. They wasn't great as hinge-pins on coffins.

Don't mean folk didn't ask her to *try.*

Not if they was sufficient desperate.

Not if they was, say, a dear neighbour suddenly short a wife. A lover. A chop-house helpmeet.

For two, Gerta may well have been discreet with her charms and spells, but she weren't one to keep no secrets. Not from her gals, anyways. Ask about anything—are mer-ladies *really* real, what's that grunting in Pa's room at night, can foxes sniff out ghosts, why all the fuss about resurrection—and Gran would come up with an answer. Groaning and creaking, she'd pull up the very stool Daisy's now standing on. Roll a couple smokes, dole 'em out, then gab 'til the cherries burnt their fingertips. Weren't no conversation off limits with old Gerta.

For three, Daisy figures Mag herself must of been going on thirteen—her own age, practically a woman grown—when Gerta started saying how *special* she were. How there *ain't no-one else like her*, not a single gal. Weren't a day passed when Gran didn't show Mag she were appreciated, even loved, but this new kind of flattering were different. It came with whispered lessons, ointments, incantations. It came with rags. It were serious as bloods, moon cycles, all the responsibility of the tides.

And Daisy seen how it spooked Miss Maggie, Gerta's praise, how it clammed her right up. Weren't nothing magick about the other girl before then, were there? Before she'd grown hot like that. Before she'd spilled red. Peering down at Mag's expert pin-pushing through velvet and thread, watching firelight twinkle off hair Daisy'd kill to grow her own self, she shakes her head. Nope, she thinks. Not in her recollection.

As a child, Daisy thinks, Maggie were duller'n baseball.

Weren't she just.

But once Mag were blooded? Now *that's* what changed her, Daisy knows, *that's* what let her wield magick so powerful. So permanent. So painful.

Daisy learnt *that* first-hand.

~

Maybe little Daisy'd been feeling a bit cooped that long-ago day, leashed in old Gerta's kitchen again, when outside the cross-county path were calling, begging her to dance through summer-bright woods. Maybe she were bored out of her gourd, kept at arm's length while the older gals transformed bones into gowns she had no hope, then, of ever wearing. Pinning together magicked outfits might sound exciting to folks who ain't never conjured nothing theirselves, but truth is: no-one wants to spend hours and hours and god-forsaken *hours* watching such repetitive hexings take shape. Without a doubt, the finished products always dazzle. *Always.* Often they win first prize on stage. And even when they don't, folk can't help but admire the sheer cleverness what pinned them creations together.

But hardly anyone—Daisy included—wants to while away precious days as Mag, colt-legged and bleeding, fidgets on a stool by her Gran's hearth while the old lady pins one bone shard after another and another and another. *For days.*

Exciting it sure as hell ain't.

So Daisy won't never say that what happened were all Miss Maggie's fault. Only that them tight red skin-rings on her neck is the best, most lasting proof that Mag *must* of got the knack for hexing along with her womanhood.

Itching for a change of pace, Daisy had pulled her leash taut when old Gerta grabbed a roll of toilet paper off the shelf, tucked it under her bloated arm, and headed out to the privy for some post-coffee business. Soon as the door slammed behind her, Daisy turned on Mag.

"Yer just so *special*, Magnolia," she'd teased. Or something along them lines. "Come 'n' blaze me free of these knots, if yer such a bright spark."

Don't much matter exactly what were said. Might of been the annoying sing-song tone what got the older girl's goat. Maybe it were the same boredom, the same hankering for action Daisy feels after hours playing mannequin for the pinmaker. Maybe it were the frustration of being pinned, instead of doing the pinning.

Trust me, Gran, Mag had said, not for the first time, before Gran escaped to the outhouse. *I knows what to do. I can be careful.*

"How can she trust a firecracker like you," Daisy had started up again, and *Lord* how Mags'd leapt off the low stool then, flashing across the room and over the makeshift barricade. *Lord* how she rustled little Daisy like she were a Tunesday chicken raised for the roast-pan. Comely even then, that tanned face of Mag's had purpled with fury. She'd threw Daisy down, straddled her scrawny chest, and started throttling. Her grip soon got so cruel, Daisy wished she'd kept her fool mouth shut. Flames writhed up her neck, hot and high between the black spots whirling in her vision. Desperate to howl, she couldn't muster nothing but a pathetic, mewling gasp.

Things'd gone all warm-watery and muffled when Gerta rushed back in, saving them both.

"Don't go wasting that fire, girl! Not on this! Not in *my* house."

Thinking back, Daisy reckons the old woman *had* to of magicked them apart somehow. Ain't no other way she could of got between 'em so fast, wrangling that wild granddaughter of hers while also damping the blaze 'neath Daisy's chin. Carrying the toilet roll, a faint whiff of newsprint, and a trace of lightning-shot wind, Gerta tore them apart like a hurricane. Chairs and curses flew.

Afterwards, Mag had hunkered on her heels, sobbing, palms up like she were begging for coin. Daisy splayed on the floor, stunned quiet. Blisters weeping from jaw to collarbone. The witch fading, older and more tired-looking'n ever, as she fixed them wounds best she could.

The corset Mag's fashioning now don't even cover the lowest of Daisy's scars; it's strapless and scooped so's it can easily be hid under the skimpiest one-piece swimsuit. But once the boning's in place, the laces crossed and knotted, the fretwork of pins arranged on the velvet panels *just so*—well, *then* Mag's hex will kick in, won't it just. From the outside, to any lookers-on, all Daisy's flaws will seem smoothed. Split ends will fuse back together. Crooked canines will straighten, the cheroot stains on all her teeth'll git bleached. For a spell, her rooster neck'll turn swan.

Of course, this pretty piece of magick ain't hers to keep. More's the pity, Daisy won't never catch a glimpse of it herself: Miss Maggie gots a lifelong hatred for mirrors. So if the pin-spell's done the trick, if Daisy's turned beauty queen, even for a very short whiles, ain't nothing she can do but to take the word of other folk on it. Of course, at this and every other miserable moment of her day, the only other folk round here is the witch herself.

"Turn around," Mag mumbles, strong hands brooking no argument. "Quit staring."

Daisy flinches, spins, says nothing.

"Stay put now," Mag says, stepping back to see all she done. Sweat glistens beneath her widow's peak, a delicate crown sparkling just below the hairline. The firelight adds a glow to Mag's features ain't no amount of makeup could match. Shadows soften the sharp angle of her cheekbones, pool in the perfect dip of her throat. Under sloppy coveralls and a man's sleeveless shirt is a figure spandex were made for. Not an inch of fat out of place. Not a hint of orange peel on them thighs.

What a waste. Daisy sighs, half-turns away.

Miss Maggie lifts a hand. *Wait.*

"Whatever," Daisy replies, heart and gaze sinking to the scuffed toes of her boots. No, she don't begrudge what Miss Maggie done way back then. Not always. She knows how hard it burns, being sorry. "I ain't going nowheres."

— 7 —

Hatchet in hand, Mag hacks twigs for kindling as she tramps through the woods to the riverside. A likely reason for her to be heading upstream instead of down towards Butcher's, she reckons, should prying eyes spot her creeping that way. Ain't no-one would begrudge her a bit of stockpiling, what with Fall ever-crisping the air, hardening and sharpening it into the cold axe of winter. Before that blade drops, severing folk from basic supplies, cutting them off 'til next year's melt, Mag gathers just enough tinder to keep loose lips from flapping, but not *so* much as to make her later to Jax's than already she is.

The wind nips her cheeks pink as she crunches through the undergrowth. Crabapples mash to sour cider under her feet, juice-soaked pinecones turn to pulp. Pausing every few steps, she drops her slow-growing bundle of branches. Presses the chopper between her knees to free up her hands. Lifts the hood on her long coat, tugging it over the brown knitted hat covering her vibrant hair. It won't be but a few yards 'til the breeze pesters the cowl off her head, forcing her to stop *again*. She tugs the hoodstrings, but don't bother bow-tying 'em. Just tucks them laces in with the red wisps escaping her cap. Trudges on.

Mag smells Jax's place long before she sees it.

Near his property, the woods git mangier. Leaves abandon branches, dive groundwards, all wilted and brown as the colourman's hill. Shrubs ain't no more'n sheaves of wasted sticks. On the forest floor, thimbleweeds and asters and harebells is all shrivelled like corpse-fingers, reaching skyward between clumps of mushrooms, clawing at fresh air. Breathing shallow, Mag hauls a scarf over her nose and jogs to the footbridge spanning a bend in the river.

Once—maybe the first time she called on Jax—Mag brung him a kerchief full of cinnamon sticks, licorice root, and summer posies. The first of many such small gifts. "That's some colour, ain't it," she'd said, opening the potpourri parcel. "Brighter'n any pennant on Vinesday floats."

Jax had laughed, kissed her 'til she forgot about the blossoms. Mag never did ask if he sneaked them gift-flowers into a batch of dye, though she fancied he might of. She seen the gleam in them rodeo fabrics he tinted, the dark in them deer-hunter shades, the gaud in them buntings and carnival tents. Best colourman in this or any other county, were Jax. Only uses the rankest ingredients to make his dyes—green nutshells, chalk and lime, rust shavings, yellow weed, boiling piss and lots of it. All them hues gots a lick of magick to 'em, Mag reckons, on account of how bad they *stink*.

Amazing what folk git use to, she thinks now, sighting Jax's cabin in the distance. Perched atop its small hill, as close to the river as it can git without falling in, it's surrounded by birch and sycamore, blackberry bushes, thorn-studded brambles—a natural fence what keeps deer and skunks from wandering too close, tumbling into the dyeing vats he gots honeycombed across the backyard. Mag winces as the breeze changes, carrying a great wafting reek her way. She stops to wipe the sting from her eyes. Tells herself it's a grove of lilacs compared to the off-meat tang of dead and dying bessies gusting downriver from Butcher's.

Fancy folk may keep Jax's business five miles away from their own *lah-di-dah* houses, their fresh-mown meadows, their coffee-scented Main Street—that avenue decked in awnings and pennants *he* made so pretty, where folk go a-strollin in fabrics dipped in *his* sharpest dyes—but ain't nothing they can do to stop Mag herself slinking up to his door every now 'n' again. Nor he to hers, any chance he gits.

Don't tell no-one I were here, he'd warn each time he come a-callin, softening the order with a smooch and a goose. True to her word, Mag don't let a single one slip—and why would she? The way folks natter . . . and whisper . . . and *stare*.

Ain't nobody's business, she thinks, what I do, what I done, and what not.

At the bridge, she stacks her meager bunch of firewood against the piling, then darts across the water and starts up the slope to Jax's house. Halfway uphill, she sees him come out the back door. Overalls rolled up to the knee. Barefoot, but rubber-gloved. A once-gingham cloth tied like a bank-robber's mask over his nose, mouth, and chin. Dark eyes fixed on the vats pitting his yard.

Crouching so's he won't spy her there, Mag watches Jax balance on the edge of an indigo-stained tank. He stirs the pot with a long metal pole, takes a few steps and attends to the next one. So on and so forth, he flows from colour to colour, placing his feet like a tightrope walker, careful but practised. Confident. *Graceful*, she thinks, though she won't never use that flouncy word to his face.

Boy, what a face.

Mesmerised, Mag looks on 'til the sun dips like a teabag, steeping the world in Orange Pekoe. Right as she's about to stand, Jax lifts his head. She decides to wait a spell longer. With the water sloshing behind her, Mag can't hear what might of caught his attention. After a moment, he continues stirring, eyes flick-flicking toward the gravel track leading upside his cabin, through a sad copse of pine, and round to the front drive. Must be due for a pick-up or delivery, she reckons. Mail truck drops in three times daily, regular as church bells, bringing and taking Jax's paper-wrapped parcels. Nothing out of the ordinary. Nothing worth hitching his shoulders up like that, nor putting that rabbit-twitch in his gaze. Except, when the visitor appears, striding down the path like he gots better places to be, it ain't no stiff-brimmed postman come a-knocking. It ain't no friendly, workaday caller.

From the looks of them coveralls, he drove over straight from the chop-shed. Black spatters his dark denim legs from the cuffs up to the hem of his fleece-lined jacket. Unwashed fists swinging hard by his sides.

What business does Butcher gots here, Mag wonders. And don't he look proper riled.

Sure she won't hear the end of it should Butch catch her skulking—*here*, of all places—Mag crab-walks back down the hill. Formulating excuses with each backward step, coded apologies only Jax'll decipher. She'll send Daisy on over later—innocent, whey-faced messenger—to reassure the colourman he'll git his *nails* tomorrow. When them two can conduct this business of theirs alone.

The river burbles as she draws near the bridge, a jolly rumble Mag swears is trickster-gods laughing.

What a lark, they's chuckling as she bends to scoop the bundle of firewood. *What a joke!*

"Yoo-hoo," Mag hears as she straightens. Briefly, she looks at the rushing water, a hot curse on her godforsaken tongue. Lava glubbing in her belly, she clenches 'n' unclenches her jaw, arse, fists. Hardly containing herself, she turns. Bares her teeth.

"Didn't know you made house calls, Miss Magnolia," Penny-Jean says, smugness thick as the apricot foundation on her face. Pointedly, she looks up at Jax's hill. Slow-smiles. "Just wait 'til the girls hear 'bout it!"

⌁

Foretelling, Daisy knows, ain't the same as *real* magicks. Mostly, it's gazing crooked at a straight world. Reading signs ain't no-one else cares to see. Understanding there ain't no such thing as accidents, only fateful happenings. Events taking folk where they needs and wants most to be.

Whenever she can, Daisy looks for destiny's little arrows, pointing her the hell away from Butchers Holler.

And these pointers *is* often small. So small, most folks don't even notice 'em. It ain't hexery as such. There won't be no shadow-spun horses come trotting round the room at her beckoning. No ensorcelled pollywog necklaces pulled out from her cookpots, changing hopeful young gals to mer-ladies. No muck-babies rising like dough between her glowing fingers, firming to flesh under cornflower spells. Old Gerta ain't bothered showing her none of *that* type of spellcraft; the witch only taught Miss Maggie them secret ways, then she up and croaked on 'em years before Daisy were ready for such learnings—or such losings. Long before Daisy had bled.

For now, without Miss Maggie at the bench beside her—blades scraping, mini lathe whirring, dust-brushes *clink-clink-clinking* on the rims of varnish jars—the cabin is blessed quiet. Perfect for Daisy to indulge in her foretelling mood. On the table, clusters of candles gutter in a draught, yellow tongues speaking a soft, throatless language only fire-faeries and hags understands. Overhead, the wind's loosing a pitter-patter of acorns on the rooftop. Curious squirrels skitter across the shack's timber walls. Every now 'n' again sap sizzles in the hearth, followed by startling snaps. Whooshing under it all is the pulse in Daisy's ears, thudding excitement.

Arranged on the scarred wood in front of her, four heart-shaped bone filings make a pattern she sure likes the look of, a pattern what *must* promise love. One after another, them slices was sheared off the calf shoulder she's working, each one landing just as they's now set: points inward, rounded edges facing out, just like a lucky field-clover or the yellow petals of a prairie sundrop. Each with a tiny hole bored through their tips, just begging to be pinned.

Now *that's* magick, ain't it just.

Daisy ain't a gal to ignore opportunity, especially not when it's laying right there, so obviously hers for the taking.

A few minutes to herself and she's brim-full of clever thinkings. It's so much easier reading signs when ain't nobody else around, noisying up her mind. *Trim that pin even sharper, milk that bessie one last time, watch yer Mama's ghost now, whet them chisels, clean them brushes, git yer hair out the way of my designs, scrub yer nails before touching that velvet, man the incinerator, charge the taser batteries, stack them logs for the fire, carry them bones . . .*

Daisy shakes her head. Imagine—just *imagine*—how many fortunes she could reckon if she ain't had to contend with so much racket all the damn time. Guaranteed, if Mag were here to distract her, Daisy would of whisked them bone-petals straight into the dustpan without sparing 'em a second glance. She'd of missed the true meaning behind 'em, missed the chance to hook her fate. Cruel shame, that would of been. After last night's dream of a striped mattress overflowing with carnations—symbols of passionate affairs, according to Mama's dream dictionary—and after this morning's encounter with Jax? *Well.* Someone out there were telling her to stay alert. Love were heading her way.

Ain't no rule against her helping it along, now were there.

In a coffee mug half-filled with simmered hooch and rose oil, Daisy mixes a varnish adapted from old Gerta's own potions. Sprigs of parsley, myrtle blossoms, crushed holly leaves git swirled in the warm liquid, and when the brew's perfume is strongest, she dips in a stiff paintbrush and slathers each heart on both sides. As they's drying, she rolls a leathery length of bindweed between her fingers 'til the stem's good and flexible. Wets it in the cup, then slowly threads it through each bone-petal. Gently, she snugs 'em together, fashioning a bloom about the size of a silver dollar.

All that's left is to find the right pin to make a brooch of this charm.

Problem is, ain't none on the workbench close enough to finished. Daisy considers the one Miss Maggie's been etching all week—a rectangular tie-pin, flat like a money clip, what she carved from the very tip of a Hereford's tailbone—but knows she'll git a hiding if it goes missing. What she needs is one what ain't so noticeable. One Mag might even believe she herself lost.

Pushing back her chair, Daisy goes to the table's end and tries the handles on every drawer. *Locked.* She rummages round the other gal's workspace, shifting bowls of sequins, razor blades, a wood-burning kit. Nothing useful.

In the fireplace, a seething log splits with a sharp crack. Hand to heart, Daisy jolts, head whipping up at the sound. "Sweet Jesus," she starts to say, then stops the oath half uttered.

Ain't *that* particular hanging god looking after me today, she thinks with a smile, gaze landing on Gerta's showcase above the mantelpiece. As ever, it's them beautiful fates that loves Daisy best.

Dashing across the room, she pries a hook-nosed pin from the second-last row in the frame, gives it a quick kiss, and spins back to the table. No sooner has she used it to secure the love charm out of plain sight—it fits perfect under the collar of her dress—than a *rap-rap-rap* of knuckles sounds on the front door.

As she opens it, Daisy sends silent prayers up to old Gerta, Mary's son, and all three of them hooded weavers alike. Thanking the immortal lot of 'em for pulling on their magick strings. Guiding her to this very moment. This threshold. This colourman.

"Twice in one day," she says, suddenly bold. Grinning coy, she steps aside to let him in. Bats her lashes, now thanking God she fixed her face after lunch. "You losing yer head over me, Jax?"

-8-

"Go home," Mag snaps, thundering into the workshop. "Shift's over."

Head down, she tosses the hatchet onto her cot. Heel-toes her boots off. Fumbles at coat buttons suddenly swole way too big for the slits. Fury and humiliation has clumsied her fingers, fuzzed her vision. *Gran must be twisting in her grave.* She whips back her hood, shrugs off the grimed jacket, hooks it on the doorknob. Unwinding her long scarf, she stares like it were a leash before jamming it into a muddied sleeve. *Fool girl, Gran'd say. Hound-dogging away from Jax's like that. As if it weren't right, you being there. As if you ought to be ashamed.*

Mag tears off her hat—yanking a few sweaty strands of hair in the process—and balls the thing with trembling hands. Bad enough she had to crawl through the cold, leaf-littered muck, inch by inch so's Butcher wouldn't catch sight of her. What else were she supposed to do? Saunter up for a quick *howdy-do* by the vats? Give Butch a nudge and a nod, saying *all* without saying nothing?

Don't mind us. *Nose-tap.*

Just here for a short roll. A bolt. A ream? *Wink-wink.*

Much worse, though, were bumping into Penny-Jean Maberry like that. *Didn't know you made house calls . . .* The pageant gal fluffed and primped and powdered, shimmering top to toe, asking with a flutter of false lashes how her new corset were coming along, and could she pop in to collect it today? Or would Mag prefer bringing it round to her place? *Didn't know you made . . .* Auditions is next week, remember? *. . . house calls . . .* She can't miss her first chance to *shine*, can she. And there were Mag, smeared and smutty, stammering excuses. *I don't make a habit of . . . I don't . . .* While the little snot smirked them bubble-gum lips of hers, and—

Giggles.

Mag spins round. Flushes to the golden roots of her hair. Ain't no surprise Jax gots secret shortcuts from his far-off place to what's closer to town—Mag ain't stupid enough to believe hers is the only door he's ever slunk up to after sundown—but even so, he could of shown some discretion, some common decency, and waited out on the stoop when he got here and found she weren't home. Like any *passing acquaintance* would.

Far as folk know—and what they *gots* to keep knowing—is that's all she and Jax is. Fellow crafters with a perfectly reasonable interest in one another's trade. Some might go so far as to call them two the lifeblood of the pageant industry—ain't no frills or frocks without *their* makings, right?—but can't no-one see nothing more in their meetings. Mag don't want none of that attention. Neither does she want no-one saying—with straight tongues or crooked— that she's riding Jax's coat-tails. That her pins ain't worth the cloth they's holding together . . .

And now Penny-Jean, of all goddamn people, is seen Mag where she shouldn't of been . . .

And now Jax is got it into his head to make a *house call*, in broad daylight, with Maberry's loose-lipped daughter nearby . . .

And now Butcher's own gal is all doe-eyed and primed for blabbing . . .

"What you doing here?"

At the far end of the workbench, Jax gots one hand on the back of Daisy's chair, the other on the table. Leaning in for a better look at the knife in the girl's hands. Blowing bone shavings off the blade's edge while she whittles a cow's rib, trimming it into a harp's tuning pin. Shoddy, unsellable work—Mag can see that plain across the room. The ridges is too deep, the shaft too thin; the thing'll snap if a string's so much as waved at it. Don't take two guesses to figure out what's stole the child's focus, what with the colourman bending so close like that. His whispering. Her blushing. Their giggling.

Slipping the chain out from under her collar, Mag trudges to the bank of drawers and unlocks the smallest one, hardly thicker'n a paperback romance. From its padded felt innards, she plucks three bobby pins, each capped with amethyst flowers. "Take these on over to Penny-Jean's place," she says, elbowing Jax out the way as she hands the bribe to Daisy. "With our apologies for the hold-up on her order. Tell her we ain't in the habit of making no house calls, never will be. This here's a one-off. Free of charge, no questions asked. And Daisy? Make it sound sincere, no matter how haughty the wench gits. Put on yer sweetest, sorriest face, and lie 'til she's happy. Once yer done, call it a night."

"But—"

Any other afternoon, Daisy would of skipped right out the cabin, trilling on this being her lucky day. A long lunch break *and* an early punch out? Seems Vinesday is come early this year. Not so, Mag realises, with the colourman here, dizzying her fool head like strong wine.

Sober up, she wants to say. *Good, wholesome gal like you can do so much better . . .*

Grubby palm flat out in front of her, Daisy holds the pins like they's firecrackers with lit fuses. Lip curling as her mind whirs for an excuse to stay. Wide eyes twitching back 'n' forth. Pins. Jax. Pins. Jax.

Jax.

"But *nothing*," Mag says, shoving the girl off her chair. "See ya in the morning."

Before the door's full-shut behind the sullen gal, Jax sidles up to Mag. Lovey-dovey, he tugs at the breast pocket on her overalls. Smiles and waggles his brows. Even in the dim candlelight, his irises is fetching. The pupils tiny black dots in a sea of malamute blue.

"Checking up on me?" she asks, crossing her arms. "Or what."

Dimples darken Jax's scruffy cheeks. Fiddling with the brass buttons on Mag's gear, he stops just short of undoing 'em. "May well be. Then again, maybe I just missed ya. Gits right lonely, y'know. All that waiting . . . "

"Does it now," Mag says, slapping his hands away. Not playful. Serious. "Way I seen it, y'all had plenty enough company today."

Pale blue circles flicks toward the door, confirming Mag's suspicions. *Fool girl's gointa git a talkin-to . . .* Jax steps back, fails to read her expression, his forehead gathering around secrets. "What you gitting at, Firebug?" The nickname stings, but Mag schools her features. Ain't no-one but Jax uses it—whips it out when he's in a tight spot, hoping to red-flag her bull temper. Not this time, she thinks, cold smiling. She won't let him razz her blind and dangerous.

"Seen Miss Maberry lately? How about Butcher?"

"So what if I has?" Jax pulls her in firm now, no arguments. Scrapes his five o'clock shadow against her temple, smooching and cooing into her ear. "No harm done. I likes a fresh bit o' meat every now 'n' again, is all."

Mag stiffens. "I ain't in the mood, Jaxon."

"Not even for this?" Thumbing her lips, he steals another kiss then turns to hoist a saggy canvas rucksack off the floor. Two buckles and a drawstring later, he gots the top flap open, a stank of sour milk heaving out from inside. "Batch gone and spoiled yesterday," Jax says, "and, more fool me, I dunked a few sheets in the mix anyhow. Testing how bad it turned, if it were at all salvageable." His tongue clicks over that piece of stupidity. "No-one else won't shell out so much as a nickel for it. But then I looks at it and thinks, *I'll be a monkey's uncle if the very drabness of it don't catch Miss Magnolia's*—" Pausing, he glances at her lap, breasts, back up to her '—*eye*."

At the first flash of the cobweb-hued fabric, Mag knows it's well worth trading for. That smock of hers needs longer ties, plus a wider trim along the hem. And if there's any material left over, she can attach a row of pockets . . .

They both knows she's game.

Can't give it up *that* easy though, Mag reckons, else the colourman won't never give her no peace. So she hesitates, puts on a show of calculating. Considering. *A spread for a spread*, that's the contract. That's the regular bargain.

For now.

Dollars to ducks, Jax won't be so keen to come a-calling once Mag's finally pinned herself plain.

"Deal," she says, reaching up to unlatch her straps. Two sizes too big, the coveralls instantly bag down to her hips, then slide into a puddle round her socks. "I'll want a good yard of that cotton, a good tumble, and not another word out of you 'til we're done."

~

When Daisy finally gits home, Mama's ghost is in the Shaker chair she loved, a crocheted afghan draped cross her lap. Cherrywood runners creak as she rocks, slow and steady, watching night drop its moth-eaten curtain over the kitchen's small window.

Just short of stomping, Daisy makes a beeline for the fireplace. "What ye reckon they's gabbing about," she asks, no preamble. Clawing the useless brooch off her dress, she crushes the flimsy bone-petals and chucks 'em onto the coals. The pieces blacken immediately, fizzle with a whiff of singed fingernails. Always first to opine in life, now Mama's ghost simply see-saws, keeping all thoughts wrapped under her messy topknot. Nothing like death for cooling a hot tongue, Daisy thinks. Still, she can't help but pester for a response.

"Well? Don't be shy, Mama."

No answer.

That'd be right, she thinks. Just her luck: even here, she can't escape older gals set on wasting her precious time today.

Now she really *is* stomping. Over to the sink, where she fishes a near-clean cutting board out the scummy water, then to the butcher's block where Pa insists they store the knives. Six of 'em, good 'n' sharp. The mood Daisy's in, only a cleaver will do. Soon it's *sshhhnnnk*ing through yams and blind potatoes, chopping 'em up skin 'n' all.

Ain't fair, she thinks. Miss Maggie sending her off on a mule-run like that, just as her spell were taking effect. Working its magick. Daisy beheads a cauliflower, hacks it to crumbs. Jax shows up and—*wham*, carrots become coins—Mag shoos her away like a pigeon. Tells her not to come back, even. Never mind that it weren't all that long a hike to Penny-Jane Maberry's. A skip through the eastern forest, the cornfields, the roadside paddock. Daisy were there and back in forty-five minutes, tops. And maybe if Penny-Jane ain't dithered so, maybe she might of made it back to Mag's before quitting time. Oh but didn't the greedy cow just *have* to *tsk* at the gift Daisy brung. Didn't she just *have* to lift that narrow chin of hers and peer down that perfect snout.

Think Magnolia could swap these stones for me? Purple's nice 'n' all, only . . . Red's the colour always gits girls to nationals. Can't y'all git me some rubies?

Sure, whatever, she'd replied, eager to head. And *still* Penny-Jean held her up, chatting all friendly-like. Acting like the best friend Daisy ain't never knew she had.

I hear Jax Kellermin had hisself a sweetheart visit today, said the beauty queen, leaning close, hush-hush. *Didn't he just.*

Colour rising, Daisy breathed in the gal's tea-rose perfume, failed to suppress a grin. *Word sure gits round*, she said. *How'd it land in yer ears?*

Penny-Jean shrugged, but kept on talking. *Ain't so far a walk from yer neck of the woods to this one, now is it. Even closer from there to Jaxon's hill . . .*

Don't I know it, Daisy'd said proudly. *Made it there 'n' back this morning—even had a drink after—before Miss Maggie knowed I were gone.*

Oh darlin, Penny-Jean said, rocking and tittering like she'd heard the best damn joke on earth. *Ain't that* precious. *The two of you—and him!—together! Today!*

Yeah, Daisy'd said, forcing a laugh though she sure didn't think it were all that funny. *Me 'n' Jax. He even come round to the workshop just now. To see me?*

Well, didn't Penny-Jean find that hilarious.

Now, glancing into the stewpot, Daisy realises there ain't no onions in there. She fetches a couple from a crate stowed next to her bed, starts slicing. Fumes git up her nose, set her eyes a-leaking.

She lets the tears flow.

Everyone knows the pinmaker's a cheapskate when it comes to wicks, wax, and oil. She hoards them bright-makers as though the end of days is nigh, doles them out drop by tiny drop, inch by stingy inch. And yet, only a few moments ago, Miss Maggie's cabin were still lit up when Daisy cut cross her yard. From that high gable window, a shaft of yellow firelight were blurring a warm streak through the evening fog. Some golden lines was slipping under the front door, others highlighting thin gaps between the cabin's timbers. Standing out in the drive, with the shadow-struck woods closing in and crows cawing down the night-dark, Daisy squinted at them shining beams. Black wings flapped overhead. Smoke and feathers roiled inside her.

Only one reason Mag ain't yet snuffed them burners, Daisy reckoned, and it weren't for *her* benefit.

Why ain't Jax skedaddled yet?

Were he waiting on her?

Hoping she were coming back?

"I didn't do it," Pa says, coming in with a gust of cold air, shaking Daisy from her reverie. Raising big hands in mock surrender, he clomps through the sitting area no-one ever sits in and over to the kitchen, keeping his coat on 'til the shivers leaves his bones. "Whatever put that snarl on yer muzzle, girlie, it weren't me."

Chuckling, he pats Mama's ghost on the shoulder. Brushes a kiss across the frayed parting of her hair. "And how were *yer* day, darlin," he asks, pulling up a stool beside the rocker. For a minute or two, he watches them blued lips open and shut, head cocked like he were truly listening. While Mama's ghost silently yammers, Butch nods and laughs. Never interrupts, not even when she seems to drone on, and the rumble in his belly talks louder ever than she does. In the pauses between stories, he reaches back to filch carrot chunks off the countertop, minding his fingers near Daisy's serious blade.

Daisy's sure Jax has eyeballed her the way Pa still does Mama, despite her only being half here. She seen love like that in Jax's lookings, hasn't she just. Hasn't she.

"Alright, spill," Butch says, once it's clear Mama ain't gots no more to share. Elbows on knees, he leans forward and pulls off his wool cap. Rakes fingertips across his scalp, scraping an itch what's been building all day. Meanwhile, he looks over his shoulder at Daisy. "What's eatin ya, my girl?"

The cleaver *thunk-thunk-thunks* through a bunch of parsnips while Daisy collects her thoughts. Pa snags an off-white sliver, crunches, while she tops and tails a few turnips. "How much cloth d'you reckon it takes to kit a gal out for, oh, say, the Miss Butchers Holler pageant?"

"Depends," Pa says, turning to face her straight on. Expression grown serious, as it always done when it comes to talking beauty contests. "If yer just goin in for the hogtie round, ain't nothing stopping ya from wearing what coveralls and Stetson y'already gots. No-one expects gals to ruin new duds while they's running round in pig shit. Preserves 'n' pie contest don't take much neither—a fresh apron, maybe a nice sundress? Yer Ma stitched herself a couple different options, took turns wearing 'em so's she wouldn't never have to show up for a new pageant in the last one's losing frock. She saved for years, I reckon. Of course, if it's the whole shebang yer after—title and crown, like she were—it's bound to be a sight more pricey. Gots to git yer stretchy swim-cloth, yer spangled evening gown stuff, and something worth ironing up for the interview round . . . All that only comes cheap as yer hoping to look. Yer Ma were a real class act, weren't she just, and wanted to dress the part. Every penny she picked on them southern fruit fields gone straight into the colourman's pocket. Every red cent. By the time I caught her eye, well now, yer Ma had a rich trunkful of fabric and not a dime more to her name."

"Right," Daisy says, whacking down the knife. "So why on God's green earth would a gal need so much of the dyed stuff if she ain't never had no intention of running? Why keep ordering cloth by the bolt-load—gitting it hand-delivered, no less!—if she ain't never gointa show it off?"

Suddenly, the fire's lickspittle murmur is the loudest sound in the kitchen. Water in the dinner pot burbles as it steams to a boil. Outside, the wind takes a breather; the windowpanes stop rattling, the pinecones and maple-keys avoid the roof. With a quiet squeak of boot leather, Butch stands. Behind him, Mama's chair quits its steady rocking.

"I gather we ain't talking bout yer Ma."

"Course not, Pa." Daisy hears the sharp whine in her voice, but can't do nothing to blunt its edge. Unfairness turns even the best folk into squeakers, every once in a while. "It's just," she huffs, "how greedy can she git? She ain't never had to pay for nothing—*nothing*—no, we never made her, did we—and now she's taking handouts, taking freebies what should be *mine*. And what's Mag want all that cloth for anyway? Already she gots more than most gals ever will—never mind that she covers most of it with bone-sticks and charms and what have you. Don't think I ain't seen her do it! May as well go pinning garbage bags together, for all the fabric she don't leave showing through them prickly clusters. But no, that just ain't good enough for Miss Magnolia. Course it ain't. She wants more and more and more! So now Jax is there, open-armed, giving it to her—"

"He's giving it to her?"

The hollow growl under his belt suddenly forgotten, Pa snatches up his hat, shunts it back on, and is out the door before Daisy can blink.

In the Shaker chair, Mama's ghost lifts a pale hand. Fails to cover a grin.

"What," Daisy snaps.

Cocking a brow, the woman resumes her rocking. Says nothing, just like she use to when Daisy were little and peppering her with questions too easy to warrant answers.

How *has* Miss Maggie been paying for all that fabric, Daisy wonders. Old Gerta's last will and testament ain't left much worth trading. And there ain't no sign she's been magicking Jax over to her place. No proof Daisy can see that he's been hexed . . . Why else would the colourman be so keen to come calling at closing time?

Ain't so far a walk . . .

The ghost nods, gaze leading Daisy on the short path from one to one equaling two. Once more, Butch's words play through her mind, but now the emphasis is changed. Now it ain't, "He's giving it to her?" so much as: "He's *giving it* to her."

"No," Daisy says, stomach dropping. It's the other way round, ain't it just. *She's* giving it to him. Nod nod. Wink wink. And he wouldn't be, would he, if Daisy were there instead. Jax's gal.

His one 'n' only.

"Back in a tick," she says, slamming the knife down. Waving off the ghost's scowl. "Seems I left something what's mine over at Miss Maggie's."

— 9 —

Truth be told, Mag thinks: it ain't awful, these *dealings* with Jax.

Stirring them dye vats day after day, lifting miles of waterlogged cloth, wringing and pressing and baling it up—all by his lonesome; he's a stickler for quality—sure has done wonders on the man's muscles. Them broad shoulders of his, slicked with effort, feel right nice under Mag's palms. The groove of his spine sits so pretty between the hard curves of his back, a nice deep trail leading her fingers down to his arse. Them firm buns is the perfect size for her hands. His thighs is bigger than hers, which is heartening, though his hips is narrower, his chest and stomach flatter. Mag's gots enough padding to keep their pelvises from knocking together, a feature Jax's been known to admire, and the wherewithal to turn over if he gits tired of doing it missionary. He ain't overly hairy, but ain't bare as a boy—a right turn-off, that is—and like most men Mag's known, Jax don't give a second thought to having his parts on show. Not that he's boasting; he ain't huge, after all, though he does just fine with what he gots. Just fine indeed. With only them two in the snug cabin, he wears nakedness easy as flannel pyjamas: as comfortable now with his rolls and folds as when he were a kid.

Starkers, Jax sure is a sight to behold—not to mention much friendlier on the nose. Most of the dye-house reek peels away with his clothes, chucked off at the foot of the bed. Once he really gits going, the clean smell of sweat washes the vinegar pall off his skin. Then there's a musk about him, strong and natural, what matches the way he ruts. Eager and a bit rough—he likes a good tumble, likes tumbling *her*—grinding and touching and nibbling and licking with a confidence bolstered by instinct. He don't never overthink it, only follows his body's lead 'til it feels good.

It always feels good in the end.

They've been at it a while now, almost long enough, when Mag hears a thud outside. On the bottom, she can't see much round Jax hunching over her, watching her expression change as the heat builds in their nethers. When he's in the groove, he don't grunt like a hog or huff his day-old breath in her face. He simply grins. True to their deal, he don't talk. He don't break rhythm, don't do nothing fancy. Only puts his hands where they's most needed. Helps things along with fingers and tongue.

He's had lots of practice.

So much so, he don't even miss a thrust when there's a quick *knock-knock* on the front door, and Butcher barges in. Mag flails to cover herself, but Jax keeps her pinned. Hips pumping, he glances over a shoulder at the older man. Hardly blinks.

"Won't be long," he says, picking up the pace.

"Thought I told you to lay off," says Butcher. Cheeks red and puffing, he's staring at the colourman so's not to stare at Mag. Torso hinging toward the bed, urging him forward, but his legs is rigid. His feet ain't taking him nowheres. "Daisy, Mags, whoever-the-hell-else y'all are drilling—*lay off*. These gals gots enough on their plates without yer filling 'em up with this nonsense."

Daisy. Mag's guts churn as she thinks on the girl's weirdness today. *Of course*. All them questions about competing . . . That hound-dog look she threw when Mag sent her home early . . . The stains on her sweater and calico dress, all them blotches what must've soaked in when Jax sprawled Butcher's daughter on her back . . .

"Twice in one day?" Mag whispers. Soon a different heat starts a-roiling inside her, familiar and dangerous. If she don't git up, *now*, things is gointa take an ugly turn. Someone's gointa git hurt. Smoke seethes from her handprints on Jax's arms as she shoves, but he don't pay it no mind.

"Seem to recall you saying something about *laying*," he comments, holding onto Mag's shoulders, grunting with another hard thrust. "As for gitting off? Well, I'd be lying if I said your presence weren't slowing us down on that front."

"Funny man," says Butch through clenched teeth. He takes a few steps forward. Raises a white-knuckled fist. "Think this is a joke?"

"Git off," Mag says, trying to push Jax away without touching him. Between 'em, sweat turns to steam. Furnace air seeps from her pores, her nostrils, her mouth. "Git off!" She bucks and writhes, but can't dislodge him. "This were a mistake."

Yet another in a long line of 'em, she thinks, bracing her forearms against Jax's chest. Heaving.

How else you gointa learn? Gran use to say, ever the philosopher. *Besides, ain't nothing worth doing what can't be done wrong a few times.*

Except, Mag knows—and she seen this truth clear as Gran's wrinkles, every crease and line a final boundary between *before* and *after*—when it come to life or death. Ain't no magicks in Butchers Holler can undo the kinds of mistakes what lead from one state to the other.

Not that Gran ain't never tried.

Drawing on every bit of lore, every spell, every herb and tisane and bone, every last bit of hand-me-down hexcraft she owned, Gran begged and bullied and bartered with gods and fates to undo what Mag done. All while Ma and Pa was staggering in the house-shaped inferno. While they was half-dragged, half-carried in Gran's skinny embrace, dropped onto the grit Ma once shoveled on the path to keep folk from slipping in winter. While their moans was choked with coughs, then their coughs was smoke-throttled. While they wheezed 'til they didn't make no sound at all. While their eyes rolled, searching for but never spying the culprit what killed them. While little Mag crawled out the house after them, ember-freckled and hair aflame, afraid of the whupping she'd git for singing that hearth-song, for snapping along, for starting that blaze.

Gran tried and tried and tried to revive 'em, but the effort were more'n enough to mark her limits. Seemed there weren't no hauling 'em back when folk slipped, accident or otherwise, into death. Not really. Not *fully*. Even when they was unknowingly pushed.

Still, she tried.

By the time she were finished, Gran were crinkled like newsprint thrown on coals, shrivelled to a third of her height. Precious life sapped from her own body—years, decades—transferred to Ma 'n' Pa by touch and by glance. A forty-something witch suddenly turned ancient crone. Crook-backed and gap-toothed, soon suffering tremors. Weeping over two perfectly unchanged, perfectly unchangeable corpses.

An accident, the Sheriffs called it. *No sign of foul play.*

But it *were* foul, Mag reckons. Fouler'n hot trash. A stupid, irreversible mistake.

~~

"Knock knock," Daisy calls, racing across Mag's stoop. Hardly pausing at the cabin's threshold, she grips the doorknob and twists. Unlocked. *Good.* Shoulders straight, chin up, chest out, she throws the door wide. Deep breath. *Dimples.* She barges in, aiming for the far end of the room, since she gots a knowing that Jax 'n' that traitor'll be over there. Flirting by the fireplace—yeah, that's it for sure—guzzling corn whiskey beside the hearth, gazing at each other over the cups' rims. Gitting all hot 'n' bothered from the booze and the blaze . . .

Five or six steps in, she stops at the foot of Miss Maggie's single bed. Pa's on the other side, face screwed up like he just trod barefoot in a cow-flop, mouth open, shut, open. No words coming out. At least, none what Daisy can hear. All of a sudden, it's like she's bobbing for apples. Head plunged in a barrel, frigid water *whoosh-whoosh-whoosh*ing as she dunks in and out, splashing so loud ain't no other sound can compete. Hard little surprises punch her right in the face. Chill drips down her neck, shoulders, soaking her chest and belly. Her eyes well-blinded with water.

The whole time she's shivering but also can't feel nothing. Nothing at all. Tangled on top the quilt—the rutting boors ain't even had the decency to git under the blankets—their shirtless arms is all akimbo, bare legs rubbing cricket-like, flesh sleek and shining but also straining, jiggling. Jax's pale arse is wagging, his bollocks on view. Below him, a glimpse of breast, full and feminine despite Mag's tomboy clothes. Abs that would rock the swimsuit round. Wild red hair fanned across the mattress. Lying there flushed and hood-eyed, the pinmaker looks proper womanly. She looks *gorgeous.*

Daisy bends and snatches the kindling axe Miss Maggie trots out for her daily walks. The handle's dangling over the bed's footboard, the half-moon blade snagged on the patchwork coverlet. Tool's an easy fit in her small grip, with a good solid heft to the business end. Don't take much grunt to raise it high, nor to bring its sharp edge down, *hard*, on bare back and shoulders, harder still on the corded neck.

She gits in three solid whacks before Pa launches one of his own, sends the weapon clanking to the blood-spattered floor. Daisy ain't long in following it down. When she sees the red mess, her fury drains fast as it first boiled, taking her gumption with it. Every one of her blows was off, her sights skewed. The axe were powerful, no doubt about it, but flat missed her target. She missed. Oh Lord, she missed.

And she hit.

— 10 —

Folk round here don't go more'n a day or two without encountering some form of dying. On the roads. In the fields. Bodies is brung low all the time. Animals and people alike. One and the same in the grim reaper's eyes. Anyone could be croaked in an instant. Obliterated. Flesh and bone and spirit turned from something *being* into something *gone*. Just like that.

Weren't nothing out of the ordinary.

Daisy seen her own Mama pass, hadn't she. Curled on the bed beside her. She'd held Ma's chapped hand. Waited for the wheeze in her sunken chest to subside. She'd propped herself on one elbow, after. Kissed her powdered cheek. Plucked the cigarette from her dead mouth. Wrapped her own lips round the filter, and shared Ma's last smoky breath.

Weren't nothing special about it.

Folk die every day, don't they just.

But *this*.

Daisy knows she couldn't of saved Mama. She weren't no doc. She weren't no hexwoman, neither. She ain't gots her bloods, ain't gots no true magick. Even old Gerta ain't had the know-how to keep Mama fully alive—so what more could Daisy do? She were just a young kid, then. Weren't she.

But *this*.

This were different.

"Wake up," she cries, but nobody's listening. "Please wake up."

This were the ugliest nightmare Daisy ever conjured.

Face-down on the bed, Jax is already stopped twitching.

For a minute there, she thought maybe, *just maybe*, the damage weren't so bad as it looked. Like that time Pa got gored by one of

Maberry's bulls. The Charolais' horn had tore clear through him. Gouged an awful chunk out his side before the beast were tranqued. Daisy ain't never seen so much blood as what pulsed out her Pa that day, but *he* survived. And he were *way* worse off than Jax. Weren't he.

For a minute there, she thought the wild in her swings might of stole some of their force. That the wounds bled all out of proportion to any actual harm done. Like fingers nicked while dicing onions. Toes slashed on sharp river rocks. Tiny slices pretending they was amputations.

"Sweet Jesus, wake up."

For a minute there, she almost believed she weren't a killer.

Cross-legged under the worktable, Daisy pinches and pinches and pinches herself. Upper arms and ribs and thighs. Feels nothing.

"Undo it," she begs, garbled with snot and tears. "Pin him back together."

But Miss Maggie's walking across the room empty-handed. No pins, no potions, no cure-alls. Leaving Jax sprawled, she untucks the quilt from her bed, neatly swaddles his body. Pulls the blanket over his head. Covers his face.

"No," Daisy cries. "Yer smothering him."

She knows it's crazy. There ain't no movement under that cloth. No breath. No life. If Miss Maggie had the skill to undead someone, she would of done it already. She would of saved Gerta, right? When the old witch kicked the bucket. Decades too young for the end, despite the hundred-year-old mug she were cursed with wearing. With a bit of makeup, she could of looked her age—forty-five? Fifty? She could of lived that many years again if Mag knew the right pin-patterns. The right chants. The right spells to revive her.

She would of saved her parents, too.

So, no. There weren't no undoing *this*, not by charm nor by prayer.

"Wake up," Daisy repeats, over and over. Talking only to herself.

∿

"Burn him," Butcher says, tossing a fresh log on the fire. It ain't but busy-work for his hands; the flames is already roaring so hot, there ain't much air left in the cabin for breathing. Dark patches is soaked clean through Butch's jacket, a deep vee spilling under his beard, half-moons pooling under each thick arm. Sweat beads on Mag's temples, collects on her upper lip, slides down her spine, in her cleavage. It trickles like piss on her inner thighs.

Droplets scatter as she shakes her head, shakes it hard.

"Please." Hard to talk round the wad of ash in her throat. There's a pain under her ribcage, panic batting its wings. "I can't."

"That so."

Butcher ain't a vicious man, Mag knows that full well. Only, he's protective. He's a problem-solver. He keeps a tidy slaughterhouse, no matter where that turns out to be.

Even so, he ain't never burnt no bodies before.

Beheading, dismembering, rendering, deboning—ain't none of that a problem for a man in his trade. But when it comes to fire, when it comes to setting human beings alight, he don't know how much wreckage gits left over, how very much remains. How much of that shit he'll have to live with afterwards, nor for how long.

He don't have the slightest clue.

"Anything else, Butch. Don't make me do that."

"Can't afford a scandal, girl. We're only just making ends meet as it is. Folk find out about this . . . " He stops, shakes his head. Starts again. "You said Penny-Jane seen you earlier. Reckon she's onto you 'n' Jax? Onto yer, yer—" He flaps a paw at the bed, at Mag's mussed self. "Reckon she knows he come a-calling? Folk hear he's gone missing, you reckon she'll point 'em this way?"

"Can't say," Mag replies. "Don't think so."

"Maybe," Daisy pipes up from the floor. Hard to separate the words from the bawling, but it sounds kinda like: "Told . . . her . . . me . . . 'n' Jax . . . so *funny* . . . "

"It weren't yer fault, darlin," Butch interrupts. "Ain't that so, Mags? Call it an accident, right? Could of happened to anyone."

"No fire," Mag says, crossing her arms. "Too obvious."

Though Butcher sighs, she notes the tension easing in his face, his shoulders unbunching, and reckons she's won. Letting him think his own way to Plan B, she goes over to the bed. Starts shrouding the corpse. Butch can't very well cross their yards with a naked, blood-bathed Jax slung over his back, now can he. What he can and will do, however, is lug a roll of cloth home for Daisy to stitch up nice. And on the way, he'll drop past the chop-shed as he does every night. It's an old habit, running the lights one last time, spinning the power-blades, giving the place a final hosing. Keeping everything in regular working order.

Nothing strange in that.

"Alright, Mags. Alright," Butcher says after a minute. With another sigh, he pinches the bridge of his nose. Peers over his fingers at the gal sobbing on the floor. "I'll do my bit, you do yers. Don't let nothing happen to my girl, y'hear? Take good care of her."

Mag nods. "One thing," she begins. Ain't no decent way to say this, not really, so she steels her nerve and blurts it. "Before he's disappeared . . . " She swallows. "Save me his shins. Thighs, too, if it ain't too—"

Too *what*? Too hard to separate a dead man from his limbs? Too grotesque? Mag shakes her head, but don't take back the request. Her and Daisy was gointa need them long striders of Jax's, weren't they just, to help walk 'em both out this mess.

"Bit lean," Butcher says, wriggling an arm under the legs in question. Sliding the other under Jax's torso, he straightens with a grunt. Shuffles to git his balance, hups the bundle off its bier. "Couldn't of asked that *before* he were tucked up tight as corn in the cob?"

"Please." Mag's voice quivers, but it don't break. Not yet. As Butcher adjusts his grip on the body, she searches for the tool what brung 'em to this sorry state. It ain't on the mattress, nor on the workbench, neither leaning up against the door-side wall where it belongs. Following the dark spattertrail drip-dropping from bed to table, she spots it sitting there on the floor. Dull, but not useless.

"Daisy," she says, crouching beside her. "Move yer arse." Grief's deafened the gal, so it seems. Hiccoughing, rambling something about a wake, she don't respond. Arms girding her middle like they's the only things can keep her guts from shivering out. Teeth chattering between blubs.

Mag *shoves*. Tipping Daisy against the table leg, she yanks the axe out from under her. As she stands, candle and firelight reflects off the blood-smeared blade, flashes of yellow and orange amid the red. Catching sight of it only makes Butcher's daughter cry harder.

Holding the weapon out handle-first, Mag squares her shoulders. Glowers at the slaughterman. "*Please*," she says again.

"Fine," he grumps. "Git the door."

A few moments later, a steady rhythm of grunts beats in from outside. A *whump-whump-whump* of steel fighting its way to the chopping block. Bass notes to counter Daisy's high-pitched sniveling.

"Git yerself together," Mag says to the girl as the pace of Butch's hacking speeds up. She goes to the fireplace and drags Gran's favourite cast-iron cauldron over the hearth. It's too big and heavy to haul up to the kitchen sink—balled up as she were right now, skinny Daisy could fit inside it easy, with only head and shoulders poking above the rim—so Mag scrapes it over the stones, nestles it empty in the coals. Chucks in a few handfuls of flaked soap, takes a rusted tin off the shelf and glugs in a shot of cinnamon whiskey. A vial of Gran's special spirits goes in next, a pale amber liquid magicked to speed up the process, then another. Another.

Soon, mustard-coloured steam is wafting up from the boiler's dark belly, stinking like a fish market on a hot summer's day. Mag adds a pinch of black salts and grinded fox-teeth, counts *five Missapeqwas* then shakes in a bit more. Each ingredient quickens the spell, but don't do nothing to quell the reek. When blue cheese and gasoline clouds start billowing out the depths, she goes and pumps water into a copper soup-pot, and fills the boiler gallon by gallon.

"C'mon, Daisy-gal," Mag urges, building the fire higher and higher around the blackened pot. With the extra kick Gran's magicks is giving the brew, won't be long 'til it's full-spitting. "We gots plenty to git done before mourning."

— 11 —

It weren't a hard heart what had set Gran to fossicking her daughter's burnt home before the wreckage 'n' bodies had cooled. Tears had streaked the black grime on her face as she raked through the rubble; they'd dripped and dripped and dripped from her chin as she scooped ash and soot, shifted beams and joists, salvaging what she could. Iron rivets and nails was piled in a barrow, charred timbers in the back of Butcher's truck. She'd dug up small gold-plated charms what had been buried along with the house's corner-posts: one for good health, one for joy, one for luck, and one—largest of 'em all—to appease gods of forest and stone, to beg protection for those sheltered within this here log cabin, this insult of wood-blood and tree-bone. Them worthless scraps had got tossed in the river, hard and far as Gran's tired hands could throw.

True, the old woman *were* determined. She were driven by some force little Mag couldn't fathom then, one she were gitting well-acquainted with now. It weren't coldness sending Gran back, again and again, into the smoking shambles while Ma and Pa had greyed and stiffened out in the gravel yard. It were practical urgency.

To claim survivors—of timber or spirit—hexenfolk gots to act before the shell is scorched hollow, the bones too brittle to work.

Gran ain't never undeaded a soul, but weren't nothing gointa keep her from trying. Nor failing.

But maybe she'd tried too hard. Maybe she took too long carting all that raw material home to her workroom. Maybe, come dawn, Gran herself were too shattered to put anyone else together again. Mag never asked, so she don't rightly know. What were clear—then as now—is there ain't bringing no-one back in the same state they was before. Not exactly. But that don't mean they ain't still useful, once they's changed. It definitely don't mean all's lost.

Bent down in front of the fireplace Gran built solely from reclaimed lumber, her folks' remains whittled 'n' spinned and pasted on the pin-board above the mantel, Mag focuses. Channels the old witch's grit. Tightens her grip on the carving knife and gits to separating Jax's flesh from his bones.

She works quickly.

Fillets and skin goes straight into the garbage bag she's throwed down to catch the muck. Butcher's done her the favour of removing feet and knees before carting off what else remains, so she don't gots to worry about cleaning all them nooks and crannies where sinews and fats likes to stay stuck, even after the bones is washed. All the same, it's a task scraping the tendons loose, holding the shafts upright with hands what won't stop shaking. The blade slips, more'n once, grazing knuckles and fingers. Mag wipes them on her shirt, wipes and wipes 'em again. Ain't nothing can unslick 'em.

Half in the flames, half on the hearth, the great cauldron is now simmering, good and steady. *Don't boil them bones, girl*, Gran use to say. *Nothing lasts forever, but while they's here you want them pins strong and white, not yellowed-up and ugly with lard.* Boiling cleans 'em up fast, so Mag were sore tempted to risk it—but one look at Daisy blubbering under the table firmed her against being reckless.

If only Daisy weren't so rash, Mag thinks. If only she'd of stopped a second, just stopped and *thunk* . . .

Weren't no point finishing the thought. She shakes her head, slowly feeds Jax's clothes to the fire. Britches first, which alight with a quiet *whoomph* as though they was oil-dipped. The slim-fitting tank top what still smells like the dye vats. The flannel button-up what's soft everywhere Jax were tough, cuffs and collar frayed where they rubbed against him. Buckling for a moment, Mag presses the shirt to her face. Breathes in the chemically, too-strong aftershave. Underneath, the salt scent of him. After mopping the damp from her eyes, she straightens. Wraps the sleeves round an iron poker and jams the whole thing deep in the coals. Shame to waste such good fabric, she tells herself—urgent, practical—but ain't no-one else could wear it. Not now. Not without raising eyebrows, nor setting town gums a-flapping. And ain't no-one could wear it as *he* done.

Retrieving the glowing rod, she skewers Jax's shoes, one at a time, and shoves 'em in far, all the way to the chimney back. The leather catches faster than expected. The laces he'd always left half-strung crumble, the tongue curls in on itself, the soles puddle. Mag covers her mouth, tries not to gag. Regret stings, the taste of it foul as burning rubber. Swallowing hard, she pushes herself up and away from the heat. What's done were done.

Ain't nothing permanent in this world, my girl.

Start over.

Finally Daisy's quit her lowing, but ain't no sign them waterworks will switch off any time soon. Pink blotches creep up the gal's neck, spreading like lichen round her scars, then across her pale jaw and cheeks. Mascara's smeared round her sockets, not dripping down her face like it always do in the movies, giving her grief a hollow, horror-skull look. Peering over her shoulder, Mag can see Daisy's mind ticking over: denial in the ugly bunching of her features, disbelief when they go all slack. Reality washes in and out like the tide. With each wave, the truth of her situation slowly rises. Bit by bit, understanding fills her eyes 'til they spill.

These ain't tears for Jax's death, Mag reckons. Not no more. Now the girl's blubbing against consequences.

"I didn't mean it," she whimpers. "Honest to God, it *were* an accident."

"Later," Mag says, weariness dragging the word long and low. Around the cauldron, the clothes is more or less gone to cinders. Stumpy beer bottles filled with Gran's strongest elixirs is lined on the shelf above, waiting to be poured. Most likely one dose would do the trick, speeding up the simmering process right nice. In normal circumstances, she'd of glugged in half a bottle's worth, propped open the cabin's window and door, then left the bones to soak for two days—skimming off fat and scum, topping up the brew, 'til the rot of small tissue were almost too much to bear. But tonight's circumstances sure as shit ain't normal. Tonight, she ain't gots two days spare.

At most she gots 'til midday, Mag figures. Round about then, the second delivery truck'll pull up to Jax's shed lugging twice the usual shipment. The first postman would of come 'n' gone by then, after knocking and receiving no answer. It weren't the first missed shipment Mag's worried about—no-one round these parts won't never question a man's feeling dull after the previous night's shine—but if Jax weren't up by noon as always, signing for his parcels, offering a bottle of ginger beer for the road, *well then*. Mag knows one thing for certain: folk'll consider it their Christian duty to pry.

Ain't nothing but trouble ever comes from them good Samaritans.

Mag upends seven of Gran's best concoctions into the pot, stirs the greenish broth, then tongs the bones in. As they sink to the bottom, the brew goes quiet. The surface belches a few grassy bubbles, then settles into a still bog. Through the water, Jax's remains waver and seem to shrink. Disconnected, they look so damn *small*.

Maybe I should of brung it to the boil again first?

The sudden tightness in her throat and a twist in her insides tells her she's ruined it. If only she'd kept the feet after all, done a test batch. If only she'd been stingier with the accelerant. Mag feels Gran looking over her shoulder, clicking them false teeth of hers as she nods. As she grins.

Ain't nothing worth doing what can't be done wrong a few times.

This were a mistake, Mag thinks. Ain't no do-overs in life nor magicks.

Careful as a surgeon, she slips a metal prong into the slurry. Swirls it widdershins, *willing* the stuff to start frothing. Steam damps her curls as she leans close, closer, the fine hairs on her bare legs crisping this near to the fire. *Ain't nothing worth doing* . . . She prods a thighbone. A shin.

"Git up," she says, shuddering out a breath as the bones begin to float. Giving it another swirl, the cloudy liquid clears and gently bubbles. *Thank Christ*, Mag thinks out of habit. Convinced the next few moments is crucial—what if it thickens again soon as she turns away? what if it boils over? what if that many potions mixed with them other vials *was* too many after all, and Jax's limbs turn brittle underwater, and all the power they hold seeps out the cracks?—Mag watches and stirs, stirs and watches. Meantime, she unclasps her necklace. After the key slides off the chain into her free hand, she turns and tosses it over to Daisy. It clunks on the floor, landing an easy stretch to the girl's left.

"Third drawer," Mag says, tilting her head at the workbench.

Daisy blinks at the thing like it were a roach playing dead, bound to skitter at the slightest touch. Wariness soon gives way to curiosity; she sniffs and knuckles more makeup into her puffy eyes. Ain't every day Daisy's allowed into Mag's private cabinets—in fact, ain't no day before this one—so she pulls tight the blanket shawled round her, snatches the unlocker, and shuffles to the bank of drawers.

Her face falls when she opens the third one down. Puzzled, she takes out the pageant gal's unfinished corset and squints up at Mag. "We're doing a fitting *now*?"

"One step at a time." Mag dips a ladle into the cauldron, spooning out a beautiful bronze liquid. Clear as scotch, it gots a mulled wine aroma what lets her know things is coming along as they's meant to: fast and fine. Clanking the handle against the boiler's rim, she looks over at Daisy and feels a pang of guilt. Like Gran before her, Mag ain't in the habit of welching on deals. Penny-Jane Maberry's already paid off more'n the raw materials cost, plus half the labour. And she were expecting the finished corset yesterday . . .

For once, Mag thinks, Penny-Jane's just gointa have to live with living without.

"Seam-ripper's in the basket to yer right," she says. "Yeah, that one. Calm yerself, Daisy. That's a girl. With your steadiest hand, unpick the ribbing and pull them bessie-shanks clean out—oh, don't give me that look. You can do this, hear? I knows you can. Now go'on and prove it."

While Daisy gits to work, Mag fishes Jax's bones out the cauldron and lays 'em on the hearth, spreading 'em out across towels Gran's own Gran embroidered back when Butchers Holler weren't yet named on no maps. White sigils and runes was stitched on the white cotton fields, near-indistinguishable to the naked eye—but all them fancy letters casts a whole nother language of shadows if 'n' when candles is placed round the borders just right. Mag knows exactly the configuration—she set it up for Gran time and again—and soon the wicks is blazing. Soon the bone shafts is changing hue, fading from clay to porcelain as they dries, as they set good and true. In round about an hour, even that green tinge from the quickening draught is gointa pale up right pretty.

Turning, Mag sees Daisy's gots five of the twenty ribs slid out the corset and discarded on the tabletop. "Try not to break 'em, if you can," she says. Might be they'll have to reuse a few of them cowbones, if Jax's thighs don't stretch that far. Concentrating, the girl simply nods. She don't roll her eyes as Mag would of, had Gran said something so bleeding obvious. She don't so much as smirk.

Gotta hand it to her, Mag thinks. Daisy sure can respond to direction. Heading to the workbench, she sighs. Damn pity the gal won't never git to perform that obedience for no audience. *Pose, twirl, sparkle for the camera.* Reckon them pageant judges would of creamed their pants over a simple little sheep like her.

Now Daisy's freed seven of them sticks, Mag has gots to git a move on herself. The key's still turned in the third lock; she slides it out, snicks it up to the first drawer. Mothball and cedar air wafts out as she retrieves the magicked smock, lingering as she slings it onto the dressmaker's dummy. Ain't been folded all that long, but for the first time ever it's hanging crooked. The skirt's rippling funny: bagging at the thighs, dipping at the crotch. Looks less like a potato-sack frock from this angle, more like a romper. A shapeless, short-legged jumpsuit.

This, Mag thinks. She ain't so crass as to smile, not given the unfoldings tonight. But inside her a knot of anxiety unclenches, a surprising and welcome jolt of relief, like joints popping into place after sitting on them high stools for too long. All them hours pinning and patterning a plain girl apron-dress—and *this* were the linchpin in her design from the git-go. She just ain't seen it 'til now.

It takes a half-turn of the clock to unstick hundreds of pins from the front and back of the smock. Working from hem to waist, she clears a triangle of fabric more'n a handspan wide, narrowing sharply toward the belt. It's fiddly, undoing them intricate whorls on the skirt, but eventually the pins come away neat enough; she can tidy up the edges when she rejigs the outfit, re-hems and re-fixes it together. Repurposing the back's gointa be a sight harder,

Mag reckons, since she only needs to free up a space about the length and width of a zipper. Problem is, all them pins back there is herringboned across the shoulder blades, each chevron fitting perfect with the next. Removing a full row is gointa be too much—even a half row'll leave too big a gap for her purpose. When she's wearing the thing, the pins has gots to touch—end to end, criss-crossed, or overlapping—else there'll be a chink in the armour, a breach that'll leak out all her fine hexwork. Won't do no good whatsoever if the glamour it casts ain't *whole*.

Then again, the magicks won't work one iota if she can't put the suit on in the first place.

Rummaging through a cutlery tray on the worktable, Mag finds a pair of nail clippers and puts them to one side. Next she grabs the biggest, meanest pair of shears in the pile—Gran's favourites: good 'n' heavy, perfectly balanced, blades merciless sharp—and turns round to face the smock. Behind her, the *crick-crick-crick* of the seam-ripper slows. Seems Daisy's pulled out the last bit of boning from the corset, so now her hands is gone still. A nasal, hound-dog whine starts up a second later, breaking the midnight silence. If Mag don't set the gal another task, she's gointa fold in on herself again. Wallow in useless crying.

"Them pins I just unstuck," Mag says. "Bring 'em here."

Sliding off her stool, Daisy folds the corset lengthwise and does as she's bid. Halfway there, she gasps. Mag's took them scissors and slit the dress from knee-level to groin, first at the front, then the back.

"You *wrecked* it," Daisy says, stopping short. The dish of pins rattles in her grip. Her voice shrills up an octave. "Can't nothing stay in one piece round here? Not even *that* hideous old thing?"

"Bear with me." Mag steers Daisy closer to the dress-form then crouches, gits to work. "Things is gointa come back together soon enough."

Starting at the frock's nether crux, she weaves sturdy new inseams—a railroad track of pins transforming the once-skirt into knee-length shorts. On the hearth, the fire's winked down to embers by the time the pants is shaped to fit comfortable round her lean thighs. Them thighs is quivering, and her lower back's spasming, before Mag's finished connecting and reconnecting the hexed pin-prints. Purple twilight filters in the gable window as she finally stands and knuckles the knots from her muscles.

"Nearly there," she whispers, startling Daisy from a stupor. Picking up the nail clippers, she fractures a thin line through the bones leading from the nape of the neck straight down to the rump. The pin-heavy fabric flaps open, the weight of it all pulling the garment off the dummy and down to the floor.

"Reckon it's now or never," Mag says, taking the mannequin off its stand so's she can free the jumpsuit. "Prep the new bones. Thighs, then shins."

A dark crease shoots up between Daisy's plucked brows. Her lower lip juts out, wibbles. "Please," she whines. "I can't."

Mag cuts her off with a scowl. "Ain't all that different from any others you've split," she says firmly, sympathy softening the lie. This were the most personal, the most powerful piece of bonework the girl's ever gointa fashion. "A mite thinner, sure, a tad more fragile. Mind the grain as you go, same as always. Use the smallest chisel, the finest sandpaper. You *can* do this, Daisy-gal. So git to it."

⁓

It's a rush-job, Mag thinks. No doubt about it.

Jax's right thighbone is split and planed, but unpolished. The dozen shafts destined for the beauty queen's corset gits their rough edges coiled in braided strands of Mag's copper hair, then sealed with potent resins—fast-drying varnishes charmed for strength, camouflage, hoax-light, *twinning*—and finally slid into the velvet channels Daisy bloodied her fingertips emptying. Each rib is fixed in place with tiny straight-pins splintered from the colourman's right shin. Hasty, ugly work secured with precise words.

Dawn had broke into the cabin window hours ago, a gentle wash of rose and coral what sneaked in when they wasn't looking, too light and carefree to penetrate the gloaming below. Splurging, Mag had brung out a week's worth of lamp oil, sparked all the glass danglers to life. Shadows was chased well away from the workbench, above which a battalion of fire-folk now flits and flickers and flails bright swords of flame. Despite the pall hanging over them, Daisy's delighted—she ain't never seen such extravagance—and Mag tries to smile, telling herself it ain't self-indulgence what's making her waste them supplies. It ain't that she's set on using up what she hoarded all these years, before none of it's hers anymores. No, sir. Not at all.

"Miss Maggie," Daisy breathes, boldly reaching up to brush the fresh-shorn patches on the pinmaker's head. "Yer beautiful curls."

"Just you wait." Wielding Gran's shears, Mag hacks off another thick red tendril. Then another. Another just for good measure. "Things always gits worse before they gits any better."

What few pins they'd had time to turn from the left thigh— the sinister side, Gran use to say, and more powerful for it—was reserved for Mag.

Both she and Daisy stripped Jax to the bone, in one way or another; both of 'em turned him from something *being* into something *gone*. Both of 'em oughta wear the truth of that turning, Mag reckons. Now and always.

Closer'n close to the skin.

"Take off yer sweater and dress," Mag says. "Undies don't matter." To anyone else, the command might seem perverted, but Daisy's use to it. She don't do much more'n sniff at being barked at before gitting started on her buttons. While the girl's stripping down, Mag unthreads the corset, yanking out the silken ribbon zigzagging across its back. Throughout the night her fingers has cramped into talons from all the close-work, but they's still nimble enough to plait a single slender hair-rope from the tresses she's chopped. Still deft enough to use it for lacing Daisy into the undergarment, to stuff the bosom with feathers and a mirrored-steel amulet, to pull the stays in tight, tighter. To knot the girl forever in place.

As Daisy looks down, smoothing her hands over a newly-trim waist, Mag leans in and presses her lips against the girl's crown. Lifting her chin, she mutters an incantation. Holds the spell along with Daisy's gaze. Transfers what life—what future—she can by touch and by glance.

Mag ain't never seen the girl so serious. So focused. "Sorry, darlin," she says, the words cracking as her drained vocal chords change.

"What for?"

She pat-pats Daisy's cheek. Admires the smooth curve of her neck. "My turn," she says.

Quickly peeling off her oversized shirt, she signals for the smock-suit. Already Daisy's taller and more svelte than she were a minute ago—she gathers the outfit, lithe as a nymph. Holding it out for Mag to step into, the girl stretches, elongates, morphs from pre-teen to teen to young woman in a shimmer, a blink. Fiery curls tumble down to her shoulders, replacing the drab fall of straight hair. Unfurling like vines, the new locks soon reach halfway down her proud back.

"Help me," Mag croaks. Hitching the suit's top-half onto her shoulders and sliding her arms through is a real effort. Not just on account of them pins spiking round the arm and neck holes, nor because the whole thing's stiff as a day-old corpse, but because conjuring two glamours at once is more draining than she bargained for. The prettier Daisy gits—now there's embers freckling those cheeks of hers, now her skin's toasting to a gorgeous tan—the more Mag withers and pales.

"Hurry," she says. Instructing every puncture, personally selecting every shard, she coaxes Daisy into pinning her inside the jumpsuit.

"How y'ever gointa git out," the girl asks in a new, familiar voice. "How y'ever gointa piss?"

Sealing up the suture, Daisy jabs flesh more'n cloth. Mag don't answer, only sucks air in sharp bursts. Hundreds of tiny gashes and holes scrape up her back, matching the red now blooming under her pits, around her throat, between her legs. Warm dampness seeps through the narrow lines in the smock's pattern, blood rimming the off-white pins the same way it does over-brushed teeth. Inch by inch, Mag feels the magicks changing her shape, making her brittle, rickety. The bodice is a bit too short, the pants gouge, the hips square her pelvis like a man's. Soon she's stooping, wheezing. What's left of her hair greys, whitens, falls out. The bone-suit creaks when she moves. So do her bones.

Most of the fire once blazing deadly inside her is now lighting up Daisy instead. While she still can, Mag summons what's left of that heat she ain't never wanted, channels it into her palms. Rubbing them up 'n' down 'n' all over herself, she cauterizes them pin-gashes, sears them holes, fuses flesh and bone. Her skin blisters with a god-awful stink. Burnt hair. Frying cartilage. Overcooked fat.

Still, she ain't never felt so cold. So settled. So *permanent*.

Weren't no gitting out of this suit, she knows. Not now, not later.

"Daisy," she whispers. "Run. Fetch me a looking glass."

The girl gapes, unmoving.

To git her attention, Mag quick-snaps her fingers. Their blunt tips don't so much as strike up a spark.

— 12 —

Daisy can't stop staring at herself.

Sure, she's been known to bore eyeholes into Mama's mirror every now 'n' again—she ain't never denied it—but this morning's brung her a whole new world of looking. Appreciating. *Loving* what she sees more'n anything ever she loved before.

Despite her self-proclaimed knack for reading futures, Daisy ain't never seen *this* good fortune a-coming.

"D'you reckon it's possible," she says, hands on corseted hips, glancing at that perfect hourglass from *this* angle then *that*, "I'm even more gorgeous than Miss Maggie were? I mean, I *know* it's the very same face I gots on, the very same figure, but . . . " She turns and peers over a shoulder, smiling at the perfect perk of her caboose. Not for the first time since she come home, Daisy waggles her arse like a cottontail, picturing how amazing it's gointa look up on the catwalk. "Maybe me being younger'n her on the inside is showing through to the outside?"

Huddled small on the edge of her bed, Mama's ghost plays with the fringe of her lap-blanket. Yarns unravel between her ragged nails. Black 'n' white fluffs of wool tumbleweed across her legs. She watches 'em roll off the cliff of her knees.

"Well?" As Daisy spins, Mag's brilliant red tresses swirl round her like a princess cloak. She ain't yet accustomed to the weight of all that hair, but wearing it makes her stand even taller. Haughtier. It pulls her head slightly back, so she gots to look at folk down the speckled slope of her nose. This is a pose she intends to strike often, for the way it highlights the length of her flawless, scarless neck. *If only Jax could see me now . . .*

"Can't y'all muster even a *bit* of excitement for me?" she says, overly brash, trying to shout down the remorse nagging at her perfect bod. "This is my chance, Mama. This is *it*."

Then again, Jax ain't never paid her sufficient attention. Who's to say *this*'d change anything? With the pinmaker's features plastered all over her, Daisy don't need no two-timing, good-fer-nothing colourman to pretty her up. Long as she were wearing this beaut corset, she could put on any of Mama's old rags and snag herself a worthy man's eye, not to mention a winning place on the circuit.

Finally, she thinks, afraid to pinch blush into her cheeks lest this were all just a dream. Ain't no way she wants to wake up before dominating the county pageant. Hell, ain't no way she won't be going all-state! Then she'll nab the national crown, and after that . . . Oh Lord, how Daisy *dimples* now. With a queen's sash draped over her banging figure, she'll git out of this shithole of a Holler, won't she just. Think of the travel! Think of the postcards and souvenirs. Maybe she'll even git far as the Red Apple. Maybe she'll take a plane ride overseas.

Sure will, she thinks, stroking the unblemished skin under her jaw. Sure as hell will.

Mama's ghost shakes its head.

The two of 'em look up as the front door swings open. Sparrow and finch songs trill in after Pa, them happy little warbles sharp and clear as the afternoon breeze. Lack of sleep's darkened the bags under his eyes, staved in his cheeks, and roughed up his mood.

"Quit yer prancing," he says. From under his arm, he pulls out a scrunched set of denim coveralls and whips 'em across the room. They snag on the bed's footboard. "Whack them on over that hussy git-up, grab yer gumboots and some rubber gloves, then meet me in the chop-shed. We gots our work cut out fer us today, gal, and the late start don't help none. Five hogs needs spitting, a load of sausages needs mincing and sheathing, a pair of Herefords wants to git hacked and roasted for the Vinesday barbeque at Town Hall . . . and that's just fer starters. What with that extra *carcass* I had to truss up last night, I ain't so much as touched a bessie all day."

"But," Daisy begins—

"Hop to it, girl. After the cutting's done and the steaks is weighed, y'all can decide what bones to keep fer them pins of yers. Orders gots to be filled, today same as yesterday. Ain't that right, *Miss Magnolia?*"

"But," Daisy tries again. "What about all this?" A swagger of hips, a flourish of tapered hands, a cute tilt of the chin. Bewildered, she looks down at the incredible magick of *her*. "Ain't this worth more'n a few slabs of beef?"

"Count yer blessings, *Mags*," Butch says, tone grave. "Yer alive and breathing when *some* folk ain't. You done stole two lives in one night, and won't never pay for neither. That girl swapped her future fer yers, understand? Thanks to her, ain't no-one gointa git pinched fer murder. Ain't no-one gointa spend no time in the clink."

Butcher grabs the battery he come in for, then gestures at the overalls he brung. *Put 'em on*, his hands say, while his tongue goes on a-wagging. "Sure, Mags'll miss that Daisy-girl who gone scampering off while *she's* stuck here working. *Won't she just.* But she sure ain't gointa to honour that stupid, runaway child—she ain't gointa reward that fool's selfishness—by parading round in no goddamn pageant. Mags ain't never wanted to enter before, and she ain't gointa change her mind now. *Is she.*"

"'Spose not," Daisy admits. In the mirror, Mag's elfin face blurs. So pretty, so ridiculous pretty, even when she cries.

Mama's ghost gits up off the bed and shuffles over to the makeshift vanity dresser. She takes a lace-edged hankie from Daisy's big makeup kit. Gently presses it into the girl's hand. And with a sweep of her arm, the ghost collects all the bottles, tubes, brushes, lipsticks, and compacts her daughter gots scattered on the table. Zips them into the quilted bag and carries it into the kitchen. Without a word, she tosses the whole lot into the fire.

~~

Clutching a willow-stick axe like a cane, the old hag stops at the crossroads to ease the stitch in her side. An ankle-length drover's coat fights the early evening chill, while flint and steel in her pocket promise to work just as hard come nightfall. With a leather pack full on her back, a pouch of spare pins rattlin on her belt, she pauses. Scrubs a fist across sweaty lips. Recoils at the stiff whiskers she finds sprouting there, scritching against her over-large knuckles. Took her longer'n ever to git here, so she ain't all too keen on lingering, but knows she ain't gots a snowball's chance of reaching the county line before sundown if she pushes her tired legs too hard now. So she waits for the jackrabbit to quit thumping 'gainst her ribcage. Pounds the end of her walking-stick into the gravel, scaring up a raucous murder of crows.

As the corn-thiefs once again settle on power-lines and fragrant stalks, a strange sound greets her. At first, seems it's a rusted gate *screeking* open. Muscles in the hag's neck click as she looks at the pasture on her left, but its fence ain't gots no such postern. To the right, them cornfields is likewise penned behind sturdy timbers. No hinges in sight. No doors. A few seconds later, seems a pebble's clattering round a pickup's tailpipe—the witch frowns, mouth lemon-puckered. Ain't no trucks drove by in ages, she reckons. Ain't none approaching neither. As the pulse hushes in her ears, she gits to hearing better.

That ain't no vehicle, she thinks. That ain't no gate . . .

Wincing, she recognises the new crackle 'n' hum of her own sorry breath. Coughing don't clear the lung-butter none, but she sputters and hacks all the same. The performance raises a decent colour in her crumpled cheeks. Masks the shame already pinking her there.

When the fit subsides, she inhales deep as her tight chest can manage. Straightens only so much as the satchel—and the crick in her spine—allows. Closes her lashless eyes. Pretends the watery sun overhead carries even a white lie of warmth to defy the promise of winter in the breeze. She's gitting good at such tricks of the mind. Such delusions.

A black beak caws her eyes open. Bracing herself, she takes a shaky step forward. Resolves not to look back twice.

Not two or three hours past, she'd took a last labored lap round her yard before hitting the road. Bid farewell to the chooks, freed the goats and rabbits so's Butcher wouldn't have to feed 'em— then kicked herself for the stupid bit of whimsy what robbed the slaughterman of a few extra pounds of good meat. She wandered through Gran's kitchen garden, stopping more and more to skim a wrinkled palm over lavender and rosemary bushes, to crush rosehips and poppy pods, to scatter herbs what had long gone to seed. Reaching the stoop out front of her cabin, she looked up and splayed her fingers above the tips of the nearest pines. Counted how many widths 'til the sun speared its guts on them spikes. Reckoning it were time enough, she took another last lap. Then another. And just one more.

"Fool girl," she chid herself in a voice eerie-close to Gran's. *No use looking back, child. Ye gots to face forwards to see what's a-coming.* And though she felt the truth in them words sharper'n the aches in her hexed body, it still took her a few more turns to let the past go.

Just as she were set to make tracks at last, Butcher rang the lunch bell downriver. After two or three clanks, the tin clapper stopped short. Weren't no reason for Butch to call her over for grub, were there. Force of habit. And easy as that—realising that bell wouldn't sing out for her, not even once more—she were yearning for one last bowlful of Butch's rich stew, one last serve of his biscuits. One last shared lull in the middle of their days. And before she knowed it, her unsteady legs was lurching across the drive, shuddering down the slope and back up the ditch, creeping through the long sweetgrass swaying between their properties—

No, she'd corrected, forcing them willful legs to halt. It weren't *her* property no more. Her cabin and the land what it stood on were *Daisy's* now, and for always. Don't matter that folk in town won't never know it changed hands—they'll see Magnolia Brawm tending to her beasts in the yard, carting bones over from the chop-house, heading up-pasture to eyeball steers and bessies with Butcher. They'll see the pinmaker fishing bones from the river nearby, hewing busted apple crates for firewood, standing on the porch to welcome another batch of bleach-blonde callers into her studio. Folk'll note how she's took up smoking them foul cheroots all sudden-like, but they won't say nothing—living out on so many acres like that, all on her lonesome, is turned that gal a bit queer, that's all. No matter what folk see or say, that whole lot now belonged to Daisy. Now that Butcher's gal wears Mag's old face.

Or her *young* face, she should oughta say.

The visage Mag's got on instead is so withered and seamed, it's well-nigh unrecognisable. No freckles, no tan, no striking peepers. Scalp hacked to pieces, bald and sizzled like it were set too close to the hearth. No curls. No hint of red. Every bit of her's gone so greyed and faded, she's practically blank. Hell, for what it's worth, she's damn-near invisible.

The pinmaker cracks a gap-toothed grin.

Her cane scrapes on the roadside's soft shoulder as she hitches her pack and gits back to walking. Up ahead, a slender silhouette struts towards her, moving three or four times faster'n than she herself can. Backlit against the dipping sun, the figure could be almost anyone—*almost*. But the haughty swing of her ponytail, the determined but still sexy gait, marks her as Penny-Jane Maberry. And the way she's angling cross the road, aiming for that breach in the cornfield—well, that speaks loud 'n' clear, don't it just. Saying she's gots that narrow path in her sights, the trail what leads through them nodding crops, through them chattering woods, and round to the pinmaker's house. Seems the gal's intent on paying the new Mag a visit. Seems she's fixed on collecting a certain corset she won't never git her manicured paws on.

"Afternoon," the witch says as Penny-Jane trots past without so much as a nod or a howdy-do. For a few steps, the crone's bunioned feet practically skip down the path. *Invisible.*

Ain't no wrath like a beauty queen spurned, she reckons, laugh sharpening into a cackle. Miss Maberry's gointa git wound up tighter'n the yarn Mag spins her: how Butcher's no-good daughter hightailed it with the magicked costume, leaving not a trace. "Lovesick gal bewitched and run off with the colourman," the new Mag'll repeat, again and again, 'til every nose in town's got a sniff of the story. "Little thief won't dare show her face round here again!"

Again, the hag chuckles.

For years to come, the new Mag's gointa *have* to spread lies about Daisy. Ain't nothing else for it, lest she's keen to leave Butchers Holler in cuffs. The firmer her fibs, the firmer new Mag's reputation will hold—though the quality of her pinwork won't never be the same, more's the pity. But eventually, if she stays lucky, every last memory of her one-time apprentice will sour, turn rank, then dissolve. Same way Jax's parts 'n' pieces done last night in them metal tubs out in Butcher's chop-shed.

Some of his pieces, the old woman corrects. Not all his parts.

From the cornfield over the fence, a gangly shadow falls across her path. Blackbirds is squawking above and through it, flying and alighting on outstretched arms. Gobbets of meat drop from caw-cawing beaks, the spiced morsels snapped up again almost before they hits the dirt. Shading her eyes with a palsied hand, the witch looks up at the scarecrow. Butcher's done a bang-up job ensuring the rot sinks in slow, she reckons. Parboiling Jax's head then packing it with cumin and salt, stripping the skeleton clean as he could—he ain't gots Mag's skills, after all—then padding the scrawny form with beetle-rich hay. Can't tell it's him no more, which suits the old lady just fine. Ain't nothing noteworthy about him now. Nothing to mark him as special.

Peppered as he is with them spices and seasonings, Jax's straw-man smells better'n ever he did churning dyes.

That's one change'll take some adjustment, she reckons. She don't mind so much moving house—there's an abandoned cabin five miles from town what fits her needs just dandy, a little log-home nestled between the county line and the river, well away from the Holler's fuss and bustle—it's the *stink* she's dreading. Them putrid colour-vats was reeking up the waterways long before Jax took on the job; ain't no reason the stench won't outlast the source. But it's the least she can do, ain't it: setting up within sniffing distance of Jax's land, keeping watch on his place 'til folk gits bored with poking round. And even once they do—well, by then, she'll be good 'n' settled. Probably won't want to leave, will she. Despite the smell haunting his tumbledown property across the way. Despite that god-awful smell.

To combat it, she'll ingnite a forest of scented candles. Hang herbs to dry on the rafters of her one-room hut. Simmer broths and stews and potions. On shelves loaded with vials 'n' jars 'n' all-sorts of Gran's concoctions, she'll scatter incense and lavender. She'll brew geranium oils, marigold, wild rose. And when the wind blows hot 'n' rank from the south, she'll pour them perfumes into hurricane lanterns. She'll set them pretty little things on fire.

Ain't it amazing, she'll think, what an old gal can git use to.

Folk'll track her down eventually, the cunning woman out in the boonies, she who clicks like thousands of knitting needles with every move. They'll come for tisanes and poultices, love charms and poisoned spindles, cure-alls and leaf-readings and a fortunate roll of the bones. Sure, she'll throw knuckles or runes carved from antlers and shins—but she won't never take a chisel to any of 'em, not in this life. She'll never so much as whittle a safety pin.

Truth is, she won't miss it.

Year in, year out, she'll stay in that new-old cabin. She'll decide, once 'n' for all, to stay put. Alone and happier for it. Oh, she ain't hard-hearted. Never were. When the mood strikes, she'll venture out to visit them dear old friends of hers. Over the river, through the corn, and back across them woods. Bearing a pack full of gifts to keep 'em long-lived and healthy. And a mind full of memories to keep 'em steadfast and true.

∞

ACKNOWLEDGMENTS

"Soft Sister Sixty-Six" copyright © 2020 Lisa L. Hannett. Original to collection.

"The Coronation Bout" copyright © 2013 Lisa L. Hannett. First published in *Electric Velocipede*, December 2013.

"A Grand Old Life" copyright © 2020 Lisa L. Hannett. Original to collection.

"Four Facts About the Ursines" copyright © 2020 Lisa L. Hannett. Original to collection.

"Something Close to Grace" copyright © 2017 Lisa L. Hannett. First published in *Murder Ballads*, 2017.

"The Canary" copyright © 2015 Lisa L. Hannett. First published in *The Dark*, 2015.

"Little Digs" copyright © 2017 Lisa L. Hannett. First published in *The Dark*, January 2017.

"Surfacing" copyright © 2016 Lisa L. Hannett. First published in *Postscripts*, May 2016.

"Snowglobes" copyright © 2013 Lisa L. Hannett. First published in *Chilling Tales II*, 2013.

"Blues Eater" copyright © 2020 Lisa L. Hannett. Original to collection.

"Sugared Heat" copyright © 2015 Lisa L. Hannett. First published in *Spectral Book of Horror Stories 2*, 2015.

"The Wail in them Woods" copyright © 2020 Lisa L. Hannett. Original to collection.

"By Touch and By Glance" copyright © 2020 Lisa L. Hannett. Original to collection.

LIMITED HARDCOVER EDITIONS

978-0-9806288-1-4   The Infernal BY Kim Wilkins
978-1-921857-54-6   Black-Winged Angels BY Angela Slatter

EBOOKS

978-0-9803531-5-0   Ghost Seas BY Steven Utley
978-1-921857-93-5   The Girl With No Hands BY Angela Slatter
978-1-921857-99-7   Dead RED Heart ED Russell B. Farr
978-1-921857-94-2   More Scary Kisses ED Liz Grzyb
978-0-9807813-5-9   Heliotrope BY Justina Robson
978-1-921857-36-2   Dreaming of Djinn ED Liz Grzyb
978-1-921857-40-9   Prickle Moon BY Juliet Marillier
978-1-921857-92-8   The Year of Ancient Ghosts BY Kim Wilkins
978-1-921857-28-7   Bloodstones ED Amanda Pillar
978-1-921857-04-1   Damnation and Dames ED Liz Grzyb & Amanda Pillar
978-1-921857-31-7   Midnight and Moonshine BY Lisa L. Hannett & Angela Slatter
978-1-921857-44-7   The Bride Price BY Cat Sparks
978-1-921857-60-7   Everything is a Graveyard BY Jason Fischer
978-1-921857-64-5   The Assassin of Nara BY R.J. Ashby
978-1-921857-78-2   Death at the Blue Elephant BY Janeen Webb
978-1-921857-82-9   The Emerald Key BY Christine Daigle & Stewart Sternberg
978-1-921857-57-7   Kisses by Clockwork ED Liz Grzyb
978-1-925212-06-8   Angel Dust ED Liz Grzyb
978-1-925212-17-4   The Finest Ass in the Universe BY Anna Tambour
978-1-925212-37-2   Hear Me Roar ED Liz Grzyb
978-1-921857-38-9   Bloodlines ED Amanda Pillar
978-1-925212-37-2   Crow Shine BY Alan Baxter
978-1-925212-37-2   Ecopunk! EDS Liz Grzyb & Cat Sparks

THE YEAR'S BEST AUSTRALIAN FANTASY & HORROR SERIES
EDITED BY LIZ GRZYB & TALIE HELENE

Year's Best Australian Fantasy & Horror 2010 (hc,tpb,ebook)
Year's Best Australian Fantasy & Horror 2011 (hc,tpb,ebook)
Year's Best Australian Fantasy & Horror 2012 (hc,tpb,ebook)
Year's Best Australian Fantasy & Horror 2013 (hc,tpb,ebook)
Year's Best Australian Fantasy & Horror 2014 (hc,tpb,ebook)
Year's Best Australian Fantasy & Horror 2015 (hc,tpb,ebook)

Ticonderoga Publications is an Australian-based independent publisher specialising in science fiction, fantasy, horror and paranormal romance. Founded in 1996, 2020 marks our 25th year as a publisher.

THANK YOU

The publisher would sincerely like to thank

Lisa L. Hannett, Helen Marshall, Vince Haig, Liz Grzyb, Donna
Maree Hanson, Pete Kempshall, Karen Brooks, Jeremy G. Byrne,
Marianne de Pierres, Jonathan Strahan, Peter McNamara,
Ellen Datlow, Grant Stone, Sean Williams, Simon Brown,
David Cake, Simon Oxwell, Grant Watson, Sue Manning, Steven
Utley, Lewis Shiner, Bill Congreve, Janeen Webb, Jack Dann,
Amanda Pillar, Angela Slatter, Garth Nix, Anthony Phillips,
Anna Tambour, Alan Baxter, Deborah Biancotti, Stephen
Dedman, Jason Fischer, Dirk Flinthart, Kim Gaal, Kate Forsyth,
Kim Wilkins, Kathleen Jennings, Joanne Anderton, Lucy
Sussex, Stephanie Gunn, Cat Sparks, Juliet Marillier, Angela
Rega, Susan Wardle, Robert Hood, Jane Routley, Martin
Livings, Rivqa Rafael, Kirstyn McDermott, Jason Nahrung,
Kaaron Warren, the Mt Lawley Mafia, the Nedlands Yakuza,
Shane Jiraiya Cummings, Angela Challis, Kate Williams,
Andrew Williams, Talie Helene, Kathryn Linge, Al Chan, Brian
Clarke, Alisa and Tehani, Mel & Phil, Jennifer Sudbury, Paul
Pryztula, Helen Grzyb, Debbie Lee, Hayley Lane, Georgina
Walpole, Rushelle Lister, Nerida Fearnley-Gill, everyone we've
missed . . .

. . . and you.

IN MEMORY OF
Eve Johnson
Sara Douglass
Steven Utley
Brian Clarke